TO DANCE WITH
A PRINCE

CARA COLTER

To Rose and Bill Pastorek
with heartfelt thanks for creating such
an incredible garden, a 'mini-vacation'
for everyone who experiences it.

CHAPTER ONE

THE HOWL OF PURE PAIN sent icicles down Prince Kiernan of Chatam's spine. He shot through the door of the palace infirmary, and came to a halt when he saw his cousin, Prince Adrian, lying on a cot, holding his knee and squirming in obvious agony.

"I told you that horse was too much for you!" Kiernan growled.

"Nice to see you, too," Adrian gasped. "Naturally, the moment you told me the horse was too much for me, my fate was sealed."

Kiernan shook his head, knowing it was all too true. His cousin, seven years his junior, was twenty-one, reckless, but usually easily able to deflect the consequences of his recklessness with his abundance of charm.

A fact Adrian proved by smiling bravely at a young nurse. Satisfied that the girl was close to swooning, he turned his attention back to Kiernan.

"Look, if you could spare me the lecture," Adrian said, "I am in desperate need of a favor. I'm supposed to be somewhere."

First of all, his cousin was never desperate. Secondly, Adrian rarely worried about where he was supposed to be.

"DH—that's short for Dragon-heart—is going to kill

me if I'm not there. Honestly, Kiernan, I've met the most fearsome woman who ever walked."

And thirdly, as far as Kiernan knew his cousin had never met a woman, fearsome or not, he could not slay with his devil-may-care grin.

"Do you think you could stand in for me?" Adrian pleaded. "Just this once?" The nurse probed his alarmingly swollen knee, and Adrian howled again.

What Kiernan was having trouble fathoming was how Adrian, who would be the first to admit he was entirely self-focused, was managing to think about *anything* at this particular moment besides his injury.

"Just cancel," Kiernan suggested.

"She'll think I did it on purpose," Adrian said through clenched teeth.

"Nobody would think you had an accident on purpose to inconvenience them."

"*She* would. DH, aka Meredith Whitmore. She snorts fire." An almost dreamy look pierced Adrian's pain. "Though her breath is actually more like mint."

Kiernan was beginning to wonder what his cousin had been given for pain.

"The fact is," Adrian said sadly, " DH eats adorable little princes like me for her lunch. Barbecued. She must have the mint after."

"What on earth are you talking about?"

"You remember Sergeant Major Henderson?"

"Hard to forget," Kiernan said dryly of the man in charge of taking youthful princes and turning them into disciplined, rock-hard warriors, capable of taking commands as well as giving them.

"Meredith Whitmore is him. The Sergeant Major. Times ten," Adrian said, and then whimpered when his knee was probed again.

"You're exaggerating. You must be."

"Would you just stand in for me? Please?"

"What would make me agree to stand in for you with a woman who likes her princes barbecued and who makes Sergeant Major Henderson look like a Girl Scout leader? I don't even know what I'm standing in *for*."

"It was a mistake," Adrian admitted sadly. "I thought it was going to be a lark. It sounded like so much more fun than some of the other official *lesser prince* options for Chatam Blossom Week."

Blossom Week was the Isle of Chatam's annual celebration of spring. Dating back to medieval times, it was a week-long festival that started with a fund-raising gala and ended with a royal ball. Opening night was a little over a week away.

Adrian continued, "I could have given out awards to the preschool percussion band, given the Blossom Week rah-rah speech *or* done a little dance. Which would you have picked?"

"Probably the speech," Kiernan said. "Have you given him something?"

"Not yet," the nurse said pleasantly, "but I'm about to."

"Lucky you," Adrian said, batting his eyes at her, "because I have the cutest little royal backside—ouch! Was that unnecessarily rough?"

"Don't be a baby, Your Highness."

Adrian watched her walk away. "Anyway, I said I'd learn a dance. I was going to perform with an up-and-coming troupe at the fund-raising evening. It's a talent show this year. My suggestion to call the fund-raiser *Raise a Little Hell* was vetoed. Naturally. It's going to be called *An Evening to Remember*, which I think is *totally* forgettable."

"I'm not taking your place for a dance number! We both know I can't dance. Prince of Heartaches causes Foot Aches, Too." It was a direct quote from a newspaper headline, with a very unflattering picture of Kiernan crushing some poor girl's foot at her debutante ball.

"Ah, the press is hard on you, Kiernan. They never nickname me. But in the past ten years you've been the Playboy Prince—"

That had been when Kiernan was eighteen, fresh out of an all-boys private school, one summer of freedom before his military training. He had been, unfortunately, like a kid let out in a candy shop!

"Then, the Prince of Heartaches."

At the age of twenty-three, Prince Kiernan had become engaged to one of his oldest and dearest friends, Francine Lacourte. Not even Adrian knew the full truth behind their split and her total disappearance from public life. But, given a history that the press was eager not to let him shake, it was assumed Prince Kiernan was to blame.

"Now," Adrian continued, "since Tiff, you've graduated to Prince Heartbreaker. Tut-tut. It would all lead one to believe you are so much more exciting than you are."

Kiernan scowled warningly at his cousin.

"Don't give me that look," Adrian said, whatever the nurse had given him relaxing the grimace on his face to a decidedly goofy grin. "Your tiff with Tiff."

While the press *loved* the high-spirited high jinks of Adrian, Kiernan was seen as too stern, and too serious. Particularly since two broken engagements to two very popular women he was seen as coldly remote.

He knew the title Prince Heartbreaker was probably going to be his mantle to bear forever, even if he lived out the rest of his days as a monk, which, after what he'd been through, didn't seem entirely unappealing!

After all, the future of his island nation rested solidly and solely on Kiernan's shoulders, as he was the immediate successor to his mother, Queen Aleda's, throne. That kind of responsibility was enough for one man to bear without throwing in the caprice of romance.

Adrian was fourth in line, a position he found deliciously relaxing.

"You should have thrown that Tiffany Wells under a bus," Adrian said with a sigh. "She deserved it. Imagine tricking you into thinking she was pregnant. And then do you let the world know the true reason for the broken engagement? Oh, no, a man of honor—"

"We're not talking about this," Kiernan said fiercely. Then, hoping to get back on one topic and off the other, "Look, Adrian, about the dancing thing, I don't see how I could help—"

"I don't ask much of you, Kiern."

That was true. The whole world came to Kiernan, asking, begging, requesting, pleading causes. Adrian never did.

"Do this, okay?" Adrian said, his words beginning to slur around the edges. "It'll be good for you. Even if you make a fool of yourself, it'll make you seem human."

"I don't seem human?" He pretended to be affronted.

His cousin ignored him. "A little soft shoe, charm the crowd, get a little good press for a change. It bugs the hell out of me that you're constantly portrayed as a coldhearted snob."

"Coldhearted? A snob?" He pretended to be wounded.

Again, he was ignored. "That's if you can survive the fire-breather. Who, by the way, doesn't like tardiness.

And you…" his unfocused eyes shifted to the clock, and he squinted thoughtfully at it "…are twenty-two minutes late. She's waiting in the Ballroom."

The smart thing to do, Kiernan knew, as he left his cousin, would be to send someone to tell the fire-breather Adrian was hurt.

But the truth was he had yet to see a woman who had managed to intimidate Adrian. Because if Kiernan was legendary for his remoteness, his cousin was just as legendary for his charm.

The press loved Prince Adrian. He played Prince Charming to his darker cousin's Prince Heartbreaker. And, oh, how women loved Prince Adrian.

Kiernan just had to see the one who did not.

Kiernan decided to go have a look at Adrian's nemesis before giving Adrian's excuses and dismissing her. In his most warmhearted and non-snobby fashion.

Meredith glared at the clock.

"He's late," she muttered to herself. The truth? She couldn't believe it! It was the second time Prince Adrian had been tardy!

She'd been intimidated by the young prince and his status for all of about ten seconds at their first meeting at her upscale downtown Chatam dance and fitness studio.

And then she'd seen he was like a puppy—using the fact he was totally adorable to have his way! Including being late. Meredith was so beyond being charmed by a man, even one as cute as him.

So, she'd laid down the law with him. And she'd been certain he wouldn't dare be late again, especially since she had conceded to changing their meeting place to the Chatam Palace Great Ballroom as a convenience to him.

Which just showed how wrong she could be when it came to men, even while she thought she was totally immune to sexy good looks and impossible charm!

Meredith glanced around the grandeur of the room and tried not to be overly awed at finding herself here.

She breathed in the familiar scents of her childhood. Her mother, a single woman, had been a cleaning lady. Meredith recognized the aromas of freshly shined floors, furniture wax, glass cleaners, silver polish.

Her mother would have been as awed by this room as Meredith was. Her mother had dreamed such big dreams for her daughter.

Ballet will open doors to worlds we can hardly imagine, Merry.

Worlds just like this one, Meredith thought gazing around the room. Wouldn't her mother be thrilled to know she was here?

Because every door that ballet could have opened for Meredith—and her mother—had slammed shut when Meredith had found herself pregnant at sixteen.

Morning sunshine streamed in the twelve floor-to-ceiling arched windows that were so clean they looked like they contained no glass. The light glinted across the Italian marble of the floors, and sparked in the thousands of Swarovski crystals of the three huge chandeliers that dangled from the frescoed ceiling.

Meredith glanced again at the clock.

Prince Adrian was half an hour late. He wasn't coming. Meredith had had her doubts about this whole scheme, but been persuaded by the wild enthusiasm of the girls.

Crazy to let the teenage girls, the ones she mentored

and loved and taught to dance, younger versions of herself, believe in fairy-tale dreams.

She, of all people, should know better.

Still, looking around this room, something stirred in her. She was going to dance here, prince or no prince.

In fact, that would be very in keeping with the charity she had founded, that gave her reason to go on, when all of her life had crashed down around her.

Meredith taught upbeat modern dancing as part of the program No Princes, which targeted the needs of underprivileged inner city female adolescents.

"You don't need a prince to dance," Meredith said firmly. In fact, that would make a good motto for the group. Perhaps she should consider adding it to their letterhead.

She closed her eyes. In her imagination, she could hear music begin to play. She had broken with ballet years ago, not just because her scholarship had been canceled. When she finally returned to dance, the only place that could ease the hurt of a heart snapped in two, she had found she could not handle the rigidity of ballet. She needed a place where her emotion could come out.

But even so, Meredith found herself doing the famous entrée of Princess Aurora in the Petipa/Tchaikovsky ballet, *The Sleeping Beauty*.

But then, she let the music take her, and she seamlessly joined the *allegro* movements of ballet with the modern dance that had become her specialty. She melded different styles of dance together, creating something brand new, feeling herself being taken to the only place where she was not haunted by memories.

Meredith covered the floor on increasingly light feet,

twirling, twisting, leaping, part controlled, part wild, wholly uninhibited.

She became aware that dancing in this great room felt like a final gift to the mother she had managed to disappoint so terribly.

The music that played in her head stopped and she became still, but for a moment she did not open her eyes, just savored the feeling of having been with her mother for a moment, embraced by her, all that had gone sour between them made right.

And then Meredith could have sworn she heard a baby laugh.

She spun around just as the complete silence of the room was broken by a single pair of hands clapping.

"How dare you?" she said, feeling as if Prince Adrian had spied on her in a very private moment.

And then Meredith realized it was the wrong prince!

It was not Adrian, eager and clumsily enthusiastic, like a playful St. Bernard, but the man who would be king.

Prince Heartbreaker.

Prince Kiernan of Chatam had slipped inside the door, and stood with his back braced lazily against the richness of the walnut. The crinkle of amusement around the deep azure of his eyes disappeared at her reprimand.

"How dare I? Excuse me. I thought I was in my own home." He looked astonished, rather than annoyed, by her reprimand.

"I'm sorry, Your Highness," she stammered. "I was taken off guard. That dance was never intended for anyone to see."

"More's the pity," he said mildly.

Meredith saw, instantly, that the many pictures of him printed by papers and tabloids did not begin to do him justice. And she saw why he was called Prince Heartbreaker.

Such astonishing good looks should be illegal. Paired with his station in life, it seemed quite possible he could break hearts with a glance!

Prince Kiernan was more than gorgeous, he was stunning. Tall and exquisitely fit, his perfectly groomed hair was crisp and dark, his face chiseled masculine perfection, from the cut of high cheekbones to the jut of a perfectly clefted chin.

Though he was dressed casually—it looked like he had been riding, the tan-colored jodhpurs hugging the cut of the muscle of his thigh—nothing could hide the supreme confidence of his bearing.

He was a man who had been born to great wealth and privilege and it showed in every single thing about him. But an underlying strength—around the stern line of his mouth, the way he held his broad shoulders—also showed.

And Meredith Whitmore was, suddenly, not an accomplished dancer and a successful businesswoman, but the cleaning lady's daughter, who had been trained to be invisible in front of her "betters," who had stupidly thrown her life away on a dream that had ended more badly than she ever could have imagined.

She thought of the unleashed sensuousness of that dance, and felt a fire burn up her cheeks. She prayed—desperately—for the floor to open up and swallow her.

But she, of all people, should know by now that the desperation of a prayer in no way led to its answer.

"Your Royal Highness," she said, and all her grace fled her as she did a clumsy curtsy.

"You can't be Meredith Whitmore," the prince said, clearly astounded.

"I can't?"

Even his voice—cultured, deep, melodic, masculine—was unfairly attractive, as sensual as a touch.

It was no wonder she was questioning her own identity!

Meredith *begged* the confident, career-oriented woman she had become to push the embarrassed servant's daughter off center stage. She begged the vulnerability that the memory of Carly's laugh had brought to the surface to go away.

"Why can't I be Meredith Whitmore?" Despite her effort to speak with careless confidence, she thought she sounded like a rejected actress who had been refused a coveted role.

"From what Adrian said, I was expecting, um, a female version of Attila the Hun."

"Flattering."

A hint of a smile raced across the firm line of those stern lips and then was gone.

It was definitely a smile that could break hearts. Meredith reminded herself, firmly, she hadn't one to break!

"You did give me a hard time for standing inside my own door," he said thoughtfully. "Adrian said, er, that you were something of a taskmaster."

The hesitation said it all. Meredith guessed that Prince Adrian had not worded it that politely. The fact that the two princes had discussed her—in unflattering terms— made her wish for the floor to open up redouble.

"I was actually about to leave," she said with the

haughtiness of a woman who was not the least vulnerable to him, and whose time was extremely valuable—which it was! "He's very late."

"I'm afraid he's not coming. He sent me with the message."

Meredith felt a shiver of apprehension. "Is it just for today? That Prince Adrian isn't coming?"

But somehow she already knew the answer. And it was her fault. She had driven him too hard. She had overstepped herself. He didn't want to do it anymore. She had obviously been too bossy, too intense, too driven to perfection.

A female version of Attila the Hun.

"I'm sorry. He's been injured in an accident."

"Badly?" Meredith asked. The prince, puppylike in his eagerness to please, had been hurt, and all she was thinking about was that she was being inconvenienced by his tardiness?

"He's been in a riding accident. When I left him his knee was the approximate size and shape of a basketball."

Meredith marshaled herself, not wanting him to see her flinch from the blow to her plans, to her girls.

"Well, as terrible as that is," she said with all the composure she could muster, "the show must go on. I'm sure with a little resourcefulness we can rewrite the part. We aren't called No Princes for nothing."

"No Princes? Is that the name of your dance troupe, then?"

"It is actually more than a dance troupe."

"All right," he conceded. "I'm intrigued. Tell me more."

To her surprise, the prince looked authentically interested. Despite not wanting to be vulnerable to him in any way, Meredith took a deep breath, knowing she could not pass up this opportunity to tell someone so influential about her group.

"No Princes is an organization that targets girls from the tough neighborhoods of the inner city of Chatam. At fifteen and sixteen and seventeen a frightening number of these girls, still children really, are much too eager to leave school, and have babies, instead of getting their education."

Her story, *exactly*, but there was no reason to tell him that part.

"We try to give them a desire to learn, marketable skills, and a strong sense of self-reliance and self-sufficiency. We hope to influence them so they do not feel they need rescuing from their circumstances by the first boy they perceive as a prince!"

Michael Morgan had been that prince for her. He had been new to the neighborhood, drifted in from somewhere with a sexy Australian accent. She was fatherless, craving male attention, susceptible.

And thanks to him, she would never be that vulnerable again. Though the man who stood before her would certainly be a test of any woman's resolve to not believe in fairy tales.

"And where do you fit into that vision, my gypsy ballerina?"

So, the prince *had* seen something. *His* gypsy ballerina? Some terrible awareness of him tingled along her spine, but she kept her tone entirely professional when she answered him. She, of all people, knew that tingle to be a warning sign.

"I'm afraid all work and no play is a poor equation for anyone, never mind these girls. As well as looking after a lot of paperwork for No Princes, I get to do the *fun* part. I teach the girls how to dance."

"Prince Adrian didn't seem to think it was fun," he said dryly.

"I may have pushed him a little hard," she admitted.

Prince Kiernan actually laughed, and it changed everything. Did the papers deliberately capture him looking grim and humorless?

Because in that spontaneous shout of laughter Meredith had an unfortunate glimpse of the kind of man every woman hoped would ride in on his white charger to rescue her from her life.

Even a woman such as herself, soured on romance, could feel the pull of his smile. She steeled herself against that traitorous flutter in her breast and reminded herself a man did not get the name Prince Heartbreaker because he was in the market for a princess!

In fact, before he'd been called Prince Heartbreaker, hadn't he been called the Playboy Prince? And something else? Oh, yes, the Prince of Heartaches. He was a dangerous, dangerous man.

"Kudos to you if you *could* push him hard," Prince Kiernan said wryly. "How did Adrian come to be a part of all this?"

It was a relief to hide behind words! They provided the veneer of rational, civilized thought, when something rebellious in her was reacting to him in a very upsettingly primal way!

"One of our girls, Erin Fisher, wrote a dance number that really tells the whole story of what No Princes does. It's quite a remarkable piece. It takes girls from hanging out on street corners flirting with boys, going nowhere, to a place of remarkable strength and admirable ambition. The piece has a dream sequence in it that shows a girl dancing with a prince.

"Unbeknownst to any of us, Erin sent it to the palace, along with a video of the girls dancing, as a performance suggestion for *An Evening to Remember*, the fund-raiser that will open Blossom Week. She very boldly suggested Prince Adrian for the part in the dream sequence. The girls have been delirious since he accepted."

Meredith was shocked by the sudden emotion that clawed at her throat. She shouldn't have a favorite, but of all the girls, Erin was so much like her, so bright, so full of potential. And so sensitive. So easily hurt and discouraged.

"I'm sorry for their disappointment," Prince Kiernan said, making Meredith realize, uneasily, he was reading her own disappointment with way too much accuracy.

Prince Kiernan was larger than life. He was *better* than the pictures. His voice was as sexy as a piece of raw silk scraped along the nape of a neck. He was a *real* prince.

But still, she represented No Princes. She *taught* young women not to get swept away, not to believe in fairy tales. She rescued the vulnerable from throwing their lives away on fantasies, as she had, no matter how appealing the illusion.

The abundance of tabloid pictures of actress Tiffany Wells' tearstained face since her broken engagement with this man underscored Meredith's determination not to be vulnerable in any way, to any man, ever again.

Her days of vulnerability were over.

"A little disappointment does nothing but build character," she said crisply.

He regarded her thoughtfully. She thrust her chin up and folded her arms over her chest.

"Again, I'm sorry."

"It's quite all right," she said, forcing her voice to be firm. "Things happen that are out of our control."

She would have snatched those words back without speaking them if she knew that they would swing the door of memory wide open on the event in her life that had been most out of her control.

Meredith slammed the door shut again, blinking hard and swallowing.

The prince was looking at her way too closely, again, as if he could see things she would not have him see. That she would not have anyone see.

"Goodbye," Meredith managed to squeak out. "Thank you for coming personally, Your Highness. I'll let the girls know. We'll figure something out. It's not a big deal."

She was babbling, trying to outrun the quiver in her voice and failing. She kept talking.

"The girls will get over it. In fact, they're used to it. They're used to disappointment. As I said, we can re-write the part Prince Adrian was going to play. Anybody can play a prince."

Though she might have believed that much more strongly before standing in the damnably charismatic presence of a real one!

"Goodbye," she said, more strongly, a hint for him to go. The quiver was out of her voice, but she had not slammed the door on her worst memory as completely as she had hoped. She could feel tears sparking behind her eyes.

But Prince Kiernan wasn't moving. It was probably somewhere in that stuffy royal protocol book she'd been given that she wasn't supposed to turn her back on him first, that she wasn't to dismiss *him*, but she had to. She had to escape him gazing at her so piercingly, as if her whole life story was playing in her eyes and he could see it. It would only be worse if she cried.

She turned swiftly and began pack up the music equipment she had brought in preparation for her session with Adrian.

She waited for the sound of footfalls, the whisper of the door opening and shutting.

But it didn't come.

CHAPTER TWO

MEREDITH DREW TWO OR THREE steadying breaths. Only when she was sure no tears would fall did she turn back. Prince Kiernan still stood there.

She almost yearned for a lecture about protocol, but there was no recrimination in his eyes.

"It meant a lot to them, didn't it?" he asked quietly, his voice rich with sympathy, "And especially to you."

She had to steel herself against how accurately he had read her emotion, but at least he didn't have a clue as to why she was really feeling so deeply.

It felt like her survival depended on not letting on that it was a personal pain that had touched her off emotionally. So, again, she tried to hide behind words. Meredith launched into a speech she had given a thousand times to raise funds for No Princes.

"You have to understand how marginalized these girls feel. Invisible. Lacking in value. Most of them are from single-parent families, and that parent is a mother. It's part of what makes them so vulnerable when the first boy winks at them and tells them they're beautiful.

"So when a prince, when a real live prince, one of the biggest celebrities on our island recognized what they were doing as having worth, it was incredible. I think it made them have hope that their dreams really could come true. That's a hard sell in Wentworth. Hope is a dangerous thing in that world."

Kiernan's face registered Wentworth. He *knew* the name of the worst neighborhood on his island. She had successfully diverted him from her own moment of intense vulnerability.

But before she could finish congratulating herself, Prince Kiernan took a deep breath, ran a hand through the crisp silk of his dark hair.

"Hope shouldn't be a dangerous thing," he said softly, finally looking back at her. "Not in anyone's world."

Honestly, the man could make you melt if you weren't on guard. Thankfully, Meredith's life had made her stronger than that! She had seen lives—including her own—ruined by weakness, by that single moment of giving in to temptation.

And this man was a temptation!

Well, not really. Not realistically. He was a prince, and she was a servant's daughter. Some things did not mix, even in this liberated age. Her roots were in the poorest part of his kingdom. She was not an unsullied virgin. She had known tragedy beyond her years. It had taken away her ability to dream, to believe.

The only thing she believed in was her girls at No Princes. The only thing that gave her reprieve from her pain was dancing.

No, there were no fairy tales for her.

She did not rely on anyone but herself, and certainly not a man, not even a prince. That was why she had been so immune to Prince Adrian's charms.

Merry, Merry, Merry, she could almost hear her mother's weary, bitter voice, *when in all your life has a man ever done the right thing?*

Her mother had been so right.

So Prince Kiernan shocked Meredith now. By being the one man willing to do the right thing.

"I'll do it," he said with a certain grim resolve, like a man volunteering to face the firing squad. "I'll take Prince Adrian's place."

Meredith felt her mouth open, and then snapped shut again. There was no joy in the prince's offer, only a sense of obligation.

Naturally I'll marry you, Michael had lied to her when Meredith had told him about the coming baby.

Oh, darlin', pigs will fly before that man's going to marry you. You're dreaming, girl.

Meredith had a feeling the prince would *never* run out on his obligations. Still, she had to discourage him.

Teaching Prince Adrian the steps to the dream sequence dance had been one thing. Despite his royal status, working with the young prince had been something like dealing with a slightly unruly younger brother.

This man was not like that.

There were things a whole lot more dangerous than hope.

And Prince Kiernan of Chatam, the Playboy Prince, the Prince of Heartaches, Prince Heartbreaker, was one of them.

"It's not a good idea," Meredith said. "Thank you, anyway, but no."

The prince looked shocked that anyone could turn down such a generous offer. And then downright annoyed.

"You just have no idea how much work is involved," Meredith said, a last ditch effort to somehow save herself. "Prince Adrian had committed to several hours a day. We have just over a week left until *An Evening to Remember.* I don't see how we could get you caught up. Really." He didn't seem to be hearing her, so she repeated, "Thanks, but no."

Prince Kiernan crossed the room to her. Closer, she could see his great height. The man towered over her. His scent was drugging.

But not as much as the light in those amazing blue eyes. Still cool, there was something powerful there. His gaze locked on her face and held her fast in a spell.

"Do I look like a man who is afraid of work?" he asked, softly, challengingly.

The truth? He didn't have a clue what work was. He wouldn't know it probably took a team of people hours on their hands and knees to polish these floors, to clean the windows, to make the crystals on the chandeliers sparkle like diamonds.

But she didn't say that because when she looked into his face she saw raw strength beneath the sophisticated surface. She saw resolve.

And Meredith saw exactly what he was offering. He was *saving* the dreams of all the girls. As much as she did not want to be exposed to all this raw masculine energy every single day for the next week, was this really her choice to make?

Ever since Prince Adrian had agreed to dance in *her* production, Erin had dreamed bigger. Her marks at school had become astonishing. She had mentioned, shyly, to Meredith, she might think of becoming a doctor.

Meredith couldn't throw away the astonishing gift Prince Kiernan was offering her girls because she felt threatened, vulnerable.

Still, her eyes fastened on the sensuous curve of his full lower lip.

God? Don't do this to me.

But she already knew she was not on the list of those who had their prayers answered.

The prince surprised her by smiling, though it only intensified her thought, of *don't do this to me.*

"I'm afraid," he said, "it's probably you who doesn't know how much work will be involved. I have been called the Prince of Foot Aches. And you have only a short time to turn that around? Poor girl."

His smile heightened her sense of danger, of something spinning out of her control. Meredith wanted, with a kind of desperation, to tell him this could not possibly work.

Dance with him every day? Touch him, and look at him, and somehow not be sucked into all the romantic longings a close association to such a dynamic and handsome man was bound to stir up?

But she had all her pain to keep her strong, a fortress of grief whose walls she could hide behind.

And she thought of Erin Fisher, and the girl she herself used to be. Meredith thought about hopes and dreams, and the excited delirium of the dance troupe.

"Thank you, Your Highness," she said formally. "When would you be able to begin?"

Prince Kiernan had jumped out of airplanes, participated in live-round military exercises, flown a helicopter.

He had ridden highly strung ponies on polo fields and jumped horses over the big timbers of steeplechases.

He had sailed solo in rough water, ocean kayaked and done deep-sea dives. The truth was he did not lead a life devoid of excitement and, in fact, had confronted fear often.

What came as a rather unpleasant surprise to him

was the amount of trepidation he felt about *dancing*, of all things.

He knew at least part of that trepidation was due to the fact he had made the offer to help the No Princes dance troupe on an impulse. His plan, he recalled, had been to see the Dragon-heart with his own eyes, make Prince Adrian's excuses, and then dismiss the dance instructor.

One thing Prince Kiernan of Chatam was not, was impulsive. He did not often veer from the plan. It was the one luxury he could not afford.

That eighteenth summer, his year of restless energy, heady lack of restraint, and impulsive self-indulgence had taught him that for him, spontaneity was always going to have a price.

The military had given him an outlet for all that pent-up energy and replaced impulsiveness with discipline.

Those years after his eighteenth birthday had reinforced his knowledge that his life did not really belong to him. Every decision was weighed and measured cautiously in terms, not of his well-being, but the well-being of his small island nation. There was little room for spontaneity in a world that was highly structured and carefully planned. His schedule of appointments and royal obligations sometimes stretched years in advance.

Aware he was *always* watched and judged, Kiernan had become a man who was calm and cool, absolutely controlled in every situation. His life was public, his demeanor was always circumspect. Unlike his cousin, he did not have the luxury of emotional outbursts when things did not go his way. Unlike his cousin, he could not pull pranks, be late, forget appointments.

He was rigidly *correct*, and if his training and inborn sense of propriety did not exactly inspire warm fuzziness, it did inspire confidence. People knew they could trust him and trust his leadership. Even after Francine, the whispers of what had happened to her, people seemed to give him the benefit of the doubt and trust him, still.

But then his relationship with Tiffany Wells, an exception to the amount of control he exerted over his life, seemed to have damaged that trust. His reputation had escalated from that of a man who was coolly remote to a man who was a heartless love-rat.

There would be no more losses of control.

And while it was not high on his list of priorities to be popular, he did see performing the dance as an opportunity to repair a battered image. His and Tiffany's breakup was a year ago. It was time for people to see him as capable of having a bit of fun, relaxing, being human.

Was that why he'd said yes? A public relations move? An opportunity to polish a tarnished image, as Adrian had suggested?

No.

Was it because of the girls, then? He had been moved by Miss Whitmore's description of the goals of No Princes. Kiernan had felt a very real surge of compassion for underprivileged young women who wanted someone they perceived as important to value them, to recognize what they were doing as having merit.

But had that been the reason he had said yes? The reason he had been swayed to this unlikely cause that was certainly going to require more of him than signing a cheque, or giving a speech or just showing up and shaking a few hands? Was that the reason he'd said yes to a cause that had his staff running in circles trying to rearrange his appointments around his new schedule? Again, *no.*

So, was it her, then? Was Meredith Whitmore the reason he had said *yes* to something so far out of his comfort zone?

Kiernan let his mind go to her. She had astounding hazel eyes, that hinted at fire, unconsciously pouty lips, a smattering of light freckles and a wild tangle of auburn locks, the exact kind of hair that made a man's hands itch to touch.

Add to that the lithe dancer's body dressed in a leotard that clung to long, lean legs, and a too-large T-shirt that hinted at, rather than revealed, luscious curves. There was simply no denying she was attractive, but not in the way one might expect of a dancer. She was at odds with the dance he had witnessed, because she seemed more uptight than Bohemian, more Sergeant Major than free-spirited gypsy.

Beautiful? Undoubtedly. But the truth was he was wary of beauty, rather than enchanted by it, particularly after Tiffany. The face of an angel had hidden a twisted heart, capable of deception that had rattled his world.

Meredith Whitmore did not look capable of deception, but there was something about her he didn't get. She was young, and yet her eyes were shadowed, cool, measuring.

Not exactly cold, but Kiernan could understand why Adrian had called her Dragon-heart, like something fierce burned at her core that you would get close to at your own peril.

So, he had said yes, not because it would be a good public relations move, which it would be, not wholly on the grounds of compassion, though it was that, and not because of Meredith's beauty or mystery. It was not even her very obvious emotional reaction to her disappointment and her valiant effort to hide that from him.

No, he thought frowning, the answer to his agreeing to this was somewhere in those first moments when she had been dancing, unaware of his presence. But what *exactly* it was that had been so compelling as to overcome his characteristic aversion to spontaneity eluded him.

So, the astounding fact was that Prince Kiernan, the most precise of men, could not pinpoint precisely what had made him agree to do this. And the fact that he could not decipher his own motivations was deeply disturbing to him.

Now, he paused at the doorway of the ballroom, took a deep breath, put back his shoulders, and strode in.

He hoped to find her dancing, knowing the answer was in that, but she was not to be caught off guard twice.

Meredith was fiddling with electronic equipment in one corner of the huge ballroom, her tongue caught between her teeth, her brow drawn down in a scowl. She looked up and saw him, straightened.

"Miss Whitmore," he said.

She was wearing purple tights today, rumpled leg warmers, and a hairband of an equally hideous shade of purple held auburn curls off her face. She didn't have on a speck of makeup. She did have on an oversized lime green T-shirt that said, *Don't kiss any frogs.*

He was used to people trying to impress him, at least a little bit, but she was obviously dressed only for comfort and for the work ahead. He wasn't quite sure if he was charmed or annoyed by her lack of effort to look appealing.

And he wasn't quite sure if he felt charmed or annoyed that she looked appealing anyway!

"Prince Kiernan," she said, a certain coolness in her tone, which was mirrored in the amazing green gold of those eyes, "thank you for rearranging your schedule for this."

"I did as much as I could. I may have to take the occasional official phone call."

"Understandable. Thank you for being on time."

"I'm always on time." He could see why she intimidated Adrian. No greeting, no polite *how are you today?* There was a no-nonsense tone to her voice that reminded him of a palace tutor. He could certainly hear a hint of Dragon-heart in there!

"Brilliant," she said, and then stood back, folded her arms over her chest, and inspected him. Now he could also see a hint of Sergeant Henderson as her brows lowered in disapproval! He felt like he had showed up for a military exercise in full dress uniform when the dress of the day was combat attire.

"Do those slacks have some give to them? I brought some dance pants, just in case."

Dance pants? He disliked that uncharacteristic moment of spontaneity that had made him say yes to this whole idea more by the second. He wasn't going to ask her what dance pants were, exactly. He was fairly certain he could guess.

"I'm sure these will be fine," he said stiffly, in a voice that let her know a prince did not discuss his *pants* with a maiden, no matter how fair.

She looked doubtful, but shrugged and turned to the electronics. "I have this video I want you to watch, if you don't mind, Your Highness."

As he came and stood beside her, the scent of lemons

tickled his nostrils. She flicked a switch on a bright pink laptop. The light from the chandeliers danced in her hair, making the red threads in it spark like fire.

"This has had twelve million hits," she said, accessing a video-sharing website.

He focused on a somewhat grainy video of a wedding celebration. A large room had a crowd standing around the edges of it, a space cleared in the center of it for a youthful-looking bride and groom.

"And now for the first dance," a voice announced.

The groom took one of his bride's hands, placed his other with a certain likeable awkwardness on her silk-clad waist.

"This is the bridal waltz," Meredith told him, "and it's a very traditional three-step waltz."

The young groom began to shuffle around the dance floor.

Kiernan felt relieved. The groom danced just like him. "Nothing to learn," he pronounced, "I can already do that." He looked at his watch. "Maybe I can squeeze in a ride before lunch."

"I've already lost one prince to riding," she said without looking up from the screen. "No riding until we're done the performance."

Kiernan felt a shiver of pure astonishment, and looked at Meredith Whitmore again, harder. She didn't appear to notice.

She tacked on a *"Your Highness"* as if that made bossing him around perfectly acceptable. Well, it wasn't as if Adrian hadn't warned him.

"Excuse me, but I really didn't sign up to have you run my—"

Meredith shushed him as if he was a schoolboy. "This part's important."

He was so startled that he thought he might laugh out loud. No one, but no one, talked to him like that. He slid her a look as if he was seeing her for the first time. She *was* bossy. And what's worse, she was *cute* when she was bossy.

Not that he would let her know that. He reached by her, and clicked on the pause button on the screen.

It was her turn to be startled, but he had her full attention. And he was not falling under the spell of those haunting gold-green eyes.

"I am already giving you two hours a day of practice time that I can barely afford," he told her sternly. "You will not tell me what to do with the rest of my time. Are we clear?"

Rather than looking clear, she looked mutinous.

"I've set aside a certain amount of my time for you, not given you run of my life." There. That should remind her a little gratitude would not be out of order.

But she did not look grateful, or cowed, either. In fact, Meredith Whitmore looked downright peeved.

"I've set aside a certain amount of time for you, also," she announced haughtily. "I'm not investing more of my time to have you end up out of commission, too! We're on a very limited schedule because of Prince Adrian's horse mishap."

Prince Kiernan looked at Meredith closely. Right behind the annoyance in her gorgeous eyes was something else.

"You're deathly afraid of horses," he said softly.

Meredith stared up into the sapphire eyes of the prince. The truth was she was not deathly afraid of horses.

But she was deathly afraid of a world out of her control.

The fact that he had got the *deathly afraid* part of her with such accuracy made her feel off balance, as if she was a wide open book to him.

She felt like she needed to slam that book shut, and quickly, before he read too much of it. Let him think she was afraid of horses!

It wasn't without truth, and it would be so much better than the full truth. That Meredith Whitmore was afraid of the caprice of life.

"Of course I'm afraid of horses," she said. "They are an uncommon occurrence in the streets of Wentworth. My closest encounter was at a Blossom Festival parade, where a huge beast went out of control, plunged into the crowd and knocked over spectators."

"You're from Wentworth, then?" he asked, still watching her way too closely.

He seemed more interested in that than her horse encounter. Well, good. That alone should erect the walls between them. "Yes," she said, tilting her chin proudly, "I am."

But instead of feeling as if the barrier went up higher, their stations in life now clearly defined, when he nodded slowly, she felt as if she had revealed way too much of herself! She turned from the prince swiftly, and clicked on the Play button on the screen, anxious to outrun the intensity in his eyes.

She focused, furiously, on the video. As the groom looked at his new wife, something melted in that young man's face. It was like watching a boy transform into a man, his look became so electric, so filled with tenderness.

Too aware of the prince standing beside her, Meredith scrambled to find sanctuary in the familiar.

"If you listen," she said, all business, all dance

instructor, "the music is changing, so are the steps. The dance has a more *salsa* feel to it now. Salsa originated in Cuba, though if you watch you'll see the influences are quite a unique blend of European and African."

"This really is your world, isn't it?" Kiernan commented.

"It is," she said, and she prayed to find refuge in it as she always had. It was just way too easy to feel something, especially as the dance they watched became more sensual. It felt as if the heat was being turned up in this room. Prince Kiernan was standing so close to her, she could feel the warmth radiating off his shoulder.

On the video, the young groom's whole posture changed, became sure and sexy, his stance possessive, as he guided his new bride around the room to the quickening tempo of the music.

"Here's another transition," Meredith said, "He's moving into a toned down hip-hop now, what I'd call a new school or street version rather than the original urban break dancing version."

A man's voice, an exquisite tenor soared above the dancing couple. *I never had a clue, until I met you, all that I could be—*

And the man let go of his wife's hand and waist and began to dance by himself. He danced as if his new bride alone watched him. Gone was the uncertain shuffle, and in its place was a performance that was nothing short of sizzling, every move choreographed to show a love story unfolding: passion, strength, devotion, a man growing more sure of himself with each passing second.

"You'll see this is very sporty," Meredith said, "and these kind of moves require amazing upper body strength, as well as flexibility and good balance.

It's part music, part dance, but mostly guts and pure athleticism."

She cast him a look. The prince certainly would have the upper body strength. And she had not a doubt about his guts and athleticism.

What she was doubting was her ability to keep any form of detachment while she worked with him trying to perfect such an intimate performance.

The dancer on the computer screen catapulted up onto one hand, froze there for a moment, came back down, and then did the very same move on his other side. He came up to his feet, tossed off his jacket, and loosened his tie.

"If he takes anything else off I'm leaving," Kiernan said. "It's like a striptease."

She shot him a look. Now this was unexpected. Prince Kiernan a prude? Where was the man of *Playboy Prince* fame?

They watched together as the groom's feet and hips and arms all moved in an amazing show of coordinated sensuality. The bride moved back to the edges of the crowd, who had gone wild. They were clapping, and calling their approval.

As the final notes of the music died the young groom took a run back toward his bride, fell to his knees and his momentum carried him a good ten feet across the floor. He caught his wife around her waist and gazed up at her with a look on his face that made Meredith want to melt.

The young groom's face mirrored the final words of the song, *I have found every treasure I ever looked for.*

There was something so astoundingly intimate about the video that in the stillness that followed, Meredith found herself almost embarrassed to look at Kiernan, as if they had seen something meant to be private between a man and a woman.

She pulled herself together. It was dancing. It was theater. There was nothing personal about it.

"What did you think?"

"I thought watching that was very uncomfortable," Kiernan bit out.

So, he'd picked up on the intimacy, too.

"It was like watching a mating dance," he continued.

"I see we have a bit of prudishness to overcome," she said, as if the discomfort was his alone.

But when his eyes went to her lips, Meredith had the feeling that the prince had a way of persuading her he was anything but a prude.

Something sizzled in the air between them, but she refused to allow him to see she was intimidated by it. And a little thrilled by it, too!

Meredith put her hands on her hips and studied him as if he was an interesting specimen who had found his way under her microscope.

"You didn't see the romance in it?" she demanded. "The delight of entering a new life? The hope for the future? His love for her? His willingness to do anything for her?"

"Up to and including making a fool of himself in front of—how many did you say—twelve million people? Every male in the world whose bride-to-be has insisted they look at this video is throwing darts at a target with his face on it!"

"He didn't look foolish! He looked enraptured. Every woman dreams of seeing *that* look on their beloved's face."

"Do they?" He was watching her again, with that look in his eyes. Too stripping, too knowing. "Do you?"

Did she? Did some little scrap of weakness still exist in her that wanted desperately to believe? That did want to see a look like the one on that young groom's face directed at her?

"I'm all done with romantic nonsense," she said, not sure whom she was trying to convince. Prince Kiernan? Or herself?

"Are you?" he asked softly.

"Yes!" Before he asked *why*, before those sapphire eyes pierced the darkest secrets of a broken heart, she rushed on.

"Prince Kiernan, the truth is I am an exception to the rule. People generally *love* romantic nonsense. Romance is the ultimate in entertainment," Meredith continued. "It has that feel-good quality to it, it promises a happy ending."

"Which it doesn't always deliver," he said sourly.

The ugly parts of his life had been splashed all over the papers for everyone to read about. He was, after all, Prince Heartbreaker.

But Meredith was stunned that what she felt for him, in that moment, was sympathy. For a moment, there was an unguarded pain in his eyes that made him an open book to her.

Which was the last thing she needed.

"All I'm saying," Meredith said, a little more gently, "is that if you can do a dance somewhat similar to that, it will bring down the house. What do you think?"

"How about I'm not doing anything similar to that? Not even if the entertainment value is unquestionable."

"Well, of course not that dance precisely, but that

video captures the spirit of what we want to do with this portion of the dance piece."

"It's too personal," he said firmly.

"It's for a dream sequence, Your Highness. This kind of dancing is very much like acting."

"Could we *act* more reserved?"

"I suppose we could. But where's the fun in that? And the delicious surprise? You know, you do have a reputation of being somewhat, um, stodgy. This would turn that on its head."

"Stodgy?" he sputtered. "Stern, remote, unapproachable, even snobby I can handle. But stodgy? Isn't stodgy just another word for prudish?"

He looked at her lips again, and again his eyes were an open book to her.

Meredith had to keep herself from gasping at what she saw there, something primitive in its intensity, a desire to tangle his hands in her hair, yank her to him, and find out who was really the prude, who was really stodgy.

But he shoved his hands deep in his pockets, instead.

Was she relieved? Or disappointed by his control?

Relieved, she told herself, but it sounded like a lie even in her own mind.

"We'll modify the routine to your comfort level," she said. "Now, let's just see where you're at right now. We can try and tweak the routine after that."

She turned her back to him, gathering herself, trying to regain her sense of professionalism. She fiddled with her equipment and the "bridal waltz" came on again.

She turned back to him and held out her hand. "Your Highness?"

It was the moment of truth. She had a sudden sense,

almost of premonition. If he accepted the invitation of her hand *everything* was going to change.

He must have felt it, too, because he hesitated.

Meredith took a deep breath.

"Your Highness?"

He took her hand.

And Meredith felt the sizzle of it all the way to her elbow.

CHAPTER THREE

"THIS IS HOW WE WOULD open the number," Meredith said, "with a simple three-step waltz, just like the one in the video."

Prince Kiernan moved forward, trying not to think of how her hand fit so perfectly into his, or about the softness of her delicately curved waist.

He was also trying not to look at her lips! The temptation to show Miss Meredith Whitmore he was no prude, and not stodgy, either, was overwhelming. And since he didn't appear to be convincing her with his stellar dance moves, her lips were becoming more a temptation by the minute.

"Hmm," she said, "Not bad *exactly*. I mean obviously you know a simple three-step waltz. You just aren't, how can I say this? Fluid! Mind you, that might just work at the beginning of the number. It would be great to start off with a certain stand-offishness, an armor that protects you from your discomfort with closeness."

Was she talking about the theatrics of the damned dance or could she seriously read his personality that well from a few steps? The urge to either kiss her or bolt strengthened.

He couldn't kiss her. It would be entirely inappropriate, even if it was to make a point.

And he didn't have to bolt. He was the prince. He could just say he'd changed his mind, bow out of his participation in the dance.

"But right here," she said, cocking her head at the music, "listen for the transition, we could have you loosen up. Maybe we could try that now."

Instead of saying he'd changed his mind, he subtly rolled his shoulders and loosened his grip on her hand. He wasn't quite sure what to do with the hand on her waist, so he flexed his fingers slightly.

"Prince Kiernan, this isn't a military march."

Oh, there were definitely shades of Dragon-heart in that tone!

He tried again. He used the same method he would use before trying to take a difficult shot with the rifle. He took a deep breath, held it, let it out slowly.

"No, that's tighter. I can feel the tension in your hand. Think of something you enjoy doing that makes you feel relaxed. What would that be?"

"Reading a book?"

She sighed as if it was just beginning to occur to her he might, indeed, be her first hopeless case. "Maybe something a bit more physical that you feel relaxed doing."

He thought of nothing he could offer—everything he could think of that he did that was physical required control, a certain wide-awake awareness that was not exactly relaxing, though it was not unenjoyable.

"Riding a bicycle!" she suggested enthusiastically. "Yes, picture that, riding your bike down a quiet tree-lined country lane with thatched roofed cottages and black-and-white cows munching grass in fields, your picnic lunch in your basket."

He changed his grip on her hand. If he wasn't mistaken

his palm was beginning to sweat, he was trying so hard to relax.

She glanced up at him, reading his silence, "Picnic lunch in the basket of a bicycle is not part of your world, is it?"

"Not really. I'm relaxed on horseback. But then that's not part of your world."

"And," she reminded him, a touch crankily, "horses are the reason why you're in this position in the first place."

Again, he felt that odd little shiver about being spoken to like that. It could have been seen as insolent.

But it wasn't. Adrian had warned him, after all. But what he couldn't have warned him was that he would find it somewhat refreshing to have someone just state their opinion so honestly to him, to speak to him so directly.

"In the pictures of you in the paper," she went on, "your horses seem absolutely terrifying—wild-eyed and frothy-mouthed." She shuddered.

"Don't be fooled by the pictures you see in the papers," he said. "The press delights in catching me at the worst possible moments. It helps with the villain-of-the-week theme they have going."

"I think it's 'villain-of-the-month'," she said.

"Or the year."

And unexpectedly they enjoyed a little chuckle together.

"So, you've seriously never ridden a bike?"

"Oh, sure, I have, but it's not a favorite pastime. I was probably on my first pony about the same time most children are given their first bicycles. Am I missing something extraordinary?"

"Not extraordinary, but so *normal*. The wind in your

hair, the exhilaration of sweeping down a big hill, racing through puddles. I just can't imagine anyone not having those lovely garden variety experiences."

He was taken aback by the genuine sympathy in her tone. "You feel sorry for me because I've rarely ridden a bike down a country lane? And never with a picnic lunch in the basket?"

"I didn't say I felt sorry for you!"

"I can hear it in your voice."

"Okay," she admitted, "I feel sorry for you."

"Well, don't," he snapped. "Nobody ever has before, and I don't see that it should start now. I occupy a place of unusual privilege and power. I am not a man who inspires sympathy, nor one who wants it, either."

"There's no need to be so touchy. It just struck me as sad. And it occurred to me that if you've never done that, you've probably never played in a mud puddle and felt the exquisite pleasure of mud squishing between your toes. You've probably never had a few drinks and thrown some darts. You've probably never known the absolute anticipation of having to save your money for a Triple Widgie Hot Fudge Sundae from Lawrence's."

"I fail to see your point."

"It's no wonder you can't dance! You've missed almost everything that's important. But what's to feel sorry about?"

He was silent. Finally, he said, "I didn't know my life had been so bereft."

She shrugged. "Somebody had to tell you."

And then he chuckled. And so did she. He realized she had succeeded in making just a little of the tension leave him. But at the same time, they had just shared something that took a little brick out of the wall of both their defenses.

"Well," he said dryly. "Imagine doing a bike ride with an entourage of security people, and members of the press jumping out in front of you to get that perfect picture. Kind of takes the country lane serenity out of the picture, doesn't it?"

"The peaceful feeling is leaving me," she admitted. "Is it a hard way to live?"

"I don't have a hard life," he said. "The opposite is probably true. Everyone envies me. And this lifestyle."

"That's not what I asked," she said quietly. "I wondered about the price, of not knowing if people like you for you or your title, of having to be on guard against the wrong photo being taken, the wrong word being uttered."

For an astounding moment it felt as if she had invaded very private territory. It annoyed him that the one brick coming out of the wall seemed to be paving the way for its total collapse.

For a moment he glimpsed something about himself being reflected back in her eyes.

He was alone. And she knew it. She saw what others had not seen.

He reminded himself that he *liked* being alone.

He allowed the moment to pass and instead of telling her anything remotely personal, he said, "How about fly-fishing a quiet stream? For my relaxing thing that I think about?"

Ah, he was shoving bricks back in the wall. Thank goodness!

"Perfect," she said. The perfect picture. Impersonal. "That kind of fishing even has a rhythm, doesn't it? See? Hold that picture in your head, because the way you are moving right now is much better."

Of course the minute she said that, it wasn't!

"I've fished on occasion," she said. "Nothing as fancy as fly-fishing. A pole and a bobber on a placid pond on a hot day."

"Really? I've always found women make scenes when they catch fish."

She rapped him with sharp playfulness on his shoulder. He was so startled by the familiarity of the move he stumbled.

"What a terrible stereotype," she reprimanded him. "I can't stand that fragile, helpless, squeals-at-a-fish stereotype."

"So, you're not a squealer?" he said, something like a smile grazing his lips.

She blushed, and it was her turn to stumble. "Good God, I didn't mean it like that."

He studied her face, and his smile deepened with satisfaction. He drew her closer and whispered in her ear, "Now who's the prude?"

But he didn't quite pull it off. Because she was blushing. He was blushing. And suddenly a very different kind of tension hissed in the air between them. He narrowly missed her toe.

With a sigh, she let go of him, moved a few steps away, regarded him thoughtfully.

"Adrian, I mean Prince Adrian, did not have these kinds of inhibitions."

"Adrian could use a few inhibitions in my opinion."

She sighed again. She was exasperated already and they'd been at this for all of fifteen minutes. "Are you going to be difficult every step of the way, Your Highness?"

"I'm afraid so."

"I'm up for a challenge," she told him stubbornly.

"I'm afraid of that, too." He said it lightly, but he was aware he was not kidding. Not even a little bit.

Meredith marshaled herself.

"Okay, let's start again." She moved closer to him, held up her hand. He took it.

"Deep breath, slide your foot, forward, one, two, right, one, two…slide, Your Highness, not goose-step! Look right into my eyes, not at your feet. Ouch!"

"That won't happen if I look at my feet," he said darkly.

"It's an occupational hazard. Don't worry about my feet. Or yours. Look into my eyes. Not like that! I feel as if you're looking at something unpleasant that got stuck to your shoe."

He scowled.

"And now as if you are looking at a badly behaved hound."

He tried to neutralize his expression.

"Bored, reviewing the troops," she pronounced.

"I am not bored when I'm reviewing the troops!"

She sighed. "Your Highness?"

"Yes?"

"Pretend you love me."

"Oh, boy," he muttered under his breath.

"Ouch," she said as her foot crunched under his toe. Well, it wasn't really his fault. What a shocking thing to say to a prince.

Pretend you love me.

Oh, God, what had made her say that? As if the tension in the air between them wasn't palpable enough!

Thankfully, the prince had no gift for pretense. He was glaring at her with a kind of pained intensity, as if she was posed over him with a dentist's drill. It was making her want to laugh, but not a happy laugh.

The nervous laugh of one who might just have to admit defeat.

Meredith had never met anyone she couldn't teach to dance. But then, of course, anyone who showed up at her studio *wanted* to learn.

And the truth?

She'd never been quite so intimidated before.

And not solely by the fact that Kiernan was a prince, either.

It was that he was the most masculine of men. He oozed a certain potent male energy that made her feel exquisitely, helplessly feminine in his presence. Her skin was practically vibrating with awareness of him, and she was on guard trying to hide that. Twice she had caught him staring at her lips with enough heat to sizzle a steak!

Unfortunately her job was to unleash all that potent male energy, to harness the surprising but undeniable chemistry between them, so that it showed in dance form. If she could manage that, she knew her prediction—that he would bring down the house—was entirely correct.

But Kiernan seemed as invested in keeping control as she was in breaking through it to that indefinable something that lurked beneath the surface of control.

"Maybe that's enough for the first day," she conceded after another painful half hour of trying to get him to relax while waltzing.

He broke his death grip on her hand with relief that was all too obvious.

"Same time tomorrow," she said, packing her gear. "I think we'll forget the waltz, and work on the next section tomorrow. I think you may find you like it. Some of the moves are amazingly athletic."

He didn't look even remotely convinced.

And an hour into their session the next morning neither was she!

"Your Highness! You have to move your hips! Just a smidgen! Please!"

"My hips are moving!"

"In lock step!"

Prince Kiernan glared at her.

Meredith sighed. "You want them to move more like this." She demonstrated, exaggerating the movement she wanted, a touch of a Tahitian fire dance. She turned and looked back at him.

The smoldering look she had wanted to see in his eyes while they were dancing yesterday was in them now.

It fell solidly into *the be careful what you wish for* category.

"Your turn," she said briskly. "Try it. I want to practically hear those hips *swishing*."

"Enough," he said, folding his arms over the solidity of his chest. "I've had enough."

"But—"

"No. Not one more word from you, Miss Whitmore."

His expression was formidable. And his tone left absolutely no doubt who the prince was.

Prince Kiernan was a beautifully made man, perfectly proportioned, long legs, flat hips and stomach, enormously broad shoulders.

But the way he moved!

"I'm just trying to say that while your bearing is very proud and military, it's a terrible posture for dancing!"

"I said not one more word. What part of that don't you

understand?" His tone was warning. "I need a break. And so do you."

He turned his back on her, took a cell phone from his pocket and made a call.

She stared at his broad back, fuming, but the truth was she was intimidated enough not to interrupt him.

When he turned back from his call, his face was set in lines that reminded her he would command this entire nation one day. He already shouldered responsibility for much of it.

"Come with me," he said.

Don't go anywhere with him, a voice inside her protested. It told her to stand her ground. It told her she had only days left to teach him to dance! They had no time to waste. Not a single second.

But Prince Kiernan expected to be obeyed and there was something in his tone that did not brook argument.

Meredith was ridiculously relieved that he didn't seem to need a break from *her*, only from dancing. He had already turned and walked away from her, holding open the ballroom door.

And Meredith was shocked to find herself passing meekly through it, actually anticipating seeing some of his palace home. She had always entered the palace grounds, and the ballroom directly through service entrances.

He went down the hallway with every expectation that she would follow him.

She ordered herself to rebel. To say that one more word that he had ordered her not to say.

But for what purpose? Why not follow him? Things were going badly. They certainly couldn't get any worse.

They hadn't even shared a chuckle this morning. Everything was way too grim, and he was way too uptight. Except for the *warrior about to ravish maiden* look she'd received after demonstrating how hips were supposed to move, the prince's guard was way up!

As it turned out, all she saw of the interior was that hallway. Still, it was luxurious: Italian marble floors, vases spilling over with fresh flowers set in recessed alcoves, light flooding in from arched windows, a painting she recognized, awed, as an original Monet. She had a cheap reproduction of that same painting in her own humble apartment.

The prince led her out a double French-paned glass door to a courtyard, and despite the freshness of the insult of being ordered not to say another word, something in Meredith sighed with delight.

The courtyard was exquisite, a walled paradise of ancient stone walls, vines climbing them. A lion's head set deep in one wall burbled out a stream of clear water. Butterflies glided in and out of early spring blooms and the warm spring air was perfumed with lilacs.

A small wrought iron table set with fine white linen was ready for tea. It was laid out for two, with cut hydrangeas as a centerpiece. A side table held a crystal pitcher, beaded with condensation from the chilled lemonade inside it. A three-tiered platter, silver, held a treasure trove of delicate pastries.

"Did you order this?" she asked, astounded. She barely refrained from adding *for me?* She felt stunned by the loveliness of it, and aware she felt her guard was being stormed.

As an only child she had dreamed tea parties, acted them out with her broken crockery, castoffs from houses her mother had cleaned. Only her companion then had been a favorite teddy bear, Beardly, ink stained by some disdainful rich child who'd had so many teddy bears to choose from that this vandalized one had made its way to the cleaning lady's daughter.

This time her companion was not nearly so sympathetic or safe!

"Sit down," he told her. Not an invitation.

The delight of the garden, and the table set for tea, had stolen her ability to protest. She sat. So did he. He poured lemonade in crystal goblets.

She took a tentative sip, and bit back a comment that it was fresh, not powder. As if he would know that lemonade could be made from a pouch!

"Have a pastry," he said.

Pride wanted to make her refuse the delicacies presented to her, but the deprived child she'd been eyed the plate greedily, and coveted a taste of every single treat on it. In her childhood she had had to pretend soda crackers and margarine were tea pastries. She selected a cream puff that looked like a swan. She wanted to look at it longer, appreciate the effort and the art that went into it.

And at the same time she did not want to let on how overawed she was. She took a delicate bite.

She was pretty sure Prince Kiernan had deliberately waited until she was under its influence before he spoke.

"Now," he said sternly, "we will discuss *swishing*."

The cream puff completely undermined her defenses, because she said nothing at all. She made no defense for swishing. None. In fact, she licked a little dollop of pure white cream off the swan's icing-sugar-dusted feathers.

For a moment, he seemed distracted, then he blinked and looked away.

But there was less sternness in his tone when he spoke.

"I am not swishing my hips," he told her. "Not today, not tomorrow, not ever."

The sting was taken out of it completely by the fact he glanced back at her just as she was using her tongue to capture a stray piece of whipped cream from her lips and seemed to lose his train of thought entirely.

"I think," she said reverently, "that's about the best thing I've ever tasted. Sorry. What were you saying?"

He passed the tray to her again. "I don't remember."

She was sure a more sophisticated person would be content with the cream puff, but the little girl in her who had eaten soda crackers howled inwardly at her attempt to be disciplined.

She mollified her inner child by choosing a little confection of chocolate and flaky pastry. He was doing this on purpose. Using the exquisiteness of the treats to bribe her, to sway her into seeing things his way.

"It was something about swishing," she decided. The pastry was so fragile it threatened to disintegrate under her touch. She bit it in half, closed her eyes, and suppressed a moan.

"Was it?" he growled, the sound of a man tormented.

"I think it was." She opened her eyes, licked the edge of the pastry, and a place where chocolate had melted on her hand. "That was fantastic. You have to try that one."

He grabbed the chocolate confection in question and

chomped on it with much less finesse than she would have expected from a prince. He seemed rattled.

"Do these have drugs in them?" she asked.

"I was just about to ask myself the same thing. Because I can't seem to keep my mind on—"

"Swishing," she filled in for him, eyeing the tray. "Never mind. It's not as important as I thought. We'll figure out something you're comfortable with."

He smiled, at first she thought because he had been granted reprieve from swishing. Then she realized he was smiling at her. "You have a sweet tooth. One wouldn't know to look at you."

Between his smile and the confections, and the fact he *looked* at her, she didn't have a chance.

"Yes," Meredith conceded, "let's forget swishing. It would have been fun. There's no doubt about that. The audience would have gone wild, but it's not really *you* if you know what I mean."

"Why don't you try that one?"

He was rewarding her for the fact he had gotten his way. She could not allow herself to be bribed. "Which one?"

"The one you are staring at."

"I couldn't possibly," she said wistfully.

"I'd be disappointed if you didn't."

"In that case," she said blissfully and took the tiny chocolate-dipped cherry from the tray. "Do you eat like this every day?"

"No," he said a trifle hoarsely, "I must say I don't."

"A pity."

Outside the delightful cloister of the garden, she heard the distinctive clop of hooves on cobblestone.

"Ah," he said with a bit too much eagerness, getting

up. "There's my ride. Please feel free to stay and enjoy the garden as long as you like. Tomorrow, then."

Again, it was not a suggestion or a question. No, she had just been given a royal dictate. He was done dancing for the day, whether she was or not.

He strode away from her, opened an arched doorway of heavy wood embedded in the rock wall and went out it.

Do something, Meredith commanded herself. So she did. She took a butter tart and popped the entire thing in her mouth. Then, ashamed of her lack of spunk, she leapt from her chair and followed him out the gate. She had to let the prince know that time was of the essence now. If he rode today they would have to work harder tomorrow. She'd made one concession, but she couldn't allow him to think that made her a pushover, a weakling so bowled over by his smile and tea in the garden that he could get away with anything.

She burst out of the small courtyard and found herself in the front courtyard of the castle. She stood there for a moment, delighted and shocked by the opulence of the main entrance courtyard in front of the palace.

The fountain at its center shot geysers of water over the life-size bronze of Prince Kiernan's grandfather riding a rearing warhorse. The courtyard was fragrant, edged as it was with formal gardens that were bright with exotic flowering trees.

The palace sat on top of Chatam's most prominent hill, and overlooked the gently rolling countryside of the island. In the near distance were farms and red-roofed farmhouses, freshly sown fields and lush pastures being grazed by ewes and newborn lambs.

In the far distance was the gray silhouette of the city of Chatam, nestled in the curves of the valley. Beyond that was the endless expanse of the sea.

Ancient oaks dappled the long driveway that curved up the hill to the palace with shade. At the bottom of that drive was a closed wrought iron and stone gate that guarded the palace entrance. To the left side of the gate was a tasteful stone sign, with bronze cursive letters, *Chatam Palace*, on the right, an enormous bed of roses, not yet in bloom.

Finding herself here, on this side of the gates, with the massive stone walls and turrets of the castle rising up behind her, was like being in a dream but Meredith tried to remind herself of the task at hand. She had to make her expectations for the rest of this week's practice sessions crystal-clear.

In front of the fountain, a groomsman in a palace stable uniform held a horse. Prince Kiernan had his back to her, his hand stroking one of those powerful shoulders as he took the reins from the groomsman and lifted a foot to the stirrup.

Meredith was not sure she had ever seen a man more in his element. The prince radiated the power, confidence and grace she had yet to see from him on the dance floor.

He looked like a man who owned the earth, and who was sure of his place in it.

The horse was magnificent. It was not one of the frightening horses she had seen in pictures, of that she was almost positive. Though large, and as shiny black as Lucifer, the horse stood quietly, and when he sensed her come out the gate he turned a gentle eye to her.

Except for nearly being trampled by that runaway

at the Blossom Festival parade all those years ago, Meredith had never been this close to a horse.

Instead of her planned lecture, she heard an awed *ooh* escape her lips.

Prince Kiernan glanced over his shoulder when he heard the small sound behind him.

And she, the one he thought he had successfully escaped, the one who could make eating a pastry look like something out of an X-rated film, stood there with round eyes and her mouth forming a little O.

He could leap on the horse and gallop away in a flurry of masculine showmanship. But there was something about the look on her face that stopped him.

He remembered she was afraid of horses.

He slipped his foot back out of the stirrup, and regarded Meredith Whitmore thoughtfully.

"Come say hello to Ben," he suggested quietly, dismissing his groomsman with a nod.

The debate raged in her face. Well, who could blame her? They had already crossed some sort of invisible line by having tea together. She was obviously debating the etiquette of the situation, wanting to be strictly professional.

And after watching her eat, he could certainly see the wisdom in that!

But he was aware of finding her reaction to the impromptu tea in the garden refreshing.

And he was aware of not being quite ready to gallop away.

And so what was the harm in having her meet his horse? He could tell she didn't want to, and that at the same time it was proving as irresistible to her as the crumpets had been. She moved forward as if she was being pulled on an invisible string. He could see her pulse racing in the hollow of her throat.

"Don't be afraid," Kiernan said.

She stopped well short of the horse. "He's gigantic," she whispered.

Prince Kiernan reached out, took her hand and tugged her closer.

They had been touching while they danced, but this was different. Everything about her was going to seem different after the semi-erotic experience of watching her devour teatime treats.

Still, he did not let her go, but pulled her closer, and then guiding her, he held her hand out to the horse.

"He wants to get your scent," he told her quietly.

The horse leaned his head toward her, flared his nostrils as he drew a deep breath, then breathed a puff of warm, moist air onto her hand where it was cupped in Kiernan's.

"Oh," she breathed, her eyes round and wide, a delighted smile tickling her lips. "Oh!"

"Touch him," Kiernan suggested. "Right there, between his mouth and his nose."

Tentatively, she touched, then closed her eyes, much as she had done when she decapitated the pastry swan with her lovely white teeth.

"It's exquisite," she said, savoring. "Like velvet, only softer."

"See? There's nothing to be afraid of."

But there was. And they both knew it.

She drew her hand away quickly from the horse's nose, and then out of the protection of Kiernan's cupped palm.

"Thank you," she said, and then rapidly, "I have to go."

He knew that was true, but he heard, not the words, but the fear, and frowned at it. The place where her heartbeat pulsed in her throat had gone crazy.

"Not yet," he said.

There was something in him that would not be refused. It went deeper than the station he had been born to, it went deeper than the fact he spoke and people listened.

There was something in him—a man prepared to lay down his life to protect those physically weaker than him—that challenged him to conquer her fear.

"Touch him here," he suggested, and ran his hand over the powerful shoulder muscle under the fringe of Ben's silky black mane.

She glanced toward the gate, but then made a choice. Hesitantly Meredith laid her hand where Kiernan's had been.

"I can feel his strength," she whispered, "the pure power of him."

Kiernan looked at where her hand lay just below the horse's wither, and felt a shattering urge to move her hand to his own chest, to see if she would feel his power, too, his strength.

Insane thoughts, quickly crushed. How was he supposed to dance with her if he followed this train of thought? And yet still, he did not let her go.

"If you put your nose to that place you just touched, you will smell a scent so sweet you will wonder how you lived without knowing it."

"I hope I'm not allergic," she said, trying for a light note, he suspected, desperately trying to break out of the spell that was being cast around them. But it didn't work. Meredith moved close to the horse, stood on tiptoe and drew in a deep breath.

She turned back to the prince, and he smiled with satisfaction at the transparent look of joyous discovery on her face.

"I told you," he said. "Do you want to sit on him?"

"No!" But the fear was gone. He saw her refusal, not as fright, but as an effort to fight the magic that was deepening around them.

"It's not dangerous," Kiernan said persuasively. "I promise I'll look after you."

He didn't know what he had said that was so wrong, but she suddenly went very still. The color drained from her face.

"Maybe another time," she said.

"You're trembling," Prince Kiernan said. "There's no need. There's nothing to be afraid of."

Meredith knew a different truth. There was so much to be afraid of people couldn't even imagine it.

But when she looked into Prince Kiernan's eyes, soft with unexpected concern, it felt as if the fear was taken from her. Which was ridiculous. The fact that she was inclined to trust him should make her feel more afraid, not less!

"Here, I'll help you up. Put your foot here, and your other hand here."

And she did. Even though she should have turned and run, she didn't. The temptation was too great to refuse.

She was a poor girl from Wentworth. And even though she had overcome her humble beginnings, she was still only a working woman.

This opportunity would never, ever come again.

To sit on a horse in the early spring sunshine on

the unspeakably gorgeous grounds of the Palace of Chatam.

With Prince Kiernan promising to protect her and keep her safe.

I promise I'll look after you. Those words were fair warning. She had heard those words, exactly those words, before.

When she had told Michael Morgan she was going to have his baby. And he had told her not to worry. He'd look after her. They would get married.

She could see the girl she had been standing on the city hall steps, waiting, her baby just a tiny bulge under her sweater. Waiting for an hour and then two. Thinking something terrible must have happened. Michael must have been in an accident. He must be lying somewhere hurt. Dying.

Her mother, who had refused to attend the ceremony, had finally come when it was dark, when city hall was long closed, and collected Meredith, shivering, soaked from cold rain, from the steps.

That's where trust got you. It left you way too open to hurt.

But even knowing that, Meredith told herself it would be all right just to allow herself this moment.

She took Kiernan's instructions, put her foot in the stirrup and took the saddle with her other hand. Despite her dancer's litheness, Meredith felt as if she was scrambling to get on that horse's back. But then strong hands lifted her at the waist, gave her one final shove on her rump.

Despite how undignified that final shove was, she settled on the hard leather of the saddle with a sense of satisfaction.

For the first time—and probably the only time—in her life, Meredith was sitting on a horse.

"Should we go for a little stroll?"

She had come this far. To get off without really riding the horse seemed like it would be something of a shame. She nodded, grabbed the front of the saddle firmly.

With the reins in his hands, Kiernan moved to the front of the horse. Instead of taking her for a short loop around the fountain, or down the driveway to the closed main gate, he led the horse off the paved area and onto the grass that surrounded the palace.

The whole time, his voice soothing, he talked to her.

"That's it. Just relax. Think of yourself as a blanket floating over him." He glanced back at her. "That's good. You have really good balance, probably from the dancing. That's it exactly. Just relax and feel the rhythm of it. It goes side to side and then back and forth. Do you feel that?"

She nodded, delighting in the sensation, embracing the experience. She thought after a moment he would turn around and lead her back to the courtyard, but he didn't.

"You'll see the first of the three garden mazes on your left," he said. "I used to love trying to find my way out of it when I was a boy."

He amazed her by giving her a grand tour of parts of the palace grounds that were not open to the public. But even had they been, the public would never have known that was the place he rode his first pony, that was where he fell and broke his arm, that was the fountain he and Adrian had put dish detergent in.

With the sun streaming down around her, the scent of the horse tickling her nostrils, and Kiernan out in front of her, leading the horse with such easy confidence, glancing back at her to smile and encourage her, Meredith realized something.

Perhaps the scariest thing of all.

For the first time since the accident that had taken her baby six years ago, she felt the tiniest little niggle of something.

It was the most dangerous thing of all. It was happiness.

of something.*

piness.*

CHAPTER FOUR

WHEN KIERNAN GLANCED BACK at Meredith, he registered her delight. There was something about her that
troubled him. She was too serious for one so young.
Something he could not understand haunted the loveliness of the deep golds and greens of her eyes.

And yet looking at her now those ever-present shad-
ows, the clouds, were completely gone from her eyes.
It made her lovely in a way he could not have guessed.
He turned away, focused on the path in front of him.
Her radiance almost hurt.

"Oh," she said. "Kiernan! He's doing something!"

Kiernan turned to see the horse flicking his tail. He
laughed at the expression on her face.

"Now, that's a *swish*," he said. "A bothersome fly,
nothing more."

But some tension had come into her, and he was
driven to get rid of it.

"On this whole matter of swishing," he said solemnly.
"A hundred years ago I could have had you hauled off
to the dungeon to straighten you out about who was the
boss. Ten days of bread and water would have mended
your ways."

He was rewarded with her laughter.

"And if it didn't, I could have added rats."

"Really, Kiernan," she laughed, "you've proven you can have your way for a pastry. Hold the rats."

Have his way? Having his way with her suddenly took on dangerous new meaning. He could practically feel her hair tangled in his hands, imagine what it would be to take the lushness of her lips with his own.

He risked a glance at her, and saw, guiltily, that her meaning had been innocent. He was entranced by her sunlit face, dancing with laughter.

Her laughter was a delicious sound, pure mountain water, gurgling over rock, everything he had hoped for when he had given in to a desire to chase the shadows from her eyes. More.

The laughter changed her. It *was* the sun coming out from behind clouds. Meredith went from being stern to playful, she went from being somewhat remote to eminently approachable, she went from being beautiful to being extraordinary.

He laughed, too, a reluctant chuckle at first, and then a real laugh. Their combined laughter rang off the ancient walls and suffused the day with a light it had not had before.

Kiernan knew it was the first time in a long, long time that he had laughed like this. It was as if his relationship with Tiffany had brought out something grim in him that he never quite put away.

But then the moment of exquisite lightness was over, and as he gazed up into the enjoyment on her face he realized that he was not fully prepared for what he saw there. Even though he had encouraged this moment, he did not feel ready for the bond of it. There was an utter openness between them that was astounding.

He felt like a man who had been set adrift on ice, who was nearly frozen, and who had suddenly glimpsed the promise of the warm golden light of a fire in the distance.

But his very longing made him feel weak. What had he been thinking? He needed to guard against moments like this, not encourage them.

Kiernan was not sure he had ever felt quite that vulnerable. Not riding a headstrong horse over slippery ground, not even when the press had decided to crucify him, first over Francine, ten times worse over the Tiffany affair.

He turned abruptly back toward the courtyard, but when they arrived, he stood gazing up at her, not wanting to help her off the horse.

To touch her now, with something in him so open, felt as if it guaranteed surrender. He was Adam leaning toward the apple; he was Sampson ignoring the scissors in Delilah's hand.

Hadn't Tiffany just taught him the treacherous unpredictability of human emotion?

Still, Meredith wasn't going to be able to get off that horse without his help.

"Bring that one leg over," he said gruffly, and then realized he hadn't been specific enough, because she brought her leg over but didn't twist and swing down into the stirrup, but sat on his horse, prettily side-saddle.

And then, without warning, she began to slide off.

And he had no choice but to reach out and catch her around her waist, and pull her to him to take the impact from her.

She stood there in the circle of his arms, her chin tilted back, looking into his face.

"Kiernan," she said softly, "I don't know how to thank you. That was a wonderful morning."

But that was the problem. The wonder of the morning

had encouraged this new form of familiarity. Barriers were down. She hadn't used his proper form of address.

She didn't even know she hadn't, she was so caught in the moment. And she never had to know how he had *liked* how his name had sounded coming off her lips.

But it was just one more barrier down, one more line of protection compromised. He should correct her. But he couldn't. He hated it that the moment seemed to be robbing him of his strength and his resolve, his sense of duty, his *knowing* what was right.

Aside from Adrian, who was this comfortable with him, there were few people in his world this able to be themselves around him, this able to bring out his sense of laughter.

Francine had. Tiffany never.

She did not back out of the circle of his arms, and he did not release her. The laughter was gone from her face. Completely. She swallowed hard.

The guard he had just put up felt as if it was going to crumple. *Completely*. And if it did, he would never, ever be able to build it back up as strong as it had been before, like a wall that had been weakened by a cannonball hit.

"Your Highness?"

Now, she remembered the correct form of address. Too late. Because now he longed to hear his name off her lips.

That's what he had to steel himself against.

"Yes?"

"Thank you for not letting me fall," she said.

But the truth? It felt as if they were falling, as if they were entering a land where neither of them had ever been, without knowing the language, without having a map.

"It's not if you fall that matters," he said quietly. "Everyone falls. It's how you get up that counts."

A part of him leaned toward her, wanting, almost desperately to explore what was happening between them. As if, in that new land he had glimpsed so briefly in her eyes, he would find not that he was lost.

But that he was found.

And that he was not alone on his journey.

Kiernan gave himself a mental shake. He couldn't allow himself to bask in that feeling that he had been *seen*, this morning, not as a prince, but for the man he really was. And he certainly couldn't allow her to see that her praise meant something to him.

Music suddenly spilled out an open window above them. She cocked her head toward it. "What on earth?" she asked. "What kind of magic is this?"

The whole morning had had that quality, of magic. Now, it seemed imperative that he deny the existence of such a thing.

"It's not magic!" he said, his tone suddenly curt. "The palace chamber quartet is practicing, that's all. It happens every Tuesday at precisely eleven o'clock."

He liked precise worlds. Predictable ones.

"Your Highness?"

He looked askance at her.

"Shall we?"

Of course he wasn't going to dance with her! He was too open to her, too aware of how the sun shone off her hair, of the light in her eyes, of the glossy puffiness of her lips. He had a horse that needed looking after. Her laughter and his had already made him feel quite vulnerable enough.

And yet this surprise invitation had that quality of delicious spontaneity to it that he found irresistible. Plus, to refuse might deepen her puzzlement, and if she studied the mystery long enough, would she figure it out?

That there was something about her he liked, and at the same time, he disliked liking it. Intensely.

But there was one other thing.

He had seen a light come on in her today. It still shone there, gently below the surface, chasing away a shadow he had realized had been ever-present until this morning.

He might want to protect himself.

But not enough to push her back into darkness.

And so he dropped the reins, uncharacteristically not caring if the horse bolted back to the stable. He felt like a warrior at war, not with her, but with himself. Wanting to see her light, but not at the expense of losing his power.

He felt as if he was walking straight toward his biggest foe. Because, of course, his biggest foe was the loss of control that she threatened in him.

Here was his chance to wrest it back, to take the challenge of her to the next level. He gazed down at her, and then took her hand, placed his other one on her waist.

There was something about the spontaneity of it, about the casualness of it, about the drift of the music over the spring garden, that did exactly what she had wanted all along.

Something in him *breathed*. He didn't feel rigid. Or stiff. He felt on fire. *A man who would prove he was in charge of himself.*

A man who could flirt with temptation and then just shrug it off and walk away.

A man who could see her light, and be pulled to it, and want it for her, but at the same time, not be a moth that would be pulled helplessly into the flame.

He danced her around the courtyard until she was breathless. Until she was his whole world. All he could see was the light in her. All he could feel was the sensuous touch of her fingertips resting ever so lightly on the place where his back met his hip. All that he could smell was her scent.

The last note of music spilled out the window, held, and then died. He became aware again of a world that was not Meredith. The horse stood, his head nodding, birds singing, sun shining, the scent of lilacs thick in the air.

Now, part two of the equation. He had danced with the temptation.

Walk away.

But she was finally looking at him with the approval a prince deserved. He steeled himself not to let it go straight to his head.

"That was fantastic," Meredith said softly.

"Thank you." With a certain chilly note, as if he didn't give a fig about her approval.

"I think you're ready to learn a few modern dance step moves tomorrow."

Tomorrow. He'd been so busy getting through the challenge of the moment that he'd managed to completely forget that.

There were more moments to this challenge. Many more.

Kiernan had known she would be that kind of girl.

The if you give an inch, she'll take a mile kind.

The kind where if you squeezed through one challenge she threw at you, by the skin of your teeth, only, another would be waiting. Harder.

And just to prove she had much harder challenges in

store for him, she stood on her tiptoes and brushed his cheek with her lips.

Then she stepped back from him, stunned.

But not as stunned as he was. That innocent touch of her lips on his cheek stirred a yearning in him that was devastating. Suddenly his whole life seemed to yawn ahead of him, filled to the brim with activities and obligations, but empty of the one thing that truly mattered.

It doesn't exist, he berated himself. He'd learned that, hadn't he?

For a moment, she looked so surprised at herself that he thought she might apologize. But then, she didn't. No, she crossed her arms over her chest, and met his gaze with challenge, daring him to say something, daring him to tell her how inappropriate it was to kiss a prince.

But he couldn't. And therein was the problem. She was challenging his ability to be in perfect control at all times, and he hated that.

Resisting an impulse to touch the place on his cheek that still tingled from the caress of her soft lips, Kiernan turned from her, and went to his horse. He put his leg in the stirrup and vaulted up onto Ben's back. Without looking back, he pressed the horse into a gallop, took a low stone wall, and raced away.

But even without looking, he knew she had watched him. And knew that he had wanted her to watch him and be impressed with his prowess.

Some kind of dance had begun between them. And it had nothing at all to do with the performance they would give at *An Evening to Remember*.

On the drive home from the palace, Meredith replayed her audacity. She'd kissed the prince!

"It wasn't really a kiss," she told herself firmly. "More like a buss. Yes, a buss."

Somehow she had needed to thank him for all the experiences he had given her that day.

"So," she asked herself, "what's wrong with thank you?"

Still, if she had it to do again? She would do the same thing. She could not regret touching her lips to the skin of his cheek, feeling the hint of rough stubble beneath the tenderness of her lips, standing back to see something flash through his eyes before it had been quickly veiled.

She parked her tiny car in the laneway behind her apartment, a walk-up located above her dance studio in Chatam. She owned the building as a result of an insurance settlement. The building, and No Princes, had been her only uses for the money.

Both things had given her a little bit of motivation to keep going on those dark days when it felt like she could live no more.

Tonight, when she opened the door to the apartment that had given her both solace and sanctuary, she was taken aback by how fresh her wounds suddenly felt.

It had been six years since it had happened.

A grandmother who had just picked up her granddaughter from day care walking a stroller across a street. Who could know why Meredith's mother, Millicent, had not heard the sirens? Tired from working so hard? Mulling over the dreams that had been shattered? A stolen vehicle the police were chasing went through the crosswalk. Meredith's mother, Millicent, had died at the scene, after valiantly throwing her body in front of the stroller. Carly had succumbed to her injuries a few days later, God deaf to the pleas and prayers of Meredith.

Now, the apartment seemed extra empty and quiet tonight, no doubt because today, for the first time in so long, Meredith had allowed herself to feel connected to another human being.

Meredith set her bag inside the door, and went straight to the bookshelf, where there were so many pictures of her baby, Carly. She chose her favorite, took it to the couch, and traced the lines of her daughter's chubby cheeks with her fingertips.

With tears sliding down her cheeks, she fell asleep.

When she awoke she was clutching the photo to her breast. But instead of feeling the sadness she always felt when she awoke with a photo of her daughter, she remembered the laughter, and the happiness she had felt today.

And felt oddly guilty. How could she? She was not ready to be happy again. Nor could she trust it. Happiness came, and then when it went, as it inevitably did, the emptiness was nearly unbearable.

Meredith considered herself strong. But not strong enough to hope. Certainly not strong enough to sustain more loss. She was not going to embrace the happiness she had felt today. No, not at all. In fact, she was going to steel herself against it.

But the next morning she was aware she was not the only one who had steeled herself against what had happened yesterday.

If Meredith thought they had made a breakthrough yesterday when she had ridden the horse and Kiernan had danced in the courtyard with her, she now saw she was sadly mistaken.

He had arrived this morning in armor. And he danced

like it, too! Was the kiss what had done it? Or the whole day they had experienced together? No matter, he was as stiffly formal as though he had never placed his hand on her rump to sling her into the saddle of his horse, as if he had never walked in front of her, chatting about his childhood on the palace grounds.

Meredith tried to shrug her sense of loss at his aloofness away and focus on the job at hand.

She had put together a modified version of the newlyweds' dance from the internet and Prince Kiernan had reluctantly approved the routine for *An Evening to Remember.* She had hoped to have some startling, almost gymnastic, moves in it, which would show off the prince's amazing athletic ability.

But the prince, though quite capable of the moves, was resistant.

"Does the word *sexy* mean anything to you?"

Something burned through his eyes, a fire, but it was quickly snuffed. "I'm doing my best," he told her with cool reserve, not rattled in the least.

But he wasn't. Because she had glimpsed his best. This did not even seem like the same man she had danced with yesterday in the courtyard, so take-charge, so breathtakingly masculine, so sure.

The stern line of his lip was taking on a faintly rebellious downward curve. Pretty soon, he would announce *enough* and another day of practice would be lost.

Not that yesterday had been lost.

She sighed. "You know the steps. You know the rudiments of each move. But you're like a schoolboy reciting math tables by rote. Something in you holds back."

"That's my nature," he said. "I'm reserved. Something in me always holds back." His eyes fastened on her lips, just for a split second, and she felt her stomach do a loop-the-loop worthy of an acrobatic airplane.

If he didn't hold back, would he kiss her? What would his lips taste like? Feel like? Given her resolve to back away from all those delicious things she had felt yesterday, Meredith was shocked by how badly she wanted to know. She was shocked by the sudden temptation to throw herself at him and take those lips, to shock the sensuality out of him.

But she also needed for both of them to hold back if she was going to keep her professional distance. And she needed just as desperately for him to let go if she was going to feel professional pride in teaching him!

It was a quandary.

"Is it your nature to be reserved," she questioned him, "or your role in life?"

"In my case, those are inextricably intertwined."

He said that without apology.

"I understand that, but in dancing there is no holding back. You have to put everything into it, all that you were, all that you have been, all that you hope to be someday."

The question was, if he gave her all that, how was she going to walk away undamaged?

"This is a ten-minute performance at a fund-raiser," he reminded her, "not the final exam for getting into heaven."

But that's what she wanted him to experience, *exactly*. She realized for her it had become about more than their performance.

There was a place when you danced well, where you became part of something larger. It was an incredible feeling. It was a place where you rose above problems.

And tragedies. A place where you were free of your past and your heartaches. Yes, just like touching heaven.

But somehow she could not tell him that. It was too ambitious. He was right. It was a ten-minute performance for the fund-raiser opening of Blossom Week. Meredith was here to teach him a few dance steps, nothing more.

When had it become her quest to unlock him? To show him something of himself that he had never seen before? To want him to experience *that* feeling. Of heaven.

And that she was dying to see?

It had all become too personal. And she knew that. She had to get her own agenda straight in her head.

Teach him to do the routine, perform it well, and be satisfied if the final result was passable if not spectacular. The prince putting in a surprising appearance, making a game effort at the steps would be enough. The people of Chatam would *love* his performance, a chance to see him let his hair down, even if he was somewhat wooden.

Though, for her, to only accomplish a passable result would feel like a failure of monumental proportions. Especially since she had glimpsed yesterday what he could be.

Her eyes suddenly fell on two jackets that hung on pegs inside the coat check at the far end of the ballroom. They were the white jackets of the palace housekeeping staff.

As soon as she saw them, she knew exactly what she had to do.

And as she contemplated the audacity of her plan, she could have sworn she heard a baby laugh, as if it was *so* right.

It was a memory of laughter, nothing more, but she could see the face of the beautiful child who had been taken from her as clearly as though she still had the photo on her chest.

She was aware again, of something changing in her. Sweetly. Subtly. It wasn't that she wasn't sad. It was that the sadness was mixed with something else.

A great sense of gratitude for having known love so deeply and so completely.

Meredith was suddenly aware that her experience with love had to make her a better person.

It had to.

Her daughter's legacy to her had to be a beautiful one. That was all she had left to honor her with.

And if that meant taking a prince to a place where he was not so lonely and not so alone, even briefly, then that was what she had to do.

It wasn't about the dance they were doing at all.

It was about the kind of person she was going to choose to be.

And yes, it was going to take all her courage to choose it.

She moved past the prince to the coat check, plucked the jackets off the wall, and then turned back and took a deep breath.

Yesterday, spontaneity had brought them so much closer to the place they needed to be than all her care-fully rehearsed plans and carefully choreographed dance steps.

Today, she hoped for magic.

CHAPTER FIVE

THE PRINCE BADLY WANTED his life back. He wanted *An Evening to Remember* to be over. He wanted the temptation of Meredith over; watching her demonstrate hip moves, taking her hand in his, touching her, looking at her and pretending to love her.

It was easily the most exhausting and challenging work he had ever done, and the performance couldn't come quickly enough in his opinion.

Though, somewhere in his mind, he acknowledged over would be over. No more rehearsals. No more bossy Meredith Whitmore. Who didn't respect his station, and was impertinent. Who was digging at him, trying to find the place in him he least wanted her to see, refusing to take no for an answer.

Who could make eating pastries look like an exercise in eroticism one minute, and look at a horse with the wide-eyed wonder of a child the next. Whose lips had felt like butterfly wings against his cheek.

Stop, Kiernan ordered himself.

She was aggravating. She was annoying. She was damnably sexy. But she was also *refreshing* in a way that was brand new to him. She was not afraid to tell him exactly what she thought, she was not afraid to make demands, she was not afraid of him, not awed by his station, not intimidated by his power.

And that, he reluctantly admitted, was what he was going to miss when it was all over. In so much of his life he was the master. What he said went. No questions. No arguments. No suggestions. No discussion.

How was it that in a dance instructor from Wentworth, he felt he had met his equal?

There was no doubt going to be a huge space in his life once she was gone. It seemed impossible she could have that kind of impact after only a few days. But he didn't plan to dwell on it.

Prince Kiernan was good at filling spaces in his life. He had more obligations than he had time, anyway, and many of those were stacking up as he frittered away hours and hours learning the dance routine he was coming to hate.

"We're going to go somewhere else today," Meredith announced, marching back over from the coat room with something stuffed under her arm. "I think the ballroom itself may be lending to the, er, stuffiness, we're experiencing. It's too big, too formal."

But he knew it wasn't the room she found stuffy. It was him.

"First stodgy, now stuffy," he muttered.

"Don't act insulted. You said yourself the role you play has made you that way."

"No, you suggested it was the role I played. I said I was born this way. And I never used the word stuffy. I think I said reserved."

"Okay, whatever," she said cheerfully. "We're going to do a little experiment today. With your reserve."

Oh-oh, this did not bode well for him. He was already hanging onto his control by the merest thread.

"Here," she said pleasantly, "put this on."

She handed him one of the white jackets she had stuffed under her arm. The one she handed him had the name *Andy* embroidered over one pocket in blue thread. He hesitated. What was the little minx up to?

Mischief. He could see it in the twinkle in her eye.

He should stop her before she got started, and he knew that. But despite the fact he had told himself he wasn't going to dwell on it, soon their time together would be over. Why not see what mischief she had planned? That spark in her eye was irresistible anyway, always reminding him that there was a shadow in her.

Like the unexpected delight of taking her for tea and then on that ride, this was part of the unexpected reprieve he'd been given from the stuffy stodginess of his life. He was aware he *wanted* to see what she had up her sleeve today.

So he slipped the white jacket over his shirt and did up the buttons. It was too tight across the chest, but she inspected him, and frowned. She went back to the coat check and reappeared with a white ball cap.

"There," she said, handing it to him. "Pull it low over your eyes. Perfect. All ready to smuggle you out of the palace." She shrugged into a white jacket of her own. It said *Molly* on the pocket.

"We can't smuggle me out of the palace," he said, but he was aware it was a token protest. Something in him was already taking wing, flying over the walls.

"Why not?"

"There are security concerns. I have responsibilities and obligations you can't even dream of. I can't just waltz out of here without letting anyone know where I'm going and why."

"To improve your waltz, I think you should. See?

There's that reserve again. Your Highness—no, make that Andy—have you ever broken the rules?"

"I don't have the luxury," he told her tightly.

She smiled at him. "Prince Kiernan of Chatam doesn't. Andy does. Let's go. It's just for a little while. Maybe an hour. In some ways, you're a prisoner of your life. Let's break out. Just this once."

He stood there for a moment, frozen. Again, he had a sense of her saying what no one else said.

And seeing what no one else saw.

She didn't see the prince. Not entirely. If she did, she would not have dared to touch his cheek with her lips yesterday. She saw a man first. The trappings of his status underwhelmed her. She saw straight through to the price he paid to be the prince.

And she wanted to rescue him. There was a kind of crazy courage in that that was as irresistible as the mischief in her eyes.

Of course he couldn't just go. It would be the most irresponsible thing he had ever done.

On the other hand, why not? The Isle of Chatam was easily the safest place in the world. He was supposed to be at dance class. No one would even miss him for a few hours.

Suddenly what she was offering him seemed as impossible to resist as the mischief that made her eyes spark more green than brown.

Freedom. Complete freedom, the one thing he had never ever known.

"Coming, Andy?" she said.

He sighed. "Molly, I hope you know what you're doing."

"Trust me," she said.

And Kiernan realized he was starting to. The one

thing he wanted to do least was trust a woman! And yet somehow she was wiggling her way past his defenses and entering that elite circle of people that he truly trusted.

He followed her outside to the staff parking lot. She led him to the tiniest car he had ever seen, a candy-apple-red Mini.

She got in, and he opened the passenger door and slid in beside her. His knees were in approximately the vicinity of his chin.

"They've gotten used to me at the service entrance," she said. "I'll just give them a wave and we'll breeze on through."

And that's exactly what happened.

In moments they were chugging along a narrow country road, he holding on for dear life. Kiernan had never ridden in a vehicle that was so…insubstantial. He felt as if they were inches above the ground, and as if every stone and bump on the road was jarring his bones. He actually hit his head on the roof of the tiny vehicle.

"Where are we going?" he asked.

"Remember I asked you about squishing mud up through your toes?"

"Yes, I do."

"That's where we're going."

"I don't want to squish mud up between my toes," he said, though he recognized his protest, once again, as being token. The moment they had driven through that back service gate to the palace something in him had opened.

He had made a decision to embrace whatever the day held.

"It doesn't matter if you want to or not. Andy does."

"But why does he?" he asked.

"Because he likes having *fun*."

"Oh, I see. There's nothing stuffy or stodgy about our man, Andy."

"Exactly," she said, and beamed at him with the delight of a teacher who had just helped a child solve a difficult problem. "Andy, you and I are about to give new meaning to *Dancing with Heaven*."

"I don't know the old meaning, Molly."

"You've never seen *Dancing with Heaven*? It's a movie. A classic romantic finding-your-true-self movie that has dance at its heart. It starred Kevin McConnell."

He didn't care for the dreamy way she said that name.

"I'll have to put watching *Dancing with Heaven* on your homework list."

"Andy doesn't like homework."

"That's true."

"He likes playing hooky. But when he's at school?"

"Yes?"

"He winks at the teacher and makes her blush."

"Oh-oh," she said.

"He likes motorcycles, and black leather, driving too fast, and breaking rules."

"My, my."

"He likes loud music and smoky bars, and girls in too-short skirts and low-cut tops who wiggle their hips when they dance."

"Oh, dear."

"He thumbs his nose at convention. He's cooled off in the town fountain on the Summer Day celebrations, disobeyed the Keep Off signs at Landers Rock, kept his hat on while they sing the national anthem."

"That's Andy, all right."

"He likes swimming in the sea. Naked. In the moon-light."

Unless he was mistaken, Meredith gulped a little before she said, "I've created a monster."

"You should be more careful who you run away with, Molly."

"I know."

"But they say every woman loves a bad boy."

Something in her face closed. She frowned at the road. Kiernan realized how very little he knew about her, which was strange because he felt as if he knew her deeply.

"Do you have a boyfriend?" He hadn't thought to ask her that before. There were no rings on her fingers, so he had assumed she was single. Now he wondered why he had assumed that, and wondered at why he was holding his breath waiting for her answer.

"I'm single." Her hands tightened on the wheel.

"I'm surprised." But ridiculously *relieved*. What was that about, since if ever there was a man sworn off love it was him? Why would he care about her marital status?

Only because, he assured himself, he didn't even want to think about her with a bad boy.

She hesitated, looked straight ahead. "I became pregnant when I was sixteen. The father abandoned me. It has a way of souring a person on romance." He heard the hollowness in her voice, but he could hear something more.

Unbearable pain. And suddenly his concern for protecting his own damaged heart evaporated.

"And the baby?" he asked quietly. Somehow he knew this woman could never have an abortion. Never.

And that adoption seemed unlikely, too. There was something about the fierce passion of that first dance he had witnessed her performing that let him know that. She would hold on to what she loved, no matter what the cost to her.

He glanced at her face. She was struggling for control. There was something she didn't want to tell him, and suddenly, with an intuition that surprised him, he knew it was about the shadow that he so often saw marring the light in her eyes.

He held his breath, again, wanting, no, *needing* to know that somehow she had come to trust him as much as he had come to trust her, even if it was with the same reluctance.

"It was a little girl. I kept her," she whispered. "Maybe a foolish thing to do. My mom and I had to work night and day cleaning houses to make ends meet. But I don't regret one second of it. Not one. All I regret is that I couldn't be with her more. With both of them more."

He felt a shiver go up and down his spine.

"My mom picked her up from day care for me on a particularly hectic day. They were crossing a street when a stolen car being chased by the police hit them."

Her voice was ragged with pain.

"I'm so sorry," he said, aware of how words were just not enough. "You seem much too young to have survived such a tragedy."

In a broken whisper she went on, "She wasn't even a year old yet."

Her shoulders were trembling. She refused to look at him, her eyes glued to the road.

He wanted to scream at her to pull over, because he needed to gather her in his arms and comfort her. But from the look on her face there were some things there was no comforting for.

"I'm so sorry," he said again, feeling horrible and helpless. He reached out and patted her shoulder, but she shrugged out from under his hand, her shoulder stiff with pride.

"It's a long time ago," she said, with forced brightness. "Today, let's just be Molly and Andy, okay?"

It couldn't be *that* long ago. She wasn't old enough for it to have been that long ago.

But she had trusted him with this piece of herself.

And her trust felt both fragile and precious. If he said the wrong thing it felt like this precious thing she had offered him would shatter.

Still, he could not quite let it go. He had to listen to the voice inside him that said, *ask her.*

"Could you tell me their names? Your baby's and your mother's?" he asked, softly, ever so softly. "Please?"

She was silent for so long that he thought she would refuse this request. When she answered, he felt deeply moved, as if she had handed him her heart.

"Carly," she whispered. "My baby's name was Carly. My mother's was Millicent, but everyone called her Millie."

"Carly," he said softly, feeling it on his tongue. "Millie."

And then he nodded, knowing there was nothing else to say, but holding those names to him like the sacred trust that they were.

There was something about the way he said her daughter and mother's names, with genuine sadness, and a simple reverence, that gave Meredith an unexpected sense of being comforted. Over the past days she had come to know Prince Kiernan in a way that made it easy to forget he was still the most powerful man in the land.

Something about the way he uttered those names made her understand his power in ways she had not before. His speaking Carly's name was oddly like a blessing.

Meredith felt tears at his gentleness sting her eyes, but she did not let them flow. Kiernan reached out, and loosed her hand from the gearshift, and gave it a hard squeeze before letting it go.

Why had she told him about Carly? And her mother? She could have just as easily left it at she was single.

Was it because she was asking him to let his guard down? And that request required more of her, too? Was it because some part of her had trusted he would handle it in just the right way?

Whatever it was, she waited for a sense of vulnerability to come, a sense that she had revealed too much of herself.

But it did not. Instead, she felt an unexpected sense of a burden that she had carried alone being, not lifted, but shared.

A prince sharing your burden, she scoffed at herself, but her scorn did not change the way she felt, lighter, more open.

But for now, she reminded herself, a newfound sense of awe of Kiernan would not forward her goal. He needed to be taken off his pedestal if she ever hoped to get him to dance as if he meant it.

So for today, Kiernan was not a prince, not the most wealthy, most influential, most powerful man in Chatam. Today he would be just Andy. And she was not a woman with an unbearable sadness in her past, just *Molly*, two palace housekeeping workers playing hooky from work for the day.

They arrived at the small unmarked pullout, the trailhead for what Meredith considered one of the greatest treasures of the Isle of Chatam, Chatam Hot Springs.

Meredith opened the boot of her small car, and loaded "Andy" down with bags and baskets to carry up the steep trail that wound through the sweetly scented giant cedar woods. She was enjoying this charade already. She would have never asked a prince to carry her bags!

Meredith was relieved to see, as they came around the final twist in the trail, there was not a single soul at Chatam Hot Springs. The natural springs were a favorite local haunt, but not this early in the day and not midweek. She had taken a chance that the hot springs would be empty, and they were.

Kiernan set down his cargo and gazed around. "What a remarkable place."

Puffs of mist rose above the turquoise waters that filled a pool edged by slabs of flat black slate rocks. Freshwater falls cascaded down a mossy outcropping at the far end of the pool. Lush ferns, and bunches of grass, sown with tiny purple and blue wildflowers, surrounded the rocks and the pool.

"You've never been here?"

"I've heard of it, and seen photographs of it many times. But to come here? When the royal entourage arrives, security would necessitate closing it to the people who enjoy it most. I have so many other pleasures at my disposal that it would seem unduly selfish to want this one, also."

She was already vulnerable to him because somehow the way he had reacted to her history had been so quietly *right*. Now she saw that despite the fact he lived in a position that could have easily bred arrogance, it had not. Kiernan clearly saw his position not as one of absolute power, but one of absolute service.

Still, the time for being too serious today was over.

"Oh, Andy," she chided him. "You're talking as if you think you're royalty!"

Still, she was delighted he had never been here before, pleased that she was the one who had brought him to something new, beautiful and unexpected.

"Oh, Molly," he said contritely. "You know me. Delusions of grandeur."

"I have a plan for bringing you down a few notches, Andy."

"I can barely wait."

And it actually sounded as if he meant that, as if he was embracing this experience with an unexpected eagerness.

"Well, then, kick off your shoes, and roll up your pants," Meredith suggested. "This is what I want to show you."

He didn't even argue with her.

Hidden in a tiny glade beside the hot springs, separated from the main pool by a dripping curtain of thick foliage, was a dip in the ground, approximately a quarter the size of the ballroom, that was filled with oozing, gray mud.

Meredith waded in. "Careful, it's—" just as she tried to warn him, one of her feet slipped. But before she even fully registered she was falling, Kiernan was beside her. He wrapped his arm around her waist, took her arm, and steadied her.

"Oh, Molly, you're a clumsy one. I'd give up those dreams of being a dancer if I were you."

She felt as if she could not get enough of the playful tone in his voice.

"I'll give up my dancer dreams if you'll give up yours of being a prince."

"Done," he said, with such genuine relief they both laughed.

"It's warm," he said, astounded, apparently unaware that even though he had let go of her waist, he still held her arm. "I've never felt anything quite like this."

And neither had she. Oh, the mud was exquisite; warm and thick, it oozed up through her toes, and then around her feet, and ankles, up her calves, but it was his hand, still steadying her arm, which she had never felt anything like.

They had been touching each other for days now.

But, except for that magical moment when the music had spilled over the courtyard, their dancing together had been basically all business. Their barriers had both been so firmly up. But that kiss she had planted on his cheek had taken the first chink out of those barriers, and now there were more chinks falling.

And so this outing and this experience wasn't all business even if she had cloaked her motivation in accomplishing a goal.

Meredith looked at Kiernan's face, dappled with sunshine coming through the feathery cedars that surrounded the pool, and something sighed within her. His face was exquisite, handsome and perfect, but she had never seen the expression she saw on it now.

Prince Kiernan's eyes were closed. He looked completely relaxed, and something like contentment had crept into the normally guarded lines of his face. He tilted his chin to the sun, and took a deep breath, sighed it out.

It was good.

But it wasn't enough.

She wanted, *needed* to see with a desperation not totally motivated by her end goal, the prince lose his inhibitions, that *restraint*, that was like an ever-present palace guard, surrounding him. Keeping others away from him. But also keeping him away from others.

She let go of his hand. She stooped, and buried her own hand in the mud, closed her fist around an oozing gob of goo. For a moment she hesitated.

It was true. Kiernan was just way too restrained. He could never reach his potential as a dancer while he carried that shield around him.

But this was probably still just about the worst idea she had ever had. She lived in a land still ruled by a very traditional monarchy. Schoolchildren and soldiers started their day by swearing their allegiance and obedience to this man's mother, Queen Aleda. But in time it would be him they stood and pledged their hearts to.

He had already shouldered much of the mantle of responsibility. Meredith knew, partly from the newspapers, and confirmed by the phone calls he sometimes had to take during dance practice, his interest in the economic health of the island was keen, that he had sharp business acumen, and that some of his initiatives had improved the standard of living for many people who lived here.

He promoted Chatam tirelessly abroad. He headed charities. He sat on hospital boards. He was the commander-in-chief of the military.

This man who stood with her, his pants rolled up to his knees, had influence over the lives of every single person in Chatam.

Really, it was no wonder he had trouble relaxing! So, this was probably one of the worst ideas Meredith had ever had. She *was* too cheeky. You did not, after all, in a land ruled by a monarchy, pick up a handful of oozing soft mud and hurl it at your liege!

But Meredith was committed to her course. Knowing somehow, in her heart, not her head, this was, absurdly, wonderfully, the *right* thing, she let fly with a handful of mud.

It caught him in the chest, and he staggered back a step, startled. He opened his eyes and stared down at the mud bullet that had exploded on his shirt.

His reaction would tell her a great deal about this man.

Furious anger?

Remote silence?

Complete retreat?

But, no, a smile tickled his lips, and when he looked up at her, she felt she might weep for what she had unmasked in his eyes.

"Disrespectful wench," he said. "I'd swear you are looking for a few nights in the dungeon."

There was a delightful playfulness in his tone.

"Andy! Are you in your prince delusion again? Dungeons, for pity sake! I suppose you'll be telling me about bread and water and rats next. Poor you. Tut-tut."

"Prince delusion? Oh, no, not at all. I'm in my warrior delusion, and you have just called me to battle. But I'm going to warn you, all prisoners go to the dungeon. If you please me, I might spare you the rats."

She giggled, a trifle nervously, because something

smoked in his eyes when he talked of making her his prisoner.

What had she started? And could she really handle it?

Kiernan stooped and came up with his big hand full of mud. He squinted at her thoughtfully, drew back his arm and took aim.

She began to run an awkward zigzag pattern through the sucking mud. The dark sludge he hurled whisked by her head.

"Ha-ha," she called over her shoulder. Meredith ducked, picked up her own mud ball and flung it back at him. But he'd had time to rearm, too.

Their mud balls crossed paths with each other, midair. His hit her solidly on the arm, with a warm, soft splat. It was like being hit with a dollop of just-out-of-the-oven pudding. Her missile wobbled through the air and went straight for his head.

Despite the fact he raised his arm in defense against the slow-flying projectile, it exploded against his raised bicep, and particles of it landed on his cheek, blossoming there like the petals of a mud flower. She drew her breath, shocked by her own unintentional audacity.

"I'm so sorry!" she called.

"Not nearly as sorry as you're going to be," he warned her.

He stopped, carefully wiped the muck off his cheekbone, and glared at her with mock fierceness. But Meredith saw there was nothing mock about the fact he did now look like a warrior! Of the barbaric variety that painted their faces before they went to battle.

He let out a cry worthy of that warrior and came after

her, stooping and hucking mud as fast as he could fill his hands with it.

In moments the glade rang with his shouts and her playful shrieking. They threw mud back and forth until they were both covered in dark blotches, until their hair was lost under ropy dreadlocks of sludge, their hands were like mud mitts at their sides, and their clothes had disappeared under layers of smelly black goo. Finally, only his teeth and the whites of his eyes still looked white. Andy's shirt was probably beyond repair.

The glade filled with the sounds of their laughter and playful insults, the sounds of them gasping for breath as they struggled to run through the sucking mud to escape each other's attacks.

"Take that, Molly!"

"You missed! Andy, you throw like a girl."

"*You* missed. *You* throw like a girl."

"But I am a girl!"

"A girl? A mud monster, risen from the deep! Take that!"

They were laughing so hard they were choking on it. It rang off the rocks around them, rode on the mist.

Despite the noise, the chaos, the hilarity, something quiet blossomed in Meredith. Something she had felt, ever so briefly on that horse yesterday, but other than that not for a long, long time.

Joy.

The quiet awareness of it knocked her off balance. With Kiernan hot on her heels, his raised hand full of mud rockets, she slipped. She went down in slow motion, somehow managing to twist so she wouldn't go into the muck face first. The mud cushioned her fall, and she fell on her back with a sucking *splat*.

She watched as Kiernan, too close, tried desperately

to stop, but his arms windmilled, and he fell right on top of her, saving her from the worst of his weight by bracing his arms around her.

She stared up into the face of her warrior prince. His eyes were alight with laughter, looking bluer than she had ever seen them look. His smile, against the backdrop of his muddy face, was brilliant, white as snow against a stone.

She had never felt anything quite so exquisite. She rested in a bed of warm mud, her skin slippery and sensuous with it. And Kiernan, equally as slippery, held himself off of her, but there were places their bodies met. His hard lines were pressed into the soft curves of her legs and her hips.

She touched him every day. But his guard had always been up.

Hers had been, too.

Only something, delicate and subtle, had shifted between them.

The laughter died in the air around them, and was replaced with a silence so profound that it vibrated with a growing tension, a deep awareness of each other.

He stared down at her, and some unguarded tenderness crept into his muddy, warrior's face.

Still holding most of his weight off her with one arm, he touched her lip with the hand he had just freed, scraped gently with his thumb.

Her joy escalated into exhilaration at the exquisite sense of being touched in such an intimate place, in such an intimate way.

"You have mud right here," he whispered, by way of excuse, but his voice hoarse.

For a splendid moment it felt as if every barrier was

down between them. Every one. As if her world was as wide open as it had ever been.

Everything became remarkable: the song of a bird nearby, the feel of the mud cushioning her, the smells that tickled her nostrils, the green of the fern plumes behind him.

Where his legs were sprawled across hers, the slide of their skin together where it made slight contact at their hips, the amazing light in his sapphire eyes, the scrape of his thumb against her lip, the slick muddiness of his hair, the sensual curve of his lips.

He was so close to her she could see the dark beginning of stubble on his cheeks, and his chin. He was so close to her his breath stirred across her cheek, feather-light, as intimate as his thumb which remained on her lips. He was so close to her she could smell the scent of him, wild and clean as the forest, over the scent of the minerals in the mud that covered them.

She closed her eyes against the delicious agony of wanting a moment to last forever.

To escalate.

"I warned you there would be consequences if I took you prisoner," he said, the words playful, while his tone was anything but.

Was he going to kiss her? Even as a rational part of her knew they could never pull back from that again, a less rational part of her wanted the taste of his lips on hers, wanted to feel them.

She took her hand, as if it didn't matter it was mud-covered, and traced a possessive line down the hard plane of his jaw. She touched it to the fullness of his lip.

As if it didn't matter to him that it was mud-covered, he teased her finger gently, nibbled it with his teeth.

She felt the featherlight touch of his lip against the skin of her finger. Was it possible to die of sensation?

If this—the merest touch of his lips to something as inconsequential as her finger—could cause this unbelievable rise of sensation within her, what would it be like if he took her lips with his own?

She felt as if it would be a death of sorts.

The death of all she had been before, the rising up of something new, the rising up within her of a spirit that was stronger and more resilient than she had ever imagined, similar to that spirit that rose in her when she danced.

A place that was without thought, and without history.

Heaven.

Brazen with wanting, she slipped her muddy hands around the column of his neck, and pulled him down to her.

His weight settled on her more fully, chest to the soft curve of breast, hard stomach to delicate swell, muscled legs to slender ones, fused.

A whisper of sanity called her back from the brink.

And then called louder, *stop.*

It reminded her of the price of such a heated moment, lives changed forever.

But in that moment, she didn't care if there was a price.

And apparently neither did he.

Because his lips touched hers. The fact they were both mud-slicked only increased the danger, the sensuality, the delicious sense of being swept away, of not caring about what happened next, of being pulled by forces greater than themselves.

His very essence was in the way he kissed her.

Kiernan tasted, not of mud, but of rain in a storm, pure, clean, elemental. His kiss was tender, welcoming, and yet the strength and leashed passion were sizzling just below the surface.

It had been so long since Meredith had allowed anything or anyone to touch her, emotionally or physically.

She had not even known the hunger grew in her, waiting for something, someone to touch it off, to show her she was ravenous.

She was ravenous, and Kiernan was a feast of sensation.

Everything about him swirled around her—the light in his sapphire eyes, the line of his hard body against hers, the taste of his lips, the hollow of his mouth—all those broken places within her were being touched by sensation that was fulfilling and healing and exhilarating.

It was madness. Exquisite, delicious, compelling madness.

And she had to stop it. She had to.

Except that she was powerless, in the grip of something so amazing and wondrous she could not have stopped it if her very life depended on it. She was just not that strong.

But he was.

He pulled back from her, she saw strength and temptation war in his eyes, and she was astounded—and saddened—when his strength won. He pulled himself away from her, hesitated, dropped back down and placed one more tiny kiss on the corner of her lip, and then pulled his weight completely off her and stood gazing down at her.

Meredith saw control replace the heat in his eyes.

She watched awareness dawn in his eyes, saw his reluctant acquiescence to the guard he always surrounded himself with.

She knew, with a desperate sadness, this moment was over.

CHAPTER SIX

KIERNAN COMPOSED HIMSELF, held his hand to her. She took it, and her body made an unattractive slurping sound as he tugged, and then yanked hard to free her from the mud.

If he said he was sorry, she felt she would die.

But he did not say that, and she felt a strange sense of relief that she could tell he was not sorry. Not even a little bit.

And neither was she, even though the consequences of what had just happened hung over her.

Neither of them spoke, looking at each other, aware with an awareness that could not be denied once it had been acknowledged.

He dropped her hand, but not her gaze.

"Thank you," he said softly.

She knew exactly what he meant. That moment of being so alive, so incredibly vibrantly alive had been a gift to both of them.

She had not even been aware how much she lived in a state of numbness until she had experienced this wonderful hour with him. It had been carefree, and laughter-filled, wondrous. Meredith felt as if she had been exquisitely and fully alive in a way she had not been for a long, long time.

If she ever had been that alive, that fully engaged, that spontaneous, that filled with wonder for the simple, unexpected miracle of life.

Still, leaving the utter and absolute magic of the moment, Meredith felt as if she was going to cry.

She covered the intensity of the moment by pasting a smile on her face. "You're welcome. People pay big money for the mud treatment at the spa."

"Yes," he said, watching her closely, as if he knew she was covering, as if he knew exactly how fake that smile was. "I know."

And of course he would know. Because that was his world. Spas and yachts and polo ponies.

His world. He had playfully said he would take her prisoner, but the truth was his world was a prison in many ways.

And he could not invite her into it.

She did not have the pedigree of a woman he would ever be allowed to love.

Love. How had that word, absolutely taboo in her relationship with him, slipped past all her guards and come into her mind?

But now that it had come, Meredith was so aware how this moment was going to have a tremendous cost to her. Because, she had ever so briefly glimpsed his heart. Because she had seen the coolness leave his eyes and be replaced with tenderness. Yes, this moment had come at a tremendous price to her. Because she had let her guard down, too.

For a moment she had wanted things she could not have. Ached for them.

Still, if she had this choice to make over, how would she do it? Would she play it safe and stay in the ballroom, tolerating his wooden performance, allowing his mask to remain impenetrable?

No, she would change nothing. She would forever be grateful she had risked so much to let him out of his world, and his prison. Even if it had only been a brief reprieve.

And in return, hadn't she been let out of hers?

He turned from her, but not before she caught the deeply thoughtful look on his face, as if every realization she was having was also occurring to him.

He walked back through the fern barrier, leapt into the hot springs completely clothed. She watched his easy strength, as he did a powerful crawl that carried him across the pool to the cascading water of the falls. She quelled the primitive awareness that tried to rise in her.

Instead, she dove into the pool, too. Her skin had never felt so open to sensation. He had climbed up on a ledge underneath the falls, and she saw the remnants of their day falling off of him as if it had never happened.

It was time to clean herself of the residue of the day, too. She swam across the pool and pulled herself up on the ledge beside him.

The fresh, cold water was shocking on her heated skin. It pummeled her, was nearly punishing in its intensity.

Though she and Kiernan stood side by side, Meredith was painfully aware some distance now separated them, keeping their worlds separate even in the glorious intimacy of the cascading water world that they shared.

She slid him a look and felt her breath catch in her throat.

His face was raised to the water, his eyes closed as

what was left of the mud melted out of his hair and dissolved off his face, revealing each perfect feature: the cut of high cheekbones, the straight line of his nose, the faint cleft of his chin.

The white of Andy's shirt had reemerged, but the shirt had turned transparent under the water, and clung to the hard lines of Kiernan's chest. She could see the dark pebble of his nipple, the slight indent of each rib, the hollow of a taut, hard belly. It made her mouth go dry with a powerful sense of craving.

To touch. To taste. To have. To hold.

Impossible thoughts. Ones that would only bring more grief to her if she allowed them any power at all. Hadn't her life held quite enough grief?

Was it the coldness of the water after all that heat, or her awareness of him that was making her quiver?

Meredith felt herself wanting to save this moment, to remember the absolute beauty of it—and of him—forever.

He finally turned and dove cleanly off the ledge, cutting the water with his body. With that same swift, sure stroke, Kiernan made his way back across the mineral pond to where he had set the baskets. How long ago? An hour? A little longer than an hour?

How could so much change in such a short amount of time?

She dove in, too, emerged from the pond, dripping, and flinging back the wetness of her hair. She saw, from the brief heat in his eyes before he turned away, that Molly's shirt must have become as transparent as Andy's.

She glanced down. And she had accused him of boring underwear? Her bra—a utilitarian sports model made for athletic support while dancing—showed clearly through the wet fabric. But from the look on his face you would have thought she was wearing a bra made out of silk and lace!

She shoved by him, and rummaged through the baskets, tucked a towel quickly around herself and then silently handed him a towel and a change of clothing.

Was there the faintest smirk on his face from how quickly she had wrapped herself up?

"You're prepared," he said.

Yes. And no. There were some things you could not prepare for. Like the fact you hoped a man would tease you about being a prude, like the fact it was so hard to let go of a perfect day.

But he didn't tease her, or linger. He ducked behind a rock on one side of the glade and she on the other. She did not want to think of him naked in a garden, but she knew the temptation of Eve in that moment, and fought it with her small amount of remaining strength.

The trip back was eerily silent, as if they were both contemplating what had happened and how to go forward—or back—from that place.

Meredith drove back through the same service entrance to Chatam Palace. On the way in she had to stop and show ID, and her palace pass. She did not miss the stunned look on the face of the guard as he recognized the prince squished in the seat beside her. He practically tossed her ID back through her window, drew himself to attention and saluted rigidly.

It could not have been a better reminder of who the man beside her *really* was.

And the look of shock on the guard's face to see the prince in such a humble vehicle with a member of the palace staff, could not have been a better reminder of who she really was, too.

He was not Andy. She was not Molly.

He was a prince, born to position, power and prestige. She was a servant's daughter, a woman who had given birth to an illegitimate child, a person with so much history and so much baggage.

She let the prince out, barely looking at him. He barely looked at her.

They did not say goodbye.

Meredith wondered if he would show up for their scheduled dance session tomorrow.

Would she?

The whole thing had become fraught with a danger that she did not know how to handle.

And yet, even that tingling sensation of danger as she drove away from the palace after dropping Kiernan off there, served as a reminder.

She was alive.

She was alive, and for the first time in a long, long time, she was aware of being deeply grateful that she was alive. The pain. The glory. The potential to be hurt. The potential to love. It was all part of the most incredible dance.

There was that word again.

Love.

"Forbidden to me," Meredith said. Because of who he was. Because of who she was, and especially because of where she had already been in the name of love.

But of course, what had more power than forbidden fruit?

When Prince Kiernan walked through the doors of the ballroom the next morning, Meredith did not know whether she was relieved he had come, or sorry that she had to be tested some more.

He was right on time as always.

They exchanged perfunctory greetings. She put on the music. He took her hand, placed his other with care on her waist.

The trip to the hot springs had obviously been an error in every way it was possible for something to be an error.

This was turning out to be just like the day she had ridden his horse and they had danced in the courtyard to the chamber music spilling out the palace windows.

Prince Kiernan's guard came down, but only temporarily!

And when it went back up, it went way up!

After half an hour of tolerating a wooden performance from him, Meredith was not tingling with awareness of being alive at all! She was tingling with frustration. Was he dancing this badly just to put her off? Maybe he was hoping she would cancel the whole thing. And maybe she should.

Except she couldn't. It was too late now to start over with someone else. The girls, rehearsing separately, at her studio, had practiced to perfection. They were there night and day, putting heart and soul into this.

She wasn't letting them down because Prince Kiernan was the most confoundedly stubborn man in the world.

But really, enough was enough!

"This is excruciating," she said, pulling away from him, folding her arms across her chest and glaring at him.

Somewhere under that cool, composed mask was the man who had chased her, laughter-filled, through the mud.

"I warned you I had no talent."

"Call somebody," she snapped at him. "It's like a

game show where you have a lifeline. Call somebody, and use your princely powers. Have them find us the movie *Dancing with Heaven*. And deliver it. Right here. Right now."

It was an impossible request. The movie was old. It would probably be extremely difficult if not impossible to find.

For a moment he looked like he might argue, but then he chose not to, probably because he wanted to do just about anything rather than dance.

With her.

With some new tension in the air between them. Harnessed, it would make for an absolutely electrical dance performance.

Resisted, it would make for a disastrous dance performance.

He took a cell phone out of his pocket, and placed a call.

"Tell them not to forget the popcorn," she said darkly. "And I'd like something to drink, too."

"You're being very bossy," he said. "As usual."

Within minutes his cell phone rang back. "It's set up in the theater room," he said.

"Can't we watch it here?"

"No, we can't. I'm not sitting on an icy cold floor to watch a movie. Not even for you."

Not even for you. She heard something there that she knew instantly he had not intended for her to hear. Something that implied he would do anything for her, up to and including going to the ends of the earth.

She deliberately quelled the beating of her heart and followed the prince to where he held open the ballroom doors for her.

It was the first time Meredith had been in the private

areas of the interior of the palace. The ballroom, along with the throne room, and a gallery of collected art was in the public wing of the palace, open to anyone who went there on a tour day.

Now, Prince Kiernan led her through an arched door flanked by two palace guards who saluted him smartly. The door led into the private family quarters of the palace.

They were in a grand entranceway, a formal living room on one side, a curving staircase on the other. The richness of it was startling: original old masters paintings, Persian rugs, priceless antiques, draperies and furniture upholstered in heavy brocaded silks. A chandelier that put the ones in the ballroom to shame spattered light over the staircase and entry.

Kiernan noticed none of it as he marched her up the wide stairs, under the portraits of his ancestors, many of whom looked just like him, and all of whom looked disapproving.

"What a happy looking lot," she muttered. "They have aloofness down to a fine art."

He glanced at the portraits. "Don't they?" With *approval*.

So *that's* where he got his rigidity!

"Maybe I'm wasting my time trying to break past something that has been bred into each Chatam for hundreds of years." And that they were proud of to *boot*.

"I've been trying to tell you."

And maybe if she hadn't been stupid enough to take him on that excursion yesterday, she would have believed him.

"This floor is where guests stay," he said, exiting the staircase that still spiraled magnificently upward. He led her down a wide corridor.

Bedroom doors were open along either side of the hallway and she peeked in without trying to appear too interested. The bedrooms, six in all, three on either side of the hallway were done in muted, tasteful colors. The décor had the flavor and feel of pictures Meredith had seen of very upscale boutique hotels.

It occurred to Meredith that princes and presidents, prime ministers, princesses and prima donnas had all walked down these corridors.

It reminded her who the man beside her *really* was, and she felt a whisper of awe. He opened the door to a room at the end of the long hallway.

Meredith tried not to gape. The "theater room" was really the most posh of private theaters. The walls were padded white leather panels with soft, muted light pouring out from behind them. The carpets were rich, dark gold with a raised crown pattern in yet darker gold. There were three tiers of theater style chairs in soft, buttery distressed leather. Each chair had a light underneath it that subtly illuminated the aisle. The chairs faced a screen as large as any Meredith had ever seen.

Two chairs were in front of all the others, and Kiernan gestured to one of them. Obviously she was sitting in a chair that would normally be slated for the most important of VIP's. She settled into the chair.

"Who's the last person who sat here?" She could not stop herself from asking.

If Kiernan thought the question odd he was polite enough not to let on. "I think it was the president of the United States. Nice man."

Never had she been more aware of who Kiernan really was.

And who she really was.

A man in a white jacket, very much like the one she

had borrowed from Andy, arrived with a steaming hot bowl of popcorn for each of them. He pushed a button on the side of her seat, and a tray emerged from the armrest.

"I was kidding about the popcorn," she hissed at Kiernan, but she took the bowl anyway.

"A drink, miss?"

Part of her was so intimidated by her surroundings, she wanted to just say no, to be that invisible girl who had accompanied her mother to work on occasion.

But another part of her thought she might never have on opportunity like this again, so, she was making the most of it. She decided to see how flummoxed the man would be if she ordered something completely exotic and off the wall—especially for ten o'clock in the morning. "Oh, sure. I'll have a virgin chi-chi."

The servant didn't even blink, just took the prince's order and glided away only to return a few minutes later.

"My apologies," he said quietly. "We didn't have the fresh coconut milk today."

She had to stifle a giggle. A desire to tease and say, *see that that doesn't happen again*. Instead, she met the man's eyes, and saw the warmth in them, and the lack of judgment.

"Can I get you anything else?"

"No, thank you for your kindness," she said. And she meant it.

She took a sip, and sighed. The drink, even without the fresh coconut milk was absolute ambrosia.

The movie came on. For the first few minutes Meredith was so self-conscious that Prince Kiernan was beside her. It felt as if she was on a first date, and they were afraid to hold hands.

Dancing with Heaven was dated and hokey, but the dance sequences were incredible, sizzling with tension and sensuality.

Though she had seen this movie a dozen times, Meredith was soon lost in the story of a spoiled self-centered young woman who walked by a dance studio called Heaven, peeked in the window, and was entranced by what she saw there. The dance instructor was a bitter older man whose career had been lost to an injury. He taught dance only for the money, because he had to.

Through what Meredith considered some the best dance sequences ever written, the young woman moved beyond her superficial and cynical attitude toward life and the instructor came to have hope again.

Wildly romantic, and sizzling with the sexual chemistry between the two, the instructor fought taking advantage of the young heiress's growing love for him, but in the end he succumbed to the love he had for her and the unlikely couple, united through dance, lived happily ever after.

What had made her insist the prince see this ridiculous and unrealistic piece of fluff?

When it was over, Meredith was aware of tears sliding down her face. She wiped at them quickly before the lights came up, set down her empty glass and her equally empty popcorn dish.

"Now you know what I expect of you. I'll see myself out. See you in the morning."

Kiernan saw that Meredith was not meeting his eyes. Something about the movie had upset her.

He ordered himself to let it go, especially after yesterday. Not that he wanted to think about yesterday.

He'd kissed her, and it hadn't been a little buss on

the cheek, either. No, it had been the kind of kiss that blew something wide open in a man, the kind of kiss that a man did not stop thinking about once it had happened.

It was the kind of kiss that made a man evaluate his own life and find it seemed empty, and without color.

The problem was they had been pretending to be ordinary.

And between an ordinary man and an ordinary woman maybe such things could happen without consequences.

But in his world? If he went where that kiss invited him to go, *begged* him to go, the world she knew would be over.

She had trusted him with her deepest secrets. How would she like those secrets to be exposed to the world? If he let his guard down again, if he allowed things to develop between them, Meredith would find her past at the center ring of a three-ring circus. Pictures of her baby would be dug up. Her mother's past would be investigated. Her ex would be found and asked for comments on her character.

So, even though the movie had upset her, it would be best to let her go.

And yet he couldn't.

He stepped in front of her.

"Are you upset?" he asked quietly.

She looked panicked. "No. I just need to go. I need to—"

"You're upset," he said. "Why? Did the movie upset you?"

"No, I—"

"Please don't lie to me," he said. "You've never done it before, and you have no talent for it."

She was silent.

He tipped her chin. "Did it remind you of your baby's father?" he asked softly. "Is that the way you felt about him?"

He remembered the sizzling sensuality between the on-screen couple, and he felt a little pang of, good grief, *envy*. But this wasn't about him. He could actually feel her trembling, trying to hold herself together.

"Talk to me, Meredith."

"It had a happy ending," she whispered. "I deplore happy endings! If it weren't for the dance sequences, I would have never asked you to watch such drivel!"

But he was stuck at the *I deplore happy endings* part. How could anyone so young and so vibrant have stopped believing in a happy ending for herself?

"My baby's father was older than me, twenty-two. He was new to the neighborhood, and all the girls were swooning over his curly hair and his suave way. I was thrilled that he singled me out for his attention. Thrilled."

Kiernan felt something like rage building in him at the man had never met, the man who had used her so terribly, manipulated and fooled a young girl. But he said nothing, fearing that if he spoke, she would clam up.

And he sensed she needed to talk, she needed to say these things she had been holding inside. And he needed to be man enough to listen, without being distracted by her lips and the memory of their taste, without wanting *more* for himself. Without putting his needs ahead of her own.

"If I had married Michael, my baby's father, it would have been a disaster," she said. "I can see that now. As hard as it was for me and my mom to make ends meet, it would have only been harder with him. You want to know how bad my taste is in men? Do you want to know?"

He saw the regret in her eyes and the pain, and he wanted to know everything about her. Everything.

"He didn't even come to the funeral."

She began to sob.

And he did what he should have done yesterday in the car, what he had wanted to do.

He pulled her into his chest, and ran his hand up and down her back, soothing her, encouraging her. *Let it out.*

"I loved him, madly. I guess maybe I held on to this fantasy he was going to come to his senses, do the right thing, come back and rescue me. Prove to my mother she was wrong. Love us."

If he could have, he would have banished the shame from her face.

"Kiernan," she said softly, "he didn't care one fig about me. Not one. And I fooled myself into thinking he did. How can a person ever trust themselves after something like that? How?"

He loved that she had called him his name, no formal address. Wasn't that what was happening between them? And what he was fighting against?

Deepening trust. Friendship. Boundaries blurring. But as he let her cry against him, he knew it was more. Mere friendship was not something that would put his guard up so high. And mere friendship would never have him feeling a nameless fury at the man who had cruelly used her, walked away from his responsibilities, broken her heart as if it was nothing.

His fury at a man he had never met abated as he

became aware of Meredith pressed against him, felt the sacredness of her trust, and this moment.

He was not sure that he had ever felt as much a man as he did right now.

"You deserved so much better," he finally said.

"Did I?" She sounded skeptical.

He put her away from him, looked deep into the lovely green of her eyes. "Yes," he said furiously, "you did. As for trusting yourself? My God, cut yourself some slack. You were a child. Sixteen. Is that what you said?"

"Seventeen when Carly was born."

"A child," he repeated firmly. "Taken advantage of by an adult man. His behavior was despicable. To be honest? I'd like to track him down and give him a good thrashing!"

She actually giggled a little at that. "Maybe the dungeon?"

He felt relieved that she was coming around, that he saw a spark of light in her eyes. "Exactly! Extra rats!"

"Thank you," she said, quietly.

"I'm not finished. As for not trusting yourself? Meredith, you have taken these life experiences and made it your mission to change things for others. Do you remember what I said to you when you thanked me for not allowing you to fall off the horse?"

"Yes," she whispered, "You said it's not how you fall that matters. You said everyone falls. You said it was how you got up that counted."

He was intensely flattered that she had heard him so completely. He spoke quietly and firmly. "And how you are getting up counts, Meredith. Helping those Wentworth girls honors your baby. And your mother. And you."

She gave him a watery smile, pulled away from him,

not quite convinced. "Oh, God, look at me. A blithering idiot. In front of a prince, no less."

And she turned, he could tell she was going to flee, and so he caught her arm. "I'm not letting you go, not just yet. Let's have tea first."

Just in case he was beginning to think he was irresistible, she said, "Will it have the little cream puff swans?"

"Yes," he said. "It will."

He guided her out of the theater and to the elevator at the end of the hallway and took her to his private apartment.

"It's beautiful," she said, standing in the doorway, as if afraid to come in. And maybe he should have thought this out better.

Once she had been in here, would he ever be completely free of her? Or would he see her walking around, pausing in front of each painting like this, always?

"Is it you who loves Monet?" she asked.

He nodded.

"Me, too. I have several reproductions of his work."

"I understand," Kiernan said, "that he was nearsighted. That wonderful dreamy, hazy quality in his landscapes was not artistic license but how he actually saw the world. You know what I like about that?"

She looked at him.

"His handicap was his greatest gift. Your hardships, Meredith?"

She was looking at him as if he had a lifeline to throw her. And he hoped he did.

"Your hardships are what make you what you are. Amazingly strong, and yet good. Your goodness shines out of you like a light."

He turned away to look after tea. But not before he

saw that maybe he had said exactly the right thing after all, but maybe not enough of it. She did not look entirely convinced.

He had tea set up on the balcony that overlooked the palace grounds and the stunning views of Chatam.

"Instead of allowing your falls to break you," he insisted quietly, sitting her down, "you have found your strength."

"No, really I haven't."

Now he felt honor-bound not to let her go until she was convinced. Of her own goodness. Of her innate strength. Of the fact that she had to let go of all that shame. Of the fact she was earning her way, by the way she chose to live her life, to a new future.

"I want to know every single thing there is to know about you. I want to know how you've become the remarkable woman you are today." And he meant that.

She looked wildly toward the exit, but then she met his eyes. But just to keep him from feeling too powerful, then she looked at the tray of goodies a servant was bringing in.

"Oh," she said. "The cream puffs."

"I know how to get your secrets out of you, Meredith."

"There's nothing remarkable about me."

"Ah, well, let me decide."

She mulled that over, and then sighed. Almost surrender. He passed her the tray. She took a cream puff, and sighed again. When she bit into it and closed her eyes he knew her surrender was complete.

They talked for a long, long time. It was deep and it was true and it was real. He felt as if they could sit there and talk forever.

It was late in the afternoon before Meredith looked at her watch, gasped, and made her excuses. Within seconds she was gone. Kiernan was not sure he had ever felt he had connected with someone so deeply, had ever inspired trust such as he had just experienced from her.

Kiernan sat for a long time in a suite that felt suddenly cold and empty for all the priceless art and furniture that surrounded him. It felt as if the life had gone out of it when Meredith had.

Without her the room just seemed stuffy. And stodgy.

He'd liked having her here in his very private space. He'd liked watching the movie with her and how she had not tried to hide the fact she was awed that a president had sat in her chair. He liked how she had acknowledged Bernard who had brought their popcorn and drinks, not treated him as if he was invisible, the way Tiffany always had.

And damn it, he'd liked that movie.

Silly piece of fluff that it was, it was somehow about people finding the courage to be what they were meant to be, to bring themselves to the world, to overcome the strictures of their assigned roles and embrace what was real for them.

And, finally, he had loved how she had come into his space, and how between cream puffs and his genuine interest and concern for her she had become so open. And liked what the afternoon told him about her.

Above all things, Meredith was courageous.

A hardscrabble upbringing, too many losses for one so young, and yet he saw no self-pity in her. She was taking the challenges life had given her and turning them into her greatest assets. She had a quiet bravery to get on with her life.

That's what she was asking of him. To bring his

courage to the dance floor. To dance without barriers, without a mask, and without a safety net.

She was asking him to be who he had been, ever so briefly, when they had chased each other through the mud.

Wholly alive. Completely, unselfconsciously himself.

No guards. No barriers.

And she was asking him to be who he had been just now: deep and compassionate.

Really, what she was asking of him would require more courage than just about anything he had ever done. At the hot springs he had shown that unguarded self to her. And again today there had been something so open and unprotected about their interaction after the movie.

Prince Kiernan felt as if he stood on the very edge of a cliff. Did he take a leap of faith, trusting if he jumped something—or someone—would catch him? Or did he turn away?

"For her sake," he said to himself, "You turn away."

But he didn't know if he was powerful enough to do that. He knew he wanted these last days with her before it was over.

So he could have moments and memories, a secret, something sacredly private in his life, to savor when she was gone.

CHAPTER SEVEN

"FROM THE TOP," Meredith said. Today's dancing session, she knew, was going no better than yesterday's. The movie had changed nothing.

No, that was not true.

It had changed everything.

It had changed her. Maybe not the movie, exactly, but what had happened after.

When Kiernan had held her in her arms, it had felt as if everything she had been fighting for since the death of her mother and baby—independence, strength, self-reliance—it had felt as if those things were melting.

As if some terrible truth had unfolded.

All those qualities that she had striven toward were just distractions from the real truth. And the truth was she was so terribly alone in this world.

And for a moment, for an exquisite, tender moment in the arms of her country's most powerful man, she had not felt that. Sitting beside him on the balcony of his exquisite apartment, surveying all his kingdom, pouring out her heart, telling her secrets, she had not felt that.

For the first time in forever, Meredith had not felt alone.

And it was the most addictive sensation she had ever

felt. She wanted to feel it again. She wanted to never let go of it.

Worse, she had a tormented sense that, though Kiernan walked with kings and presidents, she had seen what was most *real* about him. It was the laughter at the hot springs, it was his confidence in his horse, it was the tenderness in his eyes as he had listened to her yesterday.

And she had to guard against the feeling that he caused in her.

Because just like the wealthy heiress and the dance instructor in the movie, their worlds were so far apart. But unlike the movie, which was pure escapist fantasy after all, they could never be joined. And the sooner she accepted the absoluteness of that the better.

This morning she felt only embarrassed that she had revealed herself so totally to him. Talked, not just about Michael and Carly, which was bad enough, but about her childhood, growing up with a single mom in Wentworth, and then repeating her family's history by becoming one herself.

She'd told him about ballet, and her mother's hope and losing the scholarship when she became pregnant. She'd told him about those desperate days after Carly was born, her mother being there for her, despite her disappointments, Millie loving the baby, but never quite forgiving her daughter.

She told him about the insurance settlement after the tragedy that allowed her to own her own dance studio and form No Princes, and how guilty she felt that her dreams were coming true because the people she had loved the most had died.

Oh, yes, she had said way, way too much. And today, it was affecting *her* dancing.

She was the one with the guard up. She was the one who could not open herself completely. She was the one who could not be vulnerable on the dance floor. She was trying desperately to take back the ground she had lost yesterday.

And she was failing him. Because she could not let him in anymore. She could not be open.

She was as rigid and closed as the prince had been on that first day. It was the worst of ironies that now he seemed as open as she was closed!

"What's wrong?" he asked.

The tender concern in his eyes was what was wrong! The fact she was foolishly, unrealistically falling in love with him was what was wrong!

"You know what?" he said, snapping his fingers. "I know I have the power to fix whatever is wrong!"

Yes, he did. He could get down on one knee and say that though the time had been short he realized he was crazy about her. That he couldn't live without her.

All this work. All this time with No Princes and Meredith's weaknesses were unabated! She despised that about herself.

"One call," he said, and smiled at her and left the room.

When he returned he had a paper bag with him, and with the flourish of a magician about to produce a rabbit, he opened it and handed her a crumpled white piece of fabric.

"Ta-da," he said as she shook out the white smock.

"What is this?"

"I think I've figured it out," he said, pulling another smock from the bag and tugging it over his own shirt.

It had Andy embossed across the breast.

She stared down at the smock in her hand. Sure enough, he had unearthed Molly's smock.

"Remember when you told me this kind of dancing is like acting?"

Meredith nodded.

"Well, I'm going to be Andy for the rest of the rehearsals. And you're going to be Molly."

She stared at him stunned. She wanted to refuse. She wanted to get out of this with her heart in one piece.

But she could not resist the temptation of the absolute brilliance of it. If she could pretend to be someone else, if she could pretend he was someone else, there was a slim chance she could save this thing from catastrophe. And maybe, at the same time, she could save herself from the catastrophe of an unattainable love.

But it seemed the responsibility for saving things had been wrested from her. Kiernan took charge. He went and put on the music, turned and gazed at her, then held out his hands to her.

"Shall we dance, Molly?"

She could only nod. She went and took his hands, felt the way they fit together. Her resolve, which she could have sworn was made of stone, melted at his touch.

"Remember Andy?" he said, smiling down at her as they began the opening waltz.

She gave herself over to this chance to save the dance. "Isn't he that devilish boy who won't do his homework?"

"Except he did watch *Dancing with Heaven*."

"Used class time, though."

"That's true."

Kiernan had those opening steps down *perfect*. A little awkwardness, a faint stiffness, a resolve to keep his distance in his posture.

The transition was coming.

"Andy," she reminded him, getting into the spirit of this, embracing it, "winks at the teacher and makes her blush."

And Kiernan became that young fellow—on the verge of manhood, able to tie his teacher in knots with a blink of sapphire-colored eyes.

"I think he makes her drop things, too," Meredith conceded, and her blush was real. "And forget what she's teaching at all."

Kiernan smiled at her with Andy's wicked devil-may-care-delight. Through dance he became the young man who rode motorcycles, and wore black leather. He was the guy who drove too fast and broke rules.

Something about playing the role of the bad boy unleashed Kiernan. He was playful. He was commanding. He was mischievous. He was *bad*.

His hips moved!

They moved to the next transition, and Kiernan released her hand. He claimed the dance floor as his own.

He claimed it. Then he owned it.

Meredith's mouth dropped open as he tore off the smock that said Andy on it, and tossed it to the floor.

Before her eyes, Kiernan became the man who liked loud music and smoky bars, and girls in too-short skirts and low-cut tops who wiggle their hips when they dance. He became the guy who cooled off in the town fountain, claimed Landers Rock as his own, kept his hat on during the anthem.

He became a man so comfortable with himself that he would delight in swimming in the sea naked under the moonlight.

And then came the final transition.

And he was no longer an immature young man, chasing skirts and adrenaline rushes, breaking rules just for the thrill of having said he had done it.

Now he was a man, claiming the woman he wanted to spend the rest of his life with.

He crossed the floor to her, and they went seamlessly to the finale—dancing together as if nothing else in the world existed except each other, and the heat, the chemistry between them.

Meredith was not Meredith. She was Molly.

And something about being Molly unleashed her just as much as being Andy had unleashed him. She didn't have a history. She was just a girl from the kitchen who wanted something more out of life: not drudgery, but a hint of excitement wherever she could find it.

By playing Molly, Meredith came to understand her younger self.

And forgive her.

Finally, with both of them breathless, the music stopped. But Kiernan did not let her go. He stared at her silently, his eyes saying what his mouth did not.

She pulled away from him. Her smile was tremulous.

"It was perfect," she breathed.

"I know. I could feel it."

She had to get hold of herself; despite this breakthrough she had to find the line between professional and personal. She had to get over the feeling of wanting to take his lips and taste them, of wanting more than she could have, of wanting more than he could offer her.

"You know what would be brilliant?" Meredith said crisply. "We can alter the real performance dream sequence slightly so that it is Andy and Molly, and Andy transforms into a prince."

He was looking at her just as he had on the balcony of his private suite. With eyes that saw right through her professional blither-blather to the longing that was underneath.

She was only human.

And he was only human.

If she was going to keep this thing on the tracks until the performance at *An Evening to Remember* she had to make a drastic decision, and she had to make it right now.

"You know what this means, don't you?"

He shook his head.

"We're finished."

"Finished?"

"We're done, Prince Kiernan." It was self-preservation. She could not dance like that with him every day until the performance and keep her heart on ice, keep him from seeing what was blossoming inside her.

Like a flower that would be cut.

"We've got two practices left," he said, frowning at her.

"No," she said firmly, with false brightness, "there's nothing left to practice. Nothing. I don't think we should do it again. I don't want to lose the freshness of what we just did. We're done, Prince Kiernan. The next time we do that dance, it will be at *An Evening to Remember*."

Instead of looking relieved that dance class was finally over, Kiernan looked stunned.

She felt stunned, too. She was ending it. The suddenness of it made her head spin. And she felt bereft. It was over. They would have one final dance together, but it was already over. She was ending this craziness right here and right now.

"So," she said with forced cheer, holding out her

hand to shake his, "good work, Your Highness. I'll see you opening night of Blossom Week, for *An Evening to Remember*. Gosh. Only a few nights away. How did that happen?"

But instead of shaking her hand, two business people who had done good work together, the prince took her hand, held it, looked with deep and stripping thoughtfulness into her eyes. Then he bowed over her hand, and placed his lips to it.

Meredith could feel that familiar devastating quiver begin in her toes.

"No," he said, straightening and gazing at her.

"No? No *what*?"

"No, it won't be opening night before we meet again."

"It won't?" It felt just like their first meeting, when he had told her she couldn't be Meredith Whitmore. He said things with the certainty of one who had the power to change reality, who *always* had his own way.

"You've shown me your world, Meredith," Kiernan said quietly. "You gave that to me freely, expecting nothing in return. You gave me a gift. But I would like to give you something in return, a gift of my own. Come experience an evening in my world."

Her mouth opened to say *no*. It wasn't possible. She was trying to protect herself. He was storming the walls.

"It's the least I can do for you. I'll send a car to pick you up tonight. We'll have a farewell dinner on the yacht."

Farewell. Did his voice have an odd catch in it when he said that?

Say *no*. Every single thing in her that wanted to survive screamed at her to say no.

But what woman, no matter how strong, no matter how independent, no matter how much or how desperately she wanted to protect her own heart could say no to an evening with a prince, a date out of a dream?

It wasn't as if she could get her hopes up. He'd been very clear. A farewell dinner. One last time to be alone together. The next time they saw each other would be very public, for their performance.

On pure impulse, Meredith decided she would give herself this. She would not or could not walk away from the incredible gift he was offering her.

She would take it, greedily. One night. One last thing to remember him by, to hold to her when these days of dancing with him, laughing with him, baring her soul to him, were but a distant memory.

"Yes," she whispered. "That would be lovely."

It wasn't a *date*, Meredith told herself as she obsessed about what to wear and how to do her hair and her makeup and her nails. It wasn't a date. He had not called it that. A gift, he had said, and even though she knew she should have tried harder to resist the temptation, now that she hadn't, she was giving herself over to the gift wholeheartedly.

She intended to not think about a future that did not include him. She was just going to take it moment by moment, and enjoy it without contemplating what that enjoyment might cost her later.

Hadn't she done that before? Exchanged heated looks and stolen kisses with no thought of the consequences?

No, it was different this time. She was a different person than she had been back then. Wasn't she?

And so, trying to keep her doubts on the back burner, with her makeup subtle and perfect, her nails varnished with clear lacquer, dressed in a simple black cocktail dress with a matching shawl, her hair upswept, the most expensive jewelry she could afford—tiny diamonds set in white gold—twinkling at her ears, she went down her stairs, escorted by a uniformed driver, to where the limousine awaited her. She thanked God that all the years of dancing made her able to handle the incredibly high heels—and the pre-performance jitters—with seeming aplomb.

Passersby and neighbors had stopped to gawk at the black limo, and the chauffeur holding it open for her.

It was not one of the official palace vehicles with the House of Chatam emblem on the door, but still she waved like a celebrity walking the red carpet, and slid inside the door.

The luxury of it was absolutely sumptuous. She was offered a glass of champagne, which she refused. The windows of the backseat were darkly tinted, so all the people staring at her as they passed could not see her staring back at them.

The car glided through the streets of Chatam into the harbor area, and finally arrived at a private dock. The yacht, called *Royal Blue*, bobbed gently on its moorings.

A carpet had been laid out to prevent her high heels from slipping through the wide-spaced wooden planks of the dock. Light spilled out every window of the yacht, danced down the dock and splashed out over inky dark waters.

The lights illuminated interior rooms. It wasn't a boat. It was a floating palace.

And against the midnight darkness of the sky, she could see Prince Kiernan. He was outside on an upper deck, silhouetted by the lights behind him, leaning on a railing, waiting.

For her.

She wanted to run to him, as if he was not a prince at all, but her safe place in this unfamiliar world of incredible wealth.

Instead, she walked up the carpet, and up the slightly swaying gangway with all the pose and grace years of dancing had given her. She knew his eyes were only for her, and she breathed it in, intending to enjoy every second of this gift.

The crew saluted her, and her prince waited at the top of the gangway.

Prince Kieran greeted her by meeting her eyes and holding her gaze for a long time, until her heart was beating crazily in her throat. Then he took her hand, much as he had in the ballroom, bowed low over it, and kissed it.

"Welcome," he said, and his eyes swept her.

Every moment she had taken with her hair and her makeup, her jewelry and her dress was rewarded with the light in his eyes. Except that he seemed to be memorizing her. He had said *welcome*, but really, hadn't he meant goodbye?

"You are so beautiful," he said, the faintest hoarseness in that cultured voice.

"Thank you," she stammered. She could have told him he looked beautiful, too, because he did, dressed in a dark suit with a crisp white shirt under it. At the moment, Kiernan was every girl's fairy-tale prince.

"Come," he said, and he slipped his hand in hers, and led her to a deeply padded white leather bench in the bow of the boat.

As the crew called muted orders to each other the

yacht floated out of its slip and they headed out of the mouth of the harbor.

"I just have to let you know in advance, that as hard as I tried to completely clear my calendar for this evening, I'm expecting an overseas call from the Minister of Business. I'll have to take it. I hope it will be brief, but possibly not. I hope you won't be bored."

Meredith was used to these kinds of interruptions from their dance classes.

"Bored? How could I be bored when I have this to experience?" She gestured over the view of dark sea, the island growing more distant. "It looks like a place out of a dream."

The lights of Chatam, reflected in the dark water, grew further away.

"It will be breezy now that we're underway. Do you want to go in?"

She shook her head, and he opened a storage unit under a leather bench, found a light blanket and settled it on her shoulders. Then Kiernan pressed against her to lend her his warmth.

As the boat cut quietly around the crags of the island, she found she and Kiernan talked easily of small things. The girls' excitement for the upcoming performance, Erin Fisher's remarkable talent and potential, Prince Adrian's recovery from his injury, the overseas call Kiernan was expecting about a business deal that could mean good things for the future of Chatam.

After half an hour of following the rugged coastline of Chatam, the yacht pulled into a small cove, the engines were cut, and the quiet encircled them as she heard the chain for the anchor drop.

"It's called Firefly Cove," he said. "Can you see why?"

"Oh," she breathed as thousands and thousands of small lights pricked the darkness, "it is so beautiful."

The breeze picked up, and he took the blanket and offered her his hand. They went inside.

It was as beautiful as outside.

There was really nothing to indicate they were on a boat, except for the huge windows and the slight bobbing motion.

Other than that the décor was fabulous—modern furniture covered in rich linens, paintings, rugs, an incredible chandelier hung over a dining table set for two with the most exquisite china.

All of it could have made her feel totally out of place and uncomfortable. But Kiernan was with her, teasing, laughing, putting her at ease.

Dinner came out, course after course of the most incredible food, priceless wines that an ordinary girl like her would never have tasted under other circumstances.

But rather than being intimidated Meredith delighted in the new experiences, made easy because of how her prince guided her through them.

They went back out on the deck for after-dinner coffee, he draped the blanket around her shoulders again, and tucked her into him. They sat amongst the fireflies and talked. At first of light things: the exquisiteness of the food they had just eaten, the rareness of the wines, the extraordinary beauty of the fireflies; the stars that filled the night sky.

But Meredith found herself yearning for his trust, the same trust that she had shown him the day they had watched the movie.

With a certain boldness, she took his hand, and said, "Tell me how you came to earn all those horrible nicknames. Playboy Prince. Prince of Heartaches. Prince Heartbreaker. I feel as if I've come to know you, and those names seem untrue and unfair."

But was it? Wasn't he setting her up for heartbreak right now? Without even knowing it? He'd been clear. Tonight was not hello. It was goodbye.

But she wasn't allowing herself to think of that.

No, she was staying in this moment: the gentle sway of the sea beneath her, his hand in hers, his shoulder touching hers.

She was staying in this moment, and moving it toward deeper intimacy even if that was crazy. She wanted him to know, even after they'd said goodbye, that she had known his heart.

"Thank you," he said with such sincerity, as if she had *seen* him that she quivered from it, and could not resist moving a little more closely into his warmth. "Though, of those titles, the Playboy Prince was probably neither untrue nor unfair."

He recounted his eighteenth summer. "I found myself free, in between getting out of private school and going into the military. Until I was eighteen, my mother had been very vigilant in restricting the press's access to me. And women hadn't been part of my all-male world, except as something desired from a distance, movie star posters on dorm room walls. So, I wasn't quite used to the onslaught of interest on both fronts.

"And like many young men of that age, I embraced all the perks of that freedom and none of the responsibility. Unfortunately, my forum was so public. There was a frenzy, like a new rock star had been unveiled to the world. I didn't see a dark side or a downside. I was flattered by the attention of the press and the young women. I dated every beautiful woman who showed the least interest in me."

"And that was many," Meredith said dryly.

Still, she could feel the openness of him, and something sighed within her. She had trusted him, and now he was trusting her.

"That's what I mean about the Playboy Prince title having truth to it," he said ruefully. "But after that summer of my whole life becoming so public, I became more discerning, and certainly more cynical. I started to understand that very few of those young women were really interested in *me*. It was all about the title, the lifestyle, and the fairy tale. I could be with the most beautiful woman in the world and feel so abjectly lonely.

"But for a short while, I searched, almost frantically for *the* one. I'm sure I broke hearts right and left because I could tell after the first or second date that it just wasn't going to work, and I extricated myself quickly. Somehow, though, I was always the one seen as responsible for the fact others pinned their unrealistic hopes and dreams on me."

Was that what she was doing? By sitting here, enjoying his world and his company, was she investing, again, in unrealistic hopes and dreams?

Just one night. She would give herself that. It wasn't really pinning hopes and dreams on him. It was about knowing him as completely as she could before she let him go back to his world, and she went back to hers.

"I'd known Francine Lacourte since I was a child," Kiernan continued. "We'd always been close, always the best of friends."

"The duchess." She felt the faintest pang of jealousy at the way he said that name. With a tender reverence.

"She was the funniest, smartest woman I ever met.

She was also the deepest. She had a quality about her, a glow that was so attractive. She shunned publicity, which I loved."

"You were engaged to her, weren't you?"

"Ever so briefly."

"And you broke it off, bringing us to nickname number two, the Prince of Heartaches. Because she never recovered, did she?"

Which, now that she thought about it, Meredith could see was a very real danger.

But Kiernan smiled absently. "The truth that no one knows? I didn't break it off. She did."

He was telling her a truth that no one else knew? That amount of trust felt exquisite.

"But that's not what the press said! In fact, they still say she is in mourning for you. She has become very reclusive. I don't think I've seen one photograph of her in the paper since you broke with her. And that's years ago. It really is like she has disappeared off the face of the earth."

"Our friends at the press take a fact—like Francine being reclusive—and then they build a story around it that suits their purposes. It has nothing to do with the truth. For a while there was even a rumor started by one of the most bottom feeding of all the publications that I had murdered her. How ridiculous is that?"

"That's terrible!"

"I am going to tell you a truth that very few people on this earth know. I know I don't have to tell you how deeply private this conversation is."

Again, Meredith relished this trust he had in her, even as she acknowledged it moved her dangerously closer to pinning unrealistic hopes and dreams on him!

"That depth and quality and glow in Francine that I

found so attractive? She had a deep spiritual longing. Francine joined a convent. She had wanted to do so for a long, long time. She loved me, I think. But not the way she loved God."

"She's a nun?" Meredith breathed, thinking of pictures of her that had been republished after his broken engagement to Tiffany Wells. Francine Lacourte was gorgeous, the last person one would think of as a nun!

He nodded. "She chose a cloister. Can you imagine the nightmare her new life would have been if the paparazzi got hold of that? Because I have a network around me that can protect me from the worst of their viciousness, I chose to let them create the story that titillated the world."

"You protected her," Meredith whispered.

"I don't really see it like that. She gave me incredible gifts in the times we spent together. I was able to return to her the privacy she so treasured."

"By taking the heat."

"Well, as I say, I have a well-oiled machine around me that protects me from the worst of it. The press can say whatever they want. I'm quite adept at dodging the arrows, not letting them affect me at all. So, if I could do that for Francine, why wouldn't I?"

Hadn't she known this for weeks? In her heart, with her sense of *knowing* him growing? That the prince was actually the opposite of how he was portrayed by the press?

"And then you graduated to being the Prince Heartbreaker," Meredith said.

"Tiffany came along later, and I was well aware it was *time*. Very subtle pressure was being brought on me to find a suitable partner. I had been deeply hurt by Francine's choice, even as I commended her for making it. At some level I think I was looking for a woman who was the antithesis of her, which Tiffany certainly was. Bubbly. Beautiful. Light. Lively. Tiffany Wells was certain of her womanly wiles in this seductive, confident way that initially I was bowled over by."

There were few men who wouldn't be, Meredith thought, with just a touch of envy.

"I was a mature man. She was a mature woman. Eventually, we did what mature adults do," he admitted. "I'm ashamed to say for the longest time I mistook the sexual sizzle between us as love. Still, we were extremely responsible. Double protected.

"But as that sexual sizzle had cooled to an occasional hiss, I realized it was really the only thing we had in common."

"She bored you!" Meredith deduced.

He looked pained. "Her constant chatter about *nothing* made my head hurt. I was feeling increasingly disillusioned and she, unfortunately, seemed increasingly enamored.

"I told her it was over. She told me she was pregnant."

Meredith gasped, but he held her hand tighter, looked at her deeply. "No, Meredith, it is not your story. I did not abandon a pregnant woman."

CHAPTER EIGHT

PRINCE KIERNAN TOLD Meredith the rest of the story haltingly. After overcoming the initial shock of Tiffany's announcement he had weighed his options with the sense of urgency that the situation demanded.

He had done what he felt was the honorable thing, a man prepared to accept full responsibility for his moment of indiscretion.

His engagement had been announced, and they had set a date for the very near future, so that Tiffany's pregnancy would not be showing at the wedding. The press had gone into a feeding frenzy. Tiffany had appeared to adore the attention as much as he was appalled by it. She was "caught" out shopping for her gown and flowers, having bachelorette celebrations with her friends, even looking at bassinettes.

"When we were together, we could not have one moment of privacy. The cameras were always there, we were chased, questions were shouted, the press always seemed to know where we were. Now, uncharitably, I wonder if she didn't tip them off. But regardless, our lives became helicopters flying over the palace, the yacht, the polo fields, men with cameras up trees and in shrubs.

"On this point, Meredith, you were absolutely correct

in what you said to me on the day we began dance practice. Romance is glorious entertainment. It sells newspapers and magazines and it ups ratings. Interest in us, as a couple, was nothing short of insatiable."

"How horrible!" Meredith said.

"You'd think," he said dryly. "Tiffany loved every moment of it. For me, it felt as if I was riding a runaway train that I couldn't stop and couldn't get off of."

"But you did stop it. But what of the baby? In all the publicity that followed, I never once heard she was pregnant."

"Because she wasn't."

"What?"

"Before that incident it had never occurred to me that a person—particularly one who claimed to love you—could be capable of a deception of such monstrous proportions as that. Luckily for me, the truth was revealed before we were married. Unluckily, it was the night before the wedding."

He went on to say a loyal servant, assigned to Tiffany, had come in obvious distress late on the eve of the wedding to tell him something that under normal circumstances he would have found embarrassing. But the fact that *pregnant* Tiffany was having her period had saved him. Despite the lateness of the hour, he had confronted Tiffany immediately, and the wedding had been cancelled.

But now the whole world saw him as the man who had coldheartedly broken a bride's heart on the eve of all her dreams coming true. The press seemed tickled by the new role they had assigned him, Prince Heartbreaker.

Tiffany, on the other hand, seemed to be enjoying the attention as much as ever, photographed often, sunglasses in place, shoulders slumped, enthusiastically playing the part of the party who was suffering the most and who had been grievously wronged.

"Why on earth wouldn't you let the world know what and who she really is?" Meredith demanded, shocked at how protective she felt of him. "Why are you taking the brunt of the whole world's disappointment that the fairy tale has fallen apart?"

"Now you sound like Adrian." He paused before he spoke. "I saw something in Tiffany's desperate attempt to capture me that was not evil. It was very sad and very sick. I glimpsed a frightening fragility behind her mask of supreme confidence.

"How fragile only a very few people know. Tiffany had attempted suicide after I uncovered her deception."

"It sounds like more manipulation to me," Meredith said angrily.

"Regardless, I was not blameless. I gave in to temptation, let go of control when I most needed to keep it. I put Tiffany in a position where she hoped for more than what I was prepared to offer, I put myself in a position of extreme vulnerability.

"I don't think Tiffany could have handled her deception being made public, the scorn that would have been heaped on her."

"She certainly seems to handle it being heaped on you rather well. Her total lack of culpability enrages me, Kiernan."

He shrugged. "I've been putting up with the attacks of the press since I was a young man. I'm basically indifferent to what they have to say."

"You protected her, too. Even though she is not the least deserving of your protection!"

He shrugged it off. "Don't read too much into it, Meredith. I'm no hero."

"Just a prince," she said and was rewarded with his laughter.

"Just a man," he said. "Underneath it all, just a man."

But a good one, she thought. A man with a sense of decency and honor. A man who had not abandoned the woman he thought carried his child.

The man of her dreams. So, so easy to fall in love with him.

A steward came and whispered in his ear.

"I'm so sorry. That's the call I have to take."

The truth? She was glad for a moment alone to sort through the new surge of emotion she felt at his innate decency, at his deeply ingrained sense of honor.

"Don't think anything of it," she assured him. She didn't mind. She wanted to sit here and savor his trust and the world he had opened to her. But she badly needed distance, too.

The steward brought her a refill for her coffee, the day's paper, and a selection of magazines.

After staring pensively at the sea for a long time, she needed any kind of distraction to stop the whirling of her thoughts. She picked up the paper.

In the entertainment section she stopped dead.

There was a picture of society beauty Brianna Morrison under the headline Prince Heartbreaker's New Victim?

But Miss Morrison looked like anything but a victim! She was hugging a gossamer green dress to her, her choice for the Blossom Week Ball, the event that would culminate the week's celebrations.

"I couldn't believe it when I was asked," she gushed to the interviewer. "It is like a dream come true."

It seemed something went very still in Meredith. She was sharing the prince's yacht tonight. But he had been very clear. This was farewell.

The prince giving the peasant girl a final gift of himself before moving back to his real life.

But he had asked another woman to the ball.

Well, of course he had. Meredith had always known she didn't belong in this world. Brianna Morrison's family was old money, the Morrisons owned factories and businesses, real estate, and shipping yards.

And tonight he had said pressure, subtle or not, was being brought on him to find a suitable partner. Brianna was beautiful and accomplished. Her family's interests and the interests of the Chatams had been linked for centuries.

And then there was Meredith Whitmore. A dance instructor, more devoted to her charity than her business, a woman with a hard past.

No, the prince had decided to give his dance instructor a lovely night out.

A small token of appreciation. He had never claimed it was anything more than a way of saying goodbye to her and the world they had shared for a few light-filled days.

She had been crazy to encourage his confidences, some part of her hoping and praying she was in some way suitable for his world and that he would see it.

She set down the paper and called the steward. "Could we go back to Chatam, please? I'm not feeling well."

In seconds, Kiernan was at her side.

"I hope you didn't end your phone call on my behalf," she said coolly, not wanting to see the concern on his face, deliberately looking to the sea that was beginning to chop under a strengthening wind.

"Of course I did! You're not feeling well? It's probably the roughening sea, but I can have my physician waiting at the dock."

"No, it's not that serious," she said, trying not to melt at his tender concern, trying to steel herself against it. "I'm sure it is the sea. I just need to go home."

"I'll give the order to get underway immediately." He rose, scanned her face, and frowned.

Then he saw the open newspaper.

She leaned forward to close it, but he stayed her hand, bent over and scanned the headline.

"You read this?" he asked her.

She said nothing, tilted her chin proudly, refused to look at him.

"Is this why you're suddenly not feeling well? It was arranged months ago," he said quietly.

"It's none of my business. I'm well aware I don't belong in your world, Prince Kiernan. That this has been a nice little treat for a peasant you've taken a liking to."

"It is not that I don't think you belong in my world," he said with a touch of heat. "That's not it at all! And I don't think of you as a peasant."

"Of course not," she said woodenly.

"Meredith, you don't understand the repercussions of being seen publicly with me."

"I might use the wrong fork?"

"Stop it."

"I thought this was such a nice outfit. You probably noticed it was off the rack."

"I noticed no such thing. It's a gorgeous outfit. You are gorgeous."

"Apparently. Gorgeous enough to see you privately."

"Meredith, you need to understand the moment you are seen with me, publicly, your life will never be the same again. Taking you to that ball would be like throwing you into a pail of piranhas. The press would have started to rip you apart. You've told me some shattering secrets about yourself. Do you want those secrets on all the front pages providing titillation for the mob? I won't do that to you."

"Of course," she said, "You're protecting me. That's what you do."

"I am trying to protect you," he said. "A little appreciation might be in order."

"Appreciation? You deluded fool."

He looked stunned by that and that made her happy in an angry sort of way so she kept going.

"You've chosen women in the past that build you up with their weakness, who need their big strong prince to protect them, but I'm not like that."

"I've chosen weak women?" he sputtered.

"It's obvious."

"I'm sorry I ever told you a personal thing about myself."

She was sorry he had, too. Because it had made her hope for things she couldn't have. She couldn't stop herself now if she wanted to.

"I'm a girl from Wentworth. Do you think there's anything in your world that could frighten me? I've walked in places where I've had a knife hidden under my coat. I've been hungry, for God's sake. And so exhausted from working and raising a baby I couldn't even hold my feet under me. I've buried my child. And my mother. Do you think anything in your cozy, pampered little world could frighten me? The press? I could handle the press with both my hands tied behind my back.

"Don't you dare pretend that's about protecting me. Your Royal Highness, you are protecting yourself. You don't want anyone to know about tonight. Or about me. I'm the sullied girl from the wrong side of the tracks. You're right. They would dig up my whole sordid past. What an embarrassment to you! To be romantically linked to the likes of me!"

"I told you everything there is to know about me," he said quietly, "and you would reach that conclusion?"

"That's right!" she snapped, her anger making her feel so much more powerful than her despair. "It's all about you!"

She banished everything in her that was weak. There would be plenty of time for crying when she got home.

After the trust they had shared, the intimacy of their dinner, the growing friendship of the last few days, this was *exactly* what was needed.

Distance.

Anger.

Distrust.

And finally, when she got home, then there would be time for the despair that could only be brought on from believing, even briefly, in unrealistic dreams.

But when she got home, she realized she had done it on purpose, created that terrible scene on purpose, driven a wedge between them on purpose.

Because she had done the dumbest thing of her whole life, even dumber than believing Michael Morgan was a prince.

She had come to love a real prince. And she did not think she could survive another love going wrong.

And the truth? How could it possibly go right?

"What is wrong with you?" Adrian asked Kiernan the next day.

"What do you mean by that?"

"Kiernan! You're not yourself. You're impatient. You're snapping at people. You're canceling engagements."

"What engagement?"

"You were supposed to bring Brianna Morrison to the ball. The worst thing you could have done is cancelled that. One more tearstained face attached to your name. She's been getting ready for months. Prince Heartbreaker rides again."

"Is that a direct quote from the tabs?"

"No. That is so much kinder than the tabs. They're having a heyday at your expense. This morning they showed Brianna Morrison throwing her ball dress off a bridge into Chatam River."

"Make sure she's charged with littering a public waterway."

"Kiernan! That's cold! You are just about the most hated man on the planet right now."

Yes. And by the only one that mattered, too.

Adrian was watching him closely. "And there's that look again."

"What look?"

"I don't know. Moody. *Desperate.*"

"Adrian, just leave it alone," he said wearily.

"If something is wrong, I want to help."

"You can't. Not unless you can learn to dance in—" he glanced at his watch "—about four hours."

Adrian's eyes widened. "I should have known."

"What?" Kiernan said. What had he inadvertently revealed?

"Dragon-heart. She's at the bottom of this."

Kiernan stepped in very close to his young cousin. "Don't you ever call her that again within my hearing. Do you understand me?"

"She did something to make you so mad," Adrian said. "I know it."

"No, she didn't," Kiernan said. "I did. I did something that made me so mad. I gave my trust to the wrong person."

Adrian was watching him, his brow drawn down in puzzlement. "I'll be damned," he said. "You aren't angry. You're in love."

Kiernan thought it would be an excellent time for a vehement denial. But when he opened his mouth, the denial didn't come out.

"With Dra— Meredith?"

"It doesn't matter. It's going nowhere. After I revealed my deepest truths to her do you know what she did? She called me a deluded fool!"

Adrian actually smiled.

"It's not funny."

"No, it's a cause for celebration. Finally, someone who will take you to task when you need it."

"Don't side with her. You don't even like her."

"Actually, I always did like her. Immensely. She wouldn't settle for anything less than my best. She was strong and sure of herself and intimidating as hell, but I liked her a great deal."

"Do you know what she said to me? She said I deliberately chose weak women. What do you think about that?"

"That she's unusually astute. Finally, someone who will tell you exactly what they think instead of filtering it through what they think you want to hear."

"You never told me you thought my women were weak," Kiernan said accusingly.

"Because they were heart-stoppingly beautiful. I thought that probably made up for it. I always knew you never dated anyone who would require you to be more than you were before. I thought it was your choice. That you had decided love would take a minor role in your life. Behind your duties."

"I think I had thought that. Until I fell in love. It doesn't accept minor roles."

"So, you do love her!" Adrian crowed.

"It doesn't matter. I had her to the yacht for dinner last night, and she opened the paper and saw I was escorting Brianna to the ball. She left in a temper."

"Uh, real world to Kiernan: any woman who is having dinner with a man will be upset to find he has plans with another woman for later in the week."

"I told her it had been planned for months."

"Instead of *I'll cancel immediately*?" Adrian shook his head and tut-tutted.

"I told her it was for her own good. She has some things in her past I don't want the press to get their hands on. I was protecting her!"

"I bet she loved that one."

"It's true!"

"She isn't the kind who would take kindly to you micromanaging her world."

"She's not. She doesn't trust me. I showed her everything I was, and she rejected it. She believed the worst of me, just like everyone else is so quick to do."

"Kiernan, you are making excuses."

"Why would I do that?"

"You are terrified of what that woman would require of you."

"I'm not."

"Don't you get it? This is your chance. You might only get one. Take it. Be happy. Do something for yourself for once. Go sweep old Dragon-heart right off her feet."

"Don't call her that."

"I can't believe I missed it!" His cousin became uncharacteristically serious. "She's worthy of you, Kiernan. She's strong. And spunky. She's probably the best thing that ever happened to you. Don't let it slip away."

And suddenly Kiernan thought of how awful she had looked when she had left the yacht. She was afraid. He'd taken that personally, as if it was about him. But of course she was afraid! She had lost everything to love once before. She was terrified to believe in him, to trust.

And Adrian was right. He was *not* doing the right thing. Sulking because she didn't trust him, not seeing what lay beneath that lack of trust. Why should she trust the world? Or him? Had the world brought her good things? No, it had taken them. Had love brought her good things? No, it had shattered her.

Instead of seeing that, he had insisted on making it about him.

He was going to have to be a better man than that to be worthy of her. He was going to have to go get her from that lonely world she had fled to in her fear and distrust.

Kiernan of Chatam was going to have to learn what it really meant to be a woman's prince.

Something sighed within him.

He was ready for the challenge. He was about to go rescue the maiden from the dragon of fear and loneliness she had allowed to take up residence in her heart.

"I don't know what to do," he admitted.

Adrian smiled. "Sure, you do. You have to woo the girl. Just the same as any old Joe out there on the street. She isn't going to just fall at your feet because you're a prince, you know. For God's sake, she runs an organization called No Princes. Playing hard to get is going to be a point of pride with her.

"And don't look so solemn. For once in your life, Kiernan, have some fun."

The show must go on, Meredith thought as she found herself, in a white smock in a crowded dressing room, waiting, her heart nearly pounding out of her chest. She had never been this nervous about a performance.

"Miss Whit," one of the girls said excitedly. "He's here. He's come. Ohmygod, he's the most glorious man I ever laid me eyes on."

"*My* eyes," Meredith corrected woodenly.

"The music's starting," Erin whispered. "Oh, I can't believe this is happening to me. My production is becoming a reality. I just looked out the curtain. Miss Whit, it's standing room only out there."

For them. She had to pull this off for them, her girls, all that she had left in her world.

"I'm on," Erin said. "I'm so scared."

Meredith shook herself out of her own fear, and went and gave her protégée a hard hug.

"Dazzle them!" she said firmly.

And then she stood in the wings. And despite her gloom, her heart began to swell with pride as she saw Erin's vision come to life. The girls in the opening number carried the buckets of cleaning ladies, or wore waitresses' uniforms. Some of them carried school bags. All had on too much makeup. They were hanging around a street lamp, targets for trouble.

And here came trouble. Boys in carpenter's aprons, and baker's hats, leather jackets with cigarettes dangling from their lips.

The girls and the guys were dancing together, shy, flirtatious, bold, by turns.

And then Erin, who had been given the starring role, was front and center in her white smock that said Molly over the pocket, and she was staring worshipfully at a boy in a white jacket that said Andy on the pocket.

The lights went off them, and the empty spot on the stage filled with mist.

It was time for the dream sequence.

The three-step bridal waltz began to play, and feeling as if she was made of wood, Meredith came on stage.

Kiernan was coming toward her.

How unfair that while she suffered, he looked better than ever! No doubt to make his costume more realistic, he had a few days growth of unshaven beard.

Meredith went to him, felt her hand settle into his, his hand on her waist.

Her eyes closed against the pain of it.

Last time.

Even as she thought it, she could hear a whisper ripple through the crowd. It became a rumble as the spotlight fell on them, and recognition of Kiernan grew.

"You look awful," he said in her ear.

"I've been working very hard with the girls," she whispered back haughtily. She stumbled slightly. He covered for her.

"Liar. Pining for me."

She tried to hide her shock. "Why would a girl like me pine for you?" she snapped at him. "We both know it's impossible."

He was looking at her way too hard.

"You're afraid," he said in an undertone. "It was never really horses you were afraid of. It was this."

The crowd was going crazy. Not only had they recognized their prince, but he was doing something completely unexpected. Kiernan and Meredith picked up the pace, and he found his feet. She tried not to look at the expression on his face.

"Don't be silly," she told him in an undertone. "I told you nothing about your world frightens me."

"You're afraid of loving me. You have been from the moment we met."

"Arrogant ass," she hissed.

"Stubborn lass," he shot back.

She could feel the fire between them coming out in the way they were dancing. It was unrehearsed, but the audience was reacting to the pure sizzling chemistry.

She couldn't look away from him. His look had become so fierce. So tender. So protective. So filled with longing.

He knew the truth, anyway, why try to hide it? Why not let it come out in this dance?

It occurred to her that even if he couldn't have her, even if she would never be suitable for his world, that he wanted her, and that he wished things were not the way they were.

One last time, she would give herself this gift.

She would be Molly and he would be Andy, just two crazy ordinary kids in love. Everything changed the moment she made that decision. She would say to him with this dance what she intended to never admit to him in person.

She found her feet. She found his rhythm.

And they danced. She let go of all her armor. She let go of all her past hurt. She let go of all her fear. She let go of that little worm of self-doubt that she was not good enough.

Meredith danced as she had never danced, every single secret thing she had ever felt right out there in the open for all the world to see.

At some point, she was not Molly. Not at all. She was completely herself, Meredith Whitmore.

For this one priceless moment, she didn't care who saw her truth. Though thousands watched, they were alone, dancing for each other.

And then he let her go, and the crowd became frenzied as he moved into his solo piece.

He tore off the white smock.

And suddenly she saw his truth. It was not dancing as Andy that allowed him to dance like this.

It was dancing as Kiernan.

Everything he truly was came out now: sensual, strong, commanding, tender. Everything.

By the time he came across the floor to her that one last time, the tears were streaming down her face for the gift he had given her.

He had given her his everything.

He had put every single thing he was into that dance. Not for the audience who was going wild with delight.

Not for the girls who cheered and screamed from the wings.

For her. He stared down at her.

It was not in any way a scripted part of the performance. He took her lips with exquisite tenderness.

She tasted him, savored, tried to memorize it.

With the cheering in the building so loud it sounded as if the rafters would collapse on them, she pulled away from the heaven of his lips, touched his cheek. Though the whole world watched it felt, still, as if they were alone.

Goodbye.

"Thank you," she whispered through her tears. "Thank you, Kiernan." And then she turned and fled.

CHAPTER NINE

IT WAS THE DAY AFTER *An Evening to Remember*. Meredith's phone had been ringing off the hook, but she wouldn't answer.

Still, people left messages. They wanted lessons from her dance school. They wanted to donate money to No Princes.

Erin Fisher's excited voice told her she had been offered a full scholarship to Chatam University.

The press wanted to know what it felt like to dance with a prince. They wanted to know if she had been the one to teach the prince with two left feet to dance like that. They especially wanted to know if there was *something* going on, or if it had all been a performance.

After several hours of the phone ringing she went and pulled the connection out of the wall.

She didn't want to talk to anybody.

Maybe not for a long, long time.

Just as she had suspected, the video had been posted online within seconds of the performance finishing.

The website had collapsed this morning, for the first time in its history, from too many hits on that video.

"Most of those hits from me," Meredith admitted ruefully. She had watched their dance together at least a dozen times before the site had crashed.

Seeing something in it, basking in it.

Was love too strong a word?

Probably. She used it anyway.

There was a knock on her door. She hoped the press had not discovered where she lived. She tried to ignore it, but it came again, more insistent than the last time. She pulled a pillow over her head. More rapping.

"Meredith, open the damn door before I kick it down!"

She pulled the pillow away from her face, sat up, stunned, hugging it to her.

"I mean it. I'm counting to three."

She went and peered out her security peephole.

"One."

Prince Kiernan of Chatam was out on her stoop, in an Andy jacket and dark glasses.

"Two."

She threw open the door, and then didn't know what to do. Throw herself at him? Play it cool? Weep? Laugh?

"Lo, Molly," he said casually.

Don't melt.

"Just wondered if you might like to come down to the pub with me. We'll have a pint and throw some darts."

"Once you lose the sunglasses everyone will know who you are." Plus, they'd probably all seen the Andy getup on the video. He'd be swamped.

"Let's live dangerously. I'll leave the glasses on. You can tell people I have a black eye from fighting for your honor."

"Kiernan—"

"Andy," he told her sternly.

"Okay, Andy." She folded her arms protectively over her chest. "Why are you doing this?"

He hesitated a heartbeat, lifted the glasses so she could look into his eyes. "I want us to get to know each other. Like this. As Andy and Molly. Without the pressure of the press following us and speculating. I want us to build a solid foundation before I introduce you to the world. I want you to know I have your back when they start coming at you."

"You're going to introduce me to the world?" she whispered. "You're going to have my back?"

"Meredith, I miss you. Not seeing you was like living in a world without the sun. It was dark and it was cold."

She could feel the utter truth of it to her toenails.

"I miss the freedom I felt with you," he went on quietly. "I miss the sense of being myself in a way I never was before. I miss being spontaneous. I miss having fun. Will you come out and play with me? Please?"

She nodded, not trusting herself to speak.

"Come on, then. Your chariot awaits."

She could not resist him. She had never been able to resist him.

"I'm in my pajamas."

"So you are. Ghastly things, too. I picture you in white lace."

She gulped from the heat in his eyes.

"Go change," he said, and there was no missing the fact she had just been issued a royal order.

"Royal pain in the butt," she muttered, but she stood back from the door, and let him in.

Surely once he saw how ordinary people lived—tiny quarters, hotplate, faded furniture—he would realize he was in the wrong world and turn tail and run.

But he didn't. True to Andy he went and flung himself on her worse-for-wear couch, picked up a book she hadn't looked at for weeks and raised wicked eyebrows at her.

"Did you dream of me when you read this?" he asked.

"No!" She went and slammed her bedroom door, made herself put on the outfit—faded jeans, a prim blouse—that was the least like the one she had worn the other night on the yacht. It was the casual outfit of an ordinary girl.

But when she reemerged from the bedroom, the look in his eyes made her feel like a queen.

Feeling as if she was in a dream, Meredith followed him down the steep stairs that led from her apartment to the alley. Leaning at the bottom of the stairs was the most horrible-looking bike she had ever seen.

Kiernan straddled it, lowered his sunglasses, patted the handlebars. "Get on."

"Are you kidding? You'll kill us both."

"Ah, but what a way to go."

"There is that," she said, with a sigh. She settled herself on the handlebars.

His bike riding was terrible. She suspected he could barely ride a bike solo, let alone riding double. He got off to a shaky start, nearly crashing three times before they got out of her laneway.

Once he got into the main street he was even more hazardous, weaving in and out of traffic, wobbling in front of a double-decker bus.

"Give 'em the bird, love," he called when someone honked angrily when he wobbled out in front of them.

She giggled and did just that.

At the pub, true to his word, he left the glasses on.

She thought people might recognize him, but perhaps because of the plain lucridness of the whole thought that a prince would be in the neighborhood pub, no one did.

They ordered fish and chips, had a pint of tap beer, they threw darts. Then they got back on the bike and he took the long way home, pedaling along the river. She wasn't sure if her heart was beating that fast because of all the times he nearly dumped them both in the inky water of the Chatam Channel, or because she was so exhilarated by this experience.

"Where is this going?" Meredith asked sternly when he dropped her at her doorstep with a light kiss on the nose.

"My whole life," he said solemnly, "I've known where everything was going. I've always had an agenda, a protocol, a map, a plan. The very first time I saw you dance, I knew you had something I needed.

"I didn't know what it was, but whatever it was, it was what made me say yes to learning the number for *An Evening to Remember*."

"And do you know what it was now?" she asked, curious, intrigued despite herself.

"Passion," he said. "My whole life has been about order and control. And when I saw you dance that day I caught a glimpse of what I had missed. The thing is, I felt bereft that I had missed it.

"Meredith, you take me to places I have never been before. And I don't mean a hot spring or a pub. Places inside myself that I have never been before. Now that I've been there, I can't live with the thought of not going there anymore."

He kissed her on the nose again. "I'll see you tomorrow."

"Look," she said, trying to gain some control back, "I just can't put my whole life on hold because you want me to take you places!"

He laughed, and leaned close to her. "But I've been saving my money so I can get us a Triple Widgie Hot Fudge Sundae from Lawrence's. To share."

"That's incredibly hard to resist," she admitted.

"The sundae or me?"

"The sharing."

"Ah." He looked at her long and hard. "Embrace it, Molly. Just embrace it."

"All right." She surrendered.

And that's what she did. She put her whole life on hold.

But not really.

She just embraced a different life.

Carefree and full of adventure.

Over the next few weeks, as Andy and Molly, they biked every inch of that island. They discovered hidden beaches. They ate ice cream at roadside stands. They laughed until their sides hurt. They went to movies. They roller-skated.

And just when she was getting used to it all, that familiar knock came on the door, but it was not Andy who stood there. Not this time.

This time it was Prince Kiernan of Chatam, in dark suit trousers and a jacket, a crisp white shirt, a dark silk tie.

He bowed low over her hand, kissed it.

"Aren't we going bike riding?" she asked.

"I love your world, Meredith, but now it's time for you to come into mine."

"I—I— I'll have to change," she said, casting a

disparaging look down at her faded T-shirt, her pedal pushers, and old sneakers.

"Only your clothes," he said quietly. "Nothing else. Don't change one other thing about you. Promise me."

"I promise," she said, and scooted back into her bedroom to find something suitable to wear for an outing with a prince. A few minutes later, in a pencil skirt of white linen and a blue silk top, she joined him.

"Are you ready for this?" he asked, holding out his hand to her.

"Ready for what, exactly?" She took his hand, gazed up at him, still unable to quite grasp that a prince was wooing an ordinary girl like her.

"My mother wants to meet you."

"She does?" Meredith gulped. "Why?"

"Because I told her I've met the woman I intend to spend the rest of my life with."

Meredith took a step back from him, not sure she had heard him correctly, her heart beating an ecstatic tattoo within her chest. "But you haven't told me that yet!"

He cocked his head at her, and grinned. "I guess I just did."

She flew into his arms, and it felt like going home. It felt exactly the way she had wanted to feel her whole life.

"You know how I feel right now?" she whispered into his chest. "I feel safe. And protected. I feel cared about. I feel cherished."

"You make me feel those things, too," he whispered back.

"And I feel absolutely terrified. Your mother? That makes everything seem rather official."

"You see, that's the thing. After you've met my

mother, it's going to be official. You're going to be my girl. And then my fiancée. And then my wife."

"Huh. Is that your excuse for a proposal?"

He laughed. "No. Just forewarning you of what's to come." And then he frowned. "If you can handle the pressure. You won't believe the pressure, Meredith. I'm afraid your life will never be the same. Be sure you know what you want before you walk out that door with me."

But she had been sure a long time ago. She knew exactly what she wanted. She placed her hand back in his, and felt her whole world was complete.

Someone with a camera had already discovered the limousine parked at her curb, because this time the royal emblem shone gold on the door. The camera was raised and their picture was taken getting into the car together.

He sighed.

But she squeezed his hand and laughed.

"I may be terrified of your mother," she said, as he settled in the deep leather of the seat beside her, "but I'm not afraid of anything else about being with you. Nothing." She laid her head on his shoulder and soaked in the strength and solidness of him, soaked in how very right it felt to be at his side.

For a moment there was the most comfortable of silences between them.

"Did you hear that?" he asked, as the car pulled away.

"I'm sorry, did I hear what?"

He looked out the window, twisted over his shoulder to look behind them, settled back with a puzzled look on his face.

"Meredith, I could have sworn I heard a baby laugh."

She smiled, and the feeling of everything in the world being absolutely right deepened around her.

"No," she said softly, "I didn't hear it. But I felt it. I felt it all the way to my soul."

Kiernan raised his hand to knock on the door of his mother's quarters. He'd been annoyed that upon delivering Meredith his mother had dismissed him with an instruction to come back in an hour. She had drawn Meredith in and closed the door firmly behind them.

He knew his mother! The inquisition had probably started. Especially after Tiffany, whom his mother had not liked from the beginning, Queen Aleda would feel justified in asking aggressive questions, making quick judgments. Meredith was probably backed into a corner, quivering and in tears.

But as he stood at the door, he was astounded to hear laughter coming through the closed door. He knocked and opened it.

Both women looked up. Meredith was seated, his mother looking over her shoulder. He saw he had underestimated Meredith again. He was going to have to stop doing that.

He noticed his mother had one hand resting companionably on Meredith's shoulder. His mother did not touch people!

Both women were focused on something on the table, and he recognized what it was.

"Photo albums?" he sputtered. "You've just met!"

"Never too soon to look at pictures of you as a baby," Meredith said. "That one of you in the tub? Adorable."

"The tub picture?" He glared at his mother, outraged.

"What could I do?" Queen Aleda said with a smile. "Meredith asked me what my greatest treasure was."

And then the two women exchanged a glance, and he was silent, in awe of the fact their mutual love of him could make such a strong and instant bond between these two amazing women.

In the days and weeks that followed, Kiernan's amazement at Meredith grew and grew and grew.

The day after their first official public outing, when he had taken her to watch a royal horse run in the Chatam Cup, speculation began to run high. Some version of the picture of Meredith leaning over the royal box to kiss the nose of the horse had made every front page of every major paper around the world.

His press corps was instantly swamped with enquiries. When had he begun dating his dance instructor? Who was she? And especially, what was her background?

"This is the beginning," he'd told her. "How do you want to handle it?" Meredith called her own press conference.

Yes, she was dating the prince. Yes, they had met while she taught him the dance number for *An Evening to Remember*. No, she was not worried about his history, because she had a history of her own.

And in a strong, steady voice, without any apology Meredith had laid herself bare. All of it. Wentworth. The too-young pregnancy. Her abandonment by the father of her child. The baby. The lost dance dreams. The grinding poverty. The tragedy that took her mother and her child. The insurance money that had allowed her to start No Princes.

She had left the press without a single thing to dig

for. And instead of devouring her, the press had *adored* her honesty, and the fact she was just one of the people. Unlike so many celebrities that the press waited breathlessly to turn on, their love affair with Meredith was like his own.

And like that of all the people of Chatam.

The more they knew her, the more they loved her.

And she loved them right back. She became the star of every event they attended, the new and quickly beloved celebrity. From film festivals at Cannes to her first ski trip to catch the last spring snow in Colorado, she bewitched everyone who met her.

She was astonishingly at home, no matter where he took her.

But the part he loved the most was that none of it went to her head. She was still the girl he had first met. Maybe even more that girl as she came into herself, as love gave her a confidence and a glow that never turned off.

Meredith could be on the red carpet at a film premiere one day, and the next day she was just as at home on her bicycle, visiting a Chatam farmer's market. She delighted in surprising brides and grooms in Chatam on their wedding days by dropping by the reception to offer her good wishes.

When he begged her to allow him to offer her security, she just laughed at him. "I've already been through the worst life can give out, Kiernan. I'm not afraid."

And she really wasn't. Meredith was born to love. It seemed her capacity to give and receive love was endless.

And since he was the major benefactor of all that love, who was he to stop her?

Besides, he knew something he had not known a few

months ago, and probably would not have believed if someone had tried to tell him.

There were angels. And Meredith had two who protected and guided her. What other explanation for the series of coincidences that had brought them together? How had she landed right on his doorstep? How had Adrian come to be injured so that the right prince could meet her? How was it that Kiernan had gone against his own nature, and agreed to learn to dance? How was it he had seen something in her from the very beginning, that he could not resist?

From that first moment, watching her dance, Kiernan had known she held a secret that could change his life. Known it with his heart and not his head.

And only angels could have made him listen to his heart instead of his head.

But angels aside, there was no ignoring the very human side of what was happening to them.

He *wanted* her. He wanted her in every way that a man could want a woman. Their kisses were becoming more fevered. The times when they were alone were becoming a kind of torture of *wanting*.

The thing was, he would never take her without honor.

Never. What that other man had done to her was unconscionable. He would never be like him, never, ever remind Meredith of him. He would not use her obvious passion for him, or her willingness to have his way with her. He always backed away at the last possible moment.

There were honorable steps a man had to take to be with his woman. He had to earn his way there. It did not matter that it was his intention to marry her, and it was, even though he knew they had only known each other a short while, only months.

But he knew his own heart, too.

And he knew it was time.

CHAPTER TEN

MEREDITH WOKE UP to a sound at her window. Something was hitting against it. She groaned and pulled the pillow over her head.

Kiernan was probably right. She was going to have to move to a building with security. That was probably some fledging reporter out there hoping to get the shot that would make his career.

Despite her attempts to ignore it, the sound came again, louder. A scattering of pebbles across her pane.

And then louder yet!

She got up, annoyed. They were going to break the window! But when she shoved it up, and leaned out, ready to give someone a piece of her mind, it was Kiernan who stood below her.

"What are you doing?" Her annoyance now was completely faked. Sometimes she could still not believe this man, a prince outside, and a prince inside, too, was looking at her like that. With such open adoration in his eyes.

Of course the feeling was completely mutual!

"I have a surprise for you."

"What time is it?" she asked with completely faked grumpiness.

"Going on midnight."

"Kiernan, go home and go to bed."

"Quit pretending you can resist me. Get dressed and come down here."

She stuck out her tongue at him and slammed the window shut, but she quickly changed out of her pajamas, yanking on an old dance sweatsuit.

"I see you are working hard at impressing me," he said, kissing her on the nose as she reached the bottom of her stairs.

"As you are me," she teased back. "Waking me at midnight. I have work tomorrow. We don't all have lives of leisure."

This was said completely jokingly. She seemed, more than anyone else, to respect how hard he worked, and how many different directions he was pulled in a day. He was still savoring the newness of having someone at his side who was willing to back him up, to do whatever she needed to do to ease his burdens, to make his life simpler.

He held open the door of an unmarked car for her. Tonight as no other he did not want the press trailing them.

She snuggled under his arm. "What are you up to?"

But he wouldn't tell her.

They sailed through the roadblock he'd had put up to close the popular road, just for this one night. Meredith peeked out the car window with curiosity, and then recognition. "Are we going where I think we are going?"

The car stopped at the pull-out for Chatam Hot Springs. He held out his hand to her and drew her out of the car, led her up the path, lit by torches tonight, that led the way to the springs.

When they got there, he savored the look on her face. No detail had been overlooked.

There were torches flaming around the pool, but the bubbling waters of the springs were mostly illuminated by thousands upon thousands of candles that glowed from every rock and every surface.

"I didn't bring a suit," she whispered, looking around with that look he had come to live for.

A kind of *pinch me I must be dreaming* look.

"There's a change tent for you over there," he said. "You'll find a number of bathing suits to choose from."

She emerged from the tent a few minutes later, and he, already changed, was waiting on the edge of a rock with his feet dangling in the water. He smiled at her choice. Though there was staff here, they were invisible at the moment.

"The black one," he said with a shake of his head. "I was hoping for something skimpier. The red one, with the polka dots."

"How did you know about the red one with the polka dots?" she demanded.

"Because I picked each one myself, Meredith."

"That must have been very embarrassing for you," she said. "Careful, the press will dub you the pervert prince."

He leered at her playfully. "And let's hope it's deserved."

This is how it was with them. Endlessly playful. Teasing. Comfortable. Fun. And yet the respect between them also grew.

As did the heat.

As she crossed the slippery rock to him he could easily see that the black tank-style suit was so much more sexy than the polka dot bikini! Instead of sitting demurely beside him, Meredith pretended to touch his shoulders lovingly and then shoved with all her might.

And then turned and ran.

He caught up with her at the mud pool.

And they played in the mud, and swam and played some more until they were both exhausted with joy.

And then he sent her back to the change tent.

Where he knew all the rejected bathing suits had been whisked away, and in their place were designer gowns like the ones she had refused to let him buy for her for all the public outings they had attended.

While she changed, a table was set up for them and waiters appeared, along with a chef fussing about the primitive conditions he'd had to prepare his food in.

When she'd emerged from the change tent this time, Kiernan's mouth fell open. Meredith had stunned him with her beauty even in the off-the-rack dresses she insisted on wearing.

But now she had chosen the most racy of the gowns that he had picked out for her. It was red and low-cut.

She had even put on some of the jewelry he had put out for her, and a diamond necklace blazed at her neck and diamond droplets fell from her ears.

"I am looking at a princess," he said, bowing low over her hand and kissing it.

"I've told you *no* to this extravagance, Kiernan."

And yet, despite her protest, he could not help but notice that she was glowing with a certain feminine delight. She knew she looked incredible.

He led her to the table, laid out with fine linen and the best of china, and the waiters served a sumptuous feast.

She knew most of the palace staff by name, and addressed each of them.

When they had finished eating, she smiled at him. "Okay. I give it to you, you can't ever top this."

"But I will."

"You can't."

He called one of the waiters and a cooler was brought to their table. Inside it was one Triple Widgie Hot Fudge Sundae and two spoons.

In that perfect environment, their worlds combined effortlessly.

"I love it all," she said. "But you shouldn't have bought all the dresses, Kiernan. I can't accept them, and you probably can't return them."

"I'm afraid as my wife you'll be expected to keep a certain standard," he said. "And as your husband I will be proud to provide it for you."

He dropped down on his knee in front of her, slid a box from his pocket and opened it.

Inside was a diamond of elegant simplicity. He knew her. He knew she would never want the flashy ring, the large karat, the showpiece.

And he knew her answer.

He saw it in her eyes, in the tears that streamed down her face, in the smile that would not stop, despite the tears.

"Will you marry me?" he asked. "Will you make my world complete, Meredith?"

"Yes," she whispered. "Of course yes, a thousand times yes."

He rose to his feet, gathered her in his arms and held her. And his world finally was complete.

* * *

Meredith stared at herself in the mirror. She was in her slip at the dressing table, the bridal gown hung behind her. For a moment her eyes caught on it, and she felt a delicious quiver of disbelief.

Could this really be her life? A wedding gown out of a dream, yards and yards of ivory silk and seed pearls. Could this really be her life? Crowds had begun to form early this morning, lining the streets of Chatam from downtown all the way to Chatam Cathedral.

"You look so beautiful," Erin murmured.

Meredith gazed at the girl behind her.

Despite the pressure to have a huge wedding party, Meredith had chosen to have one attendant, Erin Fisher.

"So do you," she said.

"It's your day," Erin said, nonetheless pleased, "just focus on yourself for once, Miss Whit."

"All right."

"Now don't you look beautiful?"

She *did* look beautiful. More beautiful than she could have ever imagined she was going to look.

And it wasn't just the wedding gown, the hair, the makeup.

No, a radiance was pouring out of her, too big to contain within her skin.

"Are you crying?" Erin asked in horror. "Don't! We just did the makeup."

Meredith had been offered a room at the palace to get ready, and ladies in waiting to help her. She had said no to both. She wanted to be in this little apartment over her studio one last time. She wanted *her* girls to be around her.

Erin handed her a tissue and scolded. "I hope those are happy tears."

Meredith thought about it for a moment. "Not really, no."

"You are about to marry the most glorious man who ever walked and those aren't happy tears? Honestly, Miss Whit, I'm going to pinch you!"

"Don't pinch me. I might wake up."

"Tell me why they aren't happy tears."

"I was crying for the girl I used to be, the one who expected so little of life, who had such small dreams for herself. I was thinking of the girl who stood on those city hall steps, in a cheap dress, holding a tiny posy of flowers. I was thinking of the girl who felt so broken, as if it was her fault, some defect in her that caused him not to come, not to want to share the dream with her.

"If she could have seen the future she would have been dancing on those steps instead of crying. The truth? A different life awaited her. One that was beyond the smallness of her dreams."

"My dreams were so small, too," Erin whispered. "What would have become of me, if all that stuff hadn't happened to you? There would have been no Fairytale Ending group for me."

By vote, just last week, the girls, with Meredith's blessing, had changed the name of No Princes.

Because sometimes there just were princes.

And because, even when there weren't, everyone could make their own fairy-tale ending, no matter what.

"I think the universe has dreams for all of us that are bigger than what we would ever dare dream for ourselves," Meredith said quietly. "I even have to trust that losing my baby was part of a bigger plan that I will never totally understand. Maybe it made me stronger, deeper, more able to love. Worthy of that incredible man who loves me."

"Okay, stop!" Erin insisted, dabbing at her eyes. "My makeup is already done, too. Promise me, Miss Whit, that this day will be just about you and him. Not one more unhappy thought."

"All right," Meredith agreed, more to mollify the girl than anything else.

"We can't be walking down the cathedral aisle looking like a pair of raccoons," Erin said.

"Maybe you should have invested in waterproof makeup," a voice behind them said.

Erin whirled. "Prince Kiernan! Get out!" She tried to shield Meredith with her body. "You can't see her right now. It's bad luck."

"Luckily, I'm not superstitious. Could you give us a moment?"

For all the confidence she was developing, Erin wasn't about to make a stand with the prince of her country. She whirled and left the room.

Kiernan came up behind Meredith, rested his hand on her nearly naked shoulder. "This is pretty," he said touching her hair.

See? That was the problem with the promise she had made to Erin. This day could not be exclusively about the two of them.

"I thought it might be a little, er, too much," Meredith said, "but Denise is in hairdressing school. It was her gift to me. How can you refuse something like that?"

"You can't," he agreed. "Besides, it truly is beautiful."

"You really shouldn't be here," she chided him gently,

but the fact that he was here was so much better than a pinch.

This man was her life, her reason, her love, her reality.

"I had to see you," he said softly, "I have a gift for you and suddenly I realized that you needed to have it now, that I wanted you to have it close to your heart today."

All the gifts he had brought her over the course of their courtship could fill a small cottage. After they had become engaged, Meredith had quit asking him to stop. It filled him with such transparent joy to give her, a girl who had spent so much of her life with nothing, lovely things. She had learned to accept each gift graciously, because by doing so, she would receive the *real* gift.

His smile. A moment together in a busy, busy world. His touch on her arm. His eyes looking into her eyes with such wonder.

Now, Kiernan produced a small silver necklace, a cameo.

He pressed it into her hand, and she hesitated. When she touched a concealed button on the bottom of the locket it sprang open, revealing two tiny photos.

One was a picture of Carly, her head thrown back in laughter. And the other was a picture of her mother, looking young and strangely joyous.

"Where did you get this? My mother hated having her picture taken. And she so rarely looked like this, Kiernan. She looks so happy here."

"Ah, princedom has its privileges. I had the whole island scoured until I found just the right photos of both of them. Do you know when that was taken, Meredith? The picture of your mother?"

"No."

He named the date.

The tears spilled. The picture had been taken on the day of Meredith's birth.

"I wanted them to be with us," he said gently, "as close to your heart as I could get them."

"There goes the makeup," she accused him, and there went her idea that the day belonged to him and her, exclusively. What a selfish thought to entertain! This day belonged to Carly and her mother, too.

"You look better without it. The makeup."

"I know, but Rachel is in cosmetology."

"Let me guess. A gift?"

"Yes."

"And by accepting it, you *give* the gift just like the day you agreed to marry me."

The door to the room whispered open again.

"Kiernan! Out!"

There was no question of talking his way out of it this time, because it was his mother who had entered the room.

"Queen Aleda," Meredith said, truly surprised. "What are you doing here?" She had never been embarrassed about her tiny apartment, but she had certainly never expected to entertain a queen here, either.

"There are days when a girl needs her mother," the queen said. "Since your own cannot be here, I was hoping you would do me the grave honor of allowing me to take her place."

"Oh, Aleda," Meredith whispered. Of all the surprises of becoming Kiernan's love, wasn't his mother one of the best of them?

She was seen as reserved and cool, much as her son was. The truth about these two people? They guarded what was theirs, and chose very carefully who to give it to. And when they did give it?

It was with their entire hearts and whole souls.

Kiernan kissed her on her cheek, and bussed his mother, too, before quickly taking his leave. He left whistling *Get Me to the Church on Time*.

Queen Aleda quickly did what she did best—she took charge.

And Meredith realized, warmly, that this day belonged to Queen Aleda, too.

"None of that," Meredith was chastened for the new tears, "It will spoil your makeup."

Queen Aleda gathered the dress, hugged it to her briefly, looked at her soon-to-be daughter-in-law tenderly.

"Come," she said, "I'll help you get into it. The carriage will be here shortly."

Meredith was delivered to the cathedral in a white carriage, drawn by six white horses.

The people of Chatam, who seemed to have embraced her *more* for her past than less, lined the cobblestone streets, and threw rose petals in front of the carriage. The petals floated through the air and were stirred up by the horses' feet. It was as if it was snowing rose petals.

So, this day also belonged to them, to those people who had patiently lined the street for hours, waiting for this moment, a glimpse of the woman they considered to be *their* princess. They called her the people's favorite princess, and every day she tried to live up to what they needed from her. It had been a thought of pure selfishness to think this day was only about her and Kiernan.

The cathedral was packed. A choir sang.

And he waited.

At the end of that long, stone aisle, Kiernan waited

for her, strong, sure, ready. Her prince in a world she had once believed did not have princes, her very own fairy-tale ending.

Meredith moved toward him with the certainty, with the inevitability of a wave moving to shore.

And realized this day, and her whole life to follow, didn't really belong to her. And not to him, either.

It belonged to the force that had served them so well, the force that they would now use the days of their life serving.

It belonged to Love.

EPILOGUE

HE WENT HERE SOMETIMES, by himself, usually when he had a special occasion to celebrate. A birthday. An anniversary. They were part of it, and he could not leave them out.

It was not the nicest of graveyards, just row after row of simple crosses, no shrubs, or green spaces, no elaborate headstones, few flower arrangements.

The world would have been shocked, probably, to see Prince Kiernan of Chatam in this place, a grim, gray yard in the middle of Wentworth.

But he was always extra careful that he was not followed here, that no one hid with their cameras to capture this most private image of him.

It had become a most special place to him. He always brought flowers, two bouquets. He paused now in front of the heartbreakingly small grave, next to a larger one, brushed some dust from the plain stones set in the ground and read out loud.

"Carly, beloved." He set the tiny pink roses on her stone.

"Millicent Whitmore, beloved." He set the white roses there.

He did not know how the world worked. He felt a

tingle as he read that word. *Beloved*. How had a child long dead, whom he had never even met, become so beloved to him?

How could he feel as if he *knew* Millicent Whitmore, Millie as he called her affectionately, when he had never met her either?

Kiernan understood now, as he had not before marrying Meredith, that there was a larger picture, and despite his power and prestige he was just a tiny part of that.

He understood, as he had not before marrying Meredith, that sometimes great things could transpire out of great tragedies.

The death of a child, and her grandmother, had set a whole series of events in motion that not one single person could have ever foreseen or predicted.

Still, this is what love did: if he could give Meredith back her baby, even if it meant he would never meet her, and never have the life he had now, he would do it in a breath, in a heartbeat.

"I want you to know, Carly," he said softly, "that the new baby in no way replaces you. You are a sacred member of our family. Always and forever."

He felt her then, as he sometimes did, a breath on his cheek, a softness on his shoulder, a faint smell in the air that was so good.

"I brought you a picture of her. We've named her Amalee." He laid the picture, framed in silver, of his new baby and her mother between the two graves.

The picture he laid down was a private portrait, one that had never been released to the press. The baby had a wrinkled face, piercing gray eyes, and a tangle of the most shockingly red hair.

And Meredith in that picture looked like what she was: a mother who had already lost a child and would guard this one with a fierceness that was both awe-inspiring and a little frightening.

She looked like what she was: a woman certain in her own power, a woman who knew she was loved above all things.

Meredith was a woman who knew that if her husband ever had the choice to make: Chatam, his kingdom, or her, he would not even hesitate.

She was his kingdom.

He stepped back then, and sighed, asked silently for a blessing on the christening that would happen today, his baby's first public appearance. Already the people of Chatam lined the streets, waiting to welcome this new love to their lives.

He was left feeling humbled by the goodness of it all.

Each day his and Meredith's relationship became closer, deeper, stronger. The new baby, Amalee, felt as if she was part of a tapestry that wove his heart ever more intricately into its pattern.

Kiernan now knew, absolutely, what he had been so drawn to that first day that he had seen Meredith dance when she thought she was alone.

He had witnessed the dance of life.

And known, at a level that went so deep, that by-passed his mind and went straight to his heart, she was the one who could teach him the steps.

He learned a new one every day.

Love was a dance that you never knew completely,

that taught you new steps, that made you reach deeper and try harder.

Love was the dance that brought you right to heaven's door.

"Thank you," he whispered. And then louder. "Thank you."

LOVING THE PRINCESS

A.C. ARTHUR

To all those daring enough to change.

'I can't go back to yesterday because
I was a different person then.'
– Lewis Carroll, Alice in Wonderland

Chapter 1

His lips were hot. His tongue licking against hers like flames raging and spurting with energy. Samantha De-Saunters moved her head slightly and he went deeper, his strong hands covering the skin left bare by the low cut of her dress. She felt like she was falling. No, he was tilting her back, leaning into the kiss with as much fervor and...dare she say, desire, as she had felt bubbling up from the pit of her belly.

The world around her ceased to exist as he nibbled on her bottom lip, just long enough for her to catch a breath before he delved deep once more. Her lipstick was done. Her hair, the careful topple of curls that had taken her maid Lucie an hour to arrange, was going to be a complete disaster. And she was certain—as was part of her ingenious plan—that everyone was staring at them.

Well, she hadn't actually wanted everyone to see. Just Morty Javis and his persistent and unwelcomed advances.

She still wasn't one hundred percent certain that doing what she had done was the best idea. Especially considering all eyes in Grand Serenity and a few of the neighboring islands were on her and the entire DeSaunters family right now. That's what happened when there were several attempts on the lives of the royal family, one of which was an explosion at the palace six weeks ago. The act of terror had injured sixteen people who had been innocently attending the annual Ambassador's Ball.

He was taking a step back now, his lips still on hers as he brought them both to an upright position. He pulled away slowly. So slowly Sam felt like she might have actually been following him to keep the contact going. When she opened her eyes, she found him already staring at her.

Dark brown eyes, bushy brows and slightly parted lips of medium thickness really had her thinking about going in for a second kiss. She didn't. It was time to get her thoughts in line, if not her traitorous body, which wanted to stay right there in this man's arms enjoying more of his kisses and possibly whatever else he had to offer. But acting on that thought would end up embarrassing them both.

Instead she flattened her palms against the lapels of his suit jacket and prepared to step away. He held her firmly, halting her exit plan.

"Excuse me," she said, her voice low, a tentative smile in place.

He didn't even blink but instead asked, "Is that what you normally say after kissing a complete stranger?"

"I—" she started to reply when Morty tapped him on the shoulder.

"Do you know who you've just accosted? I've taken the liberty of calling the palace guards, Your Highness," Morty spat.

"This is Princess Samantha DeSaunters. Her father will certainly have you jailed for daring to put your hands on her in such a familiar way, especially in this public forum."

Morty continued to talk as he reached for Sam's arm. That's when things shifted.

The man's hand clenched Morty's wrist only seconds before his fingers could touch Sam's bare skin. The glare he gave was serious and intimidating as hell. Even Sam's heart skipped a beat at the intensity transmitted through a simple gaze.

"I'll take good care of the princess," he said, his voice deep and raspy.

"Guards!" Morty yelled.

Three guards appeared at that moment and everyone in the room that had not already been staring at them was definitely on alert now.

"Wait a minute…" Sam started to say. "I can explain."

"There is no need, Your Highness," Morty told her.

The man kept his hold on her, even when the guards approached. Sam was definitely concerned now. After the explosion, her father and brothers had been adamant about increasing the palace security. She, thankfully, had been left out of most of those meetings.

It wasn't for lack of concern, her brother Kris had told her. As Grand Serenity's goodwill ambassador, it was imperative that she have a genuine smile and authentic enthusiasm for their island and the royal family at all times. If she were privy to all the safety issues and precautions, they feared she might not be as inviting to tourists or as engaging with the press. Without tourists, Grand Serenity's economy would suffer.

Was she offended by their logic? No, because she

didn't have time to be. This was not only her job, but her life, and Sam took both very seriously.

So what the hell had she been thinking by walking up to this guy—regardless of how ruggedly handsome he was—and kissing him in front of everyone attending the Caribbean Counsel dinner? Her gears were already switching toward damage control.

Her smile came quickly, naturally, as she touched the guy's arm and laughed jovially.

"Don't be silly, Morty. There's no need for the guards, especially since they already know—"

She'd intended to say his name then say something to the effect of him being an old friend, but she hadn't had the chance to learn that detail about him quite yet.

"No, darling, they don't know yet. Remember we decided to keep this our little secret," he interrupted.

The guards stood a couple feet away, each making eye contact with him but not coming any farther.

He didn't smile, but he did pull her closer to him.

Sam kept her smile intact, no matter how many questions were suddenly soaring through her mind.

"I would like to know what is going on," Morty stated, his shoulders squared, dark eyes zooming in on her.

"It's simple," the guy answered for her yet again. "Long-distance relationships suck. Which is why we've decided to stop hiding. Isn't that right, darling?"

"That's…absolutely right…dear," Sam managed to reply.

When he'd pulled her close she'd slipped an arm around his waist, her other hand flat against his chest. She leaned her head in closer as she realized they were definitely the center of attention and, just as she smiled brighter, a camera flashed. Then another and another and, before she knew what was happening, guests were clapping, the guards had disappeared and Morty looked like a cartoon character about to explode with fury.

If someone had told Gary Montgomery a year ago, or hell, even an hour ago, that he'd be in a delicious lip-lock with the princess of Grand Serenity Island, he would have called them a bold-faced liar.

Now, half an hour after the kiss, when his body was still simmering with need and his hand was still firmly on her hip, he told himself he'd done what he'd had to do. There had been no other choice. It was for the job. Yes, definitely for the sake of the job and nothing more.

"Darling Samantha, I am so excited for you," a woman Gary had earlier identified as Jacqueline Mahair, spoke enthusiastically.

Prime Minister Obari Mahair ruled a much smaller island south of the Bahamas. He was a seventy-five-year-old man with a protruding stomach and wiry gray hair. His wife was much more glamorous with her large, expressive eyes; plump, glossy-red-coated lips; and waist-length blond curls. The professional boob and butt job, however, was not so cleverly masked in a black dress that hugged her like a second skin. But her assets weren't nearly as loud a statement as Jacqueline's high-pitched, twenty-three-year-old voice with its distinct Southern twang.

"I, for one, would never have guessed you were hiding such a delectable hunk of hot chocolate from us all," Jacqueline continued. "You have great taste in clothes and you're a sly one."

Jacqueline laughed as she stepped closer to Gary, her gaze fixated on him. It made him uncomfortable, but he knew it didn't show. He was a trained sniper who could sit still for hours on end waiting on a target. Patience and deceit were two of his main traits.

"Thank you, Jacqueline," Samantha said, her voice steady and controlled, as always. "I am so happy that you and Prime Minister Mahair could join us this evening. It is important for the counsel to remain united in sharing our culture with the world."

She was back. It had only taken her a few seconds to adjust. Gary admired that about her. Princess Samantha DeSaunters was not easily ruffled. In the months he'd been on Grand Serenity, Gary had watched Princess Samantha carefully. The fact that she was, hands down, the sexiest woman he'd ever seen had nothing to do with that. It was his job and Gary always did his job.

"Well, you know, I finally talked Obari into letting me open my own restaurant on the island. It's totally Southern. I even stole my daddy's cook to come down here and show those stuffy guys with all their international degrees how to properly prepare a good Southern meal. You look like a man who was brought up on good, old-fashioned soul food, weren't you? What's your name and where are you from? I already know you're American. They just don't make 'em like this anywhere else in the world."

Jacqueline then looked Gary up and down, moving one step closer to him as she ran her long, hot-pink-polished nails down his arm.

"I'm Gary and I'm from Cambridge, Maryland," he replied.

"I'm sure visitors to your island will enjoy the offering of an American-inspired restaurant," Samantha interjected. "If you'll excuse us, Gary and I should speak with my father and his fiancée before they retire for the evening."

Her smile had been brighter than Jacqueline's, much more targeted and laced with the polite and undeniable punch she'd intended.

Seconds later Samantha was guiding them easily away from the prime minister's daring wife. They moved across the room, still encountering smiles and well-meaning nods from guests. There were dignitaries in attendance and members of the Caribbean Counsel, which was an organization of the ruling parties of a majority of the Caribbean islands. It was formed five years ago by the youngest member of the counsel, Samantha DeSaunters.

Gary had a feeling she wanted them to find a spot alone to talk—or to regroup may have been more like it. His announcement had thrown her off, even if for just a moment. However, she would never show it. Samantha was the epitome of refinement and never failed to control any situation she found herself in. He'd discovered that about her in the last few weeks. It was an enviable trait and one he thought she'd been thrust into cultivating.

Through his many conversations with Kris, Gary had learned that Samantha had been only five years old when their mother died. From that moment on she was, for all intents and purposes, the princess of Grand Serenity Island. It was a duty she'd honed and embraced for the next twenty years. Yet, in just four months, she would relinquish the bulk of her responsibilities to Malayka Sampson, the woman who was engaged to marry the reigning prince of Grand Serenity, Rafferty DeSaunters.

"Well, the couple of the hour," Kris said quietly as he fell into step easily on Samantha's other side.

They were careful to keep their conversation low and their facial expressions jovial. Masks, Gary thought. The royal family was very good at wearing masks. He knew a little about that himself, so he didn't judge.

"Had to think of something off the cuff," Gary replied while being mindful of who was around them as they moved to the farthest end of the room.

This official dinner should've been held in one of the ballrooms on the northern end of the palace, but that area was under construction after the damage from the explosion. They were still in a very formal dining area with floor-to-ceiling windows; sparkling, gold chandeliers; and enough clinking crystal to cause Gary slight discomfort. He hated social gatherings. Always had.

"However, I think it will serve a bigger purpose," he finished.

"It was my fault," Samantha added. "I set it in motion because Morty was being an ass."

She didn't sound regretful, just annoyed. Gary wasn't sure if her frustration was directed more to him and what he'd said as a follow-up to their kiss or toward herself for initiating the kiss in the first place.

"There's going to be lots of talk about this in the morning. Dad's understandably distressed. Landry tried to smooth it over, acting as if she knew about this secret affair. I'm not sure he's buying that, though," Kris continued, finishing just seconds before the three of them approached Prince Rafe; his fiancée, Malayka; and Landry.

Landry Norris was Kris's wife, the newest princess of the island. Gary recalled a time when he'd suspected Landry of being involved with the bombing that had taken place at the palace. Landry had been hired as a stylist for Malayka Sampson and the two of them were the only guests that were not in the ballroom at the time of the bombing. Fortunately, Landry had been cleared of all suspicion.

Since then, on the few occasions Gary had visited Kris's private office, he'd had the chance to talk with

Landry. They were both American, which instantly gave them a lot to talk about. The fact that she'd actually worked closely with Malayka was a bonus. Especially since Kris and Roland, the younger prince, both suspected their soon-to-be stepmother was not everything she seemed.

"I expect you two have some explanations for me," Rafe said immediately upon their approach. "However, since your little announcement has created such interest, I suggest we take this up tomorrow. In my office at ten."

Rafe then leaned in to kiss Samantha on her cheek. He gave a curt nod to Kris and reluctantly, Gary thought, to him. Afterward the prince took his fiancée's hand and led them across the room, where they began to extend their good-nights to the guests.

"He's not at all happy with you at the moment, Gary," Landry said when the four of them were alone. "I don't think he was ready to see his only daughter caught up in such a heated embrace, or to hear that she'd been having a secret affair."

"I wasn't terribly comfortable seeing or hearing that myself," Kris said as he moved to stand beside his wife.

Kris would one day take Prince Rafe's place as the head of the royal family and ruler of Grand Serenity. He had been groomed for this role and possessed the same authoritative stance and temperament as his father. The past few weeks had also allowed Gary to make that comparison. When he'd first met Kris they were both just eighteen years old and freshmen in college.

"I needed to get Morty off my trail. I should have handled it better," Samantha said.

She'd stepped away from him the moment they'd come close to Prince Rafe. The older monarch had been giving Gary a pretty lethal stare, and he'd had no intentions of keeping his hands on the man's daughter. No matter how much he missed the feel of her standing near him.

"You never told me Morty was a problem," Kris stated.

Samantha shook her head. Strands of her long hair—which Gary couldn't remember whether or not had been loose before—moved softly over her shoulders with the motion. She wore a black, lacy-type dress that was just modest enough to hide her cleavage but still painfully sexy as it left all sorts of sexual thoughts to the imagination. Her heels were high, long legs alluring, and her eyes…that's where it all came together. Well…and her mouth. That was it for him. Deep brown, expression-filled eyes and a wide and inviting mouth. Two things that, up until tonight, he'd been able to keep at a safe distance.

"It's not an issue," Samantha told her brother. "At least it won't be anymore. I'll take care of Morty and we'll spin this—" She paused and looked over to Gary. "We'll make this work to our advantage. I just need to see everyone off for the night and I'll have a plan for damage control in the morning."

She would, Gary thought, because that was her job. She was the face of Grand Serenity, the personality that drew in tourists as well as business opportunities. Everything she said and did resulted in a gain for the island because she wouldn't have it any other way. So Gary had no doubt at all that she would come up with a way to make what had happened tonight work, not only for her personally but for their family. She had no choice.

As for him and the job he'd been hired to do, he would have to be an intricate part of her plan. Whether she liked it or not.

Chapter 2

She sprayed a spritz perfume, holding the bottle a safe distance from her body but remaining close enough so that she could still feel the cool mist hitting the uncovered areas of her skin. It was a Wonderlust day, Sam thought as she glanced at the name on the perfume bottle before replacing the gold cap on top and setting it down on her dresser. The smoky-floral fragrance made her feel steady and sexy, just what she needed today. She was about to walk away but then turned back to make sure the bottle was in its correct place.

All the bottles on one side of the dressing table had been aligned according to height. She'd thought about organizing them in correlation to when and where she wore each one, but that may have been a little over the top, even for someone like her.

When she was certain the bottles were straight, Sam caught another look at herself in the mirror. She wore a periwinkle shade of blue today, pants and suit jacket with a sheer white blouse beneath it. Last night her dress had been black because she'd wanted to appear aloof but professional. Stylish but serious. Today things were different. She needed confidence and maturity to face her father and a hint of cheerfulness for the persona she would display later today when she spoke at the grand opening of Detali's new design shop.

There would not be a break in her schedule until an hour before dinner. But since Malayka had invited guests to join them, Sam couldn't even look forward to the last meal of the day for comfort. With a sigh she fastened a single button at her waist. She'd told Lucie to leave right after selecting her clothes that morning, so the neat ponytail she wore was her own design. The nude pumps almost blended with the beige carpet in her bedroom, but she dismissed that and continued through the door that led to her sitting room.

Here the floor was tiled, a deep gray color that always made her feel warm inside when she saw it. Her mother had loved dark colors, even though she'd advised her young daughter to always use them sparingly. Sam decided she'd done just that by going with the dark tiled floor and the cameo-white-painted walls. The furniture she'd chosen for the room was what one would call sleek and modern, dark gray leather couches and glass-topped tables. The whimsy came in the bright turquoise pillows resting regally on the couches and the brilliant colorful abstract art on the walls.

With one last look back as she approached the door, Sam confirmed that everything was where it should be and that she had all she needed to head out for the day. Her purse matched her shoes and her cell phone and tablet were in her bag. Gold stud earrings were at her ears and a thick choker at her neck. Her makeup was flawless. She inhaled deeply then turned and placed her hand on the doorknob, pulling the door open before releasing an annoyingly high-pitched yelp.

"Good morning," he said in his deep voice. "Sorry if I startled you."

"Why were you lurking outside my room?" she asked immediately as she resisted the urge to flatten a palm on her chest to make sure her heart was still inside.

"Not lurking. Waiting," he told her pointedly. "Are you ready to go down and meet with your father?"

He was standing directly in front of her, which prevented Sam from simply walking out and closing the door tightly behind her. She didn't want him looking into her rooms and the last time she checked, she was certain she knew her way around this palace.

"Yes, I am. However, I do not need a chaperone," she told him.

She took a step forward, praying he would follow her lead and take one or two or three back. He didn't.

Instead of waiting for him to move, Sam pulled the door closed behind her. She was forced to look up at him at that point and she did so with what she hoped was her most cordial but undeniably annoyed look.

"If you'll excuse me?" she said.

"Certainly," he replied and finally stepped aside.

Again she wanted to breathe a sigh of relief and touch her hand to her still-pounding heart. She didn't, of course. It wouldn't look dignified and would definitely cause him to ask more questions. So she began walking instead.

"Since we were both summoned to this meeting, I thought it made sense that we go together," he said as he walked beside her.

Sam didn't respond immediately. She was taking the

time to get her thoughts together. They moved ahead in silence, before she stopped and cleared her throat.

"Gary," she said, determined to stay in control of her thoughts and her words today. "Let me first apologize for what I did last night. I should have thought more before I acted. As I told my brother, it was just a way of getting Morty off my back. Your admission—false as it was—to him afterward was not required. Still, I'd like to extend my appreciation for your quick thinking in a matter that you should not have been a part of in the first place."

She paused to take a breath and then wondered the same thing she had last night when she'd first come up to her room. "Why are you here? In the palace, I mean. I've seen you around and with Kris and Roland, but I'm not certain we were ever officially introduced."

Now Sam did feel like an idiot. She'd just admitted out loud that she'd willingly thrown herself at a man she did not know. In her defense, it was the recognition from seeing him around the palace that had made her feel it was okay…well, at the very least plausible, that she'd kiss him. Still, she really did not know who he was. That fact only compounded the rough morning she'd already been having.

"No. Not officially. But I know who you are," he replied.

"That's why you kissed me back so readily?" she asked.

He paused and stared at her. Gary was a good-looking guy. He was taller than six feet. She knew this because Kris was six feet, two-and-a-half inches; Roland was six feet, one inch; and her father was six feet even. Gary was taller than all of them. He had a golden brown complexion with very low-cut black hair and penetrating brown eyes. All of those features were enough to cause a second and third look. That's without mention of the bulk of his muscles showing definitively through the suit he'd worn last night, and the dark denim jeans and long-sleeved, gray, button-front shirt he was wearing now.

"I'm certain no man would have resisted kissing you, whether or not they knew you were a princess," he finally replied.

"So you kissed me knowing very well what other people would think?" she continued. The question popped quickly into her mind as she looked at him.

"I'm not a member of a royal family. So I stopped giving a damn what people thought about me a long time ago. Now, I know that you're fanatic about being on time, so I'm going to hurry us along so as not to break your record."

This time he extended his arm. Sam looked down at it to see that he was waiting for her to lace her arm through his and walk with him like…a couple. Or something along those lines. She began walking but avoided touching him. If he wanted to say something, or to insist that she take his arm, or whatever, he didn't. Instead he fell into step quietly beside her and did not speak another word until they were both closed inside her father's office, sitting in the chairs across from Rafe's desk.

That's when he said, "It makes sense that the princess and I continue with the façade of a relationship."

"Harry Copeland and Amari Taylor are sitting in jail. Neither has requested any counsel, nor have they given any indication as to why they conspired to attack the palace. The tribunal is set to convene in two weeks, at which time they will be officially sentenced."

Kris gave the update while Sam listened intently. After the explosion she'd been whisked off to her room and left there with four guards to ensure her safety. For most of the night she'd paced the floors, wondering what was going on. First, there had been the car accident that could have taken her father's life and then the explosion. She was afraid and she was angry. And there was nothing she could do about it, either.

"In the meantime, all palace security has been revamped. We've upgraded our electronic monitoring systems, added more guards and increased our pre-certification efforts for local and off-island events," Kris continued.

Sam shook her head. "You had advised me to keep every appointment and appearance on schedule and to make sure the people of the island knew we were all safe because the culprits had been apprehended. So you lied?"

The words were bitter and she hated having to speak them to her brother, but he had left her with no other choice. While he stood beside their father's grand, dark wood desk, wearing a black suit and a gray silk tie, looking every bit the royal that he was, Kris managed to make Sam feel like an idiot. That wasn't something she planned to take lightly. She'd always thought that she had a close relationship with both her brothers. After all, besides her father, they were the only other people in the world she could truly trust. They were her life. So betrayal cut quick and painfully.

"I told you what you needed to hear in order to do your job," Kris stated. "We were handling the rest."

"'We'? As in you, Dad and Roland. The men of the family. Let me guess, you were all protecting me, keeping the bad stuff from the youngest child, so that she could continue to smile prettily for the cameras. Keeping the tourists coming onto the island no matter what danger they might encounter?"

Because her hands threatened to shake, Sam clasped them tightly together, concentrating on holding them calmly in her lap. She knew he was staring from where he sat in the chair beside her. She could feel the heat on the side of her face from his glare.

Gary had started this conversation off by declaring that they would continue to act as if they were involved. Sam had been ready to disagree with the plan, despite her own part in instigating it, but Kris had taken the opportunity to drop his little bombshell.

"We are here to keep our people safe," her father countered. "It is our priority. As Kris stated, we have instituted a complete overhaul of our security program. In addition, we've had several meetings with Captain Briggins. As a result of the rise in tourism, we had money in the budget to hire additional officers for his battalion, as well. We are keeping everyone's safety in mind."

"You're also keeping secrets from the island's goodwill ambassador," Sam countered. She'd wanted to scream this point to her brother and her father because it seemed as if they weren't getting the severity of their error. Of course, she didn't raise her voice. It wouldn't have been respectful and Sam knew how imperative it was for her to always show respect. She'd watched her mother do it so gracefully that she'd taught herself how to handle difficult situations with the same finesse.

"It was no secret, Sam," Kris added. "We handle business every day that you know nothing about."

"Yet you insist on keeping that royal calendar so that you always know where I am and who I'm with. So it's fine for me to be under your thumb, but I shouldn't worry about the things you feel I don't need to know?"

"We each have a job to do here," Rafe stated, his voice a little louder than it had been before.

"And what's his job?" she asked without looking over at Gary.

She couldn't. Not without feeling that eerie stirring in the pit of her stomach that had begun the moment her lips had touched his last night.

"My job was to examine Grand Serenity's infrastructure and to assist in implementing new security protocols," he replied.

Resisting the urge to look at him wasn't going to work this time. Sam turned to him then. That dark gaze of his already engulfing her.

"You work for us and now you're suggesting that you and I act as if we're having an affair. That's the recommendation we paid for?"

It sounded cold and harsh, and so unlike the person Sam really was, that she flinched inwardly at her words. Her emotions were getting the best of her and that was never a good thing. She was taking a deep breath and getting ready to release it slowly when he spoke again.

"If you recall, Princess, you put this play in motion. I'm only suggesting that we capitalize on an event that might otherwise bring unwanted negative attention to the family at the moment."

He was right and that was perhaps what she hated most about this situation.

"I do not like it any more than you, Sam," Rafe admitted. "I was not pleased to see my daughter running up to this man and kissing him so wantonly in public. Very unlike you."

As if embarrassment wasn't enough, now her father had to add his disappointment to the pile of burdens on her shoulders.

Sam sighed. She couldn't keep it in and she couldn't get up and run back to the safety of her room, either.

"Morton Javis has been coming on to me for the last year. In the past few months he's decided to push a little harder. Last night he was following me around, touching my shoulder, trying to hold my hand. He wanted to do exactly what I ended up doing," she admitted. "With someone else, that is."

"You mean he wanted to make everyone believe that you two were a couple?" Kris asked.

Her brother had relaxed his stance only slightly as he looked at her. As for Rafe, his scowl had come as quickly as his hands fisted on the desk blotter where they rested. Her father was a broadly built man with a dark, chocolate-brown complexion and a stern look. To say he was visibly pissed off would be an understatement.

She swallowed and continued. "Yes. I believe that's what he wanted. He's told me on many occasions that an alliance between the royal family and a top member of the monarch's staff would show the people of this island that we see ourselves as one of them."

"Bullshit!" Gary rebutted before muttering a quick, "Pardon my language, Your Highness," to Rafe.

"I agree," Kris immediately replied. "How dare he impose on you in such a way?"

"You should have said something sooner," Rafe added. "I want him in my office before the day is out and then I want him as far away from this palace as possible."

"No," Sam insisted. "That will only play into his ploy. If we fire him now he'll go straight to the press. He'll tell whatever he may know about the inner workings of our government and our family. He's sleazy and he wants attention. We cannot give it to him."

When they all remained silent, no doubt thinking of a way to go behind her back and handle this on their own again, Sam stood.

"I had hoped that if he saw me with someone else, he would think his chances were lost. That's why I kissed... um, that's why I did what I did last night."

"And that's why this plan makes sense," Gary stated. "We can give the press something else to talk about, something better to focus on besides any still-lingering questions about the explosion. At the same time, we'll be thwarting any attempts on Morty's behalf to try to discredit or disgrace the princess or the royal family."

Kris was nodding his approval while Rafe still frowned but did not verbally object. As for Sam, she hated how logical Gary's plan sounded and more so the fact that she had no one to blame for this new predicament she was in but herself.

Again.

Chapter 3

Gary nodded to Phillipe Montenegro, Samantha's driver. He'd already requested Samantha's complete schedule for the day and was discussing the route Phillipe would be taking into town. It was almost noon and already the humidity was high enough that the idea of taking a dip in the glistening nearby turquoise sea was more than a little appealing.

There was a breeze that Gary noticed weeks ago when he'd arrived on the island. It could be downright blustery at times, aiding slightly in the cool-off, but this was ultimately air-conditioner weather in Gary's mind.

He'd already rolled up the sleeves of his shirt and knew his sunglasses protected his eyes from the intense rays of the sun as he stood outside the palace.

In the eight weeks since he'd been on Grand Serenity, he had made a point to know every corner of the royal palace, without becoming too overwhelmed. It wasn't as easy as it appeared, but Gary had been trained for assignments such as this one. He'd also left all that behind him years ago when he'd walked away from the United States Army.

When in the midst of the conversation, Phillipe suddenly stood a little straighter, his shoulders squared, almost like a soldier coming to attention, Gary knew who was approaching from behind them. He'd heard the distinct footsteps, so the person wasn't a surprise, neither was what was said next.

"Are you out of your mind?" Kris asked the moment Gary turned to face him. "I didn't invite you down here for you to start messing with my sister."

Gary listened, watching the man he'd remembered from their days at Princeton. Kris had been the astute crown prince trying to fit in. But he knew that regardless of how smart or how rich the other students and their parents were, none of them was next in line to rule a Caribbean island.

Kris had filled out over the years, still a tall and toned guy, but his eyes were more serious than they had been ten years ago. He wore a black suit, regardless of the stifling heat, and glared at Gary with enough anger that Gary decided a quick, to-the-point answer would be the best way to respond.

"I'm not messing with your sister. I'm protecting her and that is what you asked me here to do," he told him.

"I wanted your expertise on strengthening our security and keeping my family safe, yes, but this…" Kris's words trailed off as he realized Phillipe was still standing within earshot.

Gary took the first steps, leading them away from where the white Mercedes-Benz C450 AMG 4Matic was parked. The soles of his black leather boots made a muted sound on the red-brick walkway. There was a bit of shade where he'd stopped closer to a doorway. The pristine white of the palace walls and the crisp green of the shrubs that surrounded this part of the building made this a picturesque scene. Despite the low level of tension emanating between him and Kris at the moment.

Kris stood with his back to where Phillipe was tending to the car. An act that wasn't totally necessary since they were about fifteen feet from where the man was at the moment, but Gary didn't bring that up. Instead he folded his arms over his chest, his legs spread slightly apart as he looked Kris straight in the eye.

"I'm doing my job. That's all," he told the crown prince.

Kris shook his head. "That's not how it looked last night. Landry pinched my arm so hard when she saw you that I had no choice but to look in your direction. Imagine my surprise when I see you, my top security chief, locked in a heated embrace with my little sister."

With all due respect, there was nothing "little" about Kris's sister. She wasn't a plus-size woman, but was tall and slimly built, with luscious curves in all the right places. Gary had observed them on various occasions during his time there. Generous breasts and a perfectly rounded backside had always been an eye-catcher for him. Samantha's attributes in those areas left absolutely nothing to be desired, especially once he'd had his hands on her and the soft cushion of her breasts had pressed so delectably against his chest. His hand had just barely whispered over the curve of her ass, which had taken tremendous restraint on his part.

"*She* kissed *me*," Gary said in defense.

Kris sighed. "I guess I cannot dispute that since she's already admitted it." He ran his hand down his tie and looked as if he was trying to figure out what to make of everything going on around him.

Being a newlywed and a member of the royal family that had recently been targeted—albeit by amateur threats—could not be easy. For as beautiful as the island and Kris's collection of antique cars was, Gary didn't envy him at the moment. In fact, when he'd climbed out of bed this morning, Gary had thought that returning to his cabin on the Choptank River in Cambridge, Maryland, seemed like a far better place to be.

"I'll be looking closely into this Morty person," Gary told Kris. It was his attempt to reassure his one and only long-term friend that he was there to help. Regardless of how things may have appeared last night.

"I've already advised my assistant to pull everything we have on him. As a staff member, he would have gone through a vigorous vetting process," Kris stated.

"More thorough than the one on Ms. Sampson's staff, I hope," Gary stated then immediately wished he'd kept that thought to himself.

It was because he viewed Kris as a friend and felt comfortable with him that he was able to say what was on his mind. With anyone else, Gary was instantly in soldier mode, keeping a tight lip on any and everything. Lack of communication was one of the things his ex-wife had complained about until his ears burned.

"I'll take the fall for that," Kris agreed. "I spent so much time studying Landry's file that I didn't look closely enough at Amari Taylor's. Still, when I went back over everything that was provided for my perusal, there still wasn't anything to indicate that he would try to harm my family."

"That's part of their job. They infiltrate and execute." Gary knew that course of action all too well.

"Guess I should have joined the military like you and Roland," Kris stated evenly.

Gary shook his head. "You took the path that was right for you. I'm the one who kept making all the wrong turns." That's what he liked to call the way he'd lived his life. A series of turns and roadblocks meant to ultimately get him to his destination. At thirty years old and, finally, after too many years to count, he'd been able to breathe and live contentedly. Gary was glad the turns and road-blocks were behind him.

"Where is Roland, anyway?" Gary asked. "The calendar you gave me access to doesn't have his location."

Kris frowned then. He looked as if he wanted to curse, or better yet, punch something, but he didn't. Gary knew he wouldn't. Kris wasn't built that way.

"He goes off for days or weeks at a time and nobody really knows where he is. I asked him to be more mindful of our situation now, but you know Roland has always had a mind of his own."

Gary nodded. "Yeah, I know how that feels." If there was one member of the royal family Gary could totally relate to, it was Roland DeSaunters. The need to be free to roam and to make whatever decision suited him, without council, was imperative to Gary. Roland, from all that Kris had told him over the years, was the same way.

"We're going to need to brief him eventually, when we finalize all the changes you've suggested," Kris told him.

Gary nodded again. "True. In a couple of days," he said. "I want to get a few more details locked down. Then we can talk about the probability of another strike on your family."

Kris stared at him then, a seriously worried and annoyed look on his face. "That's a definite probability, isn't it?"

Gary didn't hesitate. "Yes."

"What's a definite probability?" Samantha asked as she stepped through the door only a few feet behind Gary.

"That it's going to rain later," Kris answered while Gary stepped to the side, making room for her to stand with them.

When she looked to Gary, he nodded. "We should be back from your appointments by the time the rain begins."

She looked at Kris, her eyes narrowing as she finally shook her head. "Rain usually lasts about an hour here on the island, but as high as the temperatures are likely to be today, a shower might be welcomed. I'll be back by dinner," she told Kris and moved away from them, heading to her car.

For the next few seconds Gary and Kris simply stared at her walking away, until finally Kris clapped a hand on Gary's shoulder.

"You might rethink your plan after spending the day with her when she's in this type of mood," Kris told him. "So I guess this is payback for letting her kiss you in the first place."

Gary felt the corner of his mouth lift in a smile. He was certain no living and breathing man would have been able to resist kissing a woman like Samantha DeSaunters.

When Kris had walked away, feeling a little more triumphant than Gary appreciated, Gary walked over to the car. He nodded to Phillipe. The driver had remained standing by the back door, closing it only after Gary slipped onto the leather seat.

"What are you doing?" Samantha asked immediately.

"You have appointments today, correct?"

"*I* have appointments. Not you," she stated easily.

He shook his head. "I'm going where you go today."

"This is ridiculous. It doesn't make any sense at all. As far as your rationalization for why your idea is such a great one, I—"

He hadn't been able to resist. Her hair was pulled over one shoulder, the tiny earrings twinkling at her ear. The blouse she wore was cut low and her jacket was open so that he could see hints of her cleavage. But it was enough to drive him freakin' crazy in the few moments they'd been alone.

Gary had tried to focus on what she was saying by looking at her mouth, but that was a mistake. Her lips were covered in a peach-colored gloss, the bottom one a little plumper than the top. Glimpses of her straight white teeth and just a peek of her tongue had his body aching for another taste. Just once more.

So he'd quickly closed the space across the seat of the car, using one hand to grasp the back of her neck and pull her in for the assault.

The moment his lips touched hers Gary knew it was a mistake. And yet he continued. He moved in farther, thrusting his tongue deeper, letting the sound of her long and sensuous sigh drape him like a cloak. Her hand instantly came around to cup his neck in the same way he was holding her. When he tilted his head one way and deepened the kiss, she tilted hers the opposite way, taking everything he had to offer. It was like a perfectly matched battle. Only, Gary knew way back in the recesses of his mind, that they were uneven. This wasn't what they were supposed to be doing. It wasn't expected or acceptable for either of them.

And yet he continued.

The car was moving down the incline toward the front gate and came to a halting stop, as did their kiss. Gary pulled back just enough to turn his face so that he could look out the window at what was going on.

There was another vehicle at the front gate, trying to gain access.

On a curse, he pulled completely away from her and reached to open the door. Stepping out, he circled the car and headed to the gatekeeper's booth. Inside was a guard dressed in full palace regalia, the navy, gold and white colors of the DeSaunters's flag displayed prominently in the uniform. A badge hung from the guard's right lapel.

The front gates were twelve feet tall, black iron and operated on an automatic lock system. Since he'd been there, they'd been updated to also include an electronic sensor hidden in the small speed bump leading onto the property. If by chance someone decided to let an uninvited guest through the gates, monitors in the private security room in the palace would be alerted. Specially selected guards that Gary had referred, and Kris and Rafe had approved, manned these monitors.

"What's the problem?" Gary asked the guard when he entered the booth.

Turning, the pinch-faced man looked up to see him. The second week of Gary's arrival consisted of a meeting with every guard who'd previously worked at the palace and he personally met with each of the new hires, as well. They all needed to know that he was now supervising the security at the palace. His military background coupled with his relationship with Kris put him in a position higher than Salvin Gathersburg, the chief of the palace guards. Those initial meetings had come in handy for moments such as this.

"His name's not on today's log. He says he has an appointment with Prince Kristian," the guard—Rutger, as Gary recalled—informed him.

"Have you called his assistant?"

"I did. She did not see his name in her appointment book, either. She was looking for the prince, to ask him if he knew anything about this person before I send him away."

"What's his name?"

"Kendon Arnold," Rutger told him.

Gary walked out of the booth and headed to the side of the gate where there was a doorway. Reaching into his back pocket, he retrieved the key card he and every guard on staff now had for this entrance and swiped it over the pad beside the knob. The locks released with a loud clicking sound and he walked through the door and right up to the driver's side of the white SUV waiting to get inside the gates.

"You said you have an appointment with the prince," Gary began immediately. "Who are you and what's it in reference to?"

The guy, who looked to be in his early twenties, kept his hands firmly clenched on the steering wheel where Gary could see them. A glance inside the SUV confirmed the passenger seat was empty. He wore a lightweight blue jacket with a striped shirt beneath it and sunglasses covered his eyes.

"I'm interested in opening an account at Serenity Trust," he told him.

"Then you should be at the bank, not here," Gary replied.

His hands did not move, and while his head remained turned in Gary's direction, Gary wasn't sure the man was looking at him. Something wasn't right here.

"He will want to meet with me personally," the man stated.

"What's your name?"

Rutger had already given Gary this information but he wanted to hear the man say it. He wanted to see if he could tell if he was being told a lie.

"Kendon Arnold" was the easy reply. Too easy.

Gary nodded. "I'll give the prince your message. If you're right and he wants to meet with you, he'll be in touch. But there will be no meeting today, so back this truck up and leave the property. Further sightings of you or this vehicle near the palace without the prince's approval will result in your arrest. Do I make myself clear?"

There was a moment when Gary thought he was going to have to pull the man from the truck and detain him until the island police could come and arrest him but the guy shrugged.

"That is clear," he said. Then he put the SUV in Reverse and backed away from the gate.

Gary watched as the vehicle turned and drove down the driveway. At the end of the cement drive, the road split in two directions. The SUV turned to the right and Gary frowned. That direction led back to more winding dirt roads and into the forested part of the island. The same forested part that ran along the back perimeter of the palace.

Gary pulled his cell phone from his pocket and began composing a text message to Kris. The crown prince wasn't going to like this any more than Gary did, but he needed to know.

Chapter 4

Sam watched intently from the front passenger seat of the car. She'd gotten out of the vehicle and moved onto the seat beside Phillipe while Gary had been in the security booth. Yes, it was running away from the problem. But there was no other way, she insisted as she'd avoided Phillipe's questioning gaze and pulled her seat belt into place.

If she and Gary were going to be close, they would not be able to resist touching each other. She had to put some space between them.

It was a solution. Sam was good at coming up with solutions and acting on them, regardless of whether or not it seemed she was taking the easy way out. That didn't matter. Only the "out" part did.

When Gary had finished talking to the man in the truck and then stood there for a few moments as the SUV pulled off, she'd had plenty of time to decide what she would say when he asked why she'd changed seats. Of course she wouldn't say that she couldn't trust herself not to jump him in the backseat of a moving car. That wouldn't be at all appropriate—no matter how true it might be.

She also wouldn't tell him again that she didn't like his idea of them faking a relationship. That had already been said and overruled. No, Sam decided that she would do whatever was necessary to keep her family safe and out of the scandal spotlight. So she planned to go through with this false relationship until Morty was dealt with and they could all move on. She prayed that would happen sooner rather than later.

He was heading back now, stopping only briefly at the security booth before heading toward the car. Her fingers clenched on her purse as she held it firmly in her lap. She stared straight ahead even though the windows were completely tinted so he could not see where she sat from the outside. The back door opened—she heard barely a sound as she suspected he slipped onto the seat—and then the door closed. A few muted seconds passed.

"Let's go. We don't want the princess to be late for the opening ceremonies," he instructed Phillipe.

He said nothing to her and, for that, Sam was grateful. After about fifteen minutes the gratitude shifted to mild confusion. Why wasn't he saying anything? Was kissing the only way they could communicate? No, that was silly. Especially since after each kiss Sam was left feeling more confused than ever. Aroused yet still jumbled.

She hadn't chanced a look at him but knew without a doubt that he was staring at her because the back of her neck felt as if it were on fire. He was surely staring, but what was he thinking? She wondered if it was about her or about the job he'd been hired to do. She shouldn't care. The job...rather, the safety of her family and their people, was all that mattered. So he should be thinking about the job and not her. Right?

Now she drummed her fingers on her purse, wanting to say something but not knowing exactly what to say. This was new for Sam. Her entire life had revolved around her ability to talk to anyone about almost anything. The fact that she did so with a brilliant smile and a sense of compassion made her the perfect goodwill ambassador for the island.

It had been her mother's job when she was alive. Vivienne Patterson DeSaunters had been the perfect champion for everything wonderful about Grand Serenity Island. She'd helped Rafe build the island's tourism to the bustling hub of social and economic prosperity that it was today.

Forming the Tourism Board had been Vivienne's idea, as well as bringing several social organizations she'd been part of in her hometown of Sugar Land in Houston, Texas, to Grand Serenity. Sam was a member of the Flower Circle, the Arts and Entertainment Society, and the Serenade Museum Board of Directors. But not because of her own interest in flowers or plays or the paintings that hung along the museum walls. No. As with so many other aspects of her life, these things Sam did in memory of her mother.

Twenty minutes later, when the car came to a stop and she looked across the cobblestone street to a little shop painted a bright and cheery blue with white-framed windows, she smiled. Even though lately every thought she had of her mother made her sad.

Detali Signorenson had been making dresses for Sam since Sam's first middle school dance. She was a true talent when it came to design and manufacturing dresses, and Sam was ecstatic about the turn her career had taken.

It had started two months ago when Sam had brought Landry into Detali's old shop, which had also served as Detali and her daughter's apartment. During that meeting Landry, who at the time had been Malayka's stylist, had commissioned Detali to design and make an original gown for Malayka.

Sam remembered well how Malayka had embarrassed the royal family. At a press conference she'd offended every dressmaker on Grand Serenity with her dismissive remarks about the quality of fashion on the island. But after Landry had tricked Malayka into wearing the Detali original to the Ambassador's Ball, the gown had been photographed and featured on fashion blogs with Detali as a new and upcoming designer.

Today would be the grand opening of Detali Designs, the new shop that would display Detali's original dresses. In another month or so, one of the old warehouses on the east side of the island would be transformed into a state-of-the art space for the clothes to be manufactured.

Landry had invested in Detali's dream and was present today for the press conference and ribbon-cutting ceremony. Sam wondered if Kris knew what a special woman he'd found in Landry Norris. She possessed one of the first traits to being a princess: a good heart. The business and fashion sense Landry brought to the small Caribbean island was a plus that Sam was glad to expose.

The opening of the car door jolted her from her thoughts and Sam stepped out without further hesitation. Her hair blew in the breeze as she took a step onto the cobblestone path. Gary touched her elbow immediately, a firm grasp that she doubted looked imposing at all from a distance.

"From this point on, there will be two cars traveling with every member of the royal family," he said in what, to a passerby, may have sounded like a cordial tone.

Sam wasn't certain what she should gather from his voice, she was too busy trying to squash the butterflies dancing happily in the pit of her stomach at his touch.

"Guards from the second car will enter the premises first and complete a perimeter check. Once Phillipe, or the other driver, receives the okay from the guards, he'll let you out of the vehicle. You are never to exit the vehicle alone, nor are you to enter a facility that has not been pre-checked."

He walked them across the street as he talked. Sam noticed the group of women that had been heading toward the shop. They stopped and whispered. Then one of them lifted her phone, aiming it toward Sam. Another one giggled and did the same thing. Falling easily into her role, Sam lifted a hand and waved. "Hello. How are you?" she said to them.

One of the women ran up to her, pulling a canvas bag off her shoulder and holding a marker in Sam's direction. Sam immediately reached for it.

"I'm so happy to meet you, Princess Samantha. You're much prettier in person." The woman gushed.

Sam smiled. "Thank you. Ah…?"

"Oh, my name's Kelly. Kelly Upton. I'm from Washington, D.C. Our cruise ship just docked this morning. I've been waiting all year to visit Grand Serenity. And now that I've met you, it's the highlight of the trip!"

Sam wrote an uplifting message to Kelly and signed her name to the large black bag. The silver marker she used caused her writing to glisten in the sunlight.

"Thank you so much!" Kelly insisted.

"How about a picture?" Sam offered.

"Oh, my! Yes! Yes! Come on, y'all, she's going to take a picture with us!" Kelly yelled to her companions.

The next second Gary was standing a few feet in front of Sam and the women, aimed not one, not two but four different cell phones at them and snapped pictures. He took one with them all smiling and then Sam yelled, "Now, let's make a funny face!"

The women obliged and Sam stuck out her tongue. Gary snapped more pictures.

"And now we'll strike a runway pose," Sam continued, thoroughly enjoying the moment.

The women laughed and did as Sam instructed, all of them striking poses around her. When the pictures were finished, Sam hugged each one of them and wished them a great time while visiting the island. She waited as Gary gave them their phones back and hoped that he would once again take her by the arm and walk close beside her toward the shop. There was something comforting in that act. Something that didn't seem quite the same when other guards had walked beside her.

"That should stop for the foreseeable future," he said in a gruff tone, effectively jerking her mind from the pleasant thoughts she had, but taking her by the arm once again.

"What?"

"Impromptu autographs and pictures. From this point on everyone you come in contact with needs to be vetted and searched."

They'd arrived at the door of the shop when Sam pulled her arm from his grasp and stared up at him.

"Are you joking?" she asked and then continued when she realized by the stern look on his face that he was not. "Look, I know that you have a job to do and you feel as if you're doing it by being here with me. But I also have

A.C. Arthur   43

a job and I think I know by now how to best perform my duties without you showing up on my island and passing out instructions."

It sounded harsh, Sam knew. She didn't speak that way often, and yet, twice in one day, this man had taken her to this point. She'd think about why he was able to do that later. For now, she simply needed to set him straight.

He waited a beat before responding and then his words were just as stiff and cold as they had been before she'd spoken her mind.

"I'll be by your side during the press conference. Phillipe will remain at the car. We're all wearing earpieces so we can communicate with each other. At any time, if you feel uncomfortable, let me know and I'll get you out of there," he stated.

Sam could only stare at him. It was as if he hadn't heard a word she'd said. Taking a deep breath and releasing it slowly—because others had begun to gather on the sidewalk around the store—she managed a small smile as she replied, "Thank you for your service."

She turned then and entered the store, determined to do what she'd come there to do and then get the hell away from him.

Gary was true to his word, no matter how much he wanted to grab her by the waist and haul her sexy ass back to the car to finish the kiss and whatever else they'd started that morning. Of course, he'd only given his word to himself that he would keep his hands off her and focus on his job. Still, he thought the Herculean effort deserved accolades. He stood no more than three feet away from Samantha as she talked to members of the press and posed for pictures. She and Landry were being interviewed by a greasy-haired guy who was apparently a big-time editor at some fashion magazine.

"Detali Designs is just the first step that Grand Serenity will be making in the fashion industry. I am happy to also announce that *Tropical Fashions*, my in-depth magazine covering not only international fashion but also focusing on new trends being started on the islands, will sponsor its first charity fashion show in February," Landry stated.

Even as an expat, Landry stood strong and proud beside Samantha, looking almost every bit as royal as the native-born princess. Landry was a couple of inches shorter than Samantha's five-feet, nine-inch stature and just a shade lighter than Samantha's deep brown complexion.

"We are fortunate to have such talent in the royal family and among our citizens." Samantha spoke now, her smile and gaze moving from the reporter to Landry. "We've always prided ourselves on promoting our diverse culture, so it is an honor to partner with my new sister and Detali to bring the talent of Grand Serenity to the forefront. My mother had begun similar endeavors by spearheading the redevelopment of the museum and filling one complete floor with local artists' work. Now we'll have a new princess bringing forth yet another opportunity for the talented citizens of Grand Serenity. On behalf of the royal family, I cannot begin to express how excited we are."

She was very well spoken, her voice smooth and clear. She made eye contact with each of the reporters who had gathered around, giving them all that million-dollar smile and the sexy tilt of her head that Gary wondered if she even knew she did. The bright hue of her suit caused her skin to glisten so that it appeared exquisitely sun-kissed.

Her voice wasn't high-pitched but sultry and refreshing, like a tall glass of lemonade on a hot summer's day. She was fierce and confident and dedicated, all traits Gary had never thought he'd find in a woman.

Not that he was looking for a woman. He wasn't. No, sir, one time down the aisle with a woman who turned out to be the biggest pain in his ass ever was more than enough for Gary.

As much as he hated comparing Samantha to his ex, Tonya, he couldn't help it. Tonya was shorter, curvier and mouthier than Samantha, and not in a good way. Tonya had an opinion about everyone and everything, and she did not hesitate to voice it, over and over again, until a person either agreed with her or got the hell away from her. In the two years they'd been together Gary had often chosen the latter.

No, there was definitely no competition there. Samantha would come out on top every time.

Damn.

His current thoughts were so far from what should have been on his mind now or at any other moment while he was on this island. Kris hadn't requested his presence to gawk at his sister. If the unspoken warning his friend had given him only hours ago hadn't been enough, Samantha's cool disdain toward him should have spoken volumes to calm his body's raging desire for her. Not to mention the fact that he'd just congratulated himself on keeping his hands off of her.

None of that seemed to matter.

The interview was over and Gary immediately moved around the cameramen to stand close to Samantha and Landry.

"Let's head out the back way. I've already told the cars to meet us there."

He wasn't sure if Sam remained silent and followed because Landry was there or because she was simply finished talking to him for the day. He also wondered if she planned to sit in the front seat again, instead of in back with him. He wouldn't blame her if she did. Hell, he hadn't disagreed with Kris pulling him up about kissing his sister. In fact, Gary figured if it were his sister he probably would have punched the guy first and asked questions later. Thankfully, for all concerned, Kris wasn't the same type of guy Gary was.

Their friendship had always been a strange one. Freshman year, Gary had presumed the other guys in their dorm were talking about him because he was getting rides in Kris's Mercedes and sharing in all the first-class perks of being the roommate of a prince. Gary wasn't bothered by those rumors at all. He'd thought all those preppie privileged kids were jerks, anyway. As for Kris, well, Gary always got the impression that the prince was just happy to have somebody to actually be normal around. Too bad Gary hadn't been able to tough out college life for another three years. But Kris—if nobody else in Gary's life at the time—had understood his need to do something more with his life. The army had been that something, and damn if it hadn't been more than anything he'd ever expected.

"This is the third time that white SUV has circled the block. He slowed a bit and looked down this side street."

Gary heard the message through the earpiece and was immediately on alert, thankful for the interruption of his thoughts, but not at all happy with the situation. In quick steps he moved in front of the princesses to push the back door open and look out onto the narrow street.

"What's happening?"

He heard Landry's question but ignored it as guards

opened the back doors to both the cars parked just outside. Gary turned to them and said, "Landry, you'll go first. Directly to the car, no stops."

He extended his hand to her, glad that she had not questioned him but taken his hand and moved quickly through the door, out into the late-afternoon sun. Two guards had come up to the door and flanked her sides as they moved her to the first car. Closing those doors, the guards ran back to the second car and climbed inside. With a nod, Gary sent them on their way.

"Send the other cars." He spoke softly, knowing they would hear him through the earpiece.

"What is going on?" Samantha asked as she stepped closer to him. "And don't bother telling me nothing."

No, he wasn't even going to bother.

"We're just taking some extra precautions," he told her. "When the cars pull up, we'll walk out and head back to the palace."

"Landry and I were going to do some shopping."

"Not today," he said and then heard the cars pull up. He reached for her hand and, for a split second, thought that she would pull away in an act of defiance. He really did not have time for that and prayed that she was smarter than to risk her own safety.

She didn't and Gary almost sighed with relief.

Instead she took his hand and let him lead her to the car. She went into the backseat without protest and when he slid in beside her she only clasped her seat belt in place and looked out the window.

"Go!" Gary spoke to the guards and the car began to move.

They'd driven only a few seconds when she looked over at him and said in a serious tone, "There will be no more kissing or touching. I should never have imposed on you like that last night. I apologize and promise it will not happen again."

Gary only stared at her in response. The fact that the simple act of watching her lips move while she'd been speaking turned him on more than any woman he'd ever been with was going to be a problem.

A big problem.

Chapter 5

Dinner was a circus.

One that Gary paid particular attention to. He watched each guest with meticulous regard to everything that went on in that room. Later, when he was alone, he would pull out his notepad and his pencil and sit by the window in the large room that had been designated to him at the palace. Then he would write out every note he'd mentally taken throughout the hour and a half of sitting in the private dining room of the royal palace.

All of this would be recorded in his small but neat penmanship. To be truthful, Gary had always been interested in people. To the extent that in the early part of his life he'd even sought them out. As an only child, his mother had called it a "craving for attention." But Gary never wanted the attention of the people he would be around. He just liked watching them, observing their habits, their mannerisms. It all intrigued him.

That was until the heartbreak of his mother's death, followed quickly by the relief of his marriage finally coming to an end. This was when Gary decided that being around people wasn't all it was cracked up to be. At that point, he'd found his pencil, his pad and his mind to be his very best friends. They'd introduced him to a newfound hobby he'd never imagined having. One that, in retrospect, would become his new career.

However this, his purpose for being on Grand Serenity, was also a job. Well, it was a favor to a friend.

Kris had been very specific about what he'd needed Gary's help with. First, in their conversation over the phone and then when Gary had arrived on the island. Kris had personally come to the airport to pick him up and on the ride back to the palace had laid out all of his concerns. Now, Gary was concerned, as well, and he was determined to help the friend that had showed up for Gary in his time of need.

Glancing across the room, Gary wasn't so sure all of his findings were going to be pleasing to Kris, or his siblings, for that matter.

The meal was over and now there was conversation. The guests tonight had also been here a couple of months ago, right after the royal wedding was announced. They'd only stayed for a day at that time. A breakfast soirée that Rafe had insisted his children attend. Kris had been the only one to escape that meeting, which was part of the reason he'd been the one to suggest to Malayka that she once again have her bridal party visit the island. This time for the weekend. There were several activities planned for the group, all designed to witness them interacting with Malayka. For Kris, Roland and Samantha, there was a definite correlation with Malayka's arrival to the palace and the attempts on their lives.

Unfortunately, Gary had alarming news in that department. From what he'd observed in the weeks since he'd been on the island, Malayka Sampson was undoubtedly in love with Prince Rafferty DeSaunters.

It was in the way she looked at him. The way she stood beside him, almost protectively at times, her arm intimately tucked into the crook of his. When she smiled with her dimpled cheeks and caramel-toned complexion, her brown eyes rested on Rafe in a way that spoke volumes. Even to a love cynic like Gary.

They made a striking couple, Rafe with his dark and foreboding looks standing tall and formidable beside the curly haired, pretty-faced American. They photographed well and, so far, were forming a very romantic alliance between the United States and Grand Serenity. Already, the president was scheduling a visit to the island. Gary was working with the Secret Service to figure out the safest and most opportune time for that meeting.

Still, Gary could picture the headline on the front page of global gossip papers and the reputable international press: President of the United States, First Lady, Prince Rafferty and Soon-to-be Princess Malayka. The caption, he was sure, would read "A beautiful union of diversity in a time when the world needs to see it most."

To that end, Gary had made another discovery, one he was sure the DeSaunters children had not considered. Prince Rafferty was also in love with Malayka Sampson.

At first, Gary had been alarmed that he could see it so clearly, especially considering his own epic fail in the love department. He attributed both his awareness and failure to his mother. He'd married to please Maggie Montgomery and thus learned more about what true love looked and felt like because of her memories with his father. His divorce, which came only three months after his mother's death, had been a direct result of what he knew love to be and what he was certain he never had in his union with Tonya. That and a slew of gossip and lies that had begun to work every one of Gary's nerves.

Still, even with a failed marriage under his belt, Gary was certain of what he saw between the prince and his bride-to-be. They were in love. Which meant that the suspicions Kris had brought him there to confirm were slowly unraveling before Gary's eyes.

"What are you looking at? Is she getting on your nerves, too?"

Gary didn't answer but glanced at Landry, who was now standing beside him, then back to where Malayka and Rafe stood across the room. He kept his arms folded over his chest and his thoughts on the couple to himself.

"She's happy to have her *friends* here," Landry continued.

"The two over there, bridesmaids," he said, nodding to his left where a tall woman wearing a very short green dress and another woman with long, curly hair and large-framed glasses sat.

"I wouldn't exactly call them friends," Landry replied. "They're more like opportunists."

"Why do you say that?"

Gary knew she was right, but still wanted to hear Landry's insights on the matter.

"Last month, when I was back in LA—" Landry tilted her head slightly toward the tall woman "—she was hanging on every word of an R&B singer that I had styled for an awards show. This is what she does for a living—cozy up to the rich and famous. It's a very lucrative career."

"It's degrading," he snapped.

Landry chuckled. "I wholeheartedly agree."

Gary shook his head. "The one over there has been using her phone for the last ten minutes. My guess is she's Tweeting or Snapchatting everyone in this room," he stated.

"You're probably right. Which leads to my next question. Why did you and Kris allow all these people to come here for the weekend? With all that's going on, this seems to contradict the tightening of the security plan we should be promoting."

She was right. Again. The new princess of Grand Serenity was astute.

"Let me guess, you want to observe them all up close," she continued. "Weed out the good ones from the bad, possibly?"

At that moment, across the room, Samantha walked up to her father. She leaned in to whisper something in his ear. Malayka frowned at the action, clearly not pleased with her soon-to-be stepdaughter.

"How do they get along?" he asked Landry. "Samantha and Malayka. I mean, really? You and Samantha seem pretty friendly, so she would tell you if she didn't like Malayka."

Landry made a tsking sound.

"A lot of people don't like Malayka. And you're right, Sam and I do talk. I have one blood sister and now one by marriage. So I'm not about to betray her trust by telling you how she feels about her father's impending nuptials. Besides, that has nothing to do with our security."

It had everything to do with their security, Gary thought.

"What did Sam have for dinner tonight?"

Gary answered the question reflexively. "There were two entrées offered tonight in honor of the American guests. Filet mignon and cheeseburgers. Samantha had the cheeseburger with mustard, lettuce and bacon. To appease the healthy portion of her conscience, she chose broccoli instead of fries and lemon water instead of sweetened iced tea. Which, by the way, was very well done. Tasted more like a glass of Southern iced tea than some I've had in Georgia or South Carolina."

"My, my, but you are paying attention to details tonight," Landry replied.

Gary heard the laughter in her tone as she patted him on the arm before heading over to the two ladies they'd previously discussed.

He could have cursed himself for falling so easily into Landry's trap, but his ego wouldn't allow it. He'd prefer to think she hadn't trapped him into revealing anything he hadn't wanted to reveal. Yes, he'd paid close attention to Samantha at dinner. He'd also paid attention to the way Malayka had eyed her future husband's daughter. Gary wanted to know why.

"Dance lessons begin promptly at ten-thirty tomorrow morning. Lunch is at noon. Then you will be leading us on a tour of the battle ruins from two to four-thirty."

Sam turned at the sound of her voice. She took a moment to resist saying the first response to run through her mind. Instead she clasped her hands in front of her and took a steadying breath. "I am aware of tomorrow's schedule, Malayka."

With a nod of her head, the gold hoops at Malayka's ears brushed over her cheeks. The black-and-white floral maxi dress she wore was the perfect blend of sexy but casual. Landry was no longer styling Malayka and Sam knew that no one new had been hired. Now Malayka's private staff consisted only of one maid, Onyae, who had been part of the palace staff for years, and Cheryl, who was originally her makeup artist but now pulled double duty as her hair stylist, as well. Observing Malayka's casual style had Sam wondering if the woman possessed a bit of style and class of her own.

"I wanted to be sure you weren't trying to change any of the arranged plans with your whispers to your father," Malayka replied.

"My conversations with my father are private. In the event that I have something to say regarding scheduling with you, you can be assured that I will come directly to you," Sam stated evenly.

Malayka gave another slow nod. "That would be preferable."

"You should go back in to bid your guests good-night," Sam told her and began to turn away.

"And we should further discuss relinquishing of duties around here. In the future, I will take care of directing the staff and planning the meals for events in the palace. Despite what you may have read in a magazine, not all Americans are in love with beef. Tonight's dinner should have been more inclusive."

"Tonight's dinner was a nod to my mother's hometown and one of her great loves as an American. Beef and Texas often go hand in hand," Sam countered.

"I wasn't raised in Texas," Malayka snapped back. "If there is any woman residing in this palace that a dinner menu will honor, it will be me."

"Is that so? Well, tell me this, Malayka, where are you from? Where did you grow up? What are some of the things you liked doing in America? You see, it's kind of hard to do things to honor someone you know so little about. How about you and I set aside some time to get to know each other better? That way, when I plan for palace events, I can be sure to include things that more closely represent the person you are."

"What I think will work better, Samantha," Malayka said as she took a step toward Sam. "Is if you would stop acting like a spoiled brat and step aside like a good daughter should. I am going to be *the* princess of Grand Serenity and believe me when I say I do not need any assistance from you to do my job."

"She knows that, Malayka," Roland said. "We all know that you're going to be a damn fine princess. Isn't that right, Sam?"

She hadn't heard him approach, only felt the tightening of his arm around her shoulders seconds before he spoke. He was holding her still because Sam had been more than ready to pounce. Malayka had pushed the right button when she'd told Sam she was going to be the princess. There was nothing Sam hated more at this very moment than the realization that those words were true.

"She's going to be something" was all Sam could manage to mutter. "I'm certain of that."

Malayka's sickeningly sweet smile slipped as she made her way to the door of the dining room. It never stayed in place long when Malayka was not at her fiancé's side.

"My position and the duties I will hold are non-negotiable. Maybe you can get that through your sister's pretty little head, Roland. Oh, and it's good to see you back. Your father was worried."

Of course Malayka looked at Roland differently than she did Sam, and now Landry, for that matter. She'd begun smiling again and batting her fake eyelashes. The woman clearly thought she was every man's gift, especially Rafe's. However, Sam knew for a fact that Roland was not impressed.

"He shouldn't worry. I'm a grown man and I've been taking care of myself for quite some time."

"Nevertheless," Malayka continued. "A little courtesy would go a long way. He deserves that much respect from you."

The tension vibrating through Sam's body seemed to transfer to her brother's as she felt him stiffen beside her.

"Don't press your luck, Malayka. You can plan all the parties you want, but what you will not do is tell me how to treat my father. Not now, and not even after you're married. I hope that's clear," Roland said in an easy tone.

Malayka shook her head this time. "And this is why I never bothered to procreate."

She turned and walked away at that point.

"She's a piece of work," Roland said with a sigh.

"She's a bitch," Sam replied. "And she's not worthy of you trying to be polite about labeling her."

He chuckled and the sound allowed Sam to instantly relax. It was always like that with Ro. Easygoing, fun times, smiles, good vibes. He was so much like their mother in that regard. Vivienne was all about living life to its fullest and having lots of fun along the way.

"Come on, I'll walk you upstairs," Roland said, once again wrapping an arm around her shoulders.

They turned and began walking down the long hallway that would lead to the curved staircase located in the center of the palace.

"Where have you been?" Sam asked after a few steps. "Things have been very interesting around here while you were away."

"Interesting by way of seeing my sister in a hot liplock with the American she's supposedly been having a secret affair with?"

Another thing about Roland DeSaunters was that he never pulled punches. Not even with his family.

Sam sighed heavily because she didn't know what else to do. How could one split-second decision have such a huge impact on her life? Her well-ordered and sensible life, she might add.

"That was just…" she began but didn't know what else to say. "It just happened."

"The affair or the kiss?" Roland asked after a light chuckle.

"The kiss just happened. The affair was the logical excuse for the illogical lip-lock, as you so kindly put it," she replied. "I was just trying to stop one idiot from harassing me and now I've ended up with the press and all the people of the island looking at me in question."

"Ah, come on, you're used to being in the spotlight. You were born for it," he told her. "Remember how you used to stand at the top of the stairs and act as if you were holding a press conference? I don't think you were more than eight years old when you did that for the first time."

She remembered all right. Just as she remembered crying hysterically when she'd seen Alveta, the woman who used to be her mother's maid and was now the palace's maid staff supervisor, packing up her mother's belongings. To console her, Alveta had packed a box of Vivienne's shoes and dresses and put them in the back of Sam's closet.

"This way you'll always have a piece of her," Alveta had told Sam.

She'd also inherited her mother's antique tea set collection and jewelry, both of which were in a safe locked securely in Sam's bedroom. Except for her favorite set of the collection. Sam kept that one out and set perfectly on a highboy table in the office section of her rooms.

On days when she felt alone or confused, she would sit at that table and remember the first time she'd had a tea party with a real princess—her mother.

"I wanted to be just like her," Sam said quietly as she and Roland approached the stairs.

She looked up the winding marble staircase with its black-iron railing and the huge glittering chandelier in the center of the room.

"So many times I'd watched her on television or even in the palace pressroom talking to everyone as if they were all personal friends. She never seemed confused or to struggle with what her job was, where she should be, how she should say things. She just knew and was perfect at it. Every damn time, she was perfect," Sam continued.

She did not take the first step. She felt frozen at that spot and didn't know why.

"You're not our mother, Sam," Roland told her. Dropping his arm from her shoulders, he touched her arms and turned her to face him.

"No more than I am our father, or either of us is Kris. We each have our own path," he said solemnly.

Sam looked up into her brother's face. He was so handsome it was almost heartbreaking. At that word, Sam wondered how many women had looked into Roland's dark-brown eyes and fell quickly and helplessly in love. Whatever the number, their heartbreak was inevitable. If there were any of the DeSaunters siblings that knew what they wanted and what they definitely did not want, it was Roland.

"I wish I could be as strong as you are, Ro. I wish I could make a decision on how to live my life and do just that, without any thought to naysayers or repercussions. Or duty," she admitted.

He shrugged then used his fist to lightly tap her chin.

"You're the strongest woman I know," he told her. "The only woman that's ever been able to body-slam me and Kris despite all the self-defense and combat training we've gone through."

Sam couldn't help but smile as she remembered those times when the three of them would play for hours in the playroom on the first floor. That room had been the place Vivienne had wanted her children to be free to do what children did, without maids or limitations or duty. Even after her death Alveta had made sure the children had at least an hour's time in that room each week. That was where Sam's brothers had decided to teach her how to defend herself. They had no idea how fast and studious a student she was. The memory never failed to make her smile.

"I don't like them whispering behind my back," she confessed to her brother. "Anytime I've stood in front of cameras or a room full of people, I've always felt confident in my integrity and my birthright. Now, I'm deceiving them with this lie about an affair and about my confidence in Malayka becoming the princess. She's not good enough for Dad, but he doesn't see it. And I'm not capable of some grand love affair, but the world would rather believe in the fairy tale."

"People believe what's easiest for them, Sam. There's nothing we can do about changing anybody's thoughts. As for Malayka, remember what Mom always said about what's done in the dark. We just have to let things play out. I don't like her any more than you do. There's something there and we'll find it, there's no doubt in my mind about that."

He clasped his fingers in hers and took the first step, waiting a moment until she followed before he began again.

"As for this phony affair? Well, from what Kris told me in the wordy email he sent, it makes sense—for now, anyway. Though I know it's not the best situation," he said when Sam was about to debate his comment. "But like you said, you initiated it, so now you have to endure it for a while. Kris trusts Gary with his life. And I trust Kris. He's the steadiest and most intelligent man I know. So that means I've got to trust Gary, as well. Play the game until we take care of Morty—and we will take care of his delusional ass. But let me know if this guy gets too into the fake affair. You don't ever have to take any type of harassment from any guy. Not as long as I'm around."

They'd made it to the top of the stairs by then and whatever Sam had wanted to say had vanished by the time Roland finished speaking. She turned then, wrapping her arms tightly around his neck, and held him close. For endless moments she just stood there, holding her brother, reveling in the strength and steadfastness he exuded. This was what Sam knew and what she trusted, it was the only thing she had—her family.

"What was that for?" Roland asked when she finally let him go.

She stepped back and smiled at him. "You never stay still long enough for me to do that anymore," she told him. "I miss having you around when I need you."

"I'm always here for you, Sam. No matter where I am on this earth, you can always call me and I'll come to you. Don't ever forget that." He leaned forward and kissed her on the forehead.

Sam nodded. "I won't forget," she told him.

No, Sam thought. She would never forget that her brothers were always there for her. No matter what mistakes she'd made in the past, this was home and it was where she was loved and respected for just being her.

It was her safe haven, the place she wasn't about to let anyone, or anything, jeopardize.

Chapter 6

"I believe my partner should be someone from the wedding party," Sam told Gary as he stood in front of her with his arms open in invitation.

The corner of his mouth lifted and he gave a slight tilt of his head as he replied, "No way am I standing there watching some other guy dance closely to you."

Succinct and solemn, the words had her stomach clenching, fingers threatening to shake.

"At least that's how I figure any man that's madly in love with you would feel," he continued. "That lady over there in the corner is from one of those style channels. We just cleared her to be in the palace. They're doing some type of special that Malayka believes will make Grand Serenity the next best wedding destination in the world. With that said, we need to make this thing between us look good."

He took her hand, holding it up while his other arm

slipped around her waist and he pulled her close to him. "We need to make it look very good," he whispered.

"But Morty's not here," Sam replied seconds after she placed her other hand on his shoulder and attempted to relax in his embrace. "Our charade is for the purpose of keeping Morty quiet, not boosting ratings on some wedding show."

"Your father met with Morty yesterday. He denied everything you said he did."

"He's a filthy liar!" she snapped and then sighed when she realized she'd been a little too loud.

There were eight couples in the room, all standing in the center, waiting for the music to start. The guy Sam suspected she was supposed to be partnered with was standing near Malayka. The television host Gary had referred to was, in fact, sitting in a chair with her notepad, scribbling something.

"We know he's lying, but we plan to go about firing him in the most diplomatic way possible," Gary told her. "Right now Kris is looking into the man's work, press releases he's written, reporters he's had dealings with. The goal is to find something—anything—else that can be used to relieve him of his duties. Our hope is that having his own scandal wrapped around his neck will keep him from saying anything negative about the royal family."

"Great. He gets handled with kid gloves while I get put on the hot seat," she quipped, more quietly this time.

"Is this considered the hot seat?" Gary asked. "Dancing? Or am I making you hot?"

"No, no, you're not making me...hot," she argued. "What I meant to say was I shouldn't be the one in the spotlight when he was the one out of order."

"Yes," he said. "He was out of order and we're going

to take care of him. But right now we have to take care of this."

"This," she added with a sigh, "is ridiculous, too."

Then Sam chided herself. Once again, this was not the way the Samantha DeSaunters that the world knew and loved acted.

"All right, all right, listen up, listen up!"

A short, round guy whose complexion was a little too close to a tangerine for his tan to be natural, made his way to the center of the room. He wore silver rings on each of his stubby little fingers, and a chocolate-brown suit. The shirt beneath the suit was canary yellow. The gold chains hanging midway to his protruding stomach were gaudy and Sam wasn't certain they were even real. His hair was a pasty, lacquered, brown color, combed down on the sides and swerving across the front of his forehead in a fan type of design.

"My name is Gerard Parmingham of the Parmingham School of Dance." He spoke as if everyone in the room should be familiar with either his name or the school's reputation.

Sam had never heard of either.

"We're going to start with the tango," he said with a flourish of one arm going up in the air and a snap of his fingers and clapping of his feet.

Somebody chuckled.

Gerard immediately frowned. "So everyone must pay attention and listen closely to what I say. If you listen to what I say, you will look wonderful. If you do not listen to what I say, you will look like crap. If you look like crap, Princess Malayka will not be pleased. If Princess Malayka is not pleased...well, let's just not go there.

"Now," he continued, moving to stand in the center of the room as all the couples formed a circle around him, "this dance will serve as the bride and groom's first dance. They will walk to the center of the floor, do a solo performance. Very sexy. Very lovely. We'll practice that." The last was said with a smile toward Malayka.

Malayka and the man that was supposed to be Sam's partner had made their way to the center of the room, close to Gerard. The instructor was now positioning them in an intimate fashion that had the man blushing and Malayka smiling widely.

"About five minutes into the beautiful solo dance, each couple will join them on the floor. You will move gracefully." Gerard demonstrated with more flourishing of his arms and an exaggerated step of his feet. "You will form a circle around the happy couple as you are now. Your dance will start together, in an embrace like this."

The woman who wore glasses and her partner were the subject of Gerard's positioning at the moment. The man's arm went around the woman's waist, his other hand was tucked tightly into hers, and then Gerard put his hand on both of their backs and pushed them closer together.

"Tight. Tight. Together, that's what you will do. This is a very sensual dance. Think of beautiful seductive dresses, intoxicating cologne on men garbed in tuxedos, great music and then, of course, sex." He finished with a salacious smile and a bouncing of his eyebrows.

It was sort of like the circus when everyone would watch the act in the center ring for entertainment purposes. He was exuberant and excitable, and he was getting on Sam's nerves. She felt the beginnings of a headache coming on. This was going to be the longest two and a half hours of her life. And when she wanted nothing more than to run screaming out of the room, she found herself being drawn closer into Gary's embrace.

As the music began, so did his steps.

"Pay attention! Watch Gerard. Look what Gerard is doing! One, two, three. One, two, three. One, two, three."

He continued and Sam cut a glance over at him because despite hating being here, she did not want to look like a fool at the wedding. That was simply unacceptable. She watched Gerard's movements until she was turned quickly in a lavish move that literally almost swept her off her feet. When she came to her senses and looked into Gary's eyes, it was to see him smiling at her.

Sam was no stranger to ballroom dancing. She'd taken many classes as a young girl, but it wasn't high up on her list of fun things to do. As a matter of fact, the only time she ever found herself in a dancing embrace was at formal functions. But her partners were usually older men who had nothing on the easy, seductive rhythm that Gary seemed to possess.

"Don't tell me you know how to tango?"

He shrugged.

"My mother loved to watch *Dancing with the Stars*. It made her happy to perform the dances she saw on television in the middle of our living room. It was the least I could do for her and, in my eyes, she was always the grand prize winner."

Not only was there a strength he naturally exuded, Sam also realized that she would have to contend with how attractive she found him in his jeans, black boots and black T-shirt. So unlike the attire of the men she was used to being around, and yet it fit him perfectly. The sentiment and the genuine emotion she could hear in his voice when he spoke about dancing with his mother was the clincher.

"I wasn't terribly bored watching the colorful outfits and hearing the sometimes scathing commentary from the judges," he continued. "I will admit it was a little uncomfortable while I was doing the tango with my mother, but I got the hang of it. And she loved it."

He swayed to the rhythm of the music and Sam followed as best she could. The tango wasn't one of the dances she was used to doing. She vaguely remembered some of the moves she'd been taught years ago, but admitted to herself she was nowhere as good as Gary.

"Yes, this is it," Gerard said as he came up to them. "The close embrace technique. Everybody look at the way these two are connected. Not only chest-to-chest, but also at the hips, their thighs—they are blended as one."

He was right about that, Sam thought as heat radiated throughout her entire body due to said closeness. The instructor's comments seemed to give Gary more leave because he held her even tighter, his fingers just skimming the lower part of her back. His other hand held hers tightly. Their bodies were flush, almost plastered to each other in the way that a couple making love would be connected.

Sam cleared her throat and tried to focus on the dance, and only the dance.

Gerard was saying something to another woman now. Again, Sam found herself gazing at the one who had been wearing the ridiculous glasses last night at dinner. The woman complained that her partner had two left feet.

A part of Sam wanted to rejoice; not only was her partner good-looking, he was also damn good on the dance floor. Unfortunately, Sam wasn't certain rejoicing was what she should be doing at the moment. When she'd awakened this morning, she was fairly sure that the likelihood of her being in a man's arms again was slim to none. Yet here she was, not only in Gary's arms, but thoroughly enjoying being there.

Was it hot in here now?

Were her nipples hardening as her breasts rubbed against his chest seductively?

When he ground his hips into hers and used his tight grip around her waist to guide her into the same motions, did she feel a throbbing in her center? Was he awakening something in her she had long since abandoned?

Too many questions.

After talking with Roland last night, she'd come to the conclusion that she was going to take his advice. She was going to let things play out. And by "things" she meant the nuptials between her father and Malayka. Not whatever this was that was brewing between her and Gary.

And brewing it definitely was.

As the dance continued, the two of them seemed to grow more familiar. She knew when he turned her again and dipped her deep that she would be held securely in his arms. There was no fear of falling because the look in his eyes said he would never let her go. When she was pulled back up to a standing position his leg was between hers and, on instinct, Sam relaxed into the sultry rhythm of the moves mixed with the music. She swayed in a motion that had her riding his thigh. If she'd thought her body was reacting to him before, the quick jump and throb in her center, the swelling of her breasts and the quick intake of air had her admitting she hadn't imagined anything.

There was another part of the dance where his face was close to hers, their lips only a whisper a part.

She wanted to kiss him. Again.

And again.

"Perfect! Perfect!" Gerard was yelling.

Seconds later he was clapping Gary on the back. The spell was broken—or it should have been. The music had stopped. Yet Gary didn't release her. Everyone stared at them, again. Sam attempted to pull away from him but this time Gerard was the one pushing them close together the same way he had with Malayka and her partner.

"This is how it should be done. Now, let's take it from the top and everybody watch these two. They've got it! The sex, the allure, the intensity. Like passion put to music. Again! Again!" the little cherub-like man continued and the music started once more.

"Well, you heard the man," Gary said as he folded her into his embrace once more. "Let's show them how it's done."

He smiled at her this time. A wide, crooked grin that turned all that heat that had been swirling throughout her body into a blustery storm. She took his hand and this time melted into the embrace.

Let it play out. She thought back to Roland's words. Just let this play out and it, too, would be over soon. Right?

Sam spoke of the changes to the island from the late 1800s as they stood amid the ruins of an old oil refinery. At that time, Grand Serenity was under the control of Abraham Chapman and the British government, leading up to the year-long battle in the early 1950s. After lunch, the entire wedding party, Gerard and Malayka included—had traveled to the far eastern side of the island. Buildings were old mounds of rubble and decay having been left as a historic symbol marking how far the islanders had come.

Gary listened intently although he'd already read all about Grand Serenity's history and the DeSaunters family's rise to power.

"Marco Vansig had been governor of the island by this time and he ruled with an iron fist. Vansig destroyed the monuments and any remnants from the Chapman rule and basked in the riches that continued to flow through the now numerous gold mines and refineries around the island." Sam was speaking to the group.

"This is one of the early oil refineries that was eventually bled dry by Vansig, the proceeds of which never made it to the islanders. Everything went to Vansig. He was notorious for his womanizing and gambling and his overall flashy lifestyle."

She looked amazing standing tall and proud in front of a cracking tower, its stones turned dark and dirty from a combination of salty seawater; warm, humid air; and lack of care. Her hair had been pulled back, held with a colored tie that matched the light pink, sleeveless top she wore with the formfitting white skirt decorated with large pink and black flowers. She looked fresh and young, like a woman sure of her place in this world and certain that everyone was always watching her in it. Whether or not that was a good thing, Gary hadn't concluded. He did know, however, that Samantha wore it well.

Regal, rich, intelligent, sexy. All of it she wore like a second skin and made it look effortless.

"Just down the road there is a pathway leading to the beach. This is where the army of islanders led by my grandfather, Josef Marquise DeSaunters, who had grown tired of Vansig's tyrannical rule, traveled to begin their sneak attack on Vansig and the palace." She lifted an arm to point in the direction and was greeted with a few grumbles from the crowd.

"There's too much walking on this tour," the woman with the glasses complained.

Her name was Sylvia. Gary had made a point to speak with her at lunch because he'd overheard her talking about his and Samantha's dance.

"I'll bet they're getting it on in every room of that big

ol' palace," she'd said to Evelyn, the woman who had been sitting with her last night.

"Ew, I hope not in the bed I'm sleeping in," Evelyn had replied.

"Who said anything about using a bed? He looks like the type to just pick a girl up and have his way with her right against the wall. Did you see how he was holding her and looking at her? Pure, unadulterated lust, I tell you."

"You think so?" Gary had said when he'd interrupted their conversation. "I was hoping we were doing the dance correctly. From your comments, I take it that we were."

"Oh, well, we weren't gossiping about you and the princess or anything like that," Evelyn had hurried to say. "Sylvia just meant that the two of you looked so good on the dance floor. So realistic."

"Evelyn's right," Sylvia'd chimed in, not appearing the least bit apologetic. "You looked as if you two knew each other's bodies and the moves of that dance personally. Anybody watching would draw the same conclusion."

Gary doubted that, but it had felt good to let the women know he was well aware of what they thought about him and Samantha. He had left them with a warning about spreading lies. "You're too pretty to have your nose growing longer because you can't separate fact from fiction."

Evelyn had looked embarrassed but smiled, anyway. Sylvia had looked devious and hadn't bothered to hide the fact.

Now it was Sylvia who was complaining as she'd begun to walk toward Samantha. But Malayka stopped her friend and continued to approach the princess herself.

Gary, who had been standing a few steps to the left behind Samantha, moved in closer to eavesdrop.

"How much longer is this going to take?" Malayka asked. "And why are you showing us war things? I want them to see how pretty the island is, not hear about a violent past."

"Our past is the reason for our present," Samantha replied diplomatically.

Gary wanted to applaud her for taking the high road when she could've so easily responded another way.

"Whatever," Malayka quipped. "Let's just get on with this. And when we get down to the beach, let me do the talking. The TV people will want to hear about the beach being a good location for wedding ceremonies and such."

"I don't think now is the right time for that," Samantha told her. "We should keep this outing about the history. Tourists find that interesting in addition to just going for how a place looks."

Malayka chuckled. "Who are you kidding? That's just nonsense. But I should have known, especially since you've never planned a wedding. I'll take it from here."

Malayka turned back to face the crowd. She was about to speak when the first shot rang out. It exploded against the corner of the tower, directly above Samantha's head. Gary reacted instantly, throwing his body over hers as he yelled, "Get down!"

Chapter 7

Her hands were shaking as she gripped the sides of the soaker tub and lowered her body into the steaming, fragrantly bubbled water. When she was seated, Sam lay back in an even slower motion until her neck rested on the lip of the tub. She closed her eyes and tried to block out everything.

The gunshots.

The shattering rock.

The screams.

Gary's full body on top of hers.

Her eyes shot open at her last thought. Clearly keeping them closed wasn't working, anyway. She rubbed her hands down her face then pushed back the tendrils of hair that had escaped the tight high ponytail she'd made when she'd finally closed herself in her rooms.

Gary had picked her up off the ground and run to one of the parked cars. He had her in the backseat and was yelling at Phillipe to drive within seconds of the last shot. Twenty minutes later they were at the palace. Kris and Roland were both at the front doors when they came in. Salvin, the chief of guards, was also there, four other guards standing with him.

"I'm fine," she'd said immediately upon walking into the foyer.

It had been the third time she'd said it in the last few minutes. It had apparently taken more than one time for Gary to understand and not scoop her into his arms again. That whole "being carried away" scene made her uncomfortable. Not as uncomfortable as being shot at, but still. She'd decided to deal with the things she could and, at the time, that was appeasable for her.

Dammit.

"What the hell happened?" Ro had asked before grabbing her into a tight hug.

Sam had accepted the hug because, of course, her brothers would be concerned about her. But she'd pushed back from the embrace when it had lasted too long and she'd felt the dam inside her threaten to break free.

"Shooter," Gary was saying from behind her. "The entire area was checked a half hour before we arrived. Then the extra guard that rode in each car got out and checked again before the tour began."

Kris hugged her, rubbing his hand down the back of her head as he pulled back and stared at her as if his questioning gaze was going to solicit a different response.

"I'm fine, Kris," she had stated again. "Really."

He hadn't believed her, but he had backed off, releasing her so that she could turn to face Gary.

"Thanks," she had told him, taking a breath because her legs were beginning to tremble. "Thank you for being there and for saving my life."

He was shaking his head before she could finish speaking.

"No thanks necessary. I just want you to be safe," he'd told her.

Sam had been okay with that reply. Or, at least, she was going to have to be. The thought of arguing or debating at that moment was definitely going to be more than she could bear. No, she'd been wrong. In the next seconds, when Gary had stepped closer to her, he'd touched a hand to her shoulder. His next words, "I want you to be safe," had tipped the scale on her tolerance.

She had only been able to nod in reply before turning and taking the marble steps as quickly as she could without falling on her face and creating even more of a spectacle. There'd been enough eyes on her for one day, enough thoughts and glares and judgments. She hadn't been in the mood for any more.

Now she was in the tub, closed in her prettily decorated lavender, gray and white bathroom. Vanilla-scented candles were burning, the lights were turned down low and she was relaxing—or, at least, she was trying to relax. Only, her shoulders were still tight, her neck ached and, dammit, she could not stop shaking.

Every part of her body was shaking now. Her fingers, her arms, her legs, her toes. Even her head was moving as she uselessly fought back tears. She bit her bottom lip and resisted the urge to sob. She wasn't a baby. Yes, she'd been shot at, but she was still living, still breathing. She should just be grateful and…

More tears came and now her teeth were chattering. Her shoulders jerked and before she could think of how to stop it, a sob broke free.

The shots had been so loud and people had been screaming. Gerard may have been screaming the loudest. When she'd caught sight of him, he was lying on his stomach, arms folded over his head, crying like a child. Sam hurriedly used her hands to wipe the tears from her face. She took several deep breaths, releasing them very slowly so as to calm her racing heart. It worked, sort of, and the tears finally ceased.

"Okay, get it together, Sammy," she chided herself. "There's someone trying to kill your family. That's not a surprise."

No. It wasn't a surprise, she answered herself, but it wasn't a cheerful thought, either.

"At least he was there to save you," she continued. "Again."

"He" was Gary, of course. And, yes, he'd saved her. He'd pushed her to the ground with his body and lay there until the shots stopped. His broad shoulders and muscled chest were easily wider than the width of her body, which meant he'd completely covered her. His body was on top of every part of hers.

Sam shivered, even though the water was hot against her skin.

He'd been standing behind her the entire time she'd talked to the group. Just as he'd sat next to her during lunch and he'd danced with her during the lessons. Boy, had he danced with her. The memory had Sam flushing.

It was silly. All of this was just plain ridiculous. She'd seen Gary around the palace for the last two months but until the other day she hadn't even known his name or why he was there. Yet she'd kissed him twice and today they'd danced as if a night of hot steamy sex was definitely in their future.

It wasn't just silly. It was impossible.

She was attracted to him.

Very attracted to him.

That was a problem because Sam hadn't been this attracted to a man since her college years in Paris. Kris had gone to the United States for college and Roland had opted to join the Royal Seaside Navy. Sam had flown to Paris on a fashion scholarship she'd been awarded just because of who she was.

Since she was a little girl there had been agents approaching her father about the possibility of her entering into modeling or beauty pageants. Sam had never been interested in either. Both occupations would put her in the public eye much more than she actually wanted to be. Sure, as Grand Serenity's goodwill ambassador she was still in the public, but that was her duty. It was her birthright and there was nothing she could do about performing the job her mother had left vacant.

Accepting the scholarship had been Sam's way of getting off the island and finally having time to just be a young woman and not a princess or a goodwill ambassador. She'd enjoyed that time even if the curriculum was less than she'd desired. And then she'd come home to do what was expected of her.

She always did what was expected.

Her eyes closed again and this time her internal body temperature was foremost in her mind. She felt just as she had when she'd been dancing with Gary. Hot. Agitated. Aroused.

"That's it," she said with a sigh.

Last night she was restless. Yesterday and today she was irritable. Now, even after she'd had a near-death experience and fretting over the life that she'd had no choice in, she knew what the real problem was.

She was horny.

That was probably unacceptable for a lady, especially a princess. But it was just that. Sam recognized the tugging in her center and the swelling of her breasts. She should have known when the night of the council dinner she'd been so eager to run across that room and kiss a man. At that moment she'd thought it was just some man she'd seen around the palace. She definitely should have known better because she'd enjoyed that kiss way too much.

Now she was jittery and emotional and in desperate need of release. She was clearly in the desire stage of sexual pleasure. And if anyone ever heard her say such a thing aloud they'd likely think she'd lost her mind. But she hadn't. Sam knew her body well. She'd taken the time to get to know it's every warning and signal. That was her right and her decision to make.

Knowing her own body and being able to give it what it needed was the best solution for the life she had to lead. Love and relationships weren't in the cards because there was no way she could ever trust a man to want her and only her. Not the title. Not the money. Not the recognition. Only her.

She'd learned that lesson the hard and painful way when her three-month relationship with Miguel Lopata was publicized on the front page of a Parisian tabloid with pictures of them necking on the couch in his apartment. Miguel had sold those pictures and the story of their romantic affair. He'd also taught her a very valuable lesson that Sam had carried with her ever since.

With her eyes still closed she moved her now steadier hand to her breast and massaged slowly. Her body instantly reacted as her breast seemed heavier than usual, and her breath quickened. Sam knew this part well and continued without any further recriminations. She would feel better afterward, much better, and then she could deal with the other issues swirling around in her life. She just needed this little bit of leverage. Damn, she needed it.

Her other arm slipped from the side of the tub, her hand skimming down her torso until she felt the short curls of pubic hair. In seconds she was touching herself, pleasuring herself. The sound of her moans echoed in the bathroom. Her mind went void of anything but the pleasure; the moment she would reach that precipice and soar higher than she had the last time she'd done this. Each time she aimed higher, needed more, because this, right here, was all she had in her life. It was all that she would ever have.

When her legs trembled, her teeth bit into her bottom lip and her body vibrated with each spine-tingling muscle spasm that pulsated through her. She moaned slower this time, louder and longer as she rode that glorious wave.

It took a few minutes before her breathing returned to normal and, when it did, so did everything else.

"Damn!"

Sam cursed herself and felt deflated at her inability to meet her own challenge. She hadn't soared higher. She didn't feel much better than she had before. She was still worried and still afraid and, dammit all, still aroused.

Gary was mad as hell.

He'd been in Kris's office for the past hour going over everything that happened that day. It all ended with the shots being fired, just barely missing Samantha's head.

"The guards combed that entire area but didn't find anyone," Kris reported after hanging up the phone on the edge of his desk.

"This is bullshit!" Roland raged. "Now she has somebody shooting at us? How much more of this are we going to take without doing something?"

"We don't know for certain that Malayka is connected to this," Kris stated evenly. "I know we're all thinking it, but we have to have something more concrete than just our dislike of her before we go to Dad. And, yes, we have to go to him first, before we even think about slapping cuffs on the woman he's planning to marry."

Gary had been sitting in one of the guest chairs across from Kris's desk. He'd only sat because when he was standing he paced the floor like a lion stalking its cage. He definitely wanted out. He wanted to track down the shooter himself and strangle the bastard. He'd much rather have his own rifle and scope. He'd watch that fool for hours, making sure he felt perfectly safe before Gary finally pulled the trigger, killing the son of a bitch.

Yes, he wanted him dead, even though Gary knew Kris would prefer him to be alive for questioning. Gary was beyond that point. The second he'd watched that bullet pierce the stone wall just inches above Samantha's head, he'd known the capture-and-question part of this job was over. For him, anyway.

Unfortunately, however, Kris was right in what he'd just said to Roland. They still had no evidence that Malayka was involved.

"As a matter of fact, she was standing pretty close to Samantha when the first shot rang out. A few inches to the left and she could have caught the bullet. I doubt she's in on her own murder plot," Gary told them.

His elbows were planted on his thighs and he'd been holding his head down, staring at the floor as he tried to gain some semblance of control before speaking to the princess. His control wasn't really cooperating but Gary knew he had to add his comments to their conversation.

"So you're saying the bullet could have been meant

for Malayka?" Roland asked. "I'm not buying that for one minute."

Gary was shaking his head as he sat back in the chair. "I'm not trying to sell that," he replied. "I'm just stating the facts. Malayka was standing right there. So if she were in on the plot to kill one or all of you, why would whoever she's in cahoots with have fired a shot that could have easily taken her out instead?"

"He's right," Kris stated. "It doesn't add up."

"None of this adds up!" Roland continued. "Dad wants to act like its some political strike against us, but Sam swears we have no enemies on the political front. You think it might be someone who's banking with us because of the break-in at the bank just before the explosion. But even that investigation hasn't turned up any leads. So what are we supposed to do now, just sit here and wait until whoever these people are finally get it right and kill us all?"

"No," Gary said as he stood. "We're not going to wait. Not anymore. It's time to put more pressure on the prisoners and get some real answers out of them. If they still won't talk, we go to the next best source. Their family members. Find the people that are closest to them and see what they know, who they know. That's how we'll start to connect the dots and, as soon as we get a target, I'm taking him out."

Gary didn't wait for any agreement or rebuttal. He turned and headed for the door. There was something he needed to do, something more urgent than sitting there talking about a plan that needed to be put into effect ASAP.

Gary approached Samantha's room with the cautious steps of his former profession. He kind of felt like he was stalking his prey the moment he'd decided to climb the stairs to see her.

Logic and reasoning said he should have gone back to his room to go over his notes about all the players in the palace situation. He should make some calls to find out more about the two men sitting in the Grand Serenity jailhouse. They were the key. He knew that without a doubt. One of them knew exactly what the endgame to this little plan was and if Gary just applied more pressure, if he used some of his military training, he was certain he could break them.

Yet, that's not what he'd done.

He probably should not have walked out of the meeting with Kris and Roland, either. For all intents and purposes they were his employers, even though Gary had refused Kris's offer of monetary reimbursement. Roland wanted to take action. Gary could definitely understand that and he respected the fellow military man for his quick thoughts and plans for immediate action. At the same time, Gary also knew the logic in what Kris was saying. They had to be sure that when they acted, there would be no mistakes because their father's happiness was at stake. No, that wasn't more important than their lives; Gary, of course, understood that, as well. But it was important to each of them.

Regardless of how much sense that all made, it hadn't kept him in that office with Roland and Kris.

There was something much stronger than logic and reason pulling him in Sam's direction. Something he wasn't certain he knew how to handle but that he was sure he wasn't going to ignore for much longer. Not at this point.

He knocked softly, restraint biting at him as he tried to prepare what he was going to say to her. He just wanted to make sure she was all right. No, that was wrong. Gary *needed* to see that she was all right. He needed to hear her say she was fine and for those words to actually match the look in her eyes when she did. When she'd said it so many times to him over an hour ago, he'd known she was lying. Fear and trepidation had clung to her like a bad cold. She'd wanted to be fine, of that he was sure, but the emotion hadn't been there for her and the lie had just made it worse.

He should have protected her better. He should have known there would be another attempt and he should have been more prepared. He should have—

"What are you doing here?" Samantha asked the moment she opened the door.

"I need to know that you're all right," he said and then didn't wait for her to ask him in, but instead stepped so close to her that she would have had no choice but to step back.

No, that's not what Samantha did and a part of Gary almost smiled at his misstep.

Samantha DeSaunters was not like any other woman he'd ever come across in all his travels. Sure, she was pretty on the outside, but she had so much going for her beyond the beauty. More than Gary even thought her family realized.

Right now, she was looking up at him as if she were either about to push him back into the hallway and slam the door in his face, or curse him out so he'd turn and scurry off like a properly scolded pup.

She didn't know him that well. He didn't falter easily. In fact, he had no intention of backing down, regardless of how she looked at him.

"I'm not prepared for company," she told him.

He nodded. "Good, because this is not a social call. I'm here to check on you and I don't want you hurrying me off the way you did earlier. So, I'm asking you to please let me in."

It was as nice as he could manage when what Gary really wanted to do was to scoop her up in his arms and carry her into her bedroom. And then what?

He didn't have a chance to finish that thought as she huffed and finally stepped to the side.

When she closed the door, she stayed there, leaning against it with her arms folded firmly across her chest. When he realized she hadn't followed him farther into the sitting area of the room, Gary turned and looked at her. That's when he noticed that her hair was down, hanging around her shoulders in squiggly strands that told him it was wet. She wore a light pink robe that looked fluffy and soft wrapped around her body.

His gaze shot back up to her face. No makeup. The folds of the robe dipped low so that her long neck and a sizable portion of skin were visible.

Bare.

Naked.

Gary swallowed hard at the thought that she was naked beneath that robe.

"Tell me you're okay. That what happened earlier is now pushed out of your mind and you're not afraid, not worried," he said quickly. "And tell me the truth, Samantha. I really need you to be perfectly honest with me right now."

Because if she didn't he would have to stand in this room even longer. And Gary was certain that if he did that, they wouldn't remain standing. He would not remain clothed and she would not continue to hold him at bay with a look or crossed arms.

He probably should have listened to his inner reason and logic before coming to her quarters.

"I'm fine," she said and then hurried to continue. "I wasn't earlier, that's true. I was shaken up. But I've had a chance to calm down and to try to relax."

"How did that work for you?" he asked, holding her gaze.

Her eyes seemed wider now, her lashes long even without the makeup she usually wore. The skin of her face was smooth in its natural mocha hue.

She cleared her throat. "It worked," she replied. "I feel much better."

"Really?" he asked and took a step closer.

His mind screamed, *What the hell are you doing?* But his body was in full control now.

"Because I keep trying to relax when I'm around you. It doesn't work. Hell, I can't relax when I'm away from you."

"Gary," she started and tried to back away as he approached. But she was at the door. There was nowhere to go unless she planned to run out into the hallway.

"Samantha," he said her name and could hear the complete desperation in his voice. It was different and just a bit on the side of scary, but Gary admitted there was nothing he could do about that. Not now.

"When I first saw you, I knew you were going to be different," he admitted. "I've watched you every day for the past two months. I've listened to you talk. Seen you eat, laugh, smile. Every time, everything is so potent, it's like a surprise body blow."

"Stop right there," she said and held up a hand.

That hand shook and Gary stopped.

He was less than a foot away from her.

She licked her lips nervously and spoke in a voice that was less than composed.

"I saw you around the palace time after time. But I

never knew who you were or why you were here. I didn't think anything of it until I saw you at the dinner and then I just…"

"You kissed me."

"I did," she admitted with a nod.

"And you liked that kiss," he continued. "Truth. Only the truth. Here. Now. Between us."

She squared her shoulders and gave a little shake of her head as she replied, "I liked it. I didn't mean to, but…I did."

He lifted a hand, touching his fingers lightly to her chin, moving one finger until it ran along the line of her bottom lip.

"The next time I kissed you," he spoke quietly.

She sighed. "I liked that, too."

"So did I," he replied eagerly. "I liked it so much, I can't stop thinking about doing it again. And again."

"We shouldn't," she told him, the hand that she'd been holding up now crushed between their bodies.

"I know," he said, his gaze dropping from her eyes to his finger on her lip. "But I don't think I can stop it. I don't think *we* can stop."

"We have to." She gasped. "I should have never started this," she whispered.

As she spoke, his finger moved quickly, touching the tip of her tongue.

Blood pounded loud and fast in his ears and Gary leaned in closer, until his lips were only an inch from hers.

"It doesn't matter who started what and when. Now it's time to finish it."

Chapter 8

"It doesn't matter who started it." Gary spoke in a husky tone as he lifted her into his arms and moved toward her bedroom. "Tonight, it will be finished."

He kissed her again and she eagerly joined in, wrapping her arms tightly around his neck. The door to the bedroom was open and he walked quickly inside, tearing his mouth away from hers only long enough to catch sight of the bed and carry them both there. By the time his knees hit the side of the bed, he was going down with her, bracing his fall with his elbows on the mattress.

She gasped as their lips parted again. Then, with her hands at the nape of his neck, she pulled him close for another kiss. He couldn't get enough of her. The taste of her on his tongue was intoxicating. The way she was kissing him back said she felt the same. Thrusting his hands between them, Gary quickly undid the belt of the robe and pushed the material aside.

He moaned when his hands touched the bare skin of her torso.

She felt like silk, he thought as he pulled back, nipping her bottom lip one last time before breaking their contact completely. For what seemed like forever he stared down at her flawless skin. She was beautifully made, he thought as he trailed his fingers down from her neck, between the valley of her breasts and farther until he circled her navel. She was quiet as he continued to explore, as if she were waiting and wondering what he thought.

"I won't say you're beautiful," he told her when he looked up to see her staring at him.

"I didn't ask you to," she replied and reached for the edges of the robe.

She attempted to pull it around her, to cover the exquisite sight before him, but Gary stopped her. He held her wrists down at her sides and leaned in so that his nose almost touched hers.

"I won't say it because I'm sure you've been told that by other men. Many other men," he continued and tried like hell to swallow the ball of jealousy that had just formed in his throat. "I don't want you thinking of any of them now. Not when I'm with you. Not when I'm inside you."

The final words came out in a rough gravelly tone as the last lines of control in him began to fray.

"I don't sleep around," she said.

Gary shook his head. "No. You don't," he agreed.

Not for one moment did he believe that Samantha was the type to entertain multiple sex partners. He knew that, even without also knowing that there had been hardly any stories printed or spoken to the contrary. In fact, for a princess, there was surprisingly little knowledge in the world about the personal life of Samantha DeSaunters.

She was known for keeping the personal away from the public, even while traveling the globe and constantly staying in the spotlight on behalf of her island.

He released her wrists and continued to push the robe off her body completely. There were simply no words for how good she looked, from the dark tips of her nipples down to the soft pink coat of polish on her toenails. She was simply delectable.

When he gave in to another urge and cupped one perfectly sized breast and leaned in to kiss the nipple of the other, she gasped and arched into his touch. He sucked her nipple into his mouth, gorging on the delicious taste of her. His other hand kneaded the softness until his erection was pressing so painfully against the zipper of his pants he wanted to yell out in agony.

She cupped her hands at the back of his head, holding him in place. Feeding him. Gary moaned. When she grabbed the wrist of his hand on her breast, he almost removed his mouth from her to ask what she was doing. Instead he waited a beat and realized she was leading him. Down her torso, past her navel, over the thin layer of curls at her mound, between the soft petals of her core. Gary fingered her clit and she sucked in a breath with a sound and motion so quick and potent he thought he might come in his pants from the excitement.

Wet, delicious desire soared through him as he touched her intimately. She'd moved a leg, dragging it across the mattress so that he had unfettered access to her. Gary kept his eyes closed and his tongue on her breast as his fingers glided over her wetness.

"Please."

It was said in the barest whisper and, for a moment, Gary thought he'd imagined it. But she'd grabbed his hand again, placing his fingers directly over the tightened bud of her clit once more. He tore his mouth away from her breast at that moment and moved so that now he could see what his hand had been enjoying. Again, she was exquisite, especially the way she was sprawled over the bed, her dark purple comforter a contrast to her creamy brown skin.

Gary watched his fingers moving over her and then slipped two fingers inside her. She grabbed the comforter in her hands and arched up off the bed. Her bottom lip was caught between her teeth, her eyes closed as she moaned. Gary knew exactly what she was feeling at this moment. She wanted to come and he wanted nothing more than to oblige her.

With his other hand, he placed two fingers on her clit and rubbed in sync with his thrusting fingers. His tongue moved over his now-dry lips as he continued to watch his hands on her and listened to her complete enjoyment. When her thighs began to tremble, Gary moaned louder than Samantha did. It was so sweet and yet so primal, touching her this way and watching her ride toward her climax.

She was shaking her head now, her still-damp hair splayed around her in a wild halo. Her body stiffened and Gary continued his motions, loving the feel of even more moistness, warm and sticky on his fingers.

A few seconds later, breaths heavy but her limbs relaxed, Gary watched her come down from her climax. Slipping his hand out of her and leaning over her once more, he kissed her softly on the lips. She moaned again and kissed him back.

Something in that kiss, in the way she wrapped her arms around him and held on tight, changed everything Gary had previously thought about the princess.

Every damn thing.

* * *

She'd soared.

No, she'd damn near flown right out of the strato-sphere by the simple touch of his hand. Or his hands, rather. His fingers…those dangerously excitable fingers.

Her body felt like Jell-O. Quickly dissolving Jell-O. He was now kissing her. Sam's body warmed with what she knew was probably the glow from a supreme climax.

"Oh, no," she gasped as she abruptly pulled away from the kiss. "I'm sorry."

He looked perplexed and Sam had to swallow the bit-ter taste of embarrassment as she quietly asked, "What about you?"

He appeared to be trying to figure out what she was saying and Sam almost groaned. She *did not* want to ac-tually have to say it, because it was hard enough deal-ing with the fact that she'd done it. Or rather she hadn't done it.

Sigh.

This might be more embarrassing than the pictures of her kissing Miguel being on the front page of that French newspaper.

"Oooohhh, that," he said finally and began shaking his head. "No worries. I'm good."

He was lying, she thought. And he wasn't very good at it.

Following her instincts, which she had been doing since he'd backed her up against the door, Sam let her hand move between them until her fingers scraped lightly over his still-burgeoning erection.

"No worries," he repeated once more and casually moved her hand away.

"Not worried," she told him as she moved to locate her

robe and securely wrap it around her once more. "Just wanted to be fair."

"Life's rarely fair," he replied glibly.

She tried running her fingers through her hair that she knew must look hideous right about now, but her fingers got stuck in the snags. Then she thought better than to try the painful act of detangling in front of him.

At his remark she shrugged. "That's cynical, but fair to say, I guess."

"I get the impression that you agree much more than you're letting on," he replied.

"No." She sighed and moved to sit on the other side of the bed. "I don't know what gave you that impression."

"The way you deal with your soon-to-be stepmother," he replied. "Is it that you just don't like her or do you simply not believe in true love and a blissful marriage?"

"For the record," she said, tossing him a look over her shoulder, "this is the worst after-sex conversation I've ever had."

"Touché," he said with a smile and a nod of his head. "I can do better."

Because she liked his smile way too much, Sam waved a hand at him. "It's okay, I'll answer. I don't like Malayka. She's controlling and opinionated."

He only stared at her and Sam sighed.

"Okay, so I can be controlling and opinionated, as well. I can admit my own flaws and still not like her for the same reasons. And, no, I don't believe in love and happy-ever-after. Not for everyone, anyway," she replied, hoping she didn't sound scorned.

Truth be told, Sam hadn't been in love with Miguel. And thanks to her time with him, she'd never given herself the opportunity to fall in love with anyone else. That meant, at twenty-five years old, she'd never been in love.

"How about you?" she asked, deciding they'd spent enough time on her.

He rubbed both hands down his face and leaned forward so that his elbows rested on his knees. They were both sitting on the side of the bed now, just a few inches apart. It was intimate—the fact that they were in her bedroom and on her bed.

"Do you believe in true love?" At his silence, she almost slapped herself on the forehead. "Oh, no, please tell me you don't have a girlfriend or are married. I didn't see a ring but that doesn't mean anything. You could be allergic to metal or something weird like that. Just please tell me—"

He held up a hand to stop her and turned to look at her. "Stop. No, I don't and I'm not. If I were I would have never suggested we take on this charade."

She let out the breath she'd been holding after he'd cut her off. Okay, he wasn't married. And, yeah, not okay, the charade.

"Look—" she began.

He held that hand up again. "Do you want me to answer the rest of your question first?"

Sam snapped her lips shut and nodded.

"I do believe in true love. My parents had it," he told her. "They were married for forty-two years before my father died of a heart attack. Two years after that my mother was diagnosed with colon cancer. She died three years later."

"Oh, I'm so sorry to hear that, Gary. I really am. And I'm sorry I made you talk about it."

"You didn't make me do anything. You asked a question. I had the choice of whether or not I would answer it."

He was right, so Sam said nothing else. This entire situation was just too weird. They were pretending to be lovers for the sake of the press and that sleazy Morty. It was all a ruse. Yet here they were, sitting on the side of her bed, while she was naked beneath her robe, her body still humming contentedly from the fantastic orgasm he'd given her.

"So what do we do now?" she asked.

After a moment or so he stood. A quick glance, which she probably shouldn't have taken, told her his arousal had abated. Why did that not make her happy?

Sam sighed and ran her fingers over her hair. What the hell was she doing? None of this was going the way it should, and for the first time she realized she wasn't actually in control of the situation.

"I'm going to head back to my room. Even though we're having an affair, I shouldn't be seen coming in and out of your bedroom."

"We're in the palace," she told him.

Why? Because she wanted him to stay? No, she definitely did not want him to spend the night. But talking to him hadn't been so bad. It had actually been the first time she'd been able to address—even if only in her mind— what Miguel had put her through and how it had eventually affected her entire life.

"House staff are the next likely suspects when any type of conspiracy or intrigue is going on with a family. Prostitutes are the first," he said in that tone he used often.

It was aloof and noncommittal. She didn't like it, but who was she to complain? Hadn't she built her entire life on a façade? The smile, the pleasantries, the goodwill— all at the supreme cost of ever hoping to have a real personal life. Sure, it was her duty, but it wasn't her choice.

Sam stood, too, and nodded her agreement to what

he'd said. Pulling her robe tighter around her body, she looked up at him.

"I'm glad this—" she motioned between them and the bed "—isn't awkward for either of us."

"We're adults who are capable of making our own decisions. That's what we did."

"And tomorrow things will be business as usual." She'd said it as a statement but in her mind she was asking a question. She was wondering if this had all happened for a reason. If Gary Montgomery so simply walking into her life and through the shield she'd long ago erected around herself was some act of fate. Her mother had believed wholeheartedly in fate, and, up until this very moment, so had Sam. Now she wasn't sure what the hell was going on.

"Tomorrow, I'll find out who the hell was shooting at you," Gary told her simply.

Sam once again nodded. She dismissed her personal thoughts and returned to the present issues surrounding her family. The real reason Gary was there.

"My schedule is clear tomorrow, so you don't have to worry about following me around. I'll be staying in the palace," she told him, even though she knew he had access to the calendar and could see that for himself. He likely already had.

It was his turn to nod.

They still stood in her room, neither of them taking any steps toward the door. Did he not want to leave?

Sam moved first, walking past him and out the door of her bedroom. Her bare feet trekked over the plush carpet, through the sitting area, and next she was turning the knob and opening the door. As she stepped back, her arms behind her, she knew he would be standing right behind her, even though she hadn't heard a sound from him as he'd moved.

"Get some sleep," he told her as he was about to move past her.

She'd already nodded and had just opened her mouth to say something when he stopped. He moved quickly, turning to her and wrapping his arms around her waist. He pulled her up fast and close, so close she came up on her tiptoes to stare into his face.

"What happened in there isn't over," he whispered.

Then his lips were on hers, taking her on a quick and fierce ride through a pleasure-filled haze. Her entire body reacted, so that when he finally let her go, she stumbled back against the door. That damn door again.

Gary left and Sam hurriedly closed and locked it behind her, seconds before falling back against it and sliding to the floor. She sat there thinking about what crazy and pleasurable hell she'd walked herself into this time.

Chapter 9

Sam's heart had broken into a million pieces late last night when her father had showed up at her door, grabbing her into a quick and tight hug that lasted for endless moments.

"Whatever I've done, whatever I need to do to keep you safe, I will. Never did I imagine them coming after you. I couldn't stand if anything happened to you because of something I did."

Sam could only hold on to her dad as his long arms wrapped tightly around her. He smelled of his favorite cigars and the cologne he always wore. It was an old and familiar scent that always made her feel comforted and loved. In the years immediately following her mother's death, at least an hour a day was spent in her father's arms. Sam had loved every minute of his attention. As an adult, there never seemed to be enough time for the cuddling with him, as they both led busy lives. And now he was about to get married…she'd shook her head and closed her eyes, inhaling her father's scent once more.

When Rafe finally released her he'd stepped inside her sitting room and they sat on her couch, side-by-side. Sam had already taken a shower and had just finished blow-drying her hair when her father knocked at her door. For an instant she'd thought it might be Gary again. There'd been a spark of excitement in the pit of her stomach, one she wasn't sure she should be nursing.

"How are you feeling?" Rafe asked, his thick fingers entwined with hers. "I hear you didn't come down for dinner."

Sam sighed and shrugged her shoulders. Being with her father never failed to make her feel just like a little girl again. She loved that feeling, even though she knew it would be short-lived.

"I'm okay. Just wanted some quiet for a while."

Rafe nodded. "I can understand that. Did Lucie bring you a tray?"

"Yes," Sam answered.

Lucie had brought her a bowl of Caribbean Pepper Pot with chicken and shrimp about half an hour before Gary had come to her room. While this was one of Sam's absolute favorite comfort foods, she had only managed to eat a few spoonfuls before giving up. She hadn't been in the mood to eat. Now, however, as she thought about the soup again, she wondered if she could go down to the kitchen to get another bowl.

"I know it was scary, Sammy-Girl, but I gotta tell you I'm glad that army guy was there with you. Kris told me how he shielded you with his own body," Rafe said.

Yes, she recalled Gary's body being on top of hers, on more than one occasion now.

"And I'm thankful to Dante for personally sticking closer to Malayka now," her father continued.

Sam did not reply.

Rafe looked over at her and smiled.

"You don't have to say it. I know that there is tension between you two. Between all of you, I should say," Rafe told her.

He looked tired, Sam noted. His deep brown eyes didn't have the light she was used to seeing in them. Even though he'd still called her Sammy-Girl as he often did when they were alone or around family, he hadn't tweaked her nose or winked at her, which had also been part of their private ritual. He still wore the charcoal-gray suit he'd donned this morning, but the yellow tie at his neck was now loosened and the top button of his shirt was undone.

"We just don't know her that well, Dad. And we're trying to give her the benefit of the doubt," she told him.

"I know and I'm working on that. I want us all to spend more time together, but it is difficult with our schedules," he told her. "I know that she's not at all like your mother."

"No," Sam replied immediately. "She's not."

When her father only nodded and stared off toward the fireplace and the mantel where Sam kept an 8x10 photo of her mother, Sam felt bad. It had been twenty years since Vivienne had been killed in that tragic accident. All those years, while Sam mourned her mother, Rafe had been mourning his wife. He'd never been with a woman in that time. At least, he'd never brought a woman to the palace or even introduced another woman to his children. Malayka was the first.

That meant something.

"I'll try harder," she told her father as the guilt rested in her gut. "Maybe I'll go through our schedules and plan a weekend at the villa in Greece. You love it there with those breathtaking views of the Aegean Sea. We could go out on the yacht for a day or two and bond."

The words sounded hollow to her but Sam hoped they didn't to her father. She would try, for him, but she wasn't so certain any amount of trying was going to work. Malayka didn't really want to get to know her stepchildren, she wanted to control them and this palace. That was it. However, Sam was certain her father wasn't in the mood to hear that.

"That sounds like a great idea. Maybe for the new year, once we return from our honeymoon. Check the calendars and clear the time for us all. I love that idea," Rafe told her.

He'd cheered up substantially then and, as they continued to sit, their conversation turned to his business this morning at the mills and an invitation from an American hospital to join forces in a project including teenage girls. One of Sam's most cherished causes. They did not speak of the shooting again or of Malayka. Both of which were fine with Sam.

Yet, still, the next morning, both were prominently on her mind. It was a rare Friday that she had nothing on her schedule and she intended to see to some things around the palace that had been neglected in the past few months. As Sam sat at her desk, drinking her morning tea and reading over the supply lists and meal plans that Lucie had also delivered to her room last night, Sam thought she might just have to add in a meeting with Kris and Roland.

They weren't telling her everything, Sam was certain of that fact. Why would someone try to shoot her? Why the explosion? Why tamper with the car they'd presumed her father would be riding in? There had to be a reason for all of this and, as much as she disliked Malayka, Sam couldn't figure out what the woman would have to gain if they were all killed *before* the wedding.

She wore simple black capri pants and a yellow top. With comfortable sandals on her feet, Sam finished her tea and then gathered all her paperwork into a folder and set out to take care of palace business. As she walked around her desk and was about to head for the door she stopped and looked over at the corner by the window. There was a highboy table there with four cherry-oak chairs. The cushions in the chairs were a darker shade of purple than the drapes at the floor-to-ceiling windows in her office. A lacy, white tablecloth covered the glass-topped table and there was a tea set waiting for the next official tea party.

Sam walked over to that table and ran her finger over the rim of a teacup, a smile easily forming at her mouth. She loved this set and loved the memory that accompanied it even more.

"It's beautiful, Mama," four-year-old Sam had said to the beautiful and vivacious Vivienne.

They'd been sitting on a soft-as-the-clouds white blanket and Vivienne had pulled each piece of the tea set carefully from a brown wicker basket.

"It's very delicate and requires great care," Vivienne had told her.

"Can I touch it?" At that age Sam had been willing to touch almost anything. That's how Roland had gotten her to touch that hideous whistling frog that eventually jumped away, frightening Sam and sending her flailing back into the pond where they weren't supposed to be playing.

"Yes, but be very careful, darling. Remember we must

take great care of the things that are most important to us," her mother had said.

"Like Daddy and Kris and Roland," Sam had replied.

Vivienne had nodded, her glossy black curls dancing at her shoulders. "Yes, baby, just like them."

Her mother had taught her so much that afternoon. How to properly hold a teacup, how much sugar was too much and when it was time to say she was finished, even if she really wasn't. Then, her mother had told her something else.

"One day when you have pretty little girls of your own, you'll show them all these same things. It will be our tradition, Samantha. You will carry on with your family, all the things that your father and I have taught you."

Sam shook her head now, staring down at the empty teacup, her finger shaking on its rim. How would her mother feel if she knew that there would be no family for Sam? There would be no little girls for Sam to share the tea sets with, or to tell how to hold their cup and to not take too many lumps of sugar. Sadness engulfed her and Sam almost didn't hear the knock at her door.

Clearing her throat, she rolled her neck and turned away from the table.

Sam walked out of the office without looking back and when she finally made it to the door, pulled it open with a smile already affixed to her face. It didn't falter when she saw Landry standing there instead of who she'd thought it would be.

"Well, good morning to you, too," Landry said, a fake frown and almost-grin on her face.

"Good morning. Sorry," Sam said. "I was just trying to leave and get started with my day. Kept getting sidetracked."

"Oh, then that's good. I was coming to get you to talk about where we want to have the fashion show," Landry said.

Sam nodded and checked to make sure she had slipped her cell phone into her back pocket. "That's fine. We can talk about that while I do a site check of the palace."

She'd headed toward the hallway, pulling her door closed behind her. Landry was now standing beside her.

"You do site checks of your house?" Landry asked her.

"Yes. When your house and property is larger than ten city blocks, you tend to view it more like a business than a home when it comes down to keeping it running smoothly."

"Which you do awesomely by the way," Landry told her as they headed down the long hallway.

"You're just saying that because you don't want me to pass any of my duties along to you," Sam added with a chuckle. "But you do know that you're now married to the Crown Prince of Grand Serenity, which means that one day you will be doing exactly what I'm doing."

That was a grim prospect, Sam thought, not only for Landry, but also for herself. She'd trained for this job all her life, only to have to pass it along to the next highest-ranking princess that came along. In this case, Landry, as Kris's wife, would be a higher rank than Sam. Once Malayka married her dad, then she would outrank Landry for as long as Rafe lived.

"You know, when Kris asked me to marry him, that was my only reservation," Landry told her.

"Really?"

Her sister-in-law nodded. "Yes. I did not want to be a princess. Hell, it was hard enough being a preacher's kid. I knew there was no way I could deal with a whole other set of rules to follow."

They both laughed. Sam had met Landry's father, Heinz Sr., and thought he was a great guy. When Landry's family had come to Grand Serenity for the wedding, they'd all stayed at the palace.

"Your family is great and you do much better than you give yourself credit for with rules and structure. You've adapted to island life while still running your business in the States. And now you're starting the magazine and organizing this fashion show. It's like you were meant to be here."

"Like destiny," Landry said with a nod as they approached the staircase. "I've thought about that a lot in the last few months. I mean, I didn't even really want to take on Malayka as a client, but what if I hadn't? I would have never met and married Kris, and I truly cannot think of my life without him now."

"You two are adorable," Sam said, thinking of how Kris had been so uptight and reserved before Landry had come to the palace.

Theirs hadn't been a whirlwind romance, but a slow burn, from what Landry had shared with her. So slow that it had almost fizzled out when Landry returned to the States and Kris took his time getting his butt in gear to go get her. That was the kind of love that Sam used to believe in. The kind that stood the test and came out the victor. Kris hadn't thought he would find love, hadn't wanted to do anything but his job, but then he'd fallen.

Sam was different, she thought. Her circumstances were much stickier than her brother's and, for that reason, she knew that the happiness she clearly saw on Landry's face would never be mimicked on hers.

"I've been thinking a lot lately about what it would be like if Malayka hadn't come here," Sam disclosed when they came to the bottom of the stairs. "Let's check out the atrium. There's great light in there and it's the one place where I don't think Malayka has any of the wedding planners camped out."

"This is going to be one spectacular wedding," Landry said as they turned and walked toward the east wing of the house.

"Yeah, spectacular. Complete with ballroom dancing and everything."

"Oh, yes. I heard about those training classes yesterday. How did they turn out?"

Sam groaned. "They were too good to be true. I mean, it felt too real to be... I mean, it was invigorating or rather—"

Landry turned, taking Sam by the shoulders. "Stop. Take a breath."

Sam did as she was told.

"Was Gary there?"

Sam nodded.

Landry narrowed her gaze at her.

"Was he close by at that time, too? I know he was thankfully right there when the shooting took place, but we're talking about at the dance rehearsal."

Sam nodded again.

"Oookay," Landry said, exaggerating the word, her smile spreading. "He was close like dancing with you?"

"Uh-huh." Sam finally made a sound.

"Dancing really close to you?"

"Really close," Sam answered.

"And you liked it?"

Sam bit her bottom lip and contemplated a lie. It wasn't going to work and, really, she needed to talk to someone about this. Keeping it inside and rationalizing on her own certainly wasn't working.

"I liked it a lot. I also liked when he came to my room last night and we, um, we sort of fooled around a little."

"You did not!" Landry exclaimed loudly.

A little too loudly.

With a shake of her head, Sam led her sister-in-law into the atrium and closed the double doors behind them.

"Yes, we did. Yes, it was good. And, no, I don't know what that means now."

"Well, it means that hot-ass, ex-army sniper guy wants you," Landry said with a chuckle.

"He used to be a sniper?" Sam asked and then shook her head. "See, that's another thing I'm having issues with. I don't even know this guy and I'm letting him bring me to... I mean, we're doing whatever it is we're doing."

She hadn't intended to give Landry as many details as she already had. Having never had a sister or even a very close friend, Sam wasn't totally sure how this "girl talk" thing worked.

"Kris and I knew each other for just a couple of weeks before our first make-out session. It was in the dressing room at the central pool," Landry told her.

Her sister-in-law's grin spread wide across her face as Sam figured she was recalling every second of that little interlude.

"My brother in a dressing room," Sam added with a shake of her head.

"Yes indeed and, girl, it was everything!" Landry continued.

Sam shook her head because against her will a visual was forming in her mind and she didn't want to give it any chance of sticking around. "I haven't been with a guy in years," she admitted.

Landry stopped smiling. "Years?"

"Yes."

"Wow."

"I know," Sam added with a sigh.

She walked over to the wall of windows, staring through one of the evenly cut frames of glass. The view from there was of the east lawn and the gardens. Vivienne had designed the space and now Kris supervised the groundskeepers on maintaining pristine conditions in Vivienne's honor.

"I decided a long time ago not to believe in needing a man in my life," she said quietly.

She was so quiet Sam wasn't even certain Landry had heard her, until the woman spoke from a short distance away to Sam's left.

"I can definitely relate to that," Landry said. "My dad believed in all that 'someone for everyone' and 'finding a soul mate' stuff. I didn't."

Sam looked over at her. "And yet you accepted things with Kris relatively quickly. How did you do that?"

Landry, who was wearing a lovely blush-colored sundress with a lace hem, folded her arms over her chest and stared at Sam seriously.

"I didn't accept anything," Landry told her. "The attraction was instant and way too hard to ignore. I figured we'd just go with that in the beginning, and then it would wear off and we'd both move on. I was so wrong about that."

"So it's normal for the physical desire to be…almost breathtaking?" That was the only word Sam could come up with to describe how she felt each time she was near Gary.

"It had better be," Landry replied with a chuckle. "If not, Kris and I did it all wrong. We were definitely into the physical way before our emotions got all tangled up in the process. But I think that was our foundation."

Sam nodded as if she understood, but she was still wondering if what she'd allowed herself to do with Gary made any sense at all.

"Every relationship needs a foundation to build from, Sam," Landry continued. "And no relationship builds with the same blocks. Love has no rules and no guidelines. You get there whatever way works for you. Does that make sense?"

Landry was smiling at her and Sam was about to shake her head, but then she got it. She really felt like she got every word Landry had just spoken to her.

"It does."

"Okay, good." Landry laughed again. "The important thing is to just follow your instincts. You're an intelligent woman and you're the only one who can say what is right or wrong for you."

"I've spent a long time being Grand Serenity's goodwill ambassador," Sam said, looking out the windows again. "Haven't really thought of myself as a woman in a while."

"That needs to start now," Landry said. "You are more than this title and its responsibilities. Kris had a similar issue that I presume each of you harbor because of the life you were born into. But if there's one thing I know from being one of six children, it's that you have to find your own road and walk it with your head held high. Nobody or no circumstance should dictate how you take those steps."

Landry was probably going to say more but her cell phone rang at that moment. "Sorry," she mumbled as she answered the phone she'd been holding in her hand.

"Oh, no, no problem," Sam insisted as she moved a little farther away to afford Landry some privacy.

It gave Sam a few minutes to think of what Landry had said and of what it meant to her.

She wasn't sure how things would go between her and Gary today, or the days following, for that matter. When she'd finally managed to fall asleep last night she still wasn't certain that she should have allowed him into her bedroom yesterday. What she was sure of was that the pleasure he'd brought her could easily be addictive. She'd thought about it often this morning, even after scolding herself for doing so.

"Hey, I've gotta head to my office and attempt to take care of a minor catastrophe back in the States. I do like this space and I want to continue our conversation, so can we meet up in an hour or so?" Landry asked.

"Sure. No problem. I'll be around all day, just give me a call when you're ready," Sam said.

"Great." Landry leaned in to hug Sam. "And trust yourself," her sister-in-law whispered. "Trust what you feel and what you want."

Sam nodded. "I will," she said and actually vowed to do just that.

Setting the file of papers she'd been carrying down near the windowsill, Sam continued to stare out at the beautiful summer day after Landry had left the room. The sea stretched for as far as she could see. A vision that used to amaze Sam when she was little. The first time she'd sailed from Grand Serenity to Miami she'd been certain they would get lost in the long stretch of blue water. Now, each time she thought of traveling from the island, she did so with enthusiasm to see what else was out there.

Now, she wondered, what else was there for her to see and learn where Gary Montgomery was concerned?

"Nobody believes you're really having an affair with an American."

His voice was raspy and cut into her thoughts like a dull knife. Sam turned to see Morton Javis standing just a few feet away from her.

"I'll admit to being taken aback by that kiss the other night, but I must say, after hearing you talk about him, I'm more disgusted now. But don't worry, darling, we can still work things out."

He'd moved a step closer to her and the white polka dots on the hot-pink tie he wore seemed to get larger. Morty was an average-size guy at about five feet, eight inches tall. He had a honey-brown complexion, a bald head and suspicious eyes. Today he wore a black suit with a white shirt and that bright tie. The handkerchief in his lapel pocket was a shade of lighter pink. But what really stood out was, always, the way he looked at her. Like he was dissecting her slowly. It creeped her out, but she refused to look away.

"You don't take hints well, do you, Morty?" Sam asked. She hadn't seen him since the ambassador's dinner, but she knew that her father had spoken to him about the things Morty had said to her. Gary said he'd denied everything, hence the reason they hadn't fired the sneaky bastard yet.

"What hint should I have taken?" he asked, his small lips turning up into a devious grin. "If you mean kissing that ex-soldier, I didn't believe that for one minute. Now, as for your 'fooling around' comment about him… Like I said, I'm a little disappointed about that. But I'm ready to make a true offer to you, Samantha."

"There's nothing you have to offer that I want, Morty. If I were you, I would actually be spending my time doing my job instead of pursuing this pointless endeavor."

He took another step closer and Sam felt her personal space being invaded. She could step back or even move around him to put distance between them, but, damn, she did not want to give him that satisfaction.

"Not pointless," he told her before licking his lips.

He was staring at her mouth and Sam actually felt like she might vomit in response.

"Just requires a little more finesse than I've been able to provide. But now I know exactly how to get what it is I want," he told her.

Sam crossed her arms over her chest at that point because she felt like she should do something to protect herself. It wasn't much, but at least if he stepped too close she'd be ready to push him back.

"I don't care what you want and I have no intention of giving it to you," she snapped.

"Oh, you're going to care, Samantha. You're going to care very much if I decide to publish the rest of those pictures of you from Paris three years ago."

Sam swallowed.

"Yes, I see you know exactly the ones I'm referring to," he continued. This time as he moved closer to her, he lifted a hand to touch her hair.

Sam was too stunned to move or block him.

"Apparently there were some the reporter had purchased that he hadn't had the opportunity to publish before the royal solicitors swooped in to save your pretty ass."

The crass way in which he'd said the last words had her rapidly blinking and she swallowed again. Then she leaned to the side, just far enough so that his fingers were no longer touching her hair.

"You're disgusting," she told him.

Morty shook his head. "No, my dear. That would be you. I've seen all the photos and paid that photographer a pretty penny for them. So you see, the choice is now yours. You can either accept my proposal of marriage or I will go straight to the press with those pictures. Now, what do you think Daddy and your two big brothers are going to say when they see their darling princess in such a compromising position?"

"They're going to kick your ass," Gary said from across the room. "But they'll have to stand in line because I plan to do a little damage myself first."

She hadn't heard him enter. From the direction he was walking, he must have used one of the side doors. But how had he known she was in there? How had he known that Morty would be there, too?

Morty turned and began shaking his head. "I don't think this is what they paid you for, Mr. Montgomery. But if you'd really like to act like your American counterpart...what was his name? Oh, yes, G.I. Joe," he continued with a chuckle, "then you should really request a higher salary."

Gary was in his face by that time, grabbing his pink tie and wrapping it around his fist before Morty could even consider defending himself.

"I'm going to tell you this once and you're going to listen because I kind of think you like breathing," Gary told Morty as he dragged the man across the floor and slammed his back against the wall.

Sam didn't know what to do. So much was happening and she knew she should say something, do something, but her body hadn't caught up to her mind just yet.

"Let me go!" Morty coughed. He was flailing his arms, attempting to punch Gary, but Gary was at least six inches taller than Morty and much broader. Morty's punches looked like slaps falling against Gary's pronounced biceps.

They were more prominent today because he wore a

T-shirt that looked like a second skin and cargo pants that made him appear even more like a soldier out of an action movie.

"I'll have the guards…arrest…you," Morty tried to continue.

With each word it looked as if Gary was pressing his fist tighter against Morty's larynx, causing the sounds to come from him to be a lot less coherent than she knew Morty had intended.

"You're going to get your blackmailing ass down to your office and pack up all of your stuff because today is your last day working here," Gary said gruffly.

"You…don't…have…authority. You…can't," Morty gasped.

"He's right," Sam said when she'd finally crossed to stand beside Gary. "You nor I have the authority to fire him. Only my father can appoint and dismiss royal staff. In the event that he's not available, Kris can do it."

"It will be done!" Gary yelled into Morty's face. "I'm a witness now, so that's all we need to make it effective immediately."

"I'll…the pictures… I'll," Morty tried to say.

Gary pushed harder, until Morty's eyes bulged.

"Stop it," Sam said. When he didn't, she grabbed his biceps, felt the steel stiffness of his flesh, but ignored it. "I said stop, Gary. Let him go."

"You're a piece of scum," Gary said. "The kind that I take great pleasure in squashing."

With that he released Morty and the man crumpled to the floor. "I'm calling the guards," Gary said as he turned to Sam. "You go to your room and I'll go talk to Kris."

Sam opened her mouth to tell him that she wasn't a fellow soldier or a member of his team. In fact, she out-ranked him, but he'd already started talking into what she figured was some hidden microphone. He was loud as he ordered the guards to come to the atrium ASAP and to escort Morty to his office to get his things.

When he finished speaking, he looked as if he was actually surprised that she was still standing there.

Guards came running into the room and before she could tell him what she'd been waiting to say while he was on the phone, Gary simply looked at her and said, "To. Your. Room."

He stalked across the floor, grabbed one of the guards and instructed him to take her upstairs. He was gone then, moving quickly out of the room while activity swirled around her. When the guard approached her, Sam yelled, "I don't need anybody to escort me anywhere! This is my house!" She felt like stomping her feet but remembered who and where she was and instead tilted her head upward and walked regally, on her own, to her room.

"I have news! He threatened her, man! That should be enough to fire his ass without any notice or risk of being sued," Gary said the moment he burst through the door to Kris's office.

Kris was nodding as Gary approached his desk. "Just got off the phone with Salvin. He gave me a quick rundown of what just happened."

"So you can fire that bastard right now, can't you? I mean, you should have heard him basically telling her that she would agree to marry him or he would blackmail her. She was right, he did intend to drag her and the family's name through the mud. I should have bashed his face in!"

He was pacing back and forth, adrenaline buzzing through his bloodstream like a potent drug. He'd gone to her room when she hadn't come down for breakfast, wanting to make sure she was okay with everything that had happened yesterday—the shooting and the aftermath between the two of them. But she'd been leaving with Landry just as he'd turned the corner in the hallway.

Gary didn't know what had made him follow her. Hell, he'd already known her schedule for the day. There had been no need to trail her like some lovesick puppy, or worse, a stalker, especially with Landry in tow. But he was neither and had calmly reminded himself that they were pretending. The affair they wanted the world to believe they had was just for show. Regardless of how good she'd felt to him yesterday. It was a façade that would soon melt away in the shimmering island sun.

He was going home to his cabin by the lake and his fishing boat. He wouldn't see Samantha again unless it was on the cover of a magazine or on some news broadcast. So he'd followed her because, for now, she was close enough for him to touch when he wanted to, kiss when he needed to and…

When she and Landry had begun to chat, he slowed his pace. Gary knew better than to ever intrude on conversations with women and he'd received a call at the exact moment the two of them had gone into the atrium. He'd hung back and taken his call, hating afterward that he had, especially when he went back to the atrium and could hear a male voice.

"He was up in her face like he owned her, like at any moment he was going to just take what he wanted," Gary continued, ignoring Kris's steady gaze in his direction. "I wanted to toss him right out that window for daring to upset her."

"She was upset?" Kris asked.

"Hell, yeah, she was. So upset she couldn't react," Gary stated and then dragged a hand down the back of his head. "But if she hadn't stopped me, man, I don't know what I would have done to that scumbag!"

"You said he was trying to blackmail her," Kris mentioned as he leaned forward, resting his elbows on his desk. "With what? Everything Sam does is in the public eye, all the time. What could he possibly have on her?"

That stopped Gary in his tracks. He'd heard Morty talk about pictures and, from the second he'd mentioned them, Gary had known exactly what the man was referring to. He was trained in reconnaissance and in forward observing. Before stepping foot on this island he'd done thorough recon on each person in the palace, including Malayka Sampson. Of course, he'd spent more time on Malayka since he and Kris had specifically discussed the woman's past. But there'd been a day or two that he'd spent sitting on his back porch reading everything he'd pulled on Samantha DeSaunters, including the three years she'd lived in Paris and the three months she'd dated Miguel Lopata.

"Probably nothing," Gary replied. "A bluff, most likely, designed to frighten her."

He didn't tell Kris the truth.

"He's going to be fired regardless," Kris stated evenly. "His contact with Sam today was out of order and harassing. Along with whatever else we find on him, that alone is enough."

"I'm going down there to make sure he leaves the palace for good and that he knows he's not to say anything against her or this family," Gary said and headed for the door.

"Wait a minute." Kris spoke. "I've got some news, also."

Gary wasn't in the mood for any more news today. He wanted to get this situation with Morty taken care of so that Samantha could have some peace in that regard. Still, he turned slowly and looked at Kris because there was something in his tone. Something that Gary knew wasn't going to be good.

"What news?"

Kris didn't hesitate to reply. "Amari Taylor escaped from prison."

Chapter 10

"This is kidnapping," Sam said when Gary slid in beside her on the backseat of the car.

"No," he replied in that cool and aloof manner of his. "It's a dinner date."

Sam looked out the window and tried not to frown. "A person would have to be asked to go somewhere for this to be considered a date. You jumping into my car and directing my driver to go someplace else? That's kidnapping."

"You've been dodging me for the past week, so there was no time to ask you" was his stiff reply.

She sensed he was doing the same thing she was, staring out the window to avoid looking at her. That made this scenario all the more annoying.

"Your claim of 'dodging' is false. I've seen you every day in the past week," she said after a few seconds of silence. Why she didn't want him to have the last word,

Sam couldn't say. She picked up her purse, opened it and pushed things around. What was she looking for? She didn't know; it was only imperative that she did something with her hands. Or she might just strangle him. Or would she let her hands fall to his strong shoulders and glide slowly down his arms?

How many times this week had she thought about touching him? How many times had those thoughts had her on the brink of going to his room? Too many to count and too many to be comfortable with.

"That was business," he told her simply.

"And what's this?" she asked and then—because she couldn't help it, his words had surprised her—she looked at him. "If this isn't business, what is it?"

He moved slowly, turning his head and using his fingers to smooth down the dark hair of his mustache. It didn't need smoothing, neither did the wavy hair on top of his head or the thick brows that would make any woman jealous. Gary was a soldier with a distinct male-model look about him. There was the gruffness of his tone, the preference for casual attire and those damn boots that were more than out of place as he walked around sunny and humid Grand Serenity. Then there was the swagger that announced his presence the moment he entered a room. It didn't matter that his cargo pants and T-shirts were the exact opposite of what every other male in the palace wore, those garments suited him perfectly and kept anyone in proximity staring at him.

"This is a date," he answered finally. "I'm taking you on a dinner date. Is that okay with you, Samantha? Or should I have Phillipe turn the car around and take us both back to the palace?"

The stubborn and irritated part of her wanted to say yes. She wanted to lift her chin and demand that she be taken home because of the high-handed way he'd dealt with her, for the second time in a week's span. But she did not.

"Dinner is fine with me. Just as asking a person something usually goes over much better than demanding they do as you wish," she said.

When he only continued to stare, she figured she'd have to not only lead him to the water but dunk his head so he'd drink, as well.

"I do not like being ordered around. That day in the atrium you told me to go to my room like I was an insolent child. I did not appreciate that. Just as I do not appreciate you hijacking my car and telling me we're going to dinner," she said as she closed her purse with a definite snap and set it beside her on the leather seat.

"Understood," he replied.

Simple as that? No argument, no discussion? Sam wasn't used to conversations where she'd had to stand her ground or assert her position going that smoothly. Anytime she did that with her father or brothers, there was always a debate that followed.

She didn't reply because she didn't know what else to say. The argument or debate would have been easier. Immediate acquiescence required a little more thought.

More time passed and she realized they were driving north, heading toward the parts of the island tourists frequented at that time of evening. That was because there was an array of nice restaurants in this direction, along with a few nightlife entertainment venues. She prayed they weren't going to the latter.

"Phillipe recommended the View. He said it was a great restaurant featuring American and Caribbean cuisine. I made our reservation for seven thirty. Is that all right with you?"

"That's fine with me," she replied. "I've been there a couple of times and I like their chef."

She'd planned to visit with Detali to see what the woman was working on for the fashion show. Last week Sam and Landry had been to the dressmaker to pick up their outfits for the Founder's Day celebration taking place on Saturday. So there was really no need for Sam to return there so quickly, but she'd discovered that was the only place where neither reporters nor civilians really bothered her. Especially at Detali's new place. She could go in through the shop and then out the back door and across the alleyway to Detali's new house. That's where she, Detali and Landry had shared coffee and black fruit- cake. Detali made the Caribbean favorite better than even the pastry chef at the palace. Chef Murray would not like hearing that and so Sam was sure not to ever tell him.

"Good, because we're here," he told her just as the car came to a stop.

Sam knew not to make any move to get out of the car. Before the shooting, Gary had given new protocols for when they arrived at a location other than the palace. After the shooting, he'd taken those protocols to a whole other level. It would be at least fifteen minutes before he came back to the car to help her out. Sam did not argue. Memories of lying on the ground while bullets zoomed through the crowd would not let her. She did pull out her cell phone while she was waiting, a habit she had of checking her emails several times a day.

Nothing, she thought absently as she scrolled down the list, and then there was one from a name she hadn't seen in three years. A name she hadn't ever wanted to see again. She was just about to read it when the door opened and she looked up to see Gary standing there.

"It's all clear."

She looked back at the phone again and decided that he could wait. He could also go to hell, but waiting would have to do. Sam switched her phone setting to vibrate and dropped it into her purse before taking Gary's offered hand and stepping out.

He wore jeans tonight, dark navy, with a gray, button-down shirt that fit almost as snug as his T-shirts normally did. His impressive biceps were showing and when he laced his fingers through hers as they walked toward the steps of the restaurant, Sam felt a wave of something new and warm soar through her body.

It was *just* dinner, she reminded herself.

But it was a date. His words. Not hers.

So she left her hand in his, loving how comfortable that simple act seemed. Her dress was short, the bottom flaring out to barely skim her knees. Had she known she would be going into a restaurant she would have worn something a little more royal. She'd even foregone the heels and had simply slipped on nude-colored flats. As they approached the stairs on the side of the building, she decided not to let her attire bother her because this was *just* dinner.

As she also presumed, Gary's reservation had told them who she was and thus their table was toward the back of the restaurant in a private room. There were several tables in this room but only one was covered in a white-linen cloth with candles lit and wineglasses sparkling. It was closest to the window, which afforded them a glorious view of palm trees and the lights from a golf course. To be fair, all of the tables in the restaurant boasted a view thanks to the panoramic windows. Yet there was still something about what she could see, once Gary had stood behind her and helped her into her seat.

Water was poured into their glasses, menus put into

their hands, smiles offered from the waiter who'd introduced himself as Henri.

"Chef Michael makes a wonderful balsamic dressing," Sam began as soon as she opened the menu. "It's fantastic with the tomato Caprese."

At his grumbling reply, Sam lowered her menu and gazed at him. "You don't like tomatoes, or you don't like balsamic dressing?" she asked.

"I like meat and potatoes" was his quick reply.

His brow had furrowed and his lips turned up in the corner as he looked at his menu. Sam almost smiled as she quickly imagined him as a surly child with that same face whenever something didn't go his way.

"He also prepares a red snapper, Grand Serenity style," she told him.

"I can do seafood," he replied and flipped a page in his menu.

She wasn't sure he saw what he was looking for as he continued to frown, so Sam stood to lean over the table to show him. The top of her dress was loose and the material immediately draped as she moved. Deciding this date would go along much better if she didn't set her dress on fire with the candles, she moved to the chair beside him. Leaning over then, she flipped another page in his menu and pointed.

"There's red snapper, mahi and shrimp. They make the linguini fresh on the premises, too. And they have a cocktail called the Sunset that's dynamite. I'm going to order one of those as soon as Henri returns."

"That's what you smell like."

His words were strange and she looked up to see that Gary was no longer staring at his menu, but at her instead.

"What?" she asked and cleared her throat as she

backed away from him. She'd been too close, she thought now. Way too close if he was commenting on how she smelled.

"The first time I stood close to you was at Kris and Landry's wedding. You were wearing white. You had your hair pulled back tight and there was a bright pink flower, right here." He pointed to the spot just above her right ear.

Self-conscious now, she lifted her hands and tucked her hair back behind both ears.

"I stood behind you while you talked to guests and thanked them for coming on such short notice. It was windy that day and each time there was a breeze I caught this scent. At first I thought it was the flower, but it wasn't a floral aroma at all. I couldn't figure out what it was but I knew, when I stepped closer to you, where it was coming from."

He appeared to think for a moment, during which time Sam cleared her throat and struggled for what she should say.

"Sunset," he continued. "It used to be my mother's favorite time of day. She would sit on the front porch and watch the sun setting over the river."

Henri returned at that moment to take their orders.

"To start, the princess will have the tomato Caprese and the Sunset," Gary told Henri.

Sam nodded her agreement to Gary and then looked up at Henri to tell him that she would also have the grilled salmon for her entrée.

"French onion soup and the sea bass for me," Gary continued. "And whatever beer you have on tap."

When Henri walked away again, Sam took a sip of her water as she sat back in her chair trying not to stare at

Gary. He was a complex guy. A soldier. A loner. A man who loved his mother to no end.

"Your mother lived near a river," she said. "Was that your childhood home?"

He'd been unfolding his napkin and had just placed it in his lap when he looked up to answer.

"I grew up in a Cape Cod–style home in Cambridge, Maryland," he said. "Three bedrooms and a fenced-in yard for our Labrador retriever named Junebug. There was a front porch with two rocker chairs, one for my dad and one for my mom. Across the street from us was a church with a huge yard. The river ran behind the church. My parents used to sit on that porch for a while each evening and look through the side yard of the church to where the sun rested over the river."

"Sounds nice," she replied.

He nodded. "It was. Especially in the summer when it was too hot to do anything but sit still. Junebug and I would cut through the churchyard and head straight to the river after breakfast. My mom would pack a picnic lunch that all the guys ragged me about. They used to call me a spoiled mama's boy."

And there was that tentative grin again. It didn't come often, but when it did—each and every time—Sam's heart did a little pitter-patter in her chest.

"And what did you do when they called you that?"

She had a sinking suspicion calling Gary names didn't go over too well.

"No words. I've never been much of a talker, so I showed them how a spoiled mama's boy handled his business."

"I can totally see that in you. All action, less words."

"I was an only child, so I didn't usually have anyone

to talk to. Besides, action always seemed to work much better, anyway."

"And that's why you left college to join the…which branch of the military were you in again?"

"The army," he replied and then nodded his thanks to the new waiter who had come to the table to deliver their drinks.

Sam immediately sipped from hers and relished the peachy flavor of her cocktail. Gary had lifted his glass as well, taking a gulp of his beer before continuing with his reply.

"I went to college because my parents worked really hard to save money to send me there. I didn't use the money they saved. Instead I worked damn hard to get a full scholarship to college. Nobody in the town could believe it. The Bruiser. That's what some of the parents used to call me. The ones with the sons that didn't know when to shut their mouths around me, but at the same time couldn't fight their way out of a paper bag."

"Wow, were you like the neighborhood bully?" Sam asked.

"Nah," he said with a shake of his head. "More like the enforcer. Kids liked to try to take advantage of other kids they thought had less than them. I didn't care about the ones who had bigger and prettier houses, or that took the trips to Disney World during the summer, while I spent most of the sultry days at the local rec center. But I didn't tolerate trash-talking and bullying, as you put it. Not from anybody."

And that sounded exactly like him, she thought. He was the protector, even as a child.

"I can certainly see how college wasn't for you," she said. "It's not for everyone."

"You went to college," he replied.

Sam took another sip of her cocktail. "Only because it took me away from the palace. I felt like I was choking there."

That hadn't really been what she'd meant to say, but it was out and she couldn't take it back.

"That's how I felt in college."

"So we do have something in common," she said.

"Are you surprised about that? A princess having something in common with an army vet. That would probably shock a lot of people."

"I'm just a woman, Gary. And you're a man. We're both people. That's the first thing we have in common."

He'd been lifting his glass but before he sipped he leaned it in her direction for a toast. Sam picked up her cocktail, tapping her glass against his.

"To the man and the woman with something in common," he said, his lips spreading slowly into a smile.

Sam liked his words. She liked his smile even more. "Hear, Hear!" she replied and watched him over the rim of her glass as she sipped.

He was talking too damn much.

They'd finished their delicious meal and the dessert that followed forty minutes ago and he had talked the entire time. Conversation had continued during the ride back to the palace and, when he'd walked her to her rooms, she'd surprised him by inviting him inside. Now it was nearing ten o'clock at night and they were sitting on the balcony just off her living room. She kept a mini-refrigerator in her office and had brought them both bottled water.

"Did you love her?" she asked again, probably because he'd taken such a long time to answer.

Gary dragged a hand down his face. It was a nice

night. There was a gentle breeze that cooled the air of the stifling heat from earlier in the day. The sky was clear, the moon at its half phase, palm trees swaying gently in the distance. So why were his temples throbbing at the thought of talking about his marriage and its ultimate failure?

"It wasn't meant to be," he replied.

"That really didn't answer my question" was her reply.

Instead of taking one of the chairs, she'd opted to lay back on the cushioned lounge, her long legs crossed at the ankles, feet bare after she'd slipped off her shoes when she'd gone to retrieve the water. At least, that's how she'd been positioned when he'd last glanced at her. Something about the crisp evening air and her very short dress and all the skin of her bare legs and arms was making him edgy. He'd decided it made more sense not to look at her too much.

He'd done a lot of that at dinner. Looked at her, that is. Seemed like he'd been looking at her for weeks now. Watching and taking note of every little thing about her. If he weren't such a disciplined and restrained man, he would think he was obsessing over her.

"I loved the idea of marrying her because I knew it was going to make my mother happy," he finally replied. It was the first time he'd ever said that out loud.

"Your mother wanted to see you married and happy because that's what she'd had with your father," she commented softly.

She got it. He knew she did because she'd been listening to everything he'd told her so intently that night. Almost as if this were the first time anyone had actually talked to her.

"I don't have a lot of memories of my mom," she continued. "I was so young when she died. But I know that she was happy. And I know that my dad was so very in love with her. I could see it in his eyes even years after her death. Each year we would visit her grave, I could hear it in his voice when he spoke of her. I thought he would never love anyone the way he did her but—"

She sighed and Gary finished the sentence for her.

"But now he's engaged to marry Malayka. I can see how that would be hard for you to swallow."

"I believe in love," she told him. "I believe that two people can fall in love and strive for happiness. What I don't believe is that the scenario is meant for every living, breathing soul."

He turned to her then because her words were spoken so sullenly, as if she'd been forced to believe them.

"I believe in love," he replied. "I saw it with my parents, so I know it can be achieved."

She held his gaze. "Are you looking for love, Gary? Is that what you want for your life now that you're no longer in the army?"

"No," he immediately replied. "I'm not looking for anything. I'm content with what I have."

She took a few seconds before finally nodding and saying, "Yeah, me, too."

He waited a beat, wondering what the hell was happening now. He'd shared things about his past with her and she'd shared some things with him. So that now he looked at her differently and felt as if something had definitely changed between them.

He stood abruptly, rubbing his palms along the front of his pants before announcing, "I should go."

She was looking up at him, confusion clear in her gaze. He wondered if she was feeling as weird about what was happening between them as he was. Or maybe she just thought he was the crazy one. Whatever was going through her mind, Gary would have never expected what she did next.

Sam stood then, as well, stepping closer to him and placing her hand on his chest. "No, you should stay."

Chapter 11

His hands moved over her naked body.

It felt familiar and urgent and…right.

Just like when he'd touched her before, when they'd kissed, talked or simply sat near each other. It was right. As if it had been ordained in some previous life or something.

Sam closed her eyes and decided to just let the sensations rule. Thinking was taking her in too many directions. She only wanted to feel. To finally just feel.

Gary seemed on board with that plan as he hadn't hesitated a moment after she'd suggested he stay, and had taken her by the hand, leading her to her bedroom. Before doing so he'd held on to her as he locked the patio doors and then went to the main door and locked it, as well. Once in her bedroom, he closed that door, too, and made sure all the blinds and drapes were drawn. After the security efforts, he gave all of his attention to her.

Now they were both naked, both lying on her bed. He was propped up on his elbow, looking down at her body as his hand moved over her breasts and down her torso.

"This isn't going to be slow," he told her.

His voice had grown deeper, huskier. The sound rubbing along her skin as surely and as alluringly as his fingers.

"It's going to be hot and fast," he continued, his fingers tracing the V of her juncture. "And delicious."

Sam sucked in a breath, releasing it with a quiet whisper. "Yes."

He had already sheathed his length, so when he came over her, using his legs to push hers open wider, Sam was ready. Or, at least, she thought she was.

"Look at me," he said when she'd been staring down the length of their bodies, waiting anxiously to see as he joined with her.

Trying to tamp down her impatience, she looked up to see him staring at her. Would she ever get used to how intense his stare was? How dark his eyes became whenever he looked at her? Or how warm she felt all over to be the one on the receiving end of such a mesmerizing glare?

"I'm going to give you everything you need," he stated. "First and foremost."

She was nodding her agreement before she could even wonder if she should. He knew, she thought as he leaned in to touch his lips to hers. He knew what she wanted and probably that she'd pleased herself all this time. Now he was promising her something more.

Sam laced her arms around his neck and pulled him into a deeper kiss, a searing kiss, that by its end had them both struggling to catch their breath.

Sam gasped when he attempted to enter her.

"Kiss me again," he whispered. "Everything is beautiful when you kiss me."

She did as he asked and he moved slowly, pressing his hard length deeper into her tight cove. He was filling her, down there and with his kiss. Sam felt as if she'd been empty for far too long, but at this moment she was being filled with the best.

He broke the kiss and laced an arm under the lower part of her back, lifting her hips slightly off the bed. He continued to thrust deep inside her, pulling back slowly before going deeper again.

Sam had nothing to compare the feeling to because there was nothing that had ever matched it. The slow, deliberate movements were perfect, hitting every aching and needy spot she possessed. His body was tight and strong and worked hers as if he'd practiced for this very moment every second of his life.

She wrapped her legs around his waist and Gary reached behind his back to clasp them together. He came up on his knees and dove deeper into her. Her fingers dug into the bed, grabbing handfuls of the comforter as she held on tight to not only the material but to the scream of pleasure that swirled in the pit of her stomach.

When he untwined her legs and placed her ankles on his shoulders, Sam knew what would happen next. He rubbed her calves and kissed them as he pulled slowly out of her. Then he kissed the top of her foot, the tips of her toes, the arch of her foot. She gasped and panted, licking her lips as her head began to thrash against the pillows.

Gary clasped her ankles and spread her legs into a wide V as he picked up his pace, thrusting deep and fast in and out of her. It was complete bliss. With each stroke, pleasure seeped into her body like she was on a steady intravenous infusion. Her heart beat faster, her body heated, her legs began to tremble. She was right there, it was close. She could see it within arm's reach. Feel it in every spasm of her body. Hear it in his heavy breathing and the clap of their bodies joining. Then she was there and release was upon her, gripping her, lifting her into its funnel and whirling her around.

"Gary." She whispered his name and pulled at the comforter until she was certain she'd ripped the sheets beneath from being tucked under the mattress. "Gary!"

He rubbed her legs then, down to her trembling thighs and back up to her calves. He'd gone still inside her, so that she could ride that euphoric wave and still feel his rigid length deep inside. It took seconds. No, longer, much longer for her to hit the precipice, topple over that mountain of release and then fall softly back to earth.

And Gary was there to catch her.

He rolled onto his side and pulled her over with him. His lips found hers and they kissed, his tongue dueling with hers in the same masterful motion as he'd used to make her come. His hands seemed to be everywhere at once, cupping her face, moving down to graze over her hardened nipples, tracing a line along her torso and cupping her bottom. He lifted her leg up and draped it over his waist.

"You're perfect," he whispered in her ear. "I've never felt this way before and the only reason I can use to explain it is that you're perfect."

Her arms were around him again, her head tilting back as he kissed along her neck. She thrust into him as she felt his length pressing hungrily against her moist center. He moved, positioning himself at her entrance, and Sam sucked him right in. She thrust hungrily, eager to take him deep once more. It was slippery and sweet, aromatic and intoxicating, joyous and completing.

They moved in sync, as if their bodies were made for this specific purpose. In and out. Out and in. His lips on hers. Her teeth nipping the strong line of his jaw. Her hands on the muscles of his back. His cupping the soft curve of her bottom. On and on, until once again there was bliss, this time for both of them.

Gary then whispered in her ear, his voice husky as his pleasure overtook him. "Mine. Sweet and perfect. And mine."

Chapter 12

Sam squealed with delight. She was clapping her hands and had even did a little jump off the ground the moment the football soared through the little hole in the board at least fifteen feet away. She happily wrapped her arms around Gary's neck and kissed him soundly on the lips when he gave her the stuffed elephant he'd won for his efforts.

"He's gorgeous!" she yelled.

"He's an orange elephant," Gary quipped and turned to stand beside her.

Sam laced her free arm through his and leaned into him as they began to walk down the grassy patch of land where the gaming booths had been set up. It was four days after their night together, four days that they'd spent attending all of Sam's engagements and time in between on some of the most romantic dates she could ever imagine.

To put it simply, this had been an amazing time for Sam, four days filled with an intimacy she'd never imagined achieving with anyone.

Today was like the cherry on top of a delicious caramel sundae as they attended Grand Serenity's annual Founder's Day celebration. The day-long event always kicked off with a breakfast awards ceremony at the city chamber where the royal family was honored, as well as other notable figures on the island for their dedication and commitment to the island throughout the year.

The hours after breakfast were the Fun Day Festivities. Games and prizes and food booths were in abundance along the island's main thoroughfare. Later this evening they would dress elegantly and the palace would be open for its once-a-year visit from the citizens of the island.

The Founder's Day Ball was held in the main courtyard of the palace. During the hours of the ball, the first floor of the palace was open for tours. That was a tradition started by Sam's mother. One that Vivienne thought gave the islanders a chance to see how their ruling government lived.

Rafe had told Sam that her mother had thought of it as a way to show their constituents that the royal family was not above them and that they all worked together to make Grand Serenity the tropical haven it was today. Sam wholeheartedly agreed with the tradition.

"He's the first prize won for me at the Fun Day Festivities," she said, hugging the elephant to her chest. "And I love him."

The proclamation was quick and whimsical. It was her affection for a silly stuffed animal and nothing more. But for some reason or another, she'd stopped walking when she'd said it, and Gary had stopped and looked at her, as well.

"There you two are," Landry said as she and Kris approached.

It would have appeared like two couples were simply standing near a water-gun game chatting about the late-afternoon fun they were having at one of Grand Serenity's biggest public celebrations. Except for the half-dozen armed and full-regalia guards that surrounded the foursome—three of them traveled with Sam, while the other three were assigned to Kris. The extra security was obvious to the citizens of the island who, unlike at last year's event, kept their distance from the royal family today.

"I'll be glad when this is over," Sam muttered. "They're all staring at us like we're contagious or something."

"They've always stared at us," Kris stated blandly.

He'd dressed as casual as the crown prince could, wearing slacks and a dress shirt, sans the tie and suit jacket. Beside him, Landry looked as if she were enjoying herself in the white sundress with its large plum-colored belt and matching flat sandals.

"Not like this," Sam replied. "Just a couple of weeks ago tourists came right up to me and asked for pictures and autographs. Today they're keeping their distance and staring as if I'm going to suddenly grow another head."

"They're afraid for you," Gary chimed in. "Afraid for what might happen to you and the rest of the royal family."

"Nothing is going to happen to us," Sam said defiantly.

"You're absolutely right about that," Gary told her. "Nothing is going to happen to you."

"He's right," Landry added. "We're going to go over there and get us some of those delicious banana chips and a nice, stiff drink. Then we'll head home and squeeze into our gorgeous gowns for tonight's fancy party."

Sam grinned. "I like how you insist on calling every ball or formal affair we have a fancy party."

"That's what they are because we get to dress fancy," Landry said as she moved from beside her husband to grab Sam by the arm.

The two of them walked together while Kris and Gary walked behind them.

"So where'd you get that weird-looking elephant?" Landry asked as they continued to move.

"Oh," Sam said, just remembering the stuffed animal that had brought her so much joy just a few minutes ago. "It's my Founder's Day elephant. Gary won him for me."

"He did, did he?" Landry asked. "Let me see this thing."

She pulled the elephant out of Sam's hand before Sam could stop her.

"He's cute enough," she told her. "Yes, for the first boyfriend-girlfriend gift, I guess this will do."

Sam took back her elephant and shook her head. "What are you talking about? We're not boyfriend and girlfriend."

"And why would you say that?"

"For one, because we're not eight-year-olds."

"Uh-huh," Landry said with a nod.

"And, for two, because we're just playing a part. You remember that charade we agreed upon, right?"

"I remember it started out with a pretty hot kiss in front of over two hundred people," Landry quipped. "And then I remember somebody telling me about 'fooling around' with the guy she's engaged in the charade with. And now, that same somebody is clutching a bug-eyed orange elephant like it's a strand of precious pearls because he—who is *not* her boyfriend—won it for her."

Sam opened her mouth to reply then clamped her lips

shut. Landry had a point. She had several. But Sam didn't have to concede any of them.

"Weren't we supposed to find a stiff drink somewhere?" she asked.

Landry laughed.

"What are you doing here?" Sam asked as she spun around to see Gary standing in the doorway of her bedroom.

Lucie had just finished helping her into her gown and she'd been in front of the full-length mirror, admiring her new gown. The emerald-green, pleated, silk-chiffon gown was gorgeous with its fitted bodice and thigh-high split at her left side. She loved how the color gave her skin an exotic glow and the tiny diamond earrings added a bright sparkle to the dark material. Her hair was pulled up neatly with an array of curls at the top and her shoes were a sexy silver pump.

"You look amazing" was his response.

Sam smiled, forgetting that she wanted to know how he'd come to be in her bedroom while she was dressing for the ball.

"Thank you," she said to him. "And thank you, Lucie. I think that'll be all for tonight."

"Yes, ma'am. And you do look amazing," Lucie said with a tilt of her head and a meek smile across her pixie-like face.

Sam gave a nod in Lucie's direction and waited until she heard the sound of the outside door to her rooms closing before she spoke to Gary again.

"You don't look too shabby yourself," she commented. "The soldier that cleans up well."

He gave a nonchalant shrug and a murmured thank-you as he crossed the space between them. Tonight, instead of the cargo pants and fitted T-shirt she'd become accustomed to seeing him in, Gary wore a tuxedo. It was Burberry. Landry had mentioned it one day this week when they were talking. Landry had selected all the tuxedos for the men of the royal family for this event. Gary was included, although Sam hadn't been totally sure why. Landry's comments from earlier today about him being Sam's boyfriend may have been a factor.

The white dinner jacket and crisp shirt were cool accents to the black pants, bow tie and shoes. It fit him flawlessly, not too tight, not too big, just perfect. He looked like a black James Bond, Sam thought as he approached her.

"I have something for you," he said. "I doubt it will add anything to the perfection I'm already looking at, but here you go, anyway."

Sam didn't know what to say. She was still feeling happy butterflies fluttering in her stomach when she looked over to see the orange elephant sitting in the center of her bed. Another gift from him was bound to make her float through the rest of the night. However, she cleared her throat and tried to act as casual as possible when she asked, "What is it?"

Gary shook his head. "You know that's not how it works. Open it," he prodded.

Sam prayed her hands wouldn't shake as she reached for the black-velvet box. It was too big to be a ring, which of course, he would not be giving her, anyway. Right? But it was formalized with a white-satin bow wrapped around its dark casing. The gesture made her heart do a happy dance to rival what the butterflies were doing in the pit of her stomach.

She held the box in one hand and slipped the bow off with the other. Then, after a deep, steadying breath, Sam opened the box. She gasped, loudly, and then clasped her lips shut as her head snapped up and she stared at him.

"What did you do?" she asked him. "Why did you do this?"

"A little birdie told me what color you were wearing tonight and I thought this might match. What's the matter? You don't like it?"

Sam tilted her head and kept her mouth shut tightly. She was breathing a little faster now as she cursed the tears that were about to fall. With a quick shake of her head, she closed the box. "I can't take this."

"Why not?" he asked.

"Because."

Gary shook his head. "You can do better than that."

She sighed. "Because I cannot take this."

"Because you don't like it?"

"I love it," she admitted quietly. "It's beautiful."

"But you don't want it? Or is it that you just don't want it from me? I can give you a silly-looking orange elephant, but not an emerald and diamond necklace. Why? Do you not think I can afford it because I'm not some dignitary you're used to smiling at during these endless events?"

Sam was about to reply but then she heard his tone and wondered where it had come from all of a sudden. Since the first night they'd spoken to each other, Gary had always had a steely, noncommittal tone with her, and everyone else, for that matter. Just now, he sounded different. Irritated maybe?

And, no, she recalled, this wasn't the first time he'd sounded this way. The day she'd been shot at, his tone had been different, as well.

"That's not what I said, nor what I meant," she replied. "I'm just wondering why you would give this to me. And why Landry would tell you what I was wearing. When did she tell you this? How did you have time to get this?"

He, too, took a deep breath and let it out slowly. Sam couldn't help but watch the rise and fall of his muscled chest as he did so. "Can I just put it on you to see how it looks?" he asked.

He did not wait for a response, instead taking the box from her hands and opening it once more. She watched his strong fingers remove the classically beautiful asymmetrical necklace from its base. Tossing the box over to the bed, he stepped around her, holding the necklace in front and then clasping it at the back, so that it now rested coolly against her skin.

When he touched her shoulders and turned her slowly so that she was facing the mirror again, Sam's breath caught. The necklace was gorgeous and so was he. Looking at them through the mirror, Sam could easily see another headline in the papers. There'd already been a few speculating as to when the loving couple would give Grand Serenity its second royal wedding of the year. She'd read about the rumors, and listened to newscasters trying to predict the same event, with a hint of humor. If they only knew the truth...

Another part of her hadn't found the duplicity funny. At some point they'd have to either come clean about their pretend affair or fake a breakup. Wait a minute, they were sleeping together now, so Sam wasn't so sure how fake this affair actually was. Still, it wouldn't last. It wasn't meant to last or to mean anything, no matter how good they looked together.

"You make it look so much more beautiful than it was in that box," he told her, his hands resting on her shoulders now.

"That's not possible," she replied and then hurriedly

added, "But thank you. If my comments sounded un-grateful, I apologize."

He leaned down, dropping a quick kiss to the skin between her neck and shoulder.

"You never have to apologize to me," he whispered.

Now she was shaking all over and those pesky tears still threatened to fall because, damn, this felt real. It felt like nothing she'd ever felt before. New and fresh. Exciting and intense. This couldn't be fake. She knew she wasn't that good of an actress to fake everything she was feeling at that moment. Especially since these feelings were foreign to her. Standing in her bedroom in this intimate yet seemingly innocent position was also different. It felt good, but it was not something she was used to.

But could she get used to it?

"Let's go. You and the family should all be downstairs before the guests arrive," Gary said. Letting his hands slide from her shoulders, he entwined his fingers with hers.

Sam nodded.

She slowly pulled her hands away from his and moved to her bed to grab her purse. Then, before heading to the door, she held out her arm, her hand extending to him.

"Let's go."

Gary accepted her hand and gave her a smile in return.

Yes, Sam thought as they walked out of her room and down the hall toward the stairs, she could definitely get used to this.

Chapter 13

The island's colors were navy blue, gold and white, so decorations of that color scheme flanked the marble hallways and door frames of the main foyer and throughout the length of the entire first floor of the palace. The staff was dressed in all white with a sash portraying the Grand Serenity flag across their bodies. There would be trays and trays of food offered throughout the first hour as guests entered and toured the property. During the second hour everyone would be moved to the seating area in the courtyard where forty tables had been set up with white, wicker chairs and royal-blue tablecloths.

Views of Vivienne's garden and the distinct aroma from the flowers planted there wafted into the courtyard, providing an added touch to the already brilliant scenery and ambience.

Sam had just made it to the bottom of the grand staircase when Landry, Kris and Roland came to greet her and Gary.

"This looks magnificent on you!" Landry exclaimed. "I knew this would be the perfect color!"

"Yes, you did," Sam told her with a knowing look. "And you shared that knowledge, as well."

"What…oh, yes, I did. Is this what you bought her to go with it?" she asked, stepping in to get a closer look at the necklace. "You've got great taste, Gary."

"Yeah, great taste, indeed," Roland said, his look tight and discernible.

"I'd like a word before the festivities begin," Kris said seriously. "We can talk down the hall in the library. We only have about fifteen minutes before they open the doors, so that should be enough time."

Roland nodded to his brother. "You coming, Soldier Boy?" he asked Gary.

Gary frowned but nodded to Roland and stepped away from Sam.

"Stay with Landry until I come back for you," he told Sam.

"He's right," Kris added when he looked at Sam and she figured he could see she was about to argue. "Those two guards will be with you at all times tonight. Make sure you keep them in your sights. If at any moment you don't see them, find a guard or call one of us. We'll all have our cell phones on."

"Oh, for heaven's sake, can't we just have one night without all this cloak-and-dagger stuff going on?" Malayka asked as she unexpectedly walked in on their conversation.

"That depends," Roland stated flatly.

Malayka turned to him with a brilliant smile. "On what, might I ask?"

She wore a gold dress that wrapped around her body like a second skin, hugging every curve tightly. Her hair was a cascade of curls over her right shoulder, her makeup was flawless, and the diamond choker, earrings and bracelet she wore were almost blinding. Flashy did not accurately describe how she looked.

From all the reading and movie-watching she'd done as a teenager, Sam knew the look was best known as old Hollywood. Ever since Landry had married Kris, Malayka had refused to let her even so much as suggest a color for an outfit for her. Landry hadn't been the least bit offended, because it was obvious that Malayka was bitter about her stylist becoming a princess before her and within the same royal family.

Roland continued with his question. "Tell us where your old friend Amari is hiding?"

Malayka's smile never faltered, even as she looped her arm between Rafe's as he joined their little impromptu gathering.

"I have no idea where Amari is. You fired him, remember?" She directed the question to Kris.

"Why are we talking about this tonight?" Rafe interjected. "Malayka has had no contact with that lowlife since he was arrested. Now, we'll all put on our happy faces and stop thinking and talking about whatever is going on around here. We are going to enjoy Founder's Day and make sure that our guests enjoy it, as well."

"Yes, that's exactly what we're going to do," Sam said after silence had engulfed the group.

"Excuse me. What time should we open the doors, Your Highness?" one of the staff members asked.

"Right now," Malayka replied. "Let's get this party started!"

Landry looked at Sam. She wanted to frown, or roll her eyes, or do something to express that this woman was not ready to be anybody's princess. But Sam glanced at her father and saw his furrowed brow and grim expression. Sam gave a nod to the staff member who hadn't moved a muscle at Malayka's reply. Only then did the older woman scuttle off to do as she was told.

"We should be at the door to greet them, darling," Malayka said to Rafe.

He nodded stiffly in reply. "You're right. We should. I expect the rest of you to greet everyone you can as you move throughout the palace. Smiles in place, assure our people that we are just fine," he said. "Even if—"

"We will, Dad," Roland assured him. "We will."

When Rafe and Malayka walked away, Gary was the one to remind Roland and Kris about their need to talk.

Kris nodded and kissed Landry on the cheek. "Stay with the guards."

She nodded and Sam gave Gary a tentative smile as if to say she would do the same without him feeling like he had to give her the order again.

"Be good. Both of you," Roland stated with a wink as he passed them.

"Humph," Sam said to Landry when the men were gone. "We're not the ones that need that warning."

Landry shook her head and said a quick "I know that's right" before a stream of guests began making their way down the hallway toward them.

"Amari hasn't called her, but I did come across two emails that were suspect. I'm having someone trace the IP addresses now," Gary told Kris and Roland as they stood amid over two hundred books shelved in a room with twenty-foot ceilings and top-to-bottom mahogany wood shelves.

On any other day Gary would have loved to wander

through this room perusing the massive book collection. But now was definitely not the time.

"This guy is a piece of work. He sneaks into the palace, sets a bomb, gets caught, goes to jail and then escapes. Now, he's sending emails like some pen pal. What did the emails say?" Roland asked.

The prince hadn't secured his bow tie and it hung around his neck haphazardly as he thrust his hands into the front pockets of his black tuxedo pants.

Kris stood with one arm folded over his chest, the other held upward as he rubbed a finger over his chin.

"It was pretty cryptic but two things stood out to me," Gary said as he reached into his inside jacket pocket and pulled out two pieces of paper.

"Malayka had written 'I haven't found a new stylist yet. Need one ASAP.' The reply was 'Always here for you. Tell me when you need me to come.'

"Malayka then wrote 'In a couple of weeks. Too hectic right now.' The reply was 'I can make things better. You already know how. Just say the word.'"

Gary paused, giving himself a break from the paper he was reading from.

He then continued. "Next, Malayka wrote 'It's okay. I will maintain on my own.' And the reply was 'That's not wise.' Malayka then responded 'It's my decision.' And the reply was a sad-face emoji." Gary finished and looked up at the brothers.

"And you think this is from Amari to Malayka?" Kris asked.

Gary nodded. "Now, the first thing that stood out to me was that they talked about a new 'stylist.' Not a new hair stylist or fashion stylist. Just a 'stylist,'" Gary noted.

"Because they didn't want to say hair stylist and risk

tipping us off to who was corresponding with her," Kris added.

"Exactly," Gary said.

Roland replied, "In the beginning of the message Malayka complains that she has not been able to find a 'stylist' yet, but in the end, after he tells her that he can 'make it better' and that all she needs to do is 'just say the word,' she tells him she can 'maintain on her own.'"

"Yes," Gary agreed, even though he didn't appreciate being interrupted.

There was tension between him and Roland. Gary had felt it from the first time he'd met the younger prince. He'd attempted to brush it off because Kris had been the one to hire him and thus Kris was the only one to whom he owed an explanation. But Roland was Samantha's brother and Gary could only imagine how he would react if some arrogant foreigner had come along and inserted himself into his sister's life the way Gary suspected it appeared he'd done with Samantha. Still, he wasn't about to take much more of Roland's attitude without setting the guy straight on a few things.

"So once you get the IP address, you'll trace it and then what?" Kris asked.

"Then we'll pay that person a little visit," Roland stated in a tone that said that the next action should have been obvious.

"Amari will come to us," Gary said, a small part of him enjoying the moment Roland raised a brow to look at him.

"How do you know that for sure?" the younger prince asked.

"Because he's too confident not to. This guy was able to sleep in this palace and still plan to have your father's car run off a cliff, break in to the bank—something that we still can't explain—and plant a bomb, which, if it were just a little more sophisticated, could have easily destroyed this entire dwelling and killed everyone in it."

"But he's an amateur. We figured that out after the sorry-ass bomb was examined," Roland commented.

"He wants us to think he's an amateur," Kris said in a lethally low voice. "Is that what you're getting at?"

Gary nodded. "He wants to keep catching you off guard. That's why he sent someone else to shoot at Sam."

Gary hadn't told anyone about his findings. He'd admitted only to himself that the reason was that he wanted to get the bastard and shoot a few rounds at him personally before turning him over to the Grand Serenity police. Of course, by then it would be too late to consider any type of jail time.

"You know who shot at her?" Roland asked. "Why didn't you tell us?"

"I'm telling you now," Gary stated slowly. "Remember I called you about the guy at the gate trying to get in?" He directed the question to Kris.

"Yes. You said his name was Kendon Arnold," Kris answered.

Gary nodded. "Yes and that SUV was registered in his name. The day of the shooting that same SUV was parked at the bottom of the cliff two hours before we arrived for the tour. One of the guards mentioned that after my second round of questioning. He said he'd been searching the perimeter as he'd been instructed and he saw the SUV. He copied the tag number just in case it was still there when he circled around. It wasn't."

Roland was not impressed. "Then how is it that you think this is the guy who shot at Sam?"

"Because when the hotel room Kendon Arnold had

checked out from later that evening was searched, we found the gun and more ammunition there."

"The idiot left his gun?" Kris asked incredulously.

"Again," Gary told them, "they want us to believe they're amateurs, which is why I'm telling both of you that this is not about killing anyone. It's about stopping the royal wedding."

"What?" they asked in unison.

"Think about this. The first attempt was intended for Rafe, but he wasn't in the car at the time. But that road Igor was traveling back to the palace on was less than five miles from one of only two auto mechanics on this island. Meaning, help wasn't far away from where the accident occurred.

"The bomb was placed in the part of the ballroom where there was likely to be the least amount of people at any given time. It was far in the corner behind a wall of statues and artwork that nobody could get around and thus would not be standing near when the bomb went off.

"And at the shooting, as I stated the day it happened, Malayka wasn't standing a foot away from Samantha at the time. Why take that shot if you only wanted Sam dead? What if the shot was meant for Malayka? Or, better yet, what if the shooter was sent to remind Malayka that Amari knew how to make this all better?

"Or, was each of these events meant as a stall tactic because of their timing?"

Roland dragged both hands down the back of his closely shaved head, while Kris stared at something beyond Gary's shoulders.

"It's just a hunch but..." Gary stated after having said all of his inner thoughts aloud for the first time.

"You've been trained to trust your gut," Kris said quietly. "Your whole job is centered on trusting your instincts and acting accordingly. That's why I brought you here."

Gary nodded. After his evenings with Samantha he'd been returning to his room and writing in his notebook all his observations. The reports from the guards that he'd collected after the shooting were cataloged on his laptop. He reviewed them every day and late into the night hours while sitting with a beer.

The prince and his young American fiancée; Kris and his American wife; Roland; and Samantha. How was this all connected? What was the endgame?

"My gut tells me that this is about the wedding. It didn't start until after the engagement was announced and the closer we get to that date the more I believe there'll be interruptions. Distractions, so to speak," he told them.

"Distractions?" Roland asked. "From what? For what? To kill my father so he doesn't marry her? You said this wasn't about killing us."

"I don't think it is, because the bottom line is that a killer kills. Period." It was a chilling statement that fell upon them like a cool blast of water. "I think it's about the wedding and what may happen as a result of it."

"What's that?" Roland queried.

Kris said, "Malayka will become the princess."

"Who wouldn't want her to become the princess?" Roland asked. "The answer would be none of us."

"That's certainly true," Gary replied. "Still, that's my hunch so far."

Their mood was definitely grim now.

"We need to get out there," Kris said after the silence had stretched for more than a minute.

Gary nodded. "There will be a lot of people here tonight, but I've briefed all the guards and the police chief on things to look for. We're all on alert."

"So you think he'll strike again tonight?" Roland asked. "That's just great. At this rate the citizens are going to be freaking out every time they're invited to the palace. And we're not going to be able to smooth over what's going on. People aren't stupid. They're going to connect the dots and realize that someone is after us."

"It's our duty to keep them calm," Kris stated. "No matter what, we're going to do that. So let's get our game faces on and go out there. The sooner this event is over, the better."

Gary agreed. He'd been away from Samantha too long. Lately he'd begun to only feel content when she was in his sight. Preferably lying in bed next to him, but Gary was comfortable with her just standing beside him, as well. As long as he was with her he knew that she was safe, and that mattered to him. It mattered much more than he'd presumed it would ten weeks ago when he'd first stepped foot on this island.

"I agree," he replied finally. "I have to go find Samantha."

Gary had turned and was heading to the door when he was stopped.

"Wait a minute," Roland said, grabbing Gary by the arm before he could reach the door.

Gary looked down to where the man's hand was on his arm and then back up at Roland. The younger prince did not budge.

"I thought this thing with you and my sister was supposed to be fake," he said through clenched teeth.

"It was," Gary replied stiffly.

Roland continued. "It doesn't seem fake anymore. I see how you're looking at her and I've seen you coming from her room every night this week. What the hell is going on?"

Kris didn't say a word but the way he was looking at Gary said he was thinking along the same lines as his brother.

"There's nothing going on. You're trusting me to kill the son of a bitch threatening your family and that's what I'm going to do. End of story," Gary told them.

"What if she wants it to be real?" Kris asked him. "I've observed how Sam's looking at you lately and Landry has made a few comments that lead me to believe there's more going on for Sam than what was originally planned. So I guess we're both asking what your intentions are."

Gary took a deep breath and released it slowly. He thought about all the pressure his mother had placed on him to fall in love and get married and what a catastrophe that turned out to be with Tonya. He also recalled how brokenhearted his mother had been when his father died. "It's like losing half of my soul," she'd told him that night at the hospital after his father's passing.

Hell no.

Gary was not going there again.

And he wasn't about to play Twenty Questions with these two, either. He didn't give a damn what their title was.

"My intention is to take the shot," he told them evenly. "That's my job and that's what I plan to do."

"And when that's done?" Roland asked.

"So am I," Gary replied and walked out of the room.

He was moving so fast and feeling so infuriated that he didn't see Samantha standing beside the doorway.

Chapter 14

She was pacing.

She hated that.

The bottom part of her dress bunched in her hand as she moved back and forth across the floor in her office where she'd retreated. The guard who had followed her had gone in first and checked everything before she'd entered. He'd told her he would be waiting right outside the door when she was ready to return to the party. Sam wasn't sure when that was going to be.

"Nothing good ever came from eavesdropping." Her father had told her that once when she'd been following Kris and Roland around the house. It was days before Christmas and the two of them had been planning a surprise gift for Rafe. Sam had hated being left out, especially when Roland had informed her that it was a "guy's gift."

Sam had gone down into the old empty stable stalls and

hidden in one of them while she'd waited for her brothers to meet. The scary story they'd ended up telling—instead of working on a gift—had given Sam nightmares so bad that one night she'd run out of her room, down the long hall to where her father's rooms were and climbed into bed with him. In the morning he'd asked her what was wrong and she'd reluctantly told him. Rafe had shaken his head and rubbed her back. "Some things are better left unknown, Sammy-Girl."

Yeah, well, years later, Sam still felt like his words were an understatement.

Gary was a killer.

The words sent chills down her spine as they echoed in her head.

Of course, she'd known this. He'd been a sniper in the United States Army for six years. Now, he was here because her brother had hired a killer to eliminate the threat to their family. She'd deal with the fact that her brother might be a little bit insane himself later. Right now, she was trying to digest that the killer for hire had also become her lover.

And that lover was going to walk out of her life the minute his job was over.

She'd opened up to him. Dammit. She'd let down the shield that, once upon a time, she'd had no problem erecting. How many hours had they lain in her bed, cuddled together, talking about the things that pleased them?

"When you kiss my ears," he'd said just last night when their naked bodies were twined together after another breath-stealing lovemaking session, "I want to be inside you the moment your tongue touches my ear."

Sam had warmed all over to his words because she'd known for years how to pleasure herself and, learning now how it felt to offer someone else that same pleasure, was liberating and a bit intoxicating.

"I love it when you hold me from behind," she admitted. "The feel of your strong arms around my waist and the warmth of your breath when you lean in and kiss my neck is indescribable."

It was an admission she hadn't expected to make, but they were being so open, the moment was so intimate and so starkly honest, that she hadn't been able to keep it in.

"You mean like this," he'd said and shifted their bodies until he was behind her, spooning his body against hers. His arms had wrapped tightly around her waist as he'd snuggled close to her neck and kissed the sensitive skin there.

"Ahhh," she'd sighed. "Yes."

They'd fallen asleep that way, until just before dawn when he'd awakened and left to go to his room. Sam had wanted to ask him to stay. She'd wanted to wake up to the sunrise with him still holding her; had wanted to start her day with a kiss from him, a smile, a touch.

Sigh.

She was such a fool.

He was here to do a job and afterward he was leaving. How could something that sounded so simple feel like a hot blade slipping slowly into her back? She wanted to cry. Then she wanted to yell with fury. Instead she grit her teeth and paced some more.

"There you are, my sweet."

Sam whirled around at the sound of his voice.

"What? How the hell did you get in here?" she asked Morty, who was moving slowly closer to her.

"You didn't think I'd just walk away, did you?" He clucked his tongue and shook his head, coming to a stop just a couple of feet away from where Sam stood.

Morty was dressed in a tuxedo, just like most of the men at the palace tonight. Only the erratic gleam in his eyes set him apart from the excited guests. They were red-rimmed and hysterical-looking as he continued to leer at her.

"You thought you could run to Daddy and tell him all sorts of lies and then he'd fire me and I'd be gone," he continued. "You're a very beautiful woman, Samantha, but not as smart as everyone believes you are."

Sam sighed once more. "All right, Morty. You win. I'm not smart. Okay, run along and tell the world that I'm a stupid, pretty princess," she quipped and made the mistake of turning her back to him.

Morty's arm came around her waist quickly as he pulled her roughly against him. Sam gasped as her head was yanked back by his other hand going around her neck. He held her tightly as he whispered in her ear, "Oh, no, I've got another message to send to Grand Serenity's royal family, my dear. A message they'll understand loud and clear!"

"Are you insane?" she asked, her voice husky with the pressure of his hand on her throat. "What are you doing? This isn't worth what's going to happen to you, Morty. You have to know that."

"What I know is that you're a foolish, privileged bitch! I tried to give you everything, tried to be what you needed, and you just tossed it all back in my face, like I wasn't worthy."

In her mind Sam screamed that he wasn't worthy, not even of breathing the same air as normal people. He was a lunatic and right about now she wished she'd seen this part of him sooner.

"Fine, Morty. We can talk about this. We can sit down and talk about what it is you want for your future. Maybe there's something you can still do within the government," she tried telling him.

"No!" he yelled and held her tighter.

So tight Sam was having a hard time sucking in enough air to be able to speak. It felt like he was not only choking her but crushing her insides with the strength of his arms around her waist.

"This isn't a good idea, Morty. It really isn't," she told him.

"Shut up!" he yelled.

"No, you shut up, you stupid idiot!"

Malayka's voice boomed from behind Sam, just before there was a crashing sound and Morty cursed.

Sam fell to her knees when his grip loosened, and turned just in time to see Malayka holding the tray that Sam kept on the edge of her desk for mail in her hands. As Morty turned to her, Malayka swung the tray at him. The edge struck his forehead and Morty yelled, "You conniving little tramp!"

It took him only seconds to move in, slapping Malayka so hard she fell back over the end of the desk. Sam jumped up then and reached for the lamp, which she fully intended to slam into Morty's head. But he turned back to her too fast.

With a quick lunge, he tackled her until she fell over one of the guest chairs. She fought him with every ounce of strength she had, swinging her arms, kicking, scratching, screaming. But he was stronger. He grabbed her by the hair and began pulling her across the floor. Sam knew instinctively that they were moving toward the balcony. She reached out to grab hold of the leg of the couch just a few feet away. She held on tight, even though she really wanted to do everything she could to keep the stinging in her scalp from making her go cross-eyed with pain.

"All you had to do was play along!" he was yelling at her. "Just accept my marriage proposal and we would've lived happily ever after! I worked too damn hard to secure my place to have you just slap it away like I was some pesky fly on the wall. All you had to do was cooperate!"

Sam did not intend to let go of the furniture, but Morty finally cursed loudly and bent to scoop her up. It was a tug of war that she wasn't certain she could win. The muscles in her arms screamed as he pulled at her. When he eventually slapped a hand to her forehead and pulled her head so far back Sam thought he might actually break her neck, she released her hold on the furniture, hoping to live just a little bit longer.

He picked her up then, carrying her to the open balcony doors. The balmy night air hit her just as he stepped out onto the balcony and Sam screamed again. She screamed so loud and strong that her throat wheezed with the effort. Her head throbbed and every part of her body ached, but still she screamed.

"Shut up, bitch! Just shut your stupid mouth for once!" he yelled.

"How about you shut your stupid mouth and let her go."

This next voice was deadly calm. It was like a whisper on the nonexistent wind as it soared through the tension-filled room. Morty whirled around, keeping his hold on her, and Sam's head bobbed as she caught her first glance of Gary.

He stood about six feet away, still in the office while they were outside, his arms stretched forward, a gun pointing directly at Morty. Or was it pointed at her? She wasn't sure. She felt nauseous and dizzy. What was happening?

"You!" Morty spat. "Where the hell did you come from?" He moved closer to the balcony railing as he spoke.

"My plan was going along just fine until you came along. You weren't supposed to be here and you definitely weren't supposed to kiss my woman. She was mine! Damn you! Mine! All of this—" he moved in a way that had the metal railing pressing painfully into Sam's side "—it was all mine and you messed it up! You and she destroyed my plans! It was going to work! We were going to have the royal wedding, not your old-ass father and his young American slut. That wedding was never supposed to happen. She knows! She knows!" Morty yelled.

"You've got exactly three seconds to let her go," Gary said in a steely tone Sam was sure she'd never heard before. "In three seconds I'm going to kill your sorry ass. End of plan."

"You don't scare me! I know who you are and you're nothing! Nobody! You don't—"

Morty's words were abruptly cut off and Sam didn't stop to see why. She simply took advantage of the fact that his grip on her loosened. She hustled away from him, falling once more onto her knees as she attempted to get back inside. Her chest hurt as she struggled to breathe, to clear her mind of the pain, and to get up off the ground and run.

In seconds she was being lifted and carried. Someone was whispering in her ear. There were more voices, more movement, but she'd stopped trying to figure it out. She'd had no choice because the blackness engulfed her. Silence and a pain-free existence finally cradled her and Sam let it. For once in her life she went without a fight. She acquiesced and she let go.

"You killed a man in my house!" Rafe roared.

"I killed the man that was threatening Samantha—your daughter," Gary countered. "He also assaulted your fiancée, Your Highness. You can have me arrested if you like, but killing him was my pleasure."

Rafe grit his teeth. "Of course there'll be no charges. You saved the princess…my daughter's life and I'm grateful," he told Gary. "Don't mistake my anger for discord. This is going to be hell in the press."

"Where the hell were the guards that were supposed to be with her and Malayka?" Roland roared. "Why were they there alone with him in the first place?"

"That's what I plan to find out," Kris stated. "Everyone in my office in fifteen minutes. Including Salvin and Captain Briggins."

"I'm not leaving Samantha," Gary stated.

"Landry will sit with her after the doctor is finished his exam," Kris stated in a tone that wasn't meant to be argued with.

But Gary didn't give a damn.

"I'm not leaving her," he reiterated. "I'll come down once I know she's all right, but right now, I'm staying right here."

She felt like crap and likely looked like it, but Sam didn't care. She knew she was in her bedroom; the scent of her lilac bath soaps and the fresh flowers that Lucie brought to her room daily wafted through the air. It was dark. She'd been blinking into the darkness for a few minutes now. And she was not alone.

A few weeks ago it would have been startling to realize the cool sanctity of her private rooms was being invaded, but not so much now. Another part of her had been invaded, as well. The thought made her want to cry. But Sam was well over that pastime. She'd cried over Miguel and swore it would be the last time any man ever caused her to shed a tear. Her three-year streak would continue.

"Why are you here?" she asked into the darkness.

She didn't know where he was in the room, but knew for sure he was there. The other scent in the room was his. It wasn't as prominent as it should have been because he'd been here so much over the last week. It was almost as if his scent belonged there, too, like a cosmic joining of sorts. That was ridiculous and out of place. Sam didn't like things out of place, yet in all this time she hadn't quite figured out where exactly Gary Montgomery fit into her life.

"I needed to see that you were all right," he answered.

Sam sighed. "Isn't that how this all began?"

She recalled every second of the day he'd come to her room and told her he needed to be sure she was okay after the shooting incident. She also recalled the kiss that led him into her bedroom.

"That's over and done with now and I'm just fine," she said when he still hadn't responded. "Dr. Beaumont says I'll have some bumps and bruises in the morning, but otherwise I'm okay."

He still did not speak.

"I should thank you," she told him quietly. "You saved my life."

"Your life should have never been in danger," he replied.

"It's my life," she quipped. "And I'm fine now."

"Are you?"

This was ridiculous. She wanted to see him. It was a struggle as she tried to sit upright, every part of her body hurting just as the doctor had warned. He was by her side before she could blink, proving that he'd been a lot closer than she'd originally thought.

His arms went around her and the familiar warmth irritated her. She didn't want that reaction. Not now. Not anymore.

Sam pulled away, scooting across the bed until she made it to the other side and was able to lean over and switch on the lamp on the nightstand.

"Yes," she said with a huff at the exertion. Reaching behind her she adjusted a pillow and leaned against it. "Thank you for saving my life. You can see for yourself that no permanent damage has been done. Now you can leave."

He looked perplexed when she chanced a gaze at him. The white tuxedo jacket was gone and so was the bow tie. The top buttons of his shirt were undone and the sleeves were rolled up to his elbows. He looked disheveled and stressed but still fine as hell.

"You want me to leave?"

Even his words sounded off. The tone of his voice was neither as steely nor calm as it usually was. It wasn't that deathly serious tone that he'd had in the moments just before he'd shot Morty, either.

"You shot him," she whispered as she looked at him.

He seemed different from the man she'd lain with previously in this very bed. Different and yet somehow the same.

"Without any hesitation you killed him," she continued. "I'm not angry with you, nor do I mean to sound accusatory or ungrateful in any way. I guess I'm just amazed that I know somebody that can kill so easily."

"He was going to hurt you," he said simply. "I gave him an option. He didn't take it."

She nodded. "I understand," she told him.

"Yet you still want me to leave?"

She swallowed and almost cried out because her throat was so sore from the screaming, she supposed, and the tight grip Morty had placed around her neck.

"I want you to leave because there's no reason for you to be here."

He walked around to the side of the bed where she was sitting. He did not sit. He reached out a hand and touched the tips of his fingers to her neck. There was a bruise there, she knew because she'd seen it when she'd used the bathroom.

"He was hurting you," Gary said softly.

Sam eased away from his touch because the conflict within her was too painful to endure.

"So are you," she admitted.

He yanked his hand back quickly and stared down at her. "What are you talking about?"

Sam lifted her chin and swallowed once more, attempting to square her shoulders without causing too much pain.

"I heard what you said to my brothers. I know that this was all about the job. You were hired to kill someone and you did. You weren't hired to sleep with me, so that's over. Your job is done, so you can go now."

Sam watched as realization hit him slowly. No, he hadn't invested any emotion into what they were doing. It had all simply been his job. But she hadn't been part of the job. Gary had told Roland and Kris his job was to kill someone and that was it. Once that was done he was leaving. So, Sam wanted him to leave. Without any more questions, without trying to figure out why he'd involved her on such a personal level in the first place. She needed him to go before the tears she'd sworn she wouldn't shed broke free.

"I'll go," he said with a slight nod to her. "If that's what you wish, I'll do it."

Sam could only nod. She feared speaking because tears were already filling her eyes, threatening to fall at any minute.

"Okay. I'll go," he said once more. "But if you need anything. If it's a glass of water or help getting to the bathroom, call me. I'll come. I promise."

She didn't want his promises. Not now.

Sam swallowed again and finally turned away from him. She could hear him leaving the room and it was just as well because that damn tear fell no matter how many times she'd told it not to. And then another one followed and another, until she was sobbing uncontrollably.

The fear she'd felt as Morty held her too close to that balcony railing and the memory of another bullet whizzing past her head, this time killing someone, clouded her thoughts. Yes, she cried for the fear and the close call she'd just faced, but Sam knew without a doubt that she also cried for Gary. For everything she'd begun to believe they could be, when she should have known better. She should have known that nobody would ever love the princess. Not the way she needed them to.

Chapter 15

Two weeks later

"I haven't seen you here in a very long time."

Sam turned at the sound of her father's voice. Rafe stood in the doorway, his broad frame blocking the bright light from the hallway behind him. She had been sitting on the couch, legs crossed, staring at nothing in particular, but now she looked at the best man she'd ever known as he closed the door and moved toward her.

"Just felt like being in here today," she said when he finally took a seat next to her.

Immediately her father reached out to hold her hand and Sam let that familiarity wash over her, praying it would provide solace.

"I used to come in here every day after she died," Rafe told her.

"Really?"

She'd been so young at that point, and so distraught herself that memories of how her father had handled her mother's death were nonexistent.

He nodded as he looked around the space that used to be Sam and her brothers' playroom.

"I would sit in the chair over there," he said, pointing to a high-backed chair that was pushed into a corner. "From there I could see every inch of the room. I could imagine her sitting on that window seat over there, with Kris leaning against her as she read to him. Then I could look over this way to the couch where she always sat on the floor and played with Roland and his train set. He loved trains when he was a boy."

"I remember," Sam said "I tell him all the time that's when he was bitten by the traveling bug."

They both chuckled.

"And you," Rafe said, lifting her hand and dropping a quick kiss on the back. "Always at that little table over there having a tea party. Vivienne would sit facing the window and you would take the chair right next to her. You always sat next to her, no matter where we went or who was there, you were by her side. In the other two chairs there would be a doll or a stuffed animal, whichever you'd chosen to invite to your party that day."

Sam continued to smile because as she looked at the table, she could see the same scene.

"I invited you one time," she told him.

Rafe nodded, his lips spreading wide into a grin. "You did. It was my birthday. Two days before your fifth birthday and you told me that morning at breakfast that the tea party was my birthday present."

Sam squeezed her father's hand. He sounded like he enjoyed that memory.

"Sometimes I feel bad that I don't remember a lot

about her," she admitted after they'd sat in silence for a minute or so. "I mean, I can see her standing in a group of people talking and smiling. I can hear her telling me how pretty a tea set was and how much she loved me." She sighed heavily. "But that's it."

"That's enough," Rafe told her. "The last part about how much she loved you is more than enough for you to remember."

"She loved you, too, you know," Sam told him. "I can see it in all the pictures of the two of you. Especially the portrait at the museum. The one that Malayka wants taken down ASAP."

It was Rafe's turn to sigh. "Yes, she's told me about that numerous times."

"As a woman, I understand her position." Even though Sam hated that she had to side with Malayka about anything. "But as a native of this island, as someone who has seen firsthand all the good that Mom did here, I feel like it would be a dishonor to her. Don't you?"

She'd turned a little on the couch so that she could look directly at her father. He was still gazing at that table. Today he wore a black dress shirt and black slacks, which gave him a very domineering look. The lines across his forehead and the grim set of his mouth said he was stressed and Sam would give anything in the world to take that look away from him.

"Are you all right, Daddy?" she asked after another few minutes of silence.

He began nodding as he squeezed her hand this time. "It's going to be all right," he said and then turned his head to her. "I'm sorry these things are happening to you, to all of us. I don't think I've been paying as much attention as I should have been."

It was an admission Sam hadn't expected to hear

from her father. Rafe was a proud man. He knew his duty and executed it with a flawless kind of swagger that Sam knew many dignitaries envied. He was decisive yet thoughtful. Caring yet stern. Vocal yet contemplative. All things she'd always figured a person of power had to be.

"There's a lot going on," she conceded.

"Yes," he replied. "A lot that I should have been looking more closely at from the start."

"Are you talking about your relationship with Malayka?" A part of her hoped like hell he was reconsidering that one. Another part prayed that if he was, that consideration wasn't the cause of the tormented expression on his face. Because as much as she disliked Malayka, she loved her father with every ounce of her being. If not being with the woman would hurt him in some way, Sam would have to suck it up and accept her. It wasn't worth hurting her father.

"I'm speaking about everything that has been going on this year. And, yes, I do agree with you. Taking down that portrait of your mother and me in the museum would dishonor Vivienne's legacy. I will not do that. Not to my children or my country."

"Malayka isn't going to be happy about that," Sam told him, instead of smiling madly and kissing his cheek because she was so proud of her father for taking that stance.

"She's not going to be happy about a few things, I suspect."

"Do you really love her, Daddy? Is she the one you want to spend the rest of your life with? If she is, I'll understand. I just know that you and Mom had a wonderful bond, one that was noticeable even on canvas. I'd hate for you to settle for less."

Rafe kissed the back of her hand again and this time his features softened as he looked at his daughter.

"I don't want you settling for less, either," he said.

Sam shrugged. "I have no illusions about what my life is. A long time ago I accepted that I might never have the same type of love you shared with Mom, and that's okay. If I can't have that, then I don't want anything," she said firmly, determined to believe her own words. Despite the pangs in her chest every night she lay down to sleep and every morning she woke after a night of explicit dreams.

"You're strong and sensible," Rafe told her. "Just like your mother."

Sam smiled at him.

"But Vivienne would never close her eyes to what was staring her right in the face."

"I agree," she told him. "So you're rethinking things between you and Malayka?"

His brow furrowed and then he smiled slowly. "No, Sammy-Girl, that's not what I was referring to."

"Oh?" Sam said, completely confused by his words. "Then I don't understand."

"I was afraid of that," Rafe said. He took both her hands then, holding them between his own. "The thing about falling in love is that we usually don't get to pre-select the person we fall for."

Sam continued to stare at her father. She could've sworn he was referring to his relationship with Malayka…

"Wait a minute," she said.

Rafe actually chuckled. "Such a bright and beautiful child you are and you've grown into a lovely woman who looks just like her mother did at her age. But my Vivienne knew love when she first felt it. She knew it before I did and wrestled me down like a champion until I got it through my thick skull. Seems to me you inherited my thick skull."

"Daddy, I'm sure I don't know what you're talking about," Sam told him. She swallowed and tried to keep her voice as steady as possible.

"Then I'm sure you're not like your mother in that regard. You and Gary have been tiptoeing around each other for the past couple of weeks when it's obvious to everyone else that your little charade took a serious turn at some point."

Sam flushed. She felt the heat fusing every portion of her body as her hands began to tremble with embarrassment.

"No. You're wrong."

"Am I?" Rafe asked. "Why are you really sitting in this room alone? You knew nobody would look for you in here so you figured you could think. Tell me what— or, rather, who—you were thinking about, Samantha."

She took a slow breath, trying to figure out what to say to convince him.

"I was actually thinking about my life these last few years, Dad. Now that you're about to remarry and Kris has married Landry, my role here in Grand Serenity will most definitely be changing. I need to figure out how I'll deal with that."

There, she thought. That sounded good and pretty damn convincing.

Rafe wasn't buying it.

"You know you'll always have a place here. You've instituted just as many good initiatives as your mother did in her time. There's no way you can just walk away from that. I, and the people of Grand Serenity, will not let you," he told her. "So, that leaves another aspect of your life that you could have been thinking about…"

"No," she said and then stood. "There's nothing else. This is my life. It has to be this way. I learned that already and there's no use thinking I should change it." Sam huffed out a breath and then continued. "I should go and take care of some letters I've been avoiding. I also need to respond to the director of the GirlPower Program at the hospital in the US. I'll see you tonight at dinner."

Rafe did not move to stand; rather, he seemed to wait patiently while Sam leaned in and kissed him on the cheek.

He nodded to her and let her take a few steps away from him before saying, "You've got to let somebody in, Sammy-Girl. If you don't, this life isn't worth living. That's what I realized when I met Malayka. Even though I could, and had done it for many years, I was not meant to live this life alone. I don't believe you were, either."

Sam stopped, her hands clasped tightly in front of her. "You don't understand, Daddy," she said quietly.

"Oh, but I do, baby. I understand everything you went through and I wanted to break every bone in that man's body for putting you through it. But you learned the lesson you needed to learn at that time. Now, years later, it's time for you to take what you learned and do something with it. Hiding behind the incident proves he won and I'll be damned if that happens. You should feel the same."

Tears were already stinging her eyes. They'd been coming too fast and too frequently these past couple of weeks and she hated it. She hated the reason for them and the helplessness they caused her to feel. So when she probably should have said something else to her father, Sam simply shook her head and walked out of the room.

She walked pretty fast to get to her rooms, which were on the second floor and at the opposite side of the palace. But when her door was in sight she started to run, opening it and slamming it tight behind her before collapsing to the floor and letting the tears flow once again.

"I'll be going to Baltimore with her," Gary said that evening when they were sitting at the dinner table.

Sam's fork fell to her plate with a loud clatter. Malayka rolled her eyes and Landry used her napkin to cover her mouth and the grin she was obviously trying to suppress.

Rafe stared at Gary a moment before giving a slight nod of his head. "That's probably a good idea," he said after what seemed like endless moments of tense silence.

"So he'll be her private bodyguard now?" Malayka asked. "And her secret lover?"

Now, Landry gasped and Kris frowned. Roland had already taken his leave once more, but not before telling Gary that he'd done a good job of taking care of Morty.

Gary figured that might be as close to a thank-you or a truce that the two of them would manage. He'd accepted whatever it was and continued to speak to Roland after they'd finished one of several meetings they'd had with palace security and Kris over the past two weeks. While Roland had been away he'd been following up on the break-in at the bank to see if he could trace the money back to someone, anyone, who'd also had dealings with Malayka. Gary wasn't sure that Roland's investigation was going to be fruitful, but he'd admitted that it was worth a shot. After recalling Morty's comments the night of the ball about Malayka knowing that the royal wedding was never supposed to take place, Gary was certain she was connected. And since the soon-to-be princess had put Sam in the line of fire, Gary was game for investigating any and everything that would finally lead them to the truth.

"I believe he's listed as a security consultant," Sam

managed to say after taking a big gulp from the glass of wine.

Malayka waved her fork in the air in a "whatever" fashion before spearing it into the grilled chicken salad she'd opted to have for dinner. Gary and the rest of the family were having a fabulous jerk pulled-pork entrée.

"Didn't we just have a complaint about a staff member sexually harassing a member of the family? Yes, I believe we did. And that person ended up dead." Malayka forked the food into her mouth and wiggled her eyebrows as she stared at Gary this time.

Gary almost mentioned Morty's comments at that moment. In the past couple of weeks he'd had to resist the urge to simply ask Malayka what Morty was talking about that night. The only thing that kept him from doing so was that he was dedicated to obtaining all the facts before shattering the façade of Prince Rafe's happy-ever-after with this woman.

"That's enough," Rafe said in a stony tone. "Gary does work for us and as such he will travel with Samantha to oversee her safety during this trip."

"And what about the personal aspect?" Malayka continued.

She was only on her second glass of wine, but Gary had suspected when she'd stumbled toward her seat earlier that she may have had a drink or two before coming down to dinner.

"When I was at that godforsaken opening ceremony for the ridiculous garden show yesterday, a reporter asked when there was going to be another royal wedding. I, of course, assumed he was talking about our impending nuptials," she said, looking at Rafe, but then shook her head. "Nope. He was referring to the princess and her Sir Galahad!"

The last part of her statement was said in a louder tone, with her arm going up to wave the napkin she'd scooped from her lap around her head.

Rafe stood, his expression grim as he moved toward her.

"We're going to head upstairs now," he said to her.

Malayka didn't move. "I'm not sleepy," she told him. "I'm mad."

Rafe moved around to the back of her chair and put his hands under her arms to lift her up.

"This is supposed to be about me. My time. My wedding. My turn at ruling on this island. She's taking everything!"

Gary didn't know what to do except stare. Malayka sounded eerily like his ex-wife when he'd received the first offer from the publisher for his book. As a former championship gymnast, Tonya was the star of their family—at least that's what she liked to think. At first, he'd admitted it had been easy to fall back and let her have the spotlight. She went to all kinds of speaking events given she was a quasi-star. He'd attended but often felt like nothing more than her bodyguard. It was a good thing his military training had often called for him to be in the background—the watcher, he supposed—otherwise he might have been offended. Now Gary found himself watching another woman.

He looked at Samantha while Rafe was working to get Malayka out of the dining room. She didn't like what he'd said about going with her, but she wouldn't express that, not in front of her family.

"Kris and I are going to head up now, as well," Landry said, breaking Gary from the trance he'd been in. "I'm a little tired."

He watched Samantha reach for her wineglass, then

think better of it—possibly after realizing that Malayka was drunk—and set the glass down again. She'd let her hands fall to her lap at that point and now looked at Landry.

"You're a really bad liar," Sam replied to her sister-in-law.

Landry shrugged and gave Sam a smile as Kris went over to kiss his sister on the forehead.

"See me before you fly out," Kris said to Gary, who nodded his agreement.

Landry actually gave him a conspiratorial wink as she walked out and Gary couldn't help but smile at her. He liked the new princess of Grand Serenity. He liked her a lot and was glad that his friend had found such a down-to-earth and special lady to spend his life with. He could feel that way and not resent the fact that his attempt at happy-ever-after hadn't gone so well.

"I'm sure this is all very funny to you," Sam said when they were in the large formal dining room alone.

The table was huge, way too long and too pristine to be the place where a family had their dinner every night. He was used to the old oak table his father had built when he was sixteen. It still sat in the kitchen at Gary's house today, serving its only purpose of holding each one of the meals he enjoyed when he was back home in Cambridge.

"Actually, it's not," he replied and sat back in his chair. "Your father is going to have to deal with her drinking before it gets out of hand like it has before."

"What? Wait. Malayka had a drinking problem in the past? How do you know this?" she asked, her attention cleverly averted from his previous smile and the fact that he'd said he was going to Baltimore with her.

Gary wanted to give himself a pat on the back.

"I've done my homework on her. Two years ago she was picked up for a DWI in Washington, DC. No charges were ever brought against her, that's probably why it didn't show up in the background check that Kris did before she came here."

"If it doesn't show up on a background check, how do you know?"

He shrugged. "I have ways of finding out things."

She sat back in her chair as well, and stared at him. "When did you find out about my past with Miguel?"

He hadn't expected that question at all. Judging from the way she carried herself, Gary had been willing to bet money on the fact that the last person in this world Samantha ever wanted to talk about again was Miguel Lopata.

"The week before I arrived here," he replied. There was no sense in lying. Besides, if there was one thing Gary despised, it was dishonesty. He'd had enough of that to last him a lifetime.

She was angry. Or was she embarrassed? Her lips had closed tightly, her arms stiffening at her sides. But she never broke eye contact, never wanted to show anyone that she could be touched by what they said or thought.

"Is that your job?" she asked him, her voice just a notch lower than it had been before.

"My job is to know all the players, not just the target," he told her. "I compile a full picture before taking any action."

She began shaking her head slowly. "No wonder you weren't shocked when I kissed you. Not one moment's hesitation. You just went right along with it. Probably because after seeing those pictures and reading that article you classified me as the Prowling Princess, as well."

Her words ticked him off instantly.

"Don't insult me," he said through clenched teeth. "I've never been anything but respectful to you, so don't mask your embarrassment over a situation you had no control over with rude and callous remarks toward me."

"Callous? You want to talk callousness?" she asked as she leaned forward and flattened her palms on the table.

"You're the one who suggested this fake affair and then slept with me, on more than one occasion I might add, when you were supposed to be working for my family. You poked around in my past, made yourself comfortable coming in and out of my room when you pleased, hijacking my car and making plans for me. You didn't give a damn what I might have been feeling about our situation, or how I was going to react when you just packed your bags and left. I guess I was just part of the assignment!"

She shot up out of the chair, pushing it back with her legs so fast it fell to the floor.

Gary did not yell even though he was feeling pretty agitated by this point. She was accusing him of something ridiculous. He would never manipulate a woman, for any purpose. So to suggest that he'd taken advantage of their situation, or even planned to toy with her emotions, was simply ludicrous.

"Everything we did was consensual," he reminded her. "You wanted. I wanted. We did it. Period."

"You knew things about me before I even knew your name. You didn't tell me you were hired to kill someone. And, dammit, you made me feel like…you opened…I mean—" She clamped her mouth shut and made a sound that was more animalistic than coherent and Gary slowly came to his feet.

"Again, nothing happened between us that we did not both want and agree to. This was not my intention," he told her. "I haven't thought about committing to a woman since my divorce, so believe me when I say I'm just as thrown off by this as you are."

She was shaking her head again.

"I realize now that there's more here than either of us anticipated. So maybe we should take a deep breath and talk about this like the consenting adults that we are."

"No," she answered immediately. "It's too late. I mean, it's not even necessary. You're right, I consented. I knew and I should have protected myself better."

She lifted her hands and pushed her hair back behind her ears. After a deep breath she said, "But it's done, so we just need to move forward. Your job for my family isn't done. I understand that."

Now her hands ran down the front of her dress and fisted at her sides.

"I'll be ready to leave for the airport by noon tomorrow," she said stiffly before turning to walk out of the room.

"You're not a quitter," he said before she could make a fast exit. "You've been in hiding since Lopata pulled that stupid stunt three years ago. When are you going to decide he doesn't deserve that victory?"

She waited a few seconds, during which time Gary wasn't certain she would even reply. But finally she turned back to him, hands clasped calmly in front of her. She looked at him directly, those proud shoulders squared as she began to speak.

"You know nothing about me," she said slowly. "I don't care how much research you did. You have no idea who I am or what I'm capable of. Let's just leave it at that."

No, Gary decided when she'd walked away, leaving him alone in the elegantly decorated dining room. He would not leave it at that, regardless of what she'd just said.

Chapter 16

The Kennedy Krieger Institute at Johns Hopkins Hospital was proud to stand with Samantha, the goodwill ambassador of Grand Serenity Island, to announce their collaborative effort to treat, inspire, instruct and empower young ladies on an array of medical issues on a global platform.

It had been Sam's work with the Bella Club that had made her a perfect fit with the institute. For years, Sam had worked with the young ladies of Grand Serenity, teaching, guiding and being a hands-on mentor to the group. It was the one thing she felt proud of because it had been her project from the start, instead of picking up where her mother left off.

GirlPower International was commemorated with Samantha and the director of the institute's Global Outreach shaking hands.

Sam had worn a soft pink pantsuit with a simple white blouse to symbolize her femininity, as well as her power. Her jewelry was an understated brushed-silver necklace and matching earrings. On her right ring finger was the sterling silver and yellow diamond ring her father had given her for her sixteenth birthday. It was the princess version of the royal insignia ring that her brothers and father wore.

As she'd stepped out of the limousine an hour and a half ago she'd held a pink clutch in her hand and slipped on pink-framed, large-lens sunglasses. Her shoes were Badgley Mischka blossom-pink, satin-silk pumps and her hair was flat-ironed straight as a bone, hanging well past her shoulders. She exuded confidence and intelligence and she looked like a million bucks.

Now, leaving the beautifully constructed facility in Baltimore, Sam had once again slipped onto the backseat of the limousine. She dropped her purse beside her and let her head lay back against the headrest.

"You did good," Gary said from across the seat.

He hadn't left her side all day. They'd landed earlier that morning and while she'd checked into a hotel room to change and prepare for the meeting, he had been in the adjoining room, with the door between them ajar. He'd walked beside her every step of the way and stood just a few feet behind her as she'd stepped up to the podium for the ceremony. Even if she hadn't seen him, hadn't picked up the scent of his cologne, Sam would have known he was there.

Gary Montgomery had an authoritative and domineering presence. It cloaked him like a blanket, resting easily on his broad shoulders. When he spoke, people naturally listened and, to Sam's surprise, obeyed. He supervised the newly hired security detail for her trip to America with a stern yet respectful tone. Each member of the detail was ex-military, which is probably why they so easily fell in line with Gary's command. Still, it had been intriguing to watch him give orders and direct everyone, down to Lucie who had traveled with her, on what they should do and when.

"Thank you," she said without looking at him.

She took a deep breath and released it slowly, determined to stop thinking of him in any capacity.

"What time is the flight out?" she asked after a few moments of silence.

"Two of the guards will accompany Lucie back to the island later this evening," he replied.

It took her a second to realize he'd only said Lucie and then Sam did turn her head to him. "Just Lucie?"

"Yes," he replied.

He turned to look at her, as well. Both their eyes were hidden by sunglasses. Where she had a very professional, feminine look today, Gary was the slick bodyguard. His suit was black and expertly fitted to his muscular frame. His shirt, crisp and white. His tie, blue. His shoes, shiny black tie-ups. In his left ear was a clear hearing device with the squiggly cord resting behind his ear and a thinner cord going down into the collar of his shirt. He wore no jewelry. His hair was close cut, wavy on top. His goatee was trimmed neatly. She liked this look on him.

"I want to show you something before you return to the island," he told her. "It's an hour and a half ride, and if you're ready to leave when we're done, I'll arrange for the plane to come back and pick you up."

She didn't know what to say to that but finally asked, "What do you want to show me?"

His hands lay flat on his thighs as he gave a slight nod of his head. "Just something that I think you'll enjoy. Call it an outing," he said when he saw she'd been about to comment once more. "Because I know you like to have a title for everything that goes into your itinerary book."

Sam sighed as she thought of the itinerary app she had on her tablet. It synced her schedule with the calendar system Kris had implemented for the royal family, while offering a private setting for her personal appointments, as well.

"There's nothing wrong with being organized," she told him.

"No, nothing at all wrong with it," he replied. "Just saying that now you have a title for what we're going to do for the rest of the day."

"I need to go back to the hotel to change," she informed him.

"I've taken care of it," he replied.

"Have you taken care of everything?"

"I tried," he told her with a half smile.

It was a very sexy half smile, but Sam didn't want to acknowledge that. She looked out the window.

"Is this an outing I will enjoy?"

"We're both going to enjoy it."

Something in his tone had Sam clasping her thighs tightly together. It had been weeks since he'd touched her, or kissed her, or held her in his arms. She'd tried pleasuring herself when the need became too intense, but it hadn't worked. The edge of desire was still there. As long as he stayed close, Sam was afraid it would remain. For that reason she prayed this little outing would involve a public place and a lot of people, or the resolve she'd been trying to rebuild would be shot completely to hell.

* * *

It was nothing like she'd expected, Sam thought as she walked through the front door.

Maybe she should have suspected this because when the door to the limousine had opened, she'd stepped out onto a dirt road. That road had given way to a stone pathway leading in two directions. One stopped at a wood-planked dock that stretched a few feet out onto a magnificent river. There were two boats there: a large, older one and a smaller, faster-looking vessel. But the river was really what caught her breath. Where Sam was used to looking out to the gorgeous turquoise-blue sea and seeing nothing but water on the horizon, here the water appeared darker and not as calm. Lush green grass formed the banks as opposed to dazzling white sand, and not a far distance across the water was more grass and more houses. Boat slips and boats. People actually sailing along the river. All of it gave a communal feel that Sam hadn't been used to.

Turning in the direction that Gary had already begun to travel, Sam walked along the stone path, noting that the dirt had given way to thick, perfect, green grass. Her pink peep-toe pumps seemed woefully out of place as she moved onto stone steps and made her way up to the porch of the most picturesque little cabin she'd ever seen. Well, okay, it wasn't actually little. There were two stories and a gable roof. Part of the porch—toward the left end—was screened. This part, where the massive wood door and full-length side windows were, was open, with two welcoming rockers on each side.

His parents, she thought immediately. They would have sat here to watch the sun set over the river. No matter how hard Sam tried to fend against it, the thought warmed her heart.

"I figured you'd want to change clothes. So I had Lucie

pack your bags and they were delivered while we were in Baltimore," Gary said as he unlocked the door to let them inside.

Sam stepped in, her heels clicking loudly on the wood floors before she turned to him and asked, "Where are we now?"

"Cambridge, Maryland," he replied after closing and locking the door. "It's on Maryland's eastern shore."

She nodded. "You grew up here."

"I grew up a little closer to town. I bought this place a few years ago after my father passed away." He began moving as if he didn't want to stay too long on that subject.

"There's a guest room on this level and two more bedrooms upstairs. You just head straight through the living room, down that hallway, and you'll see the room. There's also a bathroom down there. I'm going to go upstairs to change."

Sam looked around as he spoke.

The center of the room was anchored with a huge stone fireplace that looked straight out of the Colonial era. The ceilings were beamed with thick log rafters. The walls were a subtle contrast, smooth and painted a shade that reminded Sam of coffee with way too much cream. On a glance the walls could have been construed as plain, but the wide baseboards and dark wood trim matched the tone of the beams, bringing them back to life. The furniture was a combination of leather and wood, and big plump pillows in another dull beige tone that worked well with large masculine chairs and dark chocolate leather upholstery.

"Um, where are we going?" she asked when she found herself getting too caught up in the décor. "I mean, I need to know what type of outfit I should change into."

He was nearing a set of stairs that looked as if logs

had simply been cut in two and nailed together. It was a rustic look that for some reason appealed to her.

"Dress casually," he told her. Then he looked her up and down. "Well, as casually as a princess can."

If he hadn't smiled after the remark Sam might have bristled. On a sigh she realized she was ready to bite at whatever Gary said or did lately. It was the pain that still lingered. The pain of her own stupidity, she concluded. This was not personal. There was no happy-ever-after for her. She'd accepted it before and there was no reason she couldn't wrap her mind around it once again. Except that Sam was growing tired of living that way.

Still, she didn't think any longer on Gary's princess remark. Instead she walked in the direction he'd told her, finding the guest bedroom and her suitcases neatly placed near the bed. A queen-size bed made entirely of wood, with drawers beneath the thick mattresses and a multicolored quilt on top sat in the middle of the room. She smiled at the huge windows that opened up to what she figured was the back of the house. Tall trees, more grass, ambience. She stood at the window for a few seconds, taking it all in.

There was a serenity to this place, to its surroundings. A quiet type of informality that she envied. The palace was nothing like this. It was big and beautiful, elegant, formal and sometimes colder than an Alaskan winter. Here there was warmth. Not just from the outside temperature—she was used to that. No, there was something else, a sort of welcoming feel that she'd experienced the moment her heels had made contact with the dirt road.

Oh, well, she thought with another sigh, better to get the outing over with so she could return to her real life. Sam opened her suitcase and found the most casual outfit she'd thought to pack. This wasn't supposed to be a long trip, but Sam had learned long ago to always pack more than she needed.

She took off the pink pantsuit that was beyond out of place there, folded it neatly and placed it on the back of a rocking chair near the dresser. That was wood, too, with a big mirror, where she examined herself after slipping on the khaki pants and peach-colored camisole. There was a jacket to the pants, but she figured she could go without it. She'd appear more casual that way. She wore sandals with a lower heel than the pumps she'd set next to the rocking chair. Feeling like she still looked too prim and proper, Sam removed her necklace and the matching earrings. She pulled out her toiletry bag, found her brush and then proceeded to pull her hair back into a high ponytail.

Her makeup hadn't been heavy, but she still felt like she looked too put together. There just didn't seem to be a point for that there. So she grabbed the toiletry bag and headed across the hall to the bathroom. There she washed her face and then used a light bronzer over her cheeks, chin and forehead. A stroke of eyeliner, some mascara and a neutral-toned lip gloss completed the look.

"There," she said to herself in the mirror with a satisfied smile. "You look almost normal."

Almost, she thought, because deep down she still knew who she was. No amount of dressing down would change that she was a princess.

The only other purse she had was a large Givenchy bag that she didn't think was casual at all, so she'd decided to forego the purse altogether. She slipped her cell phone into her front pants' pocket, spritzed a little perfume—a soft vanilla-type scent—and headed back to the living room.

He was already there, waiting for her.

"Is this casual enough?" she asked as she moved farther into the room.

"Perfect," he said with barely a glance at her. "As always."

"You are, too," Sam said without thinking first.

When he looked at her in surprise, she cleared her throat and continued, "You're always so composed. Your objective is clear and you move toward it, no questions or hesitations. And that's just your mental state. But even your clothes are on point with whatever situation you've planned to be in. I would say it was methodical, but I think it's more ingrained than that. It's simply your personality."

There was silence when she finished. Gary stared at her and she glared back at him. Like a standoff but without the requisite tension. Just a casual acknowledgment, Sam thought before she moved toward the door. He stepped quickly in front of her and opened it.

"Thanks," she said when what she'd really been thinking was that she knew how to open doors for herself.

It was silly, especially considering her position. People opened doors for her all the time. They pulled out chairs, asked what she needed and provided it for her. She wouldn't classify herself as a pampered princess, but to an extent, it could be true. No matter how she wanted it to be different.

For Gary, it was the polar opposite. He hadn't been pampered. He'd been teased until he'd had no choice but to fight back, and he'd loved his parents to the end. So Sam walked through that door and did not say a word when Gary led them to a bright red pickup.

She couldn't help it, she giggled.

"Something funny about my truck?" he asked as he

lifted his arm and pointed the remote toward the truck, disengaging the locks and alarm system.

"It's red," she said and shook her head. "I'm sorry. It's not funny, it's just odd. I would never guess you would have a candy-apple-red truck."

He opened the passenger door and waited for her to walk around it before saying, "It's called Barcelona Red Metallic."

She chuckled again. "Still doesn't quite fit you."

He extended his hand and Sam put hers in his.

"Step up on the running board," he told her. "Or I can lift you up and put you inside."

A choice. Sam liked the idea that he'd given her a choice this time.

With her hand in his, Sam stepped up onto the running board and lifted herself into the cab of the truck. Gary climbed inside just as she finished clicking her seat belt in place. He started the engine and backed up without saying another word. Sam didn't speak, either. Instead she sat back and enjoyed the sights. There was lots of greenery—grass, trees, shrubbery in front of the large houses they began to pass. The sky was a pristine type of blue today, complete with the puffy clouds Sam remembered seeing as she'd lain on the beach staring up when she was a young girl.

"That one right there looks like an elephant," she said after using the remote to lower the window.

She was shocked when Gary jumped right in. "And that one over there looks like a unicorn. See the horn stretching over that way?"

Sam leaned forward as Gary was looking out the front windshield. "Yeah, I see it. If it moves a step or two closer, its horn will definitely poke the elephant. That won't be a pretty scenario."

"Not at all," he said and chuckled.

Sam laughed, too, as she settled back in her seat and continued to stare out the windows. They drove a bit farther until she could see out of one window that they were riding along the shore of more water.

"The Choptank River is a tributary to Chesapeake Bay. It flows all the way down this way," he told her.

She nodded. "It's serene here. I like it."

"I like it, too," he told her.

A while later they were pulling onto a stretch of grass where other vehicles were parked. Gary cut the ignition and undid his seat belt. Sam figured this meant they were getting out, so she undid her seat belt, as well. She was just about to reach for the door handle when Gary touched her arm to stop her.

"My mom's favorite color was red," he told her. "Just before my dad died, he picked out a red dress online and had me order it for her. I buried her in that dress because she said it was her favorite gift from my dad, besides me."

He looked momentarily uncomfortable, so Sam covered the hand he had on her arm. She let her fingers rest over his and then looked up at him.

"It's a wonderful tribute to her," she told him. "You were a great son and I'm sure she was bursting with pride for you."

He nodded and then moved to get out of the truck. He was at the passenger-side door by the time she was about to jump down. Gary clamped his hands around her waist and lifted her out of the truck. When her feet touched the ground his hands stayed on her. Sam let hers fall to her sides as he stared down at her. She smiled and backed away.

"What's this place?"

"It's the Maryland Seafood Festival," he said just after

she heard the truck door close. "Great food. Wine. Gorgeous scenery. Just what was prescribed to unwind after a long day's work," he told her.

"It was a two-hour tour and press conference," she told him.

"It was work and that's all you ever seem to do. I think this will be a good place for you to unwind a bit. To just relax for a while."

Sam was about to say something to that when a voice from behind stopped her.

"Well, well, well. Look what the sunshine brought in," a slow and seductive voice said.

Sam turned just in time to see the woman brush past her and grab Gary around the neck, pulling him down for a tight hug. Well, it was tight on her part. As for Gary, he'd given her a little pat on her back before letting his arms fall to his sides.

"Hello, Tonya," he said in a tone that was less than enthusiastic.

"Hi, sweetie. I was beginning to think you were never coming back to town," the woman replied after Gary grabbed her wrists and unwrapped them from his neck.

"Hello," Sam said because she was beginning to feel like a third wheel and did not like that feeling one bit.

The woman turned slowly and looked at Sam as if she'd just realized she was standing there. Sam may have grown up in a palace and thus had a different type of childhood and introduction to the social niceties, but she wasn't stupid. She recognized an unhappy woman when she saw one.

This Tonya person was definitely unhappy.

She was a very pretty woman with caramel-toned skin and blond dreadlocks. She wore black shorts and a white T-shirt with a huge red crab on its front with Maryland

is for Crab Lovers written in red, black and gold script.
She was smiling but it was a different type of smile. The
kind that didn't reach the eyes.

"Well, hi," Tonya said and stepped in Sam's direction.
"Who are you?"

"Samantha DeSaunters," Sam said, extending her hand
to her. "It's nice to meet you."

Tonya looked at the hand a second longer than was
polite before shaking.

"Oh, okay, Samantha. Are you a visiting relative? I
don't recall you having any other family around, Gary."

Tonya spoke to Gary but she did not take her gaze off
Sam. She was looking at everything from the band holding Sam's hair together to the polish on her nails and the
straps on her shoes. Or at least, that's the way it appeared
to Sam. She wasn't unnerved because Sam was more than
used to people staring at her. What did bother her was
the look of disdain Tonya was giving her. Now, that was
something Sam was not used to. Not until Malayka had
entered the scene, anyway.

"She's Princess Samantha DeSaunters from Grand
Serenity Island," Gary corrected.

He came to stand beside Sam and they both looked at
Tonya whose eyes had grown wider.

"You're a princess?" she asked in disbelief. Then she
actually laughed. "Are you serious? Or is that just what
she told you to get you into bed?"

"Okay, that's enough," Gary said. "We're leaving." He
took Sam's hand and turned away from Tonya.

They hadn't taken more than three steps before she
yelled out, "He's a liar and a cheater!"

Sam stopped walking before Gary did. She turned
to look at Tonya, which, from the way she'd folded her

arms across her chest in triumph, was exactly what the woman had wanted Sam to do.

"That's right. I was married to him. For a year and a half, and I tried to be everything a wife should be to her husband. But it wasn't enough for him. No, I think he was intimidated by my success as a star athlete and all the attention that drew. But that was no reason for him to sleep with our neighbor. Bastard!"

Sam couldn't believe what she was seeing and she didn't believe what she was hearing, either. Just a few minutes ago this woman had had her arms wrapped around Gary's neck. She'd been smiling up into his face, rubbing her ample breasts against his chest, very happy to see him. Now she seemed just as happy to embarrass him.

"Oh, that's okay," Sam replied much to the woman's surprise. "You see, I'm known as the Prowling Princess. That means I go through men quicker than I do tiaras. So he won't be breaking my heart if he cheats on me. In fact, I'm likely to cheat on him first."

At her words Tonya's mouth opened then closed, then opened once more as she slapped her hands on her hips. The woman didn't know what to say, which made Sam feel triumphant.

"That's not funny!" Tonya snapped.

Sam turned to see that the woman was staring at Gary, who was, in fact, laughing. She'd never heard him laugh like that before.

"Look, Miss...whoever you are—'cause I'm not believing that princess crap at all. He's not worth your time and wherever you purchased those shoes, you should send them back because they're horrible knock-offs."

With that Tonya sashayed her very generous bottom away from where they stood.

Gary's chuckles subsided when they were once again alone. He then looked at Sam and said with a victorious grin, "I wish you lived in Cambridge."

Chapter 17

Samantha moaned and the sound sent pleasure tendrils throughout Gary's body. Like, literally, he shivered from the jolt of arousal that shot through him when he heard the sound. He looked up to see her lying on her back, her hands splayed over her abdomen, mouth partially open and eyes closed.

"I ate too much," she complained. "Why did you let me eat so much?"

Gary cleared his throat as a way to also clear his mind. It didn't work because he was still thinking about ripping her clothes off and taking her right there on the blanket where they lay close to the water.

"I didn't tell you to sample everything you saw," he said and continued to massage one of her feet on his lap.

"You said, and I quote, 'This is some of the best food you will ever taste in your life. Everything is freshly caught from the Chesapeake Bay and seasoned generously with Maryland's signature Old Bay Seasoning.' Those were your words exactly."

Because she'd lifted an arm and dropped it over her eyes Gary could smile at her pouting lips. Well, he could smile until he imagined those lips on him, around him… Damn, this wasn't going the way he'd imagined.

When he'd realized Samantha had needed to come to the States for a business trip, he'd felt like his mother was actually reaching down and giving him a little push. Well, considering what he'd gone through with Tonya, it had actually taken a pretty big push to get him to go after another woman. This time, however, Gary had finally admitted to himself that he didn't think he needed his mother's push at all. He'd already fallen completely, head-over-heels in love with Samantha.

It hadn't been a quiet or sneaky type of fall, either. Nor had it been foreseen or even cultivated the way he had attempted with Tonya. No, this time it had smacked him in the face the moment he'd first seen her. But no matter how high his IQ was judged by a written exam, he hadn't seen it until the night she'd first placed her lips on his.

"I did say that," he replied. "But I didn't fix two plates after I'd had samples of everything, either."

"Ugh." She groaned this time. "Two plates! You let me eat two whole plates of food? And that fruit punch had to have contained at least a gallon of sugar. I feel sick."

"You look beautiful," he told her.

Her arm slid from her face and she stared at him through partially parted lids. "What? You think my bloated look and the greenish color of my skin, because I'm afraid I might puke at any moment, is beautiful?"

Gary smiled, now touching both her feet as he stared up at her.

"Yes," he said. "That's what I think."

She waited a minute, processing his words, he thought. Then she shook her head. "You had too many beers."

He chuckled.

"Yet you let me drive you back here and convince you to sit out under the night sky, instead of telling me to call your limo back and get your plane ready to take you to Grand Serenity."

Saying the words aloud made him irritable, but he had thought it so many times this afternoon, it was no wonder he would speak them now. Sending her maid and her jet home without Samantha was a gamble. She didn't like it when he made decisions for her. While he figured she was used to people doing that, he could also see why it bothered her. The only problem with that was that he was used to giving commands. He'd led an elite team of snipers in the army, calling the shots for adult men. She was a princess in a family of powerful and authoritative men, it was no wonder she hated being told what to do and when to do it. Yet she was loyal and astute enough to disagree with pride and elegance.

That was only one of the things he adored about her.

The quick and efficient way in which she'd cut Tonya off at the knees this afternoon was another.

"I didn't want to go back," she said, her voice softer this time.

"That worked in my favor," he said and let his hands move over her feet to grip her ankles.

"I hate saying it," she conceded. "Admitting that I don't want to go home. It sounds so juvenile. Besides, I have responsibilities. I've always had duties. I was born with them."

"You were also born to live," he told her as his hands pushed her pants up a bit so that he could touch the skin of her calves.

He loved how her skin felt beneath his touch. Smooth, warm skin gliding along his big palms was like a slice of heaven.

"And you can live outside of Grand Serenity," he continued. "Outside of the crown with all its duties and responsibilities."

"No, I can't," she said. "I'm the princess, remember?"

"Not today you weren't. You were just a woman at a food festival eating and drinking too much just like everybody else."

She sat up slowly, her hair falling down around her shoulders, hands resting in her lap.

"Is that why you left the army? To be just a guy like everybody else?"

She always had questions. Gary had been trained to look for answers. They were matched in so many areas it was odd.

"I didn't like what I was doing anymore," he stated evenly. That was the easiest way he could explain feeling used and dissuaded. "I was fighting a war for a country that didn't take care of their own."

"The United States has the most powerful military in the world," she said.

"And they have a horrifically insufficient program to take care of their veterans. My father served in the Vietnam war. He was enlisted in the army for twenty years before retiring. But when he became sick, his doctor's bills soared and the supplemental insurance he had didn't do a damn thing. They exhausted their savings and my mother's pension trying to take care of him. If I hadn't left the military when I did, they would have lost their house."

Gary sighed. He looked out at the river, saw the moonlight's glossy glow over the water and shook his head slowly.

"I came home and I did what I could to make money as fast as I could to help them. All of my monthly checks from the service had been deposited directly into my parents' account and they were still drowning in debt. When I was in high school I was on the wrestling team. For a while I thought that would be my ticket to college since I knew my parents didn't have the money for me to go."

He took a deep breath and let it out slowly. "Who knew all that time I had to myself where I had spent reading books would make me smart enough to receive a full scholarship."

"Smart and cute. You were a deadly combination before you were even trained to be one," she said.

"I guess that's what got me onto the wrestling circuit. Two years in the professional league and I made more money than I had in all my life. I paid off my parents' house and those medical bills a week before my father died. The day after we buried him my mother told me to put the house on the market, that she couldn't live there without him. So I bought her a one-bedroom condo newly built closer to town and the river. A month after that I received my first book contract." He shook his head at the memory.

"Looking back now, I wish I'd had the nerve to submit my book for publication long before my dad became sick. Maybe if I had, I would have been able to use the book money to get him better medical treatment."

"I didn't know you were a writer," she said. "There's so much more to you than I originally thought."

"I could say the same about you," Gary admitted. "I had no idea how involved you were with the young ladies on the island. Helping to shape their young minds is commendable."

"Thank you," she said with a nod. "I enjoy it. But not enough to let you use that as a way to change the subject. What type of books do you write?"

"You caught on to that, huh?" he asked jokingly. "I'm a mystery writer. I write under the pen name Sampson Christopher. It's my mother's last name and my father's first name."

She tilted her head and grinned. "My brother hired a mystery writer to come to the palace and solve the mystery of who was trying to hurt us. That was very clever of him."

Gary shook his head. "Kris doesn't know about my writing. Not many people do. My mother knew and now you and, of course, Tonya."

"I have to say I do not see what attracted you to her. I mean she's a pretty woman but she seems awfully vindictive."

He didn't feel good talking about one of the biggest mistakes of his life. But from the way she was looking at him, she wasn't going to let this go, either.

"I married Tonya because my mother always wanted to see me happily married so that I could give her grandchildren. That was a colossal mistake. I should have known that when I met Tonya while I was on the wrestling circuit. Six months in, she started accusing me of sleeping around and lying to her. I don't know where it came from or why it started. In the end, I told her it was best that we go our separate ways because all the drama was much more than I could stand. She was happy with a hefty financial settlement, thanks to my first publishing contract."

"You know you don't have to keep proving how great

a guy you are. I get it now," she said after staring at him for a few moments.

"Now?" he asked and then grinned. "You didn't think I was a good guy before?" The question was meant as a joke but Gary knew there was more he needed to explain to her.

"I know you heard me telling your brothers that I planned to leave as soon as my job was done. That wasn't a lie. It was my plan. But somewhere along the way I knew that plan was beginning to change. I knew that there was something more between us than the fake affair or the job. I should have said something to you sooner, should have let you know how I was feeling."

She shook her head. "In the last couple of weeks I'll admit that I've been thinking you were a special kind of demon sent to destroy the last shreds of the woman I thought I was. But the more I look at you, the more I see what you do and how you do it, and then I hear why you do it... I just can't continue to feed that illusion.

"In the beginning," Sam continued, "I was so together, so busy believing that I'd found the answer to being hurt in relationships. I had a great job and a big bank account. I lived in a palace and had people around who loved and cared for me. I could even provide my own sexual pleasure. There was nothing I needed from a man. Nothing. Until I realized that it wasn't about what I needed from a man but what I wanted in my life." She shrugged then, a smile wavering on her lips. "So if you were a demon, I must have been a total bitch these past few years."

Gary touched her cheek. "I think you're a pretty wonderful lady," he told her.

She sighed. "Because of my title?"

"No," he answered immediately. "That's just a word. Born with or without it, you would have still been beautiful and special. And I would have wanted nothing more than to sit on a blanket in the middle of the night, beneath the stars with you."

She smiled, slow and sexy as hell, and the hormones that had settled minutely while he'd been talking about his parents and his past resurged.

"What else do you think we could do beneath these stars?" she asked him.

He could say nothing. He could remind her that she was a princess and that they should consider her privacy. But they weren't on Grand Serenity anymore. Nobody knew who she was here, or didn't immediately recognize her, not while she was dressed like a normal woman and on his arm. Besides all that, this was his property and it was private.

"So many things," Gary replied.

He moved his hands farther up her legs before grasping her by her waist. In one quick motion he had her straddling him.

"But we could start with a kiss."

Sam remembered that first kiss the second Gary's lips touched hers. She wrapped her legs around his waist, her arms around his neck and leaned in for the ride. He was kissing her so deeply, holding her so tightly, she thought at any moment they would both simply float away with the euphoria of the moment.

When she'd been lying back on the blanket she'd seen the stars, tiny pricks of light creating a dazzling landscape of the sky. There was the scent of the sea in the air, different than what she was used to but familiar enough to offer a sense of comfort. It was quiet and Gary was there. It hadn't taken her long to realize how important that was.

It seemed as if they'd been through so much in such a short amount of time. That with everything going on around them, there should have been no time for this connection between them to grow and become stronger. No time for pleasure.

He pulled at the hem of her shirt, his teeth nipping along the line of her jaw. Sam did the same, removing his shirt with a giggle after he'd already removed hers. He unsnapped her bra and tossed it to the side, leaning down to catch one nipple between his teeth while rubbing the other with his palm. She needed more. The contact of skin on skin, the complete connection, was what she desired.

So Sam didn't hesitate to unsnap the button of her pants and unzip the zipper. As if the sound was like a beacon, his head shot up and he gazed at her.

"Who would have ever guessed the princess was really a vixen?" he asked and pushed her off his lap so that they both could stand to remove their pants.

It was the craziest thing Sam had ever done in her life and it felt exhilarating. He pulled her close, kissing her again as they stood naked, behind a huge tree and just a few feet away from the water's bank. When she slipped her hand between them to cup his length, he pulled back from the kiss.

"Wait a minute, just…wait…wait," he was saying.

Sam grinned as she continued stroking him. "That'll teach you to call me a vixen," she teased. "That'll teach you good and plenty."

He groaned long and loud until Sam felt as if the sound stroked something deep inside her. Seconds later he was grabbing her wrists and gently pushing her hands away.

"Wait a second, just let me…" he tried to say, but was interrupted.

"Oh, no, Mr. Montgomery. You're the one who said there were so many things we could do beneath the stars. Don't bail on me now," she said.

"No, not bailing," Gary told her before dropping to his knees and picking up his pants.

He dug into the pocket and found his wallet where he yanked out a condom packet. Going to the ground beside him, Sam took the packet and ripped it open. She rolled the latex over his length, an act that had him groaning once more. She was grinning again when she pushed him onto his back and straddled him.

"I'll go first this time," she said as she angled herself over him. "After all, I'm a guest here, so I should get to call the shots."

His hands came up to grip her hips. He was strong and hard, and she found that she really did enjoy looking at him. All of him.

"You definitely get to call the shots," Gary told her as he held her hips until the tip of his erection fitted against her entrance. "Especially if it entails a long, slow ride."

Sam lowered herself slowly, loving the way he filled her with every thick inch of him.

"Oh, it's going to be a ride all right. A ride you will never forget."

Later that evening—or was it early morning? Sam had no idea—she'd felt chilly as she lay in Gary's bed where he'd carried her after their tryst outside. After a shower that turned into another mind-blowing love-making session where Gary was determined to pay her back for the fast and deliciously arousing ride she'd given him outside, they'd fallen onto his king-size bed and fallen asleep.

Sam recalled thinking how safe and special she felt right there in this strange country wrapped in arms that felt so familiar. Now, she didn't feel that and she was worried. She opened her eyes and bit back a gasp as she saw Gary staring down at her.

He wasn't touching her, but still lay beside her, his head propped up on his elbow as he watched her.

"I thought it was a dream," she said and rested her hands over her midsection. "But I'm really here in the United States, in your bed."

"I can't believe it, either," he replied.

Sam gave a little nod. "I thought what Miguel did to me was going to scar me for the rest of my life. I mean, even when I got that email from him a few weeks ago, I just knew my past was coming back to haunt me."

"Miguel emailed you?" he asked. "When?"

"The night we went to the View. Four days before the Founder's Day celebration. I just knew he was going to say he had more pictures or something. I figured that because I was feeling a little bit of happiness, it had to happen. You know, the bad interrupting the good. The balance of life."

"What did the email say?"

"Nothing," she replied. "I didn't open it until a day or two later when I remembered it again, and there was no message, just a link. I figured his email account was hacked, so I just deleted it."

For a moment Sam thought Gary was going to ask another question. She thought he would want to know more about her relationship with Miguel, but he didn't. Instead he lifted a hand to cup her cheek.

"You don't have to worry about him anymore," Gary told her. "I'm not going to let him anywhere near you."

She moved her hand until it gripped his wrist as she stared up at him. "I'm not worried about Miguel. I'm not worried about anyone or anything right now but us."

He smiled and she warmed all over. She loved his smile. And his scent. And the small scar on his shoulder. She loved this cabin with all its rustic charm and the soft cotton sheets that slipped farther down her body as she turned on her side to face him.

"There is an 'us,' isn't there, Gary?" she asked.

His answer was to run his hand down her side, pushing the remainder of the sheet completely away. He lifted her leg, bringing it across his hip as he scooted closer to her. Before she could speak he was slipping his length deep inside her and Sam was melting in his arms.

Slow and languid. It was a joining that took her to someplace other than that mountaintop where she would eventually soar with pleasure. No, this was a different journey altogether. When he eased her onto her back and came over her, Sam wrapped her legs around him tightly. She held him in her arms and closed her eyes to everything but the sensations moving through her at that moment.

"I can't think of anything but you now," Gary whispered in her ear.

She sighed, her nails scraping along his back. "It's just you. Nothing else."

"Nothing else," he said and sighed into her neck before dropping tender kisses there. "Just you."

They moved together in perfect sync, their bodies committing to something Sam had never imagined experiencing in her life. When he looked down at her and thrust faster, pushing her further, Sam kept her gaze fixed on his. She rode that wave and he was right beside her. They climbed together, higher and higher, until falling, together, into that beautiful haze of pleasure.

For what seemed like forever...they did not move. He was still on top of her and she was still holding him there.

"No matter what I've done in my life…" Gary began to say. "The medals I received in the war, the book awards, the honorary *Dancing with the Stars* award my mother and I gave ourselves," he said with a grin. "None of that, and I mean absolutely none of it, compares to loving Princess Samantha Raine DeSaunters."

Sam didn't know how to respond. He shifted just slightly as he talked so that he was now staring at her with that gaze that had been so potent from day one. A part of her still felt like she was floating while another part had sobered the instant he'd begun to speak. The tears came next, the pesky little things, filling her eyes as her breathing increased. She tried to breathe faster, to keep them from falling, but she was overwhelmed at this moment. Emotions swimming through her so fast and furiously that she wasn't sure if she was going to be simply swept away. But when one tear slipped down and Gary hurriedly lifted a finger to stop its trek, she knew.

Sam wasn't falling into sexual bliss this time. She wasn't going to be swept away by the intensity of this man who had come into her life under dangerous and unsavory circumstances. She was tumbling at a very high rate of speed, not grabbing on to anything to stop the journey. No excuses. No titles. No circumstances. Nothing was in her way. The path was clear.

She reached up and cupped his face in her hands, loving the feel of the stubble along the line of his jaw. Another tear fell but Sam didn't care. They could all fall, she could break down in sobs, none of it mattered. Not now.

"That was the best thing I've ever heard," she told him. "I never thought I would hear it, never knew how much I wanted to hear it, until this very moment. My heart is so full," she said softly.

"My mother used to say that when she hugged me," Sam continued. "My heart is so full of love for you, Garrison Montgomery. All for you."

Epilogue

Two months later

Today was the day.

Sam had been waiting weeks for this day to arrive. Actually, she'd been waiting all her life, she thought as she stood at the window in her bedroom looking out at the glistening turquoise sea.

It had begun that day when Sam was just four years old and she'd sat in the garden with her mother. Vivienne had taken out that blue, green and white tea set. The colors and the flowers had become a source of contentment for Sam in the years after her mother had passed away. Now, all these years later, that same tea set was the inspiration for Sam's perfect wedding.

One week after they'd returned from Maryland, Sam had been the one to propose to Gary.

"I've never been in love before," she'd told him while they'd walked along the beach.

He was holding one of her hands. In the other were her shoes. There was a warm breeze and the water was calm. It was a picturesque day and the thought had just floated into her mind.

"Neither have I," he replied.

"I kind of like it," she said.

"Me, too," he answered.

"I wonder if I'll like marriage as much."

"It's wonderful when you're in love," he said. "I know because I witnessed it."

She'd nodded and then said the very next thing that came to her mind. "Let's do it, then. Let's get married and be wonderful."

He'd stopped walking and simply stared at her. Sam had looked up at him in anticipation of his answer. When he shrugged, leaned forward and kissed her forehead, she'd been sure that was an easy letdown. Her mind hadn't had a moment to decide how she would react when he'd said, "Let's do it."

The planning had begun the next morning and the following seven weeks had been full speed ahead.

Now, today, Sam was ready for the biggest and best tea party ever.

"It's time, Ms. Samantha," Lucie said from somewhere behind her.

Sam stood at the window just a moment longer. She stared out at the sea and whispered quietly, "Thank you, Mama. For everything."

Forty-five minutes later Sam walked down the grand staircase in the foyer of the palace. Everything around her sparkled, from the huge crystal and gold chandelier to the candles that had been lit and placed on every surface as far as she could see. Her veil was pulled down over her face, her arm entwined in her father's.

When they made it to the bottom of the steps and the photographer continued to snap pictures, Rafe turned to her, his hands holding both of hers now.

"Vivienne would be so proud," he told her. "So very proud of the strong and decisive woman that you have become. She would be especially happy that you have found love."

"Thank you, Daddy," Sam said, once again blinking back tears. This morning had been a battle of keeping her eyes dry and her makeup intact. For this reason Sam was so glad she had decided on a noon wedding. It would be over soon and the threat of tears would be thankfully behind her.

"I'm glad that you've found love, too. I know Mom would have wanted you to be happy. After the wedding, I will be spending more time in Maryland with Gary, so I'll make sure to give Malayka everything she needs to run the palace," Sam told him.

Rafe smiled and Sam noticed the tears filling his eyes, as well. "I can't say that I'm happy about this man taking my Sammy-Girl to another country. But I understand that he is not just a former soldier, but that he also has a budding writing career. I commend you both for being so fearless in this ever-changing world."

"I thank you for giving me everything I needed to be prepared for this world. I love you, Daddy. More than any words can possibly express."

"I love you, too, my darling," he said and hugged her closer to him. "Now, let's go get you married. I saw Gary this morning and he looks as anxious as a kid on Christmas."

Sam chuckled. "That's a good thing, right?"

"Oh, baby, that's a wonderful thing. Love is a wonderful thing."

* * *

Samantha Raine DeSaunters walked down the white runner amid white-iron chairs placed at tables covered in white, floor-length, satin tablecloths. Large crystal vases filled with blue hydrangeas with large green leaves were used as the centerpieces. The napkins on the table were blue, a saucer and teacup at each seating in a pattern that almost exactly matched the one her mother had given her. There were carafes of water and of hot tea in three different flavors. After the ceremony a fabulous brunch would be served with mimosas and fresh fruit, individually made omelets at Gary's request and a grand buffet of foods.

Her aisle had been created with a white runner and candelabras holding tall, white candles separating the fifty tables. As she walked slowly, Sam looked around to see people she'd worked with in town. Detali and her daughter, the women from the Children's Hospital where she spent a lot of her time, as well as all the members of the Bella Club and the girls currently enrolled there. It had been one of her girls from the club that had suggested Sam wear a blue wedding gown.

Malayka had been appalled by the idea but Landry was instantly hyped by the prospect. Sam's sister-in-law had taken great care in selecting designers to send their ideas for Sam's perfect gown. And it was perfect, she thought as she came closer to the altar. The strapless, fitted bodice that flared out at the waist in a traditional ballroom style was a gorgeous shade of blue, with an overlay of white chiffon from the waist down. She felt unique and beautiful and happier than she ever imagined she would be.

Gary's smile confirmed everything she'd been thinking. Sam was happy and she couldn't wait to marry this man.

The moment their vows were said and they were pronounced man and wife, she kissed and hugged her husband, whispering in his ear, "Your mom's probably smiling down on us right now because she knows that this time you really did marry for love and that this princess has no intention of ever letting you go."

"And I'm never going to stop loving this princess," Gary told her.

* * * * *

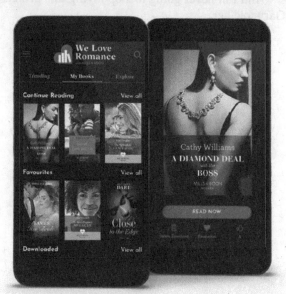

JOIN THE
MILLS & BOON
BOOKCLUB

* **FREE** delivery direct to your door

* **EXCLUSIVE** offers every month

* **EXCITING** rewards programme

50% OFF
YOUR FIRST
PARCEL

Join today at
Millsandboon.co.uk/Bookclub

MILLS & BOON
MEDICAL
Pulse-Racing Passion

Set your pulse racing with dedicated, delectable doctors in the high-pressure world of medicine, where emotions run high and passion, comfort and love are the best medicine.

LET'S TALK
Romance

For exclusive extracts, competitions
and special offers, find us online:

 facebook.com/millsandboon

@MillsandBoon

@MillsandBoonUK

Get in touch on 01413 063232

For all the latest titles coming soon, visit
millsandboon.co.uk/nextmonth

WANT EVEN MORE
ROMANCE?
SUBSCRIBE AND SAVE TODAY!

'Mills & Boon books, the perfect way to escape for an hour or so.'

MISS W. DYER

'Excellent service, promptly delivered and very good subscription choices.'

MISS A. PEARSON

'You get fantastic special offers and the chance to get books before they hit the shops.'

MRS V. HALL

Visit millsandboon.co.uk/Subscribe and save on brand new books.

MILLS & BOON

THE HEART OF ROMANCE

A ROMANCE FOR EVERY READER

MODERN

Prepare to be swept off your feet by sophisticated, sexy and seductive heroes, in some of the world's most glamourous and romantic locations, where power and passion collide.

HISTORICAL

Escape with historical heroes from time gone by. Whether your passion is for wicked Regency Rakes, muscled Vikings or rugged Highlanders, awake the romance of the past.

MEDICAL

Set your pulse racing with dedicated, delectable doctors in the high-pressure world of medicine, where emotions run high and passion, comfort and love are the best medicine.

True Love

Celebrate true love with tender stories of heartfelt romance, from the rush of falling in love to the joy a new baby can bring, and a focus on the emotional heart of a relationship.

Desire

Indulge in secrets and scandal, intense drama and plenty of sizzling hot action with powerful and passionate heroes who have it all: wealth, status, good looks…everything but the right woman.

HEROES

Experience all the excitement of a gripping thriller, with an intense romance at its heart. Resourceful, true-to-life women and strong, fearless men face danger and desire - a killer combination!

To see which titles are coming soon, please visit

millsandboon.co.uk/nextmonth